LIVING WITH YOUR PAST SELVES

BILL HIATT

Edited by
CREATESPACE EDITING SERVICES
Cover designed by
PETER O'CONNOR

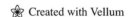 Created with Vellum

For the many students I have had the pleasure of working with during my thirty-three years of teaching. None of you are exactly like Taliesin Weaver, but each of you, like him, is capable of greatness.

UNWITTING BETRAYAL

"STANFORD, CAN YOU HURRY IT UP?" I said with mild irritation. Yeah, his name really was Stanford, though I didn't usually call him that unless I was annoyed with him. Guess where his parents wanted him to go to school.

"I'm doing this as fast as I can, *Taliesin*!" he snapped back, his fingers clicking extra hard on the keys. I knew I had pushed too hard. He never called me Taliesin unless he was genuinely mad at me. "And it's Stan."

"I know. Sorry. I'm just anxious…"

"You're always anxious! Maybe if you'd learn how to use a computer better yourself, you wouldn't have to rely on someone as slow as I am."

"You're not slow," I replied, giving him a pat on the shoulder. "Hell, you could probably work faster than the people who designed the computer in the first place." That wasn't just empty flattery. Stan knew technology like a time traveler from the future. I, on the other hand, couldn't quite figure out how to update my Facebook status.

"Okay," said Stan in a tone that suggested I was not yet quite forgiven, "the virus scan finished, and I made sure all your security software is up-to-date. Your computer is clean for now, but stop clicking on links in email from people you don't know."

"Thanks, Stan. My computer would have gotten the digital equivalent of leprosy long ago if you hadn't been around." I got a little smile out of Stan then. I made a mental note to be more careful not to call him Stanford. It wasn't that he was really that temperamental. Well, actually I guessed he was pretty temperamental, but he had good reason. His parents put as much pressure on him as if they believed he was coal and were trying to make a diamond out of him. Whatever he achieved—4.5 grade point average, getting into AP Physics (normally a senior class) as a high school freshman, creating a successful website design business with several corporate clients—nothing, and I mean nothing, was ever enough. They gave him some praise, yes, but then they started right on pushing him toward the next big achievement.

Add to the parental pressure the fact that Stan and I had known each other practically since birth, but that recently, I had been a constant reminder of what puberty hadn't yet done for him. We were both sixteen, but I had, as the adults were fond of saying, "shot up" and "filled out," so that, though I didn't exactly have the build of a basketball player or a bodybuilder, I could draw the occasional female glance and was sometimes mistaken for eighteen. Stan, by contrast, was a sixteen-year-old who looked thirteen or fourteen. It's okay to look like a cute little kid when you are a little kid, but not really all that great when you're sixteen. The fact that I could fend off the bullies that would otherwise have circled Stan like sharks should have been some consolation, but, though we never talked about it, I felt sure Stan didn't want to be dependent on me—or anyone else—for that kind of protection. He had tried martial arts, where his size wouldn't have been as much of an obstacle, but he apparently didn't have the coordination for it, so he ended up dependent on me, whether he wanted to be or not.

"Tal?" asked Stan. I glanced over, and Stan was looking back with an odd expression on his face. He looked like guys our age look when they first realize their parents have left some details out of the sex talk, and they want to ask a buddy but don't quite know how to bring the subject up without sounding completely clueless. Since I was pretty sure Stan's parents viewed him as more machine than guy anyway, I could almost see the gaping holes his dad's talk would have contained — if they had even had the talk at all.

"Yeah?" I replied curtly, mentally bracing myself.

"Can I ask you something?" Oh God, here it comes!

"Sure!" I said with very, very fake cheeriness. "Ask away."

"You remember a few weeks ago, when you stayed over at my house?" Okay, so I hadn't seen that one coming.

"Yeah," I answered, trying to figure out where he was going with this.

"Do you know you talk in your sleep?"

The question hit me like a brick right between the eyes. Hell, more like a whole brick wall. I realized that I had started breathing faster and tried to appear calm.

"I don't know," I quipped lamely. "After all, I'm asleep when it happens."

"Well, you do." Stan opened his mouth as if to continue, but he didn't.

"Okay, enough with the suspense." This time the fake cheer sounded fake even to me. "So what did I say?"

"I didn't know at first. I couldn't understand. It wasn't until later I realized I had left my computer on that night. I have a very sophisticated language recognition program on it, something my uncle, you remember, the Berkeley linguistics professor uncle, sent me as a Bar Mitzvah gift. I also have a really powerful microphone on that computer, and it picked up what you were saying. The language program identified it and tried to translate it."

And here I was, worrying about what I might have said, when the biggest problem was apparently how I said it.

"The translation part didn't work," continued Stan, sounding more and more puzzled. "The software didn't have a complete dictionary and grammar for the language you were speaking built in. But the program could at least identify the language. It was Welsh."

"You know, my family is from Wales. My parents don't speak Welsh, but I do have a few relatives who do. I must have picked up—"

"No!" shot back Stan, so vehemently that I reflexively pulled away from him. "There has to be more to it than that!" Now it was my turn to be puzzled.

"Why? Usually, you are all about the logic, and that is a perfectly logical explanation."

"Except that the language wasn't modern Welsh. The software could have translated that. It was *medieval* Welsh, apparently an early form that is actually closer to the original Celtic. Unless someone in your family has been around for fifteen hundred years, you couldn't have picked it up from them. There aren't more than a handful of specialists in the world that can read it, and no one who can speak it fluently. My uncle confirmed that!"

Well, damn your uncle to hell. "Okay, Stan, there must be a glitch in your software."

"I have double-checked…"

"So, what are you suggesting?" The cheerful tone was really wearing thin, but I didn't know what else to do at this point. "Demonic possession? I think then I'd be doing Latin backwards, not medieval Welsh. No, maybe I'm a vampire who lived in medieval Wales. Though I'd like to think my abs are really more like a werewolf's…"

"Don't make fun of me!" Stan's retort wasn't exactly a shout, but it was certainly higher volume than he needed to make his point to someone who was sitting practically right next to him. It was also high pitched enough to be funny, but I suppressed even the faintest hint of a smile. "I'm asking a serious question," Stan continued, slightly more calmly. You're my best friend. If you don't take me seriously, who else is going to?"

Choose your words carefully. "Stan, I'm not making fun of you. You have to admit, though, that the question isn't exactly scientific, and you are always scientific in the way you analyze situations. Maybe the problem is that I have no idea where you're going with this."

Stan leaned closer and almost whispered, a sharp contrast to his previous shout. "The ancient Celts believed in reincarnation."

The implicit question hung in the air for a while. I'm ashamed to admit that for a split second my old battle training almost took over. Yes, for one bloody, irrational moment I thought about how many times I had killed before, how easy it would be to kill Stan and dispose of the body, all before my parents got home. Then I got a grip on myself. All of that killing was so long ago. I hadn't killed in this life, and I didn't want to. Besides, I was an only child, and Stan was the closest thing I had to a brother, as well as my truest friend. He was almost the last person I would ever want to hurt, let alone kill. However, the fact that I was shocked enough to think such a dark thought for even a fraction of a second gives you some idea of how I dreaded what I knew was about to happen.

Stan, little human supercomputer Stan, had figured out my situation, as unscientific as it was.

Yeah, I know, unbelievable—but true, nonetheless. And now my best friend was going to hound me about it like the *Gwyllgi,* the black hound of destiny from the tales of my people.

Why the idea of my best friend knowing my secret horrified me so much, I couldn't quite say, but ever since I had known the truth myself, I had also known that if anyone else shared that knowledge, the consequences could be unimaginably horrible. It was as if I had forgotten some *tynged* ("binding spell" is the closest I can come in English) that required me to keep the secret, on pain of death or worse. My heart grew colder than the fog sweeping in from the sea on a dismal night. I could almost feel the sharp fangs of the *Gwyllgi* biting through my chest.

The question was, what could I do about the situation now? Was it already too late? Was the cliché cat out of its bag already, and was it ready to claw out my eyes?

"Reincarnation?" I finally managed. "You have got to be kidding me."

"Think about it. I didn't notice it when we were kids, but recently you have done a lot of things that can't really be explained any other way."

"Such as?" I asked, trying to sound contemptuous about the whole idea but sounding shaky instead.

"Well, there's that," said Stan smugly, indicating my harp with a sweeping gesture. "You played the guitar for years, but you never touched a harp, and out of nowhere you con your parents into getting you one, you take a few lessons, and suddenly you're a concert quality harpist? I don't buy that for a minute. But if you had played the harp in a previous life, your sudden ability makes sense. You know literature better than I do, but didn't Arthur Conan Doyle write a line for Sherlock Holmes something like, 'When you have eliminated the impossible, whatever remains, however improbable, must be the truth'?"

"Mastering the harp took more work than you think."

"No, it didn't. We hang out all the time, Tal. How much time did you spend practicing the harp? Enough for appearance's sake, I guess, but not enough to really learn it from scratch—and you know that as well as I do."

"Okay, so I'm a prodigy. Mozart was composing music when he was a toddler."

"Exactly, he didn't start when he was twelve or so. Statistically, if you are a prodigy, you are an awfully late-blooming one." Well, he had me there.

"I still play guitar, though."

Stan raised an eyebrow at that. "Yeah, in a garage band that should never have gotten out of the garage."

"Hey!"

"Don't pretend to be offended. Even you used to say you guys sucked. Then, all of a sudden, you become the Bards, and you are actually good, pretty much overnight."

"We aren't that good."

"Horse manure." That was Stan's idea of cursing. "You played at the Troubadour last summer. I was there, remember." Yeah, I'd had to do some heavy lobbying with Stan's parents to let him go to LA for a weekend with a *band*. Now I wished I hadn't.

"And then there is that." Stan pointed to my fencing foils, leaning against the wall in their carrying bag. "You were in AYSO soccer for years, all set to be starting varsity in high school—and then you just dropped it, and started fencing instead. And you were good at fencing right away, just like the harp. I've been to some of your competitions. I've seen you beat people who have been fencing for years. I heard my parents talking about it. They don't understand why you aren't trying to do what it takes to get on the Olympic team. Tal, the Olympic team! Four years ago, you didn't even know what a fencing foil was. Then there is your sudden interest in medieval reenactments." That last I used as a way to camouflage my possession of some real weapons, but I had to admit I had kind of become the star of the show—I should have been more careful.

"And just look around the room, Tal." I did, and again, he had a point. How could I have been so sloppy? I should have kept up the typical teenage boy decor: sports poster; maybe a band poster or two; images of strikingly beautiful, if unattainable, models and celebrities; something that would have made me seem more normal. Instead, I had Celtic crosses, Welsh flags, mythologically themed art reproductions. The room was altogether too medieval, not to mention too green, to seem anything like the typical teenager's lair. In retrospect, I was surprised Stan hadn't started asking questions much sooner.

Stan fell silent, clearly waiting for a response. I couldn't even begin to think of a suitable one. How could I possibly explain all the changes in my life, without letting him know who—and what—I really was?

So instead I walked over and started to play the harp and sing—in Welsh. Nothing much to lose at this point.

Stan was dumbfounded...during the brief time he remained awake. One trick I had mastered long ago, at least 1500 years ago, give or take a century, was using my music to charm someone to sleep. Needed that one for my parents more than once, I can tell you. Anyway, Stan looked as if he were trying to fight the effect, but if so he only lasted a few seconds; then he slouched over in his chair, nearly falling off. My reflexes were good enough for me to catch him in time and lay him gently on my bed. Whenever I used that kind of magic on someone, they never seemed to remember it afterward, so at least I hadn't made the situation any worse.

"Yes, Stan, I should have known I couldn't fool you," I whispered to him. "I can't just tell you the truth, or I would have, believe me. What can I say? My parents don't know it, but they named me Taliesin for a reason." Stan twitched almost as if he had heard me, but I knew he was under too deeply for that.

Not knowing what to do with Stan, or even if anything I did with him would help at this point, I listened to the slow, steady sound of his breathing and let my mind wander back over the last few years.

I remembered vividly how much I had resented my parents for naming me Taliesin, not exactly the most masculine sounding choice any way you look at it. Maybe in Wales, such a name could have worked, but in the United States? Ridiculous! Despite the name, though, I had been a fairly normal kid, good at soccer, so-so at school, someone who played my rock music louder than my parents thought necessary, and then...

And then puberty had hit, and when I say "hit," I mean "HIT"—like a sledgehammer to the skull, smashing my mind into hundreds, maybe even thousands, of little, bloody, screaming fragments. The worst part was not being able to tell anyone, not even my parents. I kept imagining spending the rest of my life in a mental institution, and the Hollywood images stirred around by my pre-teen imagination could conjure up a fairly lurid picture of what mental institutions were like. Whatever was happening inside me made me physically ill, like the sharp edges of my shattered mind were twisting around and ripping up my innards. I was even in the hospital for a few weeks. It wasn't a mental hospital, but I figured it was only a matter of time until I ended up in one.

Then, just as abruptly as my mind had come apart, it had snapped back together like someone assembling a psychic jigsaw puzzle. Sure, everything wasn't in exactly the same place, and there were days when I felt like pieces were missing, but at least I could function. You see, nothing was actually broken in the first place; it just took my adolescent mind a while to process what was happening to it.

And what was happening? People associate a belief in reincarnation mostly with eastern religions, but, just as Stan had said, the ancient Celts had a similar belief—and, if my experience was any indication, they were right. Sometimes people have fleeting memories of previous lives, but for the most part, they live in blissful ignorance of who they might have been and what they might have done. I didn't know why, but suddenly the dam that separated my past lives from my current one had dissolved, drowning me in a tidal wave, thousands of years of memories and of radically varying personalities all pouring over me, giving me no room to breathe. I might have lost myself; I might have washed up on shore, broken and rotting, and ended up in the mental institution I so dreaded. Somehow I had hung on. Eventually, my current life personality reasserted its dominance, though flavored by my newly remembered past, as my changing interests indicated.

My parents told me afterward that Stan had been at the hospital almost as much as they had, that he often held my hand and talked to me, that almost as often he cried when he thought nobody was looking. I often wondered if his friendship had somehow anchored me, saved me.

And yet here I was, standing by him as he slept, with some of my ancient and medieval past personas wanting to throw him out the window, smother him with a pillow, run him through with a sword—anything to mend the *tynged* and save me from that uncertain something waiting to swallow me up. I didn't really blame them in a way—some of them came from much more savage times in which moral dilemmas did not interfere with survival. Fortunately, they were just echoes of the past; I was the one who was in control, and if I had to face death or worse so Stan could live, then I would. Easy to say, I know, but at the time I really believed it. My past lives gave me a wild side I sometimes had to restrain, but they also gave me wisdom "beyond my years," you might say.

That did, however, leave the question of what to do with Stan. I could do more than charm him to sleep. I could, for example, make him forget, but that process posed more risks. I would have trouble wiping just the memories that threatened me, and, looking down at him and thinking about his brilliant mind, I just couldn't make myself take the chance. Besides, unless I erased much more, and took an even bigger risk, he would just come to the same conclusion again at some point in the near future. Instead of erasing his memories, I settled for a temporary fix and made him think he had dreamed the conversation with me. When he awoke, he would be a little groggy, not prone to act out the discussion he thought he had dreamed. I would walk him home—he lived just down the block—and I would buy myself a few days perhaps, to figure out what to do.

"Yes, Stan," I whispered to him again. "You were right. I am Taliesin Weaver right now, but I was also the Taliesin who journeyed with Arthur to Annwn and then wrote about the journey later. And I was the more 'historical' Taliesin who was the court poet to King Urien of

Rheged. I am betting you looked him up in *Wikipedia* and would have asked me about him had I given you half a chance. I have been other Taliesins as well, and many, many other people. The best part of all that, though it almost crushed me, is I can access any memory, use any skill from any of them; at least I can if I concentrate hard enough. Why that is true, what the purpose of all of it is, I really, really, wish we could find out together, but that, my friend, is a journey I am going to have to take alone."

With that I brought him back to semi-wakefulness, just as I had planned, walked him home to make sure he got there in one piece, went back to my place, had the usual tense dinner with my parents, played the harp a little, and then crawled into bed, though naturally, I couldn't sleep.

Around midnight I heard howling that would be enough to freeze anyone's blood, let alone someone like me who knew what it meant. The howl was followed soon enough by harsh scratching at the windows and by a moaning lament in, you guessed it, Welsh.

Over breakfast, my parents speculated about what could have caused all the racket last night, but I already knew.

We had heard the *Gwrach y Rhibyn*, the Welsh Banshee. When it spoke, it spoke to the relatives of the one who was going to die, wording its lament from their point of view.

Last night it spoke to my parents. It repeated, "Oh, my son!" to them over and over.

Now what Stan did or didn't know became the least of my worries.

The *tynged* had been broken, and the price for its breaking was death. Mine.

COMING STORM

"TAL, YOUR OATMEAL IS GETTING COLD," my mom said worriedly. She always sounded worried these days, actually ever since I had been in the hospital. She was looking more tired than usual though, I suppose because the *Gwrach y Rhibyn* had kept her up.

"Sorry, I guess I'm just a little preoccupied today." My mother smiled, just a bit, but she kept those overly inquisitive eyes on me. Most of the time she acted as if she thought I would break at any moment. Hell, maybe she was right.

"The soccer coach tells me the Simpson boy is moving out of town, so there'll be an opening in varsity this season. I think he'd like to see you go out for the team." Where my mom's blue eyes were inquisitive, my dad's gray ones were more like inquisitorial as they peered at me, the lower part of his face covered by the morning newspaper.

"Dad, you know I don't have time."

"But you used to love soccer!" The disappointed edge in his voice felt like a knife, cutting me yet again. Yeah, we had had similar conversations before.

"Junior year is especially important for college," I replied, remembering previous conversations I had had with the college counselor at school. "I have to do well in my classes, and colleges want to see sustained commitment to a few extracurriculars, not a lot of jumping around. If I drop fencing, or music, or poetry for soccer, it just won't look good."

"It's good you have a sport," said my dad grudgingly. I guess he was having a good day if he was conceding that fencing was a sport. "But fencing is so, so…" he struggled for some politically correct word and failed to find one.

I knew what he wanted to say was "fencing is so gay," but those words would never come out of his lips. He was always better at picking away at the edges of problems rather than facing them directly. The truth was he had feared I was gay ever since my collapse four years ago. He might have swallowed fencing; I think it was the harp playing that really horrified him, but the poetry writing didn't help. I knew that in some deeply hidden part of his mind, he was just waiting for me to announce I was taking up ballet. Honestly, the man would have been secretly delighted if he'd caught me in bed with a girl. Even my getting a girl pregnant would probably have been better for him than the gray dread he must have felt every time he contemplated what for him was unspeakable.

Okay, I know you are dying to ask, so for the record, I'm not gay—not that it should matter. The ancient Celts really had the right idea; if a man were brave in battle and a dutiful subject of his king, people didn't worry too much about whom he was in bed with, as long as it wasn't another man's wife.

"Dad, you know some of the football fathers would feel the same way about soccer that you feel about fencing."

"I don't feel anything about fencing," said my father defensively, burying himself in his newspaper.

I might have had the accumulated knowledge of millenniums of incarnations, but in more ways than you would think, I was a teenager. Yeah, I wanted to rebel against my parents—but I had done that in so many subtle ways already that it was getting old. Really, I wanted my dad to be proud of me, and even though I had some prestigious colleges already interested in me, I knew he just couldn't feel proud of who I was now. He wanted the little boy again. He wanted me to play soccer and be carefree, like I was before the hospital. But of course, that little boy didn't have the weight of thousands of years bearing down on him. I would never be that little boy; I didn't even remember what it was like to be him. I wanted to tell my dad that the boy was dead, but that I was alive, and I needed him—I needed him to love me, not some memory that hung between us like a pale, dull fog. However, those words would never escape my lips.

In that way, I guess in my dad and I were not that different in that way.

I looked at my mother and father then and sighed. My mother had once been beautiful, my father had once been handsome, and they were still sometimes described as "a handsome couple," but they were both graying and sagging a bit, and their faces were lined with more worry than the last four years should probably have given them. But of course, I reflected, it wasn't really the last four years that had done that, but me.

Well, I decided that was enough guilt-tripping for one day. I finished my breakfast as fast as I could and managed to get out of the house with minimal fussing on my mom's part, though I did end up with a jacket I didn't really think I needed.

However, once outside I had to admit, though grudgingly, that she might have had a point. We were only a few blocks from the beach, so a marine layer was not uncommon, especially in the morning. Still, mid-August tended to be warmer than this, if not exactly on a par with "Indian summer" in areas further inland. Despite myself, I shivered a little bit as I finished zipping my jacket. And talk about fog! It wasn't perhaps quite "John Carpenter" thick, but I really couldn't see more than a few feet in front of me.

The situation was made more uncomfortable by the fact that I had a backpack on my back, my guitar case hanging from my left shoulder, and my fencing bag hanging from my right. Carrying all that was a hassle, but I didn't want to be caught unprepared. I needed the contents of the backpack for school, and, given the ominous signs last night, I didn't want to be too far from a musical instrument. The harp would have been my first choice, but it was too large for me to drag along with me. As for the fencing equipment, let's just say one of the foils only appeared to be a foil; it was actually a little something special I might need at some point. I might be doomed, but if death came for me, I intended to die fighting.

Unless of course, something attacked me right now, in which case I was so awkwardly weighted I could be knocked over pretty easily.

I stumbled a few steps and glanced back at my house, partly to make sure Mom wasn't watching. If she was, she wasn't going to be seeing much. That Spanish colonial revival architecture-on-steroids monolith that we called home was already little more than a large grayish-white blur, the fog washing out the roof tiles to vague brown smudges, the landscaping to greenish black swirls.

I staggered on down the street, passing more Spanish colonials. Even though the neighborhood, and indeed most of the town, had been the product of a single development, the architects had gone to considerable lengths to vary the basic pattern, so that no two houses were exactly alike, but in this fog, they were just a row of more or less identical grayish white blurs. I had to really concentrate to keep track of which one was Stan's. It would be mildly embarrassing to knock on the wrong door in a neighborhood where I had lived basically my whole life.

Luckily, I got the right door, and Stan answered it. His parents were always superficially nice to me, but his mother, in particular, seemed suspicious of me, as if I had some evil plan to recruit Stan as a roadie for my band, introduce him to drugs, and just generally mess with his destiny: graduate high school with honors, graduate Stanford with honors, become a famous scientist, win a Nobel prize, the works. For the record, I wasn't even sure what use a roadie would be for such a small band, and I didn't do drugs, but one thing my parents had certainly taught me was that parental fears aren't always rational.

I said hello to him and asked if he was ready. He was—and probably had been for an hour, if only to keep his mother from fretting over him—so we got as quick a start as we could, given my load. I wasn't eager to talk to him, though, after what had happened last night, so I whistled instead, and he didn't interrupt. In fact, I was using the whistling to instill in him the feeling that the silence shouldn't be broken. Probably the damage was already done anyway, and I could just as well have shouted my secret in the center of the high school quad, but I decided to adopt a "wait and see" attitude.

And so we walked along slowly, the silence broken only by our footsteps and my soft whistling, and I thought about Santa Brígida, a town that was both home and a never-ending puzzle to me.

If you have ever passed through Santa Barbara, you might know about where my "city" (really a town) is. It's just a little east of Santa Barbara on the coast, between Coast Village and Summerland. But the best way to describe Santa Brígida is in reference to Montecito, which is just north of Coast Village, and so northwest of us. For lack of a better way of putting it, Santa Brígida is "wannabe Montecito." In fact, but for some legal snarls, the town name would have been something with Montecito in it. While Montecito traces its origins to the late 1700s, Santa Brígida, despite the historic sounding name, only goes back to 1996 — coincidentally, the same year I was born. Montecito is an enclave of prestige and wealth; Santa Brígida is an enclave of people who aren't quite as wealthy as those in Montecito but who would very much like to look like they are. Both communities are demographically very heavy with executives, entrepreneurs, and various professionals, though the average income in Montecito is considerably higher. Undaunted by that difference, the developers did their best to imply that home buyers would get the "Montecito experience" (whatever the hell that is) at a lower cost.

So why did the town leave me puzzled? It hadn't until my hospital stay. Afterward, the place always seemed just a little off, somehow, like everyone was trying too hard. The very houses themselves seemed to groan with the weight of the expectations placed upon them, if not the weight of the extra stories — I learned in architecture class last year that the Spanish colonial revival style typically only had one story, but in Santa Brígida, most of them had two or more. The square footage also tended to be big for residential properties in the area — except, of course, some of the homes in Montecito. To complete the intended effect, the developers paid extra to get fully grown trees, including the enormous palm trees on the street Stan and I were walking down, trees that, when enshrouded by fog like today's, looked even more out of place than usual.

How all this worked out financially was another puzzle. How could the developers have poured such money into extras, put the houses on such large lots, and still been able to sell the houses at reasonable rates? Rumor had it they got the land "dirt cheap," if you will pardon the cliché. The way my luck was running, the whole place would probably turn out to be built on a toxic waste dump or Native American burial ground, with ecological and/or karmic consequences one could readily imagine.

As we were nearing the school, Stan mumbled something to me. I was deep enough in my own thoughts that I answered without thinking.

"I knew it!" Stan practically yelled. He surprised me so much I almost lost my balance.

"Stan, what the hell?"

"Tal," he said, slowly and deliberately, "I just asked you a question —in Hebrew—and you answered it. In Hebrew."

Well, that was a problem.

I guess I should mention that Welsh wasn't the only language I wasn't supposed to know in this life but did. There was a poem in "The Tale of Taliesin" that was sometimes attributed to me, though I couldn't remember writing it. A lot of it was pretentious nonsense suggesting that the bard Taliesin (whom I thought of as Taliesin 1) was with God at the creation and would be in the world until the Day of Judgment. Hogwash, probably, but there were specific verses talking about being with King David when Absalom was slain and witnessing other events in ancient Israel that stirred dim memories in me, as did the references in the same work to Alexander the Great. In any case, my ability with both Hebrew and Greek was second only to my ability with Welsh— though right then, I was wishing that was not the case.

"I must have picked up enough Hebrew from you…"

"Tal, the only time you ever heard Hebrew was at my Bar Mitzvah, and you weren't exactly quoting my Torah portion just now."

The fog was still thick, but I could hear voices up ahead. We were definitely getting close to the school. If I weren't careful, Stan would out me in front of everyone. The *tynged* aside, I wasn't sure how I felt about some public revelation of my previous lives, which at best would make Stan look stupid, at worst make me look like some kind of freak.

"Anyway, when we started to really talk last night, you put me to sleep. I know you did."

The danger level just spiraled off into the stratosphere. There was no way, absolutely none, that Stan should've remembered our conversation as anything but a dream—and there was really no way he should've remembered my putting him to sleep. Over the last four years, I had had to manipulate my parents from time to time. I'm not proud of that, but I did it very sparingly, and only when necessary. (I know that sounds at best self-serving coming out of an adolescent mouth. Feel free to picture me as a wise old man with a white beard—I've been one quite often in the past—if that helps my credibility any.) Anyway, I had done the same with others as well. No one in all that time had ever resisted me or realized that I had done something to them. No one. And yet now Stan was talking as if he were somehow immune to me. Well, he hadn't been last night, so what had changed?

I really had no time to ponder that question. Shadowy figures in the fog ahead of us had to be other students. We were very, very near the front of the school.

I did my best work with both voice and instrument, but I couldn't exactly whip out my guitar at this point, or start singing, for that matter. In a pinch, I had sometimes made my speaking voice alone work, if I put enough "oomph" into it. Welsh would have been best for that, but I couldn't risk that either, so I settled for English.

"Stan," I commanded in a harsh whisper, "you will be unable to speak of this until we are alone." I could feel the power flowing through my words. This maneuver should be enough to buy me some time, and perhaps a little privacy.

Stan stopped dead in his tracks.

"What are you trying to do, Tal, cast a spell on me?" That was Stan's serious tone, not his joking one. Odd as it was to hear the campus' biggest science nerd talking about spells, there was no question. He was aware of what I was doing, and he was completely unaffected by it.

I was still trying to frame a response when the car hit me.

THE THEFT

OKAY, so I was being a little over-dramatic. The car hit at about half a mile an hour, not enough to kill or maim in this case, but certainly enough to make an ominous sounding thud, knock me over (since I was a little off balance anyway), and send my shoulder bags flying in different directions. I had been so distracted by Stan that I hadn't realized we were standing right in the middle of the street. The incident ended up being more embarrassing than anything else. The driver turned out to be one of the mothers dropping off her daughter. She seemed torn between fussing over me and getting hysterical. Getting hysterical won pretty quickly, with the result that we drew an uncomfortably large crowd, including several girls who I wished had not seen me sprawled out in the middle of the street, and Ms. Simmons, the high school's principal, who eased back on her usual sternness to fuss over me herself. Needless to say, that too was embarrassing.

There were, however, two good things that came out of the fiasco: Stan couldn't keep questioning me, and Ms. Simmons sent me to the nurse's office to be checked out—which meant I got to check out the nurse!

I'm not complaining, but really someone should have more common sense than to hire a smoking hot twenty-something nurse with long blond hair and the figure of a *Playboy* model for a high school. Usually, students just try to get sent to the nurse's office so that they can miss class, but at good old Santa Brígida High School, the guys had an additional reason for faking illness. You practically had to be dying, though, before most teachers would let you out of class. Clearly, they knew what was going on.

"Tal, your heart rate is a little fast."

No kidding! (Yeah, I know, I should have been thinking about what to do with Stan, and the *Gwrach y Rhibyn*, and the myriad of other problems I had, but again I'll point out that the combined wisdom from my previous lives couldn't completely override my sixteen-year-old body.)

"Adrenaline, I guess, Nurse Florence. You know, from the accident."

"Probably." God, even her voice was sexy. "I don't see anything else wrong with you."

Funny, I don't see anything wrong with you, either.

"But," Nurse Florence added, "I should call your mother, just to let her know what happened."

Well, that was certainly one way to derail the porno movie I had started scripting in my head.

Switching into Welsh, I said, "That won't be necessary. There is no need to call my mother."

As if I had not spoken, Nurse Florence smiled, and said, "Well, I guess there really isn't a need to call your mother—but come back here if you notice anything wrong. I mean anything."

You can count on that. "Yes, Nurse Florence." It was good to know that my Celtic mojo was still working, even if it didn't work on Stan for some odd reason.

I pulled on my backpack and left the office as slowly as I could. As I closed the door behind me, the bell rang. I must have missed first period. As they say, it is amazing how time flies when you're having fun.

I'm sure someone out there is silently cussing me out for objectifying women. Guilty as charged, but at least I don't act on every impulse I have. Indeed, I don't act on most of them. Say what you will

about my parents—and certainly I have said my share about them—
they brought me up to respect women and to set moral boundaries, and I
really do. At least my brain does—I can't always vouch for the rest of
my body, but my brain manages to stay in charge—and this despite the
whisperings from some of my past lives, during which society had a
quite different sexual morality. You know I'm not just putting you on.
Given my unique abilities, think what I could do without moral
restraint. Hell, give me a guitar and a chance for a little lunchtime
concert, and I could have the whole female population ready to jump
into bed with me right on the spot. I could, but I don't.

Damn morality! Damn free will!

And damn...down the hall came Eva O'Reilly, a fellow Celt,
straight at me.

My self-restraint was certainly being tested today.

Eva was about my height, strawberry blond with deep green eyes
and a curvaceous figure. She wasn't quite Nurse Florence, but I knew
my heart rate was a little too fast again. Now that she was closer, I
caught a whiff of the jasmine perfume she liked to wear.

"Tal, are you okay?" she asked softly. "I heard you got hit by a car."

"Rumors of my death have been much exaggerated," I said, trying
to be witty—nearly always a mistake. Somehow, Eva never seemed to
get my humor, even though I'd known her for years. Apparently, she
didn't get Mark Twain's humor either.

"Well, I knew you weren't *dead*," she replied in her stating-the-
obvious voice. "But anyway, I'm glad everything is okay."

"Yeah, Weaver," came a loud voice from right behind me, "next
time look twice before crossing the street."

I didn't need to turn around to know that Eva's boyfriend, Dan
Stevens, was right behind me.

Yeah, boyfriend. The way my luck was going, you would have to
figure Eva was attached.

Except for some well-hidden tension, Dan was stereotype incarnate: varsity football quarterback, and looking pretty much like the
all-American boy from Central Casting, with blond hair, blue eyes,
deep tan, and well-muscled body. He stood about a head taller than I
did and infinitely higher in the high school social hierarchy, so natu-

rally, he made little attempt to conceal his general contempt for me. Our relationship hadn't always been like that, though. There was a time when we had been friends—close friends actually, almost as close as Stan and me—but that seemed very long ago now, like in another lifetime, though ironically that particular memory came from this one.

"Yeah, I'll try to remember that next time," I quipped. Dan looked as if he might have wanted to get another dig in, but Eva probably wouldn't have liked that, so he pressed his lips together and said nothing.

"Anyway," I said, turning back to Eva, "thanks for asking."

"Well, I'm just glad you're okay. I'll see you later."

I smiled my best fake smile and nodded as she walked off with one arm around Dan. Women are so superficial.

Suddenly I realized what should have occurred to me a while ago: I had my backpack, but not my guitar or fencing equipment. Since the nurse's office was closer than the front of the school, that's the way I headed.

"Nurse Florence, I was carrying my guitar and fencing stuff this morning. Do you have any idea what happened to them?"

She pondered for just a second.

"I think your friend Stan picked them up." I thanked her and headed out into the hall. The students still milling around meant passing period wasn't quite over. Stan and I didn't have the same period two, and I wasn't sure exactly where he was, so I pulled out my cell phone and gave him a quick call.

He took a longer time to answer than I expected, and when he did, he sounded half dead.

"Stan? Where are you?"

"Still at home sick," he responded, almost in a whisper. "I admire your faith, but sorry, no miracle cures this morning."

"When did you get sick? You seemed fine this morning."

"You didn't see me this morning. I texted you not to come."

"Sorry to bother you, Stan. I'll call you later, to see how you are." He mumbled a goodbye, and then I started sorting through my texts. Sure enough, there was one from Stan telling me he was sick, and that I didn't need to come by his house. I had been so frazzled getting out of the house that I hadn't noticed it.

However, a missed text was the least of my worries. The fog hadn't been so bad this morning that I couldn't recognize my best friend standing right behind me.

Ever since my past selves had awakened within me, I had remembered many encounters with supernatural beings, but all of those had been many centuries ago. Except for my own abilities, I had never experienced anything out of the ordinary in this life, and I had pretty well decided that such encounters with the supernatural no longer occurred. Then, less than a day ago, the *Gwrach y Rhibyn* had shown up, and I now apparently faced another, much more immediate supernatural visitor.

There was a shape-shifter on campus, and he had stolen my stuff!

Perhaps more than just a shifter. He—or it—not only looked like Stan but acted like Stan. Either the thing had observed him quite a bit, and that thought chilled me more than I can say, or the thing had some kind of telepathy, which wasn't a much more comforting thought. I didn't remember any telepathic creatures, though. Then another thought struck me.

I had counted very carefully. I knew I was at the right door this morning, though I now realized that "Stan" had actually popped out before I had a chance to knock.

The thing had come out of Stan's house.

Obviously, Stan was still alive. I was half tempted to call his parents to make sure they were still alive, but I couldn't think of any particularly plausible reason to have called if they turned out to be alive. Anyway, Stan, even groggy as he apparently was, would certainly have noticed if his ever-hovering mother was not around. And there was still the problem of the shifter, who was running around loose at school, with at least one particularly dangerous piece of equipment.

The bell starting class rang, but I ignored it. I couldn't chance the shifter getting away with what it had stolen. I moved down the hall as stealthily as I could; even at that, I had to convince a couple of teachers that I was supposed to be out of class. As I looked around, I tried to figure out how to find the shifter. It hadn't waited for me in the nurse's office, which suggested its mission the whole time had been to steal from me. Its mission accomplished, it would probably get as far away as it could with its loot. Logical enough, but what good did any of that do me unless I knew in what direction the thing was moving or at least what its destination was?

The Celts practiced a number of methods of divination in ancient times, but most of them were impractical right now. My best option was to get outside and look for signs in nature. The high school, also a Spanish colonial revival structure, featured an enormous courtyard in the center that was almost more forest than courtyard, but enclosed nature like that wouldn't do me as much good as the real outdoors. Anyway, more people could potentially spot me, especially from the second-floor windows, if I was out in the courtyard, and I didn't want to have to magic every adult on campus. There was also a wooded area near the back entrance of the campus. It wasn't a real forest, but an artifice of the developers. Nonetheless, the trees were real enough, and perhaps they would speak to me if I were patient. Patience was in short supply at the moment, but what choice did I really have?

I got out of the back entrance of the school, across the parking lot, and almost ran toward the "woods." In their own way, they looked nearly as out of place as the ubiquitous palm trees, but even I had to admit they looked as if they had grown there naturally, though some types of trees were not native to the area. Doubtless, they, like the palms, had been brought in full grown.

As soon as I hit the edge of the woods, I reached out and touched each tree in turn, trying to hear any message that it might have for me. I was expecting that this process could take hours, but the third tree I touched actually did speak to me, though not quite with the message I had anticipated.

"HE'S HERE!" it shrieked, and the wind seemed to echo the cry. My body tensed into combat readiness, and I crept slowly around the next turn in the path.

"Stan" was indeed there. Having tossed my guitar case down roughly on the ground, he was rummaging through the fencing equipment, tossing the foils on the ground one by one, clearly disappointed so far. Without hesitation, I lunged for the guitar case. I was quick, but

"Stan" was quicker, noticing my presence, charging in my direction and smacking me aside before I could get within ten feet of the instrument. I rolled and was back on my feet almost before I hit the ground. However, "Stan's" blow had been much harder than Stan, or probably even Dan Stevens, could have administered, and it left me a little wobbly. Indeed, if the thing had pressed its advantage, I might have been dead. Instead, it made a grab for the last foil in the bag and then gave a triumphant, un-Stanlike scream as it raised high above its head, not a fencing foil, but a real sword. Its blade flashed in the sunlight as the last bits of the foil illusion that had surrounded it melted away.

Why I felt the need for a real sword when I had never faced a serious threat until today, I never knew, but it is said, "A sword always finds a wielder," and this one must have called out to me hard enough to get me to manipulate my parents into vacationing in Europe. The finding of the sword, to say nothing of the difficulty concealing it from my parents and from customs officials, was an ordeal for which even I couldn't understand the reason—until this moment. Perhaps destiny had led me on the sword quest precisely to save me today. The problem with that theory was that the shifter was the one with the sword and was charging in my direction, hell-bent on impaling me with it.

The shifter was clearly stronger than the real Stan, so it had the muscle to swing the sword, but not the months of practice to really make those swings count. I dodged without difficulty, though I knew I could not keep that up indefinitely. I started to sing a couple of times, but the physical exertion made me short of breath; the sad fact was that I couldn't very easily sing and dodge so fast at the same time.

The shifter was losing his "Stanishness" in an attempt to master the weapon. He was now a head taller than the real Stan, with longer arms and legs that bulged with muscle. The face remained superficially like Stan's, but the sheer malevolence of its expression destroyed the illusion almost completely.

I knew my music could affect the shifter now that I knew what I was dealing with, but since I could neither play (the guitar being well out of reach) nor sing, my theoretical ability to win that way was of little practical use. I continued to commune with the trees, but this forest was not sufficiently used to magic to make a very effective contribution to combat. Nor was there much wildlife, and I doubted the couple of squirrels I could sense would be much of an obstacle to this adversary.

It was then I realized that I might die today.

The shifter wanted me dead; there was no question of that. I was in decent shape, but there is a big difference between fencing, or even practicing with a long sword, and actual combat. Sure, I had seen plenty of action in my past lives; one of me had even served with Alexander the Great, and another with King David. The problem was, though I had their memories, physical skills depended to some extent on the body, and my current body, I now belatedly realized, just wasn't up to the job yet. I had been practicing the skills, but not building enough stamina. I could still dodge successfully, but my breathing was getting pretty ragged, my heart was pounding, sweat was getting in my eyes—the damned sword looked like it was getting a little closer each time. Then "Stan" managed to nick me on the left arm, and I felt blood begin to trickle down.

I could run, but I doubted I could outrun the shifter, whose stamina seemed considerably greater than mine and who might well be able to lengthen his legs if needed. Hell, the shifter wasn't even working up a sweat. Aside from that, leaving the shifter with my sword, just the proverbial stone's throw away from a whole bunch of people who wouldn't even know what hit them if the shifter took it into his head to go on a killing spree, wasn't my first choice. I won't lie—I'd probably do it if it were the only way I could survive, but not while there were other options.

Then I rolled just a little too slowly and got an even bigger gash on my left arm. My brain flicked into overdrive as I pawed desperately through the memories of my past selves, trying to find something, anything, that might save me.

I could make myself "invisible," or at least make people not notice me, but I had never tried that move in combat. I'd never even been in combat in this life, but I had the feeling I couldn't just vanish right in front of the shifter.

I could shift myself—in theory. Taliesin 1 had been able to shift, so I knew what to do, but I had always been too afraid to try, and combat didn't seem like the place to make the attempt for the first time. Anyway, there was no guarantee I could beat the shifter at his own game; Taliesin 1 had lost his biggest contest in shifting.

I could pass into Annwn, the Welsh "Otherworld." Taliesin 1 had gone there with Arthur and some knights, but I had always been too scared to try that either. Annwn was fiendishly unpredictable under the best of circumstances. I could slam right into something far, far worse, than the shifter—and that was assuming the shifter didn't follow me in, which he probably could.

Ah, there was nothing like having no options whatsoever.

Nick, this time on the right arm. At this rate, the blood loss alone would make me too weak to defend myself effectively.

I whispered to the trees, they whispered to the wind, and a call for help began radiating outward from the woods. Unless some benevolent supernatural being was nearby, though, the likelihood was that it would go unanswered. Oh, one of the security guards at the school might get a sudden itch to take a little walk in the parking lot, but the trees would block his view, and the sound of a sword cutting into my flesh wouldn't exactly be audible from a distance. Some of the students in classrooms on the back side of the building might feel uneasy and glance out the window, but again they would see and hear nothing. No, I couldn't expect help, at least not from anyone around here.

I narrowly dodged a sword stroke that bit deeply into the oak tree behind me, so deeply the blow shook the whole tree. The shifter had hit hard enough to practically sever an arm. Clearly, he was getting tired of this fight and wanted to end it. He ripped the blade loose from the oak and came at me again.

Another lunge and the shifter would have finished me, but he tripped on a tree root and staggered, missing me by inches. I guess the trees had a little fight in them after all.

I struck with all the speed I could muster, grabbing the sword hilt and wresting it from the surprised shifter's hand. I no sooner had control of the sword than the blade was engulfed in flames.

Yeah, this was no ordinary sword I had brought back from Wales. It was *Dyrnwy*, White Hilt, the sword of Rhydderch Hael, one of the thirteen magic treasures of Britain, brought back from Annwn by Arthur and Taliesin 1. Damn good thing it found me worthy enough to flame for me; that sword was pretty temperamental, or so it was said.

The shifter's eyes became slits, and he backed away a step or two, hissing at me. Knowing I had no time to lose, I pressed forward, keeping the flaming sword between us.

Fortunately, I had practiced with this blade, and I had worked on my arms enough to hold and swing it to good effect. As far as skill was concerned, I was a better swordsman than the shifter, and now I had the sword.

The problem was, the shifter wasn't bleeding from multiple flesh wounds, and his arms hadn't started to feel like lead. I could still lose if I didn't kill him fast.

The shifter dodged me skillfully, staying just far enough away to tempt me to lunge too far and lose my balance. Luckily, I knew that game from my previous lives and did not fall for it. Unfortunately, the shifter had created a standoff. He couldn't get close enough to me to try hand-to-hand combat, but he moved too fast for me to strike successfully with the sword. The subtle blurring of his outline told me that he was shifting constantly, somehow using his shifting as a tactic to dispel the fatigue poisons in his muscles. His breathing was still steady, his moves as fast as ever. I was pretty sure he couldn't keep up the shifting indefinitely, especially at that rate of speed, but he really didn't need to. I was already having trouble keeping the blade up, and the blood loss was making me light-headed; there was no way I could outlast him.

Then I realized what I had to do. The force creating the fire on the sword was magic, but the fire itself behaved as fire normally would—and I could manipulate natural forces, at least on a small scale, almost as easily as I could manipulate people. I had enough breath now for a quick chant in Welsh, and I used it. In response to my words, the flames shot out from the sword like a laser, blasting the shifter's chest and igniting him. He howled and tried to beat out the flames with his hands, but the fiery stream, fed by the magic of the sword in a way I by myself could never have sustained, just kept right on coming. In no time he was engulfed in flames. His screams echoed in my ears, and the smell of burning flesh was everywhere. Once I was sure his attention was focused completely on the fire, I moved in and took off his head in one swift, clean stroke.

I need to preface what happened next by pointing out I wasn't really as much of a wimp as I'm going to sound like. You just have to keep in mind that, for all my bravado, I had never had to deal with this kind of situation before in my current life. Many of my former selves had been hardened by numerous battles, and they took killing lightly, in some cases even when they were about as young as I was now. For me it was different. For four years I had had the echoes of those past selves in me, telling me to kill, sometimes for what seemed pretty trivial causes, like Stan's poking around near my secret. In my wildest dreams, though, I had never actually expected that I would ever need to kill somebody. Finding the sword, the training, so much else, I had done more or less instinctively, not really anticipating the immediate practical need for such things. For the last few minutes, of course, I had known that my life was on the line, that I needed to kill the shifter. But during the whole battle I had been running on autopilot, fueled by battle adrenalin and survival instinct, other feelings jammed down as far inside of me as they would go. Now, as the adrenaline faded, I knew that everything had changed. I had sometimes daydreamed about myself as a fairy-tale knight slaying a dragon. But fairy tales don't suggest any psychological aftermath. The prince finishes saving the damsel, perhaps marries her — end of story. However, my story had no end. Yes, I was alive, and that should have made me ecstatically happy, but I had killed, and I knew with a chilling certainty that I would kill again…and again…and again. Oh, it would be self-defense, or it would be defending someone else, but my current self could not yet handle the enormous weight with which such violence would press upon my soul.

As the gory reality flooded over me, I swayed, fell to my knees, and vomited repeatedly, my stomach continuing to convulse long after it was empty. The smell of burned flesh continued to assail me, and so did one sight I would never be able to forget no matter what I did — to the very end, the shifter's face had looked like Stan's. When he had realized he could not contain the flames, I saw the absolute, gut-wrenching fear in Stan's eyes. And when I took the thing's head, I could not shake the feeling that I was taking Stan's.

I lay on the ground, feeling sorry for myself and disgusted with myself, not wanting to ever get up. I began to cry, gently at first, then in long, shaking sobs.

I might have stayed that way for hours, stayed until the school authorities found me, covered in blood, with a bloody sword on the ground next to me and charred human remains nearby. But then, as seemed to be the norm in the last few days, my life went through another crazy twist.

I heard someone clearing his throat nearby. Who was it, and what could I possibly say to him?

I twisted my head just enough to see Dan Stevens standing a few feet away, his face unreadable.

UNEXPECTED SALVATION

"DAN?" I croaked, barely able to speak. My throat ached. If he were another shifter, he wouldn't have much trouble taking my sword—and my head.

"Weaver, looks like you're having a bad day." I would have expected sarcasm at the very least, but his tone was not even a little sarcastic. Much to my surprise, he actually sounded sympathetic.

"You could say that."

"Want some help?" I nodded, wondering if this was some kind of hallucination. Dan would have been the last person in the world from whom I would have expected—or wanted—help. He seemed completely unlike himself in some ways, but oddly the same in others.

I watched, still lying on the ground, as he gathered up my fencing equipment, including White Hilt, which I'd had neither the time nor the will to magic back into its disguise.

He looked up, saw me looking at him, and smiled. "Don't worry. I'm not going to remember any of this later, so the fact that I have seen your sword isn't a problem. Just don't forget to enchant it again before we're through."

Definitely, a WTF moment if ever there was one. However, I was far, far too out of it to process the full implications of what Dan was saying. In fact, by this point, I wasn't processing much of anything. I felt myself going numb, but even that was an improvement.

Dan picked up my guitar case and carried it and my fencing bag over to me. To my horror, I realized I was still crying, and so did Dan.

"Don't worry about it," he said with odd gentleness. "I've cried too. It's no big deal."

Was I hallucinating, or could Dan really be so different from the person I thought he was?

"Can you walk?" he asked, bending over me. I guess I wasn't quick enough to answer, which he must have taken as a "no." In any case, he strapped one of my bags over each shoulder, and then he picked me up and started carrying me back toward campus. I could not have been more surprised at this point if Martians had beamed me up to their spaceship.

"Somebody's going to see," I muttered, oddly embarrassed for Dan as well as for me. His carrying me out of the woods would certainly look odd, to say the least.

"Doubt it. Fog's back." I don't know how I had missed that detail. The fog had seemed to be burning off while I was fighting the shifter, but now a new, equally impenetrable wave was coming in off the sea, covering the back of the main building just as we emerged from the woods.

Then Dan veered left, toward the gym.

"Where are we going?" I asked weakly.

"Locker room. You need to clean up. We can't have people seeing you like that. I can also get some clothes for you, and there's a first aid kit."

"Won't there be other guys around?"

"Give me some credit. Period 2 is over. We're about ten minutes into period 3, which means the locker room should be empty for a good half hour at least. I'm Coach's TA this period, but he doesn't normally give me anything to do, so I doubt he will miss me. Can you walk now?"

"Yeah, I think so." He put me down gently. I still needed to lean on him a bit, but my legs were feeling much less shaky. He helped me into the back entrance to the locker room and led me to the inner sanctum (the football players' section of the locker room, separated from the main room by a wall), making it even less likely anyone would see me.

"You should shower. Can you do that on your own?" Dan looked visibly relieved when I nodded yes. "Okay. I'll go scrounge up some clothes. Stay alert, and try to stay out of sight if you hear anyone besides me coming." I nodded again, and he hurried off.

Trying hard to focus, but only on the task at hand, not on what had happened earlier, I stripped as fast as my shaky hands would let me, grimacing a little when I saw how much of my skin was bloodstained. I tried to shower as quickly as possible, but the warm water felt good, made me feel just a little bit more like my old self, so I lingered perhaps a bit longer than was wise. Then, remembering myself, I dried off quickly, wrapped the towel around myself, and headed back to the football locker room. Dan was waiting with clothes and a first aid kit.

"I'm sorry about the clothes," he said, surprisingly sheepishly. "They don't really match, and they may be a little big on you."

"Dude, I'm a 'let me grab the first clean thing I can reach' kind of guy. Whatever you brought is fine." Dan cleaned and dressed my wounds with surprising finesse. Once he was done, I got dressed, conscious of the fact that we had only a few minutes left before the locker room would fill up with people, all of whom would have questions I didn't want to answer.

Just as I reached out to shake Dan's hand, he moved over to the door of the inner sanctum and kicked it closed for no apparent reason.

"Incoming message," he said when I looked at him questioningly.

Almost immediately after that, his eyes went blank, and a voice that was clearly not his own started coming out of his mouth. The new voice spoke in Welsh.

"You almost got yourself killed today, Taliesin. You must be more careful in the future."

"Who are you?" I whispered. I had thought the day could not get any weirder. Clearly, I had been wrong.

"Who I am you may or may not find out later. For now, know that I am a friend, and be satisfied with that. You need to concentrate on what I am telling you, not who I am." I nodded, then realized I had no idea whether the voice was seeing through Dan's eyes or not. "Okay," I whispered.

"In Welsh!" snapped the voice. "I doubt anyone will overhear, but you must be as cautious as you can be from now on."

"Sorry," I replied, somewhat defensively, but in Welsh.

"The sword is valuable, but to anyone who is not worthy, it is just an ordinary sword. If it falls into the hands of evil, so be it. You are more valuable than the sword."

"How can that be?" I asked. Following simple routines like showering and dressing had helped keep the day's events at bay, but this conversation was causing them to flood back. All of the blood on me had not been mine. "You said yourself I screwed up badly today, and I...I..." I couldn't even say it, though at least I didn't fall completely apart.

The voice became oddly gentle. "If it makes you feel any better, you did not kill a man. The shifter you fought was a *pwca*, and one who would cheerfully have eaten your face for breakfast." That was the first good news I had had all day, though I was a little incredulous. A *pwca*? I knew they were natural shape shifters in Welsh mythology, but even in my earlier lives, I couldn't remember having actually seen one, let alone having fought with one.

"But," said the voice in a firmer tone, "make no mistake. There will be others who will seek to harm you. Some of them will be human. Evil, but human. The day will come when you will shed another man's blood."

"NO!" I almost shouted. "I don't think I can, and I don't know if I would even if I could. Today I let my instincts, and maybe my past selves, take over a little. But I am still me, and the person I am is not a killer."

"Would you kill if it were the only way to save Stan? Or your parents?" Nice. Now I had visions of Stan with his guts ripped out, of my parents lying in pools of their own blood.

"If, as you say, others will try to kill me, then shouldn't I get as far away from people like Stan and my parents as I can?"

"NO!" This time it was the voice that nearly shouted. "If you leave now, anyone pursuing you will go straight for those you love, as a way of drawing you back. They are actually in less danger with you here than with you gone."

"Then maybe I should search for a way to separate myself from my past lives. I have thought about that. I bet I could do it if I put my mind to it."

"Tal," said the voice calmly, almost sympathetically. "You have already carried this burden for four years, and it isn't fair that it has come upon you so early in your life or that it has already asked so much of you, but there is no help for that now. I doubt you can go back to being as you were, but if you did somehow succeed, that would just leave you defenseless. Those who would have come after you will still come after you regardless. Nothing you can do now will alter that."

Despite myself, I let out a little sob. The numbness had begun to fade, and now to the reality of today's kill was added the certainty of more and more and more. Kill or die yourself. Kill or let your family die.

You out there! Yeah, you, the one snickering about what a big wimp I am. I'll be happy to trade lives with you. Then we'll see who the wimp is.

"Tal," said the voice again, somewhat more insistently, since I hadn't responded to its last statement, "time is short. Yes, you made a mistake today. You ran after a shifter with no real plan. Yet, at a great disadvantage, you still won. The most powerful of your previous selves, the one you call Taliesin 1, would have lost and paid for it with his life under the exact same circumstances."

Okay, this was the wrong time for me to massage my ego, but I had to know what the voice meant. "What do you mean?"

"Taliesin 1 would have died because it would never have occurred to him to redirect the fire from White Hilt in the way you did. You are not as at home on a battlefield as he would have been, yet even under the pressure of the battlefield, you thought your way out of certain death. Your mind, with its modern experiences, can conceive of things Taliesin 1 could not, like lasers, for example. That is your strength. Develop that strength. And stop trying to do everything yourself. Dan will come if you call; he won't remember most of the time, but he and I made a deal that binds him to help you in time of need. However, he is just the beginning. Arthur had his knights of the round table. Urien of Rheged, the master of Taliesin 2, was never without allies. Find people you can trust, and make a fellowship of your own. Much will be asked of you, but to stand alone will never be asked of you."

"But the earlier Taliesins were subordinate to people like Arthur and Urien."

The voice sighed at that. "You may find an Arthur one day, but the ways of the world are different now. A good man cannot wait for someone else to lead; sometimes he has to lead himself. Now you must go."

"Wait! How can I contact you if I need to?"

"I will contact you if need be, perhaps through Dan, perhaps through someone else." Abruptly, Dan's eyes came back to life, and he glanced down at his watch.

"You got about two minutes, Tal. Maybe you should go see the nurse and just go home for the rest of the day."

"Oh, my God! What about the body in the woods?" Yeah, I should have asked the voice that, but my mind was working very sluggishly.

"Already gone," said Dan as matter-of-factly as if he were discussing the football team's prospects in the upcoming game. "Ashes. *Pwca* bodies disintegrate pretty rapidly after death." I didn't even ask how he knew that. What would have been the point?

I got up and started to reach for my old clothes.

"I'll find someplace to toss them. They're ruined; you'll never get all that blood out."

I shook Dan's hand, thanked him again, and left just quickly enough to avoid the period 3 students coming in to shower after PE. I took his advice and went home. God, how much I longed to sleep. But as I walked home, I knew my mind was trying to adjust to a life-changing experience far, far too rapidly.

Before yesterday, life had seemed simple—well, as simple as anyone's life could be if that person remembered all his past lives. There were even moments when I thought of my abilities as being at least a little cool. Then Stan got too close to my secret, inadvertently breaking the *tynged* and unleashing all that had followed. I now knew that supernatural creatures were not a thing of the past; indeed, the world seemed suddenly infested with them, and a good portion of them seemed out to get me, for reasons that were not immediately apparent. I had one ally, though, an ally whose power over the human mind made mine seem puny in comparison. Yes, I could manipulate people, but I could never have gotten Dan, arguably my nemesis at school, to act like my best friend, especially for such a long period of time. That kind of work required a mojo far, far beyond what I had. But why would such a powerful…being need to remain in the shadows? And how did so many creatures, both good and evil, suddenly know every little detail about me? The *pwca* had known all about my interaction with Stan the night before, as well as enough of Stan's personality to play him flawlessly, to say nothing of knowing that I was carrying White Hilt that day. The owner of the mysterious voice knew all about my previous incarnations. Was there any corner of my life, no matter how small, that was truly private anymore? I feared I knew the answer to that one.

I didn't know whether I entirely trusted the voice yet, but it had one thing right: I needed more allies. Someone I could trust more than anonymous voices or old enemies suddenly turned into friends. When I got home, I let Mom fuss just a bit, then sang her to sleep. Then I paid a call at Stan's house, put his mother to sleep, and told him everything, every secret, every relevant scrap of information, from the moment I could remember my past lives until today.

LIFE CHANGES

To say that Stan was skeptical would have been a gross understatement. Even though he had proposed the reincarnation idea himself just yesterday, he had done so only because he could not think of any other rational explanation, and perhaps also because one of the students on his science Olympiad team was both scientifically minded and a firm Hindu believer in reincarnation, making the idea seem more respectable to him. But reincarnation was one thing, outright magic quite another. He did me the courtesy of not laughing in my face, though he questioned every detail. He would have made a great investigative reporter, but right now I needed my friend, not an interview.

"Stan, even you have to admit that science can't explain everything."

"Yet," he added pointedly. "That doesn't mean there is no scientific explanation for those things. It just means we haven't found it yet."

I sighed inwardly. I couldn't really blame Stan for being who he was, and he was a born scientist. What would you expect from someone who finished the highest level high school math and science courses by the end of freshman year and now took special online college courses in both subjects as a result of some deal between UC Santa Barbara and Santa Brígida High School? I bet the powers that be at UC Santa

Barbara thought they could recruit Stan and students like him that way; if so, they obviously didn't know Stan's parents.

I glanced nervously at my watch. In theory, I could keep his mother asleep for as long as I needed, but his father would be home soon. The more people involved, the more complicated keeping them asleep would become, and I was already feeling spread thin to the point of transparency. At the same time, I didn't feel as if I could just leave Stan as things were. I wanted, no, I needed him to believe me. Well, there was not too much question about the best way to shake that skepticism.

"'There are more things in heaven and earth, Horatio, than are dreamt of in your philosophy.' What would science have to say about this?" With that, I pulled out White Hilt, realizing with a sickening jolt that I had forgotten to clean the blood off. The blood... No, I wasn't going to let myself be distracted by anything. I grasped the hilt firmly, and the blade was engulfed in flames.

Stan's eyes widened in shock, and he pulled back as far as he could.

"Tal, damn, are you trying to burn my house down?!" I hadn't meant to frighten him, but I had never seen him look so scared. I got another jolt when I realized his face looked almost like that of the *pwca* as it had been burning. I willed the blade to return to normal, and it did.

"What the hell!" exclaimed Stan, his voice shaking in a way that suggested he might be close to tears. Okay, so I had picked the wrong demonstration.

"Are you crazy? We could both have been burned."

"Stan, we were never in any danger, I swear," I said patiently. "You have been the scientist all afternoon. I need you to be the scientist again. Take the sword yourself." I held it out to him, and at first, I thought he would refuse, but curiosity got the better of him, and he grasped the hilt, moving the blade slowly in his direction and looking at it carefully. Then he smelled it.

"I don't smell anything combustible."

"What did you think I did to get it to burn like that, pour gasoline on it? Do you really think I'm nuts? More to the point, do you really think I would do anything to hurt you?"

"Well, no, but..."

"No buts. Stan, you can see for yourself there is no physical reason for the sword to burst into flames like that. It just does when it is in the right hands."

Stan spent a good twenty minutes examining the sword, making me more and more nervous about the time. My dad would be home soon, too, and he would find my mom asleep and be unable to wake her. I needed to get back home.

Finally, he handed the sword back to me. "Do it again," he said hoarsely, almost like a command.

"Are you sure?"

"Do it again," he said in a voice marginally more like his normal one. I held up the sword, and once more it burst into flames.

Stan clearly longed to be in a lab, but he made do with what observations he could make, viewing the sword from all angles, putting his hand close enough to feel the heat, that kind of thing.

"Show me how you can reshape the flame." I obliged, causing the flame to jut up toward the ceiling, though I was careful to make sure it didn't actually get too close.

"Well, I can't explain it. Will you let me take it to a friend at UC Santa Barbara?"

At that I snapped. "Stan, I came here to share something important with my friend, not be a lab rat." The intensity of my tone made him cringe away from me. "Dude, I almost died today. And I could be dead tomorrow. I need you to be my friend, Stan, not make me your project for the science fair." To my horror, I realized I was crying again, tears of exhaustion and frustration, tears of fear that I might lose his friendship. Stan started crying too, but I wasn't at first sure if he wept because he felt for me or because he thought he was alone with a dangerous lunatic. Then he hugged me, and for a few awkward moments, I wept in his arms as his body shook with his own weeping.

Eventually, we both pulled ourselves together. "I'm sorry, Tal, I'm so, so sorry for not just believing you."

"Hell, Stan, I was there, and I hardly believe it myself. But now that you know the truth, maybe you can help me."

"Sure. Anything. What kind of help do you need?"

I wouldn't have thought it possible for such a simple question to flummox me, but it did. What exactly did I want from Stan? I had to suppress a snicker as I visualized Stan stabbing a shifter with his protractor. As potential knights of the round table went, Stan was definitely going to be combat challenged.

"Ah, I think I know," he said thoughtfully. You had to give the kid credit for resilience. Just a few minutes ago his emotions had been riding roughshod over him. Now he was back in control and evidently several steps ahead of me.

"Yes, I know exactly what to do."

Well, you tell me, and we'll both know.

"Didn't that voice tell you that your strength was being able to conceptualize things differently from the way your ancestors did, and so come up with new solutions?"

"Yeah, sort of."

"So what advantage does that give you that your ancestors didn't have?" I started to formulate an answer, but the question was evidently rhetorical, since Stan continued almost immediately. "The voice referred to lasers. Your ancestors didn't have to deal with modern technology. It wasn't part of their worldview, but it is part of yours. Well, a little anyway…"

"Is that a cheap shot about my computer skills?"

"Pretty much. Anyway, you can do a lot, but can you, let's say, erase a computer hard drive by singing to the computer?"

"I have never tried."

"Well, let's try, then." Stan got out of bed and walked over to his desk. His computer, sleek, fast, and new as hell, booted up quickly. "I just made a backup earlier today."

That's sure not what I would have been doing on a "sick" day, but Stan really had been sick.

"Okay, go ahead and erase the hard drive," Stan continued. I tried for a while, but aside from entertaining Stan, who enjoyed listening to me sing in Welsh, I couldn't get as much as a momentary screen flicker from his computer, much less erase its hard drive.

Stan shook his head after a while. "This isn't working. And yet you can manipulate the human brain, a far more sophisticated computer than this."

"But if I wanted to erase the data, I could just as easily pull out White Hilt and burn the whole thing up."

"Sure, but there are some situations where subtlety would be better. What if your only option when dealing with people was to cut off their heads with White Hilt? How would that work out?" As usual, he made a compelling point. "So what then is the solution? You need to be able to interact with technology directly. If you could manipulate the digital universe as easily as you can manipulate the natural one, your power, and with it, your ability to get results in modern society, would increase exponentially, and sometimes you could get those results more covertly. You came to me so that I could help you learn how to do that."

Stan must have known he was at least fourteen steps ahead of me now, and that I was awed by the sheer brilliance of his suggestion. A hybrid of magic and science! If we could do it, we could certainly surprise whatever bad guys came my way.

"That's a great idea, Stan, but I don't really know where to begin."

"Oh, I do, but we will both have to work very hard—and you will have to pay my price." The last part sounded oddly ominous.

"Okay, so what's your price?"

"Get me a girl." *Gee, maybe I should get one for myself first!*

"I can try, but dude, you need to lose those Star Trek pajamas."

"You should talk." I had been so engrossed in spilling my guts, I forgot about my trend-setting wardrobe from the Santa Brígida High School lost and found. The purple sweater, about three sizes too big for me—now there was a bold fashion statement if ever there was one.

"But at least my room..." I began, glancing around at a unique collection of science fiction paraphernalia that might have been a turn-on if Stan's perspective sweetheart was from Vulcan, but otherwise seemed more like a massive turn-off.

"Your room? Yeah, come to think of it, maybe I'd better ask someone else to help me get a girl. Tal, your room looks like you're plotting to seduce the queen of the faeries." Yeah, unfortunately, that's what my dad thought, though in a somewhat different way than Stan meant it.

Stan and I traded friendly insults for a while, our exchange ending as it often did, with me on top of him, tickling him unmercifully. Stan was too scrawny to put up a good fight against me, but I had to give him credit; he always tried.

Being with him reminded me of just how much he had filled the "little brother" niche in my life. Maybe the "little" label wasn't fair and would even hurt his feelings if I said it to him, since we were about the same age, but as I've mentioned, he looked a lot younger, and I had a hard time remembering he wasn't. We were both only children, and in my experience, at least as far as guys were concerned, that meant each of us had a brother-sized hole in our lives. Unrelated by blood, we had become brothers by friendship. I had come to him for that reason, not to have him refine my abilities, but his idea was good, and at least now he believed me. Whatever happened next, at least I would not be alone.

That night after I went home, I managed to gag down dinner, but I couldn't sleep at all. I don't know if I was waiting for the *Gwrach y Rhibyn* to start scratching at the windows, or dreading some nightmare about having to kill—and this time a real person. Whatever was going through my head kept my nerves as tight as if they were being stretched on a rack. It was almost a relief when my alarm went off. A guy can only do so much tossing and turning in the dark, waiting for God knows what kind of horror to manifest itself.

Much to my surprise, the next day, the next week, in fact, the next several weeks went well. I was still on edge most of the time, and probably I would have been even worse if I hadn't learned how to use my music to calm myself. But there was no mass attack on the high school by supernatural beings; hell, there wasn't even any unnatural fog in the mornings, just bright August sun, shifting imperceptibly as the days shortened. During this time of year, I used to go to the beach when I was younger, but since my "awakening" I had always been too busy, and now I was that kind of busy squared.

However idyllic the end of August seemed, I always felt the watchful eyes of both allies and enemies. The latter had probably not expected me to thwart the *pwca's* attempt to steal White Hilt, much less actually beat the *pwca* in combat and kill it. Perhaps they figured they had underestimated me and wanted to plan their next move carefully, so I could just be experiencing the calm before the storm. Regardless, I had underestimated the shifter and overestimated my own preparedness.

I didn't dare make that mistake again, so every day I worked on my defense preparedness to-do list.

First, I needed to build stamina. I had always considered myself to be in pretty good shape, but real combat wore me down too fast. I kept up fencing (and occasional covert long sword) practice, but I added much more running. Stan bicycled part of the way with me at first, then most of the way. Then, much to my surprise, he started running too. In the beginning, he couldn't keep up with me at all, but I gave him props for trying so hard. I thought he was just keeping me company, but it didn't take me long to realize he had an ulterior motive: he had figured out, doubtless through very scientific observation, that girls like you better if you are buff. His mother wasn't keen on his spending so much time out running, fearing it would compromise his schoolwork, but he could use the running to get PE credit on a contract basis, and that mollified her a little, since it opened up a slot for yet another course that would build his credentials with the Stanford admissions people.

Second, I needed to build muscle. Sure, I could handle White Hilt, but not as well as I would like. I could have infinite stamina in general, but it wouldn't do me much good in combat if my arm muscles gave out from all the rapid sword swinging. In that area, I got help from an unexpected source: Dan Stevens.

Ever since the day when Dan became the pawn of some anonymous ally of mine, he had been, well, if not exactly friendly, then at least not contemptuous, and almost every day he surprised me in some way, but never more than on the day he invited me to work out with the football team. He explained that during weight training sessions, non-football players, like team managers and athletes from off-season sports, could join in if they wanted. Though there was no fencing team on campus, I did fence competitively, so technically I was a "non-football athlete," and thus qualified to join weight training if I'd like.

"What about Coach?" I asked worriedly. Some members of the coaching staff had never quite forgiven me for not playing high school soccer.

"Leave Coach to me," replied Dan with a little grin I had never seen before. Now that I thought about it, these days whatever Dan wanted from the football coach, he could get. Dan had always been a good player, but this year he was on fire, skyrocketing from someone who might get into a local college on the merits of his football career, maybe with a little scholarship support, to someone who colleges from other parts of the country were now at least hinting could get a full ride. Besides that, the team had won all its early games, including one against last year's league champion. As far as Coach was concerned, Dan walked on water, so I didn't doubt he could get me cleared to weight train with the team. With that in mind, I decided to press my luck a little.

"Do you think you can get an invite for Stan as well?" Dan looked at me as if I had suggested a new rule that would prohibit cheerleaders from dating football players.

"Dude, I know he's your friend, but he's no athlete. Mathlete, maybe..."

"He's trying to get in shape, though, and it would mean a lot to him."

I watched Dan teeter on the edge of refusal but, as if inspired by some hitherto unsuspected muse, I had the greatest lightbulb moment in months.

"You said team managers can join the workout."

"Yeah, but Schoenbaum isn't a manager, and there are no openings right now."

"Well, how about creating another position, like team tutor? Dan, I hear some of the guys are having trouble academically. Let Stan in, and he'll tutor for free in math and science, and I'll do English, history, and foreign language." And there went hours a week down the drain, but I knew how much an opportunity like this would mean to Stan, especially in his current mood.

Dan, surprised by the suggestion, nonetheless knew I was right. Some of the guys were in trouble, real trouble. The school's free tutoring program had fallen victim to budget cuts, and some football players' families were getting squeezed pretty hard by the recession. Also, the close proximity of Montecito tended to drive up tutoring rates in the area. Then there was the fact that Stan was already operating at college level, having aced every high school math and science course, most before he was even in high school. He probably had a deeper knowledge of the subject matter than many of the college-aged tutors available, making him a better bet even for those students who could afford someone else.

"Well, don't get your hopes up…but I'll see what I can do" he added grudgingly. I did get my hopes up, though—and I was right. The coach jumped on board right away. Some of the players raised objections, the right to work out with the team being a fairly closely-guarded privilege, but in the end, Dan, who was team captain as well as quarterback, had his way.

When I told Stan, he was like a kid at Christmas, or, well, actually Hanukkah, if you want to get technical. Unfortunately, his mother was a little more like the Grinch.

"Stanford, I don't want you doing weight training. Football players work out much harder than someone like you would be able to, and you might hurt yourself." Geez, Lady, why not just wrap the kid in plastic and keep him on a shelf somewhere?

"Mrs. Schoenbaum," I began, "there are three professional trainers present at all times, not to mention Coach Miller and his assistants, who are there at least part of the time. They won't let Stan do anything he can't handle."

If looks could kill, Mrs. Schoenbaum's glare at me would have gotten her convicted of homicide. "Tal, I know you *mean* well," she said, with an emphasis on *mean* that suggested I was much too incompetent to actually *do* well, "but you don't understand Stanford's situation. He isn't the same physical…type…that you are. And he doesn't have the luxury of scattering his energies in all directions." Meaning, I guess, that I could, being the slacker that I was and doubtless destined to work at McDonald's after graduation. I had always suspected that Mrs. Schoenbaum didn't like me. Now I was sure of it.

"He needs to stay focused if he wants to get into Stanford," she finished. Sometimes she seemed more like Stan's manager or agent than his mother. I knew she loved him on some level, but I thought she loved the destiny she had mapped out for him even more. There was an intensity to her, a determination that almost scared me. Like my mom, Mrs. Schoenbaum probably had been beautiful once, but unlike my mom, it wasn't worry that wore away at that beauty. Instead, it was the burning, pulsing mass of her vicarious ambition for Stan, constantly threatening to go supernova somewhere within her.

"Studies show that people who stay physically fit can achieve higher cognitive levels than those who don't," offered Stan, more timidly than if he were making the same argument to me.

"This issue is not up for discussion," replied Mrs. Schoenbaum coldly, her tone carrying the finality of a prison door clanging shut. "You will not be working out with the football team." By this point, I was readying a quick Welsh chant to wrench agreement from her no matter how much resistance she put up, and I knew she would put up a lot. Fortunately for her, at that moment, Mr. Schoenbaum walked in.

"What's this about Stan working out with the football team?" he asked cheerfully, his presence an enormous contrast to that of his wife. I knew Stan might not speak up, so I did.

"Stan's been invited to do weight training with the team. It's actually a big honor."

Mrs. Schoenbaum snorted at that. "It's actually a big danger and a big distraction." Oh, no—the two Ds!

"Dear, perhaps we should discuss this in the other room. Stanford, why don't you and Tal go upstairs for a few minutes?" Clearly, Stan was so eager to get away from his mother that he would have teleported up to his room by sheer force of will if that had been possible. I was equally eager, though in my case the ability to work a little background persuasion was my primary concern. I could tell we had Stan's father already. In his own way, Stan's father pushed just as hard on Stan as Stan's mother did, but at the end of the day, he was still a dad, and a lot of dads want their sons to be athletes, if only subconsciously. I'd be willing to bet that somewhere, at the far, far back of his mind, Mr. Schoenbaum had a vision of Stan somehow absorbing physical prowess from the team by osmosis, and becoming, if not a real football player, then at least someone who could play touch football in the park at a family picnic and not fall flat on his face.

Stan's mother, however, would not be easily won over, even by Stan's father. So I sat at the top of the stairs, singing a little "mood music," making Mrs. Schoenbaum calmer and more receptive, chipping away at her opposition rather than smashing it. Mr. Schoenbaum did the rest.

In the end, Stan got a qualified parental blessing. ("Only if you maintain your grades and fulfill all your other responsibilities.") Stan's mother was still visibly sullen, but his father was beaming, obviously delighted by whatever strange turn of events gave Stan a chance to work on self-esteem outside the arena of math and science. I could see pride in the way he looked at Stan, and at that moment, I wished that my dad would look at me that way.

The first workout was a little strained, with some of the team members ignoring us, and in particular, giving Stan the big chill, but they thawed out pretty quickly. One factor working in our favor was that the tutoring really did work. Stan was better than anyone would have thought at explaining complicated concepts in a simpler way (better actually than some of our teachers). Once some of the football players started coming back with Bs on quizzes in subjects where they had been getting Ds, Stan suddenly became one of the guys. The team members I tutored also did better, though the change was not as dramatic, since they had been having more trouble in math and science than in their other subjects. What helped them accept me was my music, oddly enough. Dan suggested I could help get the team pumped before games. How Dan knew that would work, I couldn't imagine, since the Voice had told me specifically that ordinarily, he wouldn't remember anything about my secrets. In any case, it did work. I did the school fight song and a couple other appropriate numbers, with a little some-thing extra behind them—not enough to be like cheating, but just enough to get each player to do his best, just as Dan seemed to be doing already. Even the coach noticed the difference in the way the team performed; though he didn't ever say anything directly, he looked at me differently.

For Stan, the experience was practically life-changing. A lot of the players offered him tips during his workout, complimented him on his efforts, and made small talk of a kind normally reserved for team members. It was the most sustained positive attention Stan had ever gotten from jocks in his life, not counting me, and it was clear that the whole experience was doing wonders for his self-esteem, just as I knew it would. But the workouts were just the beginning. High school society is like a complicated ecosystem, and our interaction with the team changed our relationship to the rest of that system. Sometimes the players hung out with us outside of workouts. Sometimes we had lunch with them before practice. Rapidly our social status soared far above its earlier position. I was used to being something of a loner, except for Stan, and so I didn't really care...oh, who am I kidding? I loved it, I loved it just as much as Stan did, if only because being part of the football clique gave me times during the week when I could forget about whatever diabolical forces were hiding just out of sight, waiting to pounce on me.

Stan liked our changed circumstances for a completely different reason. He put so much effort into running with me and weight training with the football team that it wasn't long before he started looking more muscular. Not that he was ripped, or anything—that would take months and months, if it happened at all. Not all guys can build muscle that way. But he was clearly getting some definition; his arms and legs looked less like matchsticks, and his chest had begun to make his shirts look a little too tight. As if on cue, puberty started giving him some breaks. In just a few weeks, his voice got decidedly less squeaky, and he began a growth spurt that made him seem, if not like a junior, then at least like a sophomore.

Imagine my surprise to overhear two cheerleaders talking about "the little cutie," and then realize that they were talking about Stan!

"That's my boy," I said to myself, and walked off whistling, not for some magic purpose, but just because I felt like it, something I hadn't done since I was twelve.

As for me, I knew I was much more combat-ready now. I also knew that my rise to social prominence made me a more desirable catch and that I even had a potential choice of girlfriends. Sure, their attraction might be somewhat superficial. I was, after all, the same person I had been when those girls hadn't really known I was alive—a little more muscle and a different rung on the social ladder hadn't changed that. But, when all is said and done, sixteen-year-old guys, with or without memories of a thousand prior lifetimes, aren't necessarily looking for spiritual fulfillment in a relationship. They are, almost invariably, looking for…oh, let's just be honest, sex. Now I would like to think that wasn't all I was looking for—I'm not a complete dog.

Nonetheless, I'd be lying if I'd said the thought hadn't crossed my mind. The societies in which my earlier selves had lived had somehow generally avoided trapping people in the weird paradoxes of our society, in which girls are discouraged from having sex and guys are encouraged to have it, by their friends (and sometimes, more covertly, by their fathers) if not by society as a whole. I had always been very careful not to lay that kind of trip on Stan, who had been until just recently too tightly wound anyway. In fact, with his social status changing, I'd actually given him a "wait for the right girl" not-exactly-abstinence-but-pretty-much-the-same-in–the-short-run talk. Stan giggled a little bit over my mixed efforts to give him brotherly advice. I didn't think he realized how close he was to getting picked up on the female radar, and perhaps it was just as well. I never told him about the cheerleaders. I didn't want to get his hopes up, or, even worse, make him feel as if he had to do something right away.

Like a rock hitting the surface of a pond and sending out ripples, the changes Stan and I were going through affected others as well. My mom gradually stopped looking at me as if she expected me to break into a million pieces. My dad's transformation was even more gradual, but I couldn't remember seeing him happier than the day I told him I was thinking about trying out for soccer. (Truth be told, Dan twisted my arm a little bit on that one, but I was glad he did.) Hell, even Mrs. Schoenbaum loosened up a bit, partly because Stan seemed to be able to take the time to work out and still be the academic star she needed him to be, and partly because the high-priced private college counselor she had hired thought the experience would be good for Stan. (It's truly amazing how the most mundane advice can sound like the wisdom of Solomon when you are paying big bucks for it.) Anyway, I got the big invite to Rosh Hashanah dinner at Stan's. For the first time I could remember, Mrs. Schoenbaum didn't treat me like some juvenile delinquent out to corrupt her son. I made what could have been a serious mistake, though. I joined in a conversation with Stan's cousins and slipped into Hebrew again without meaning to. But you know what? Nobody noticed.

It was as if I were a member of the family.

September would, in fact, have been the teenage version of bliss, except that I needed to think about more than just all the usual teenage things. That part of my life lay across the surface of a much more complicated reality, masking it but not erasing it. As well as my life seemed to be going, there was still the need for combat readiness in the background. I was taking care of the physical part, but there was also a mystical part. I needed to master all of my abilities, and I hadn't tried either shifting or entering Annwn, the Otherworld. Depending on who my enemies turned out to be, they might be capable of either—or both. I needed to be able to do whatever a potential adversary could, and as long as I could access some of my abilities only as memories from previous lives, I would not be able to count on them in a battle situation. Then there was the question of getting my magic to interact with modern technology more effectively.

So much to do, so little time to do it—in more ways than one!

PRACTICE IMPERFECT

I CONFESS I was a little nervous about trying to change into an animal. I must have watched too many werewolf movies as a kid, particularly the ones in which the wolf seems to have to rip itself out of its human form. Even though I could remember the experience from my past lives, and so I knew shifting was really nothing like that, the whole idea still gave me the creeps. As a result, I decided to start with a more familiar subject: Stan. (If the *pwca* could do it, I was sure I could as well.) That whole idea gave Stan the creeps, but he played along, letting me study him for some time.

"Okay," I said at last, "I'm ready."

"Let's get this over with, then," replied Stan.

I closed my eyes, slowed my breathing, and began to sing, letting the sound surround me and the magic flow through me. (The singing was not strictly speaking necessary, but I had learned that song made any of my magic workings stronger, and I needed to feel confident in my first shift of this lifetime.)

It took me a few minutes to achieve the right state of mind, but once I did that, I simultaneously felt a momentary, almost electrical jolt throughout my body and heard Stan gasp. I glanced over at the mirror and saw two Stans side by side, though one was wearing baggy clothes that were clearly too big for him.

"Wow!" I said and realized that the voice still sounded like mine.

And that was the biggest problem with shifting into another human form, at least if the purpose were to impersonate that person, as Uther had when he took on the shape of Gorlois to lay with Gorlois's wife, Ygraine. (Not that I had any such thing in mind, at least outside the realm of fantasy!) Changing was easy enough with a little practice. Changing in such a way that I could fool other people who knew my subject well required a high level of exactitude, which in turn required an almost excruciatingly intense focus. Other forms of magic I tried, from shifting someone's mood a bit to shifting the weather, seemed like child's play by comparison. The first time I had Stan's body right, but not the voice. The second attempt I didn't get Stan's curly black hair; I kept my straight dark brown hair instead. The third time the eye color was wrong, a darker brown than it should have been. It took days of practicing concentration before I could do a shift that Stan pronounced satisfactory. To put the transformation to a real test, I changed into some of Stan's clothes, went downstairs, and fooled his mom. So far, so good.

Next came variations. Could I be basically Stan, but deliberately get one or more characteristics to vary, as the *pwca* had been able to do? I tried taller Stan, buffer Stan, and several other alternate forms, and each one worked. Once I had the basic pattern of a person down, making custom alterations came naturally.

While I was at it, I realized that I could cheat on workouts really easily by just shifting my own body into a more muscular condition. That didn't seem right to me, but in any case, I couldn't maintain a shift indefinitely, so I still needed to keep my real body in shape. However, adding muscle mass temporarily might be a good gimmick in battle, at least if I were fighting someone much stronger than my natural form. In just a few days, I felt that my combat readiness had improved substantially.

But these successes brought me right back to the need to practice non-human forms. In some ways shifting into an animal form would be easier, unless I had to imitate a specific animal for some reason, like someone's pet dog, for instance. Then I would need the same precision I would for a human impersonation. Just being a dog, though, as long as I got all the parts in the right places, shouldn't be hard. Actually, the shift itself was less trouble than basic logistics, like what to do with my clothes before and after a shift. The first time I tried a dog, Stan and I were on a quiet stretch of beach. When we were sure no one was around, I shifted into a rather handsome German shepherd, if I do say so myself. I frolicked in the waves for a while, as some dogs like to do, and fetched a stick for Stan a few times. Stan praised my movements as being very dog-like, at which point it seemed like a good idea to become myself again, but then the reality of the situation hit me: how could I shift back to my normal self without being stark naked on the beach? Even though nobody was around, someone could always appear unexpectedly. I had to shift my German shepherd vocal cords back to a close enough approximation of my own to be able to explain the problem to Stan. He laughed himself silly, but then he laid a beach towel over me so I could change back without inadvertently flashing someone. From then on, most of the animal shifts got practiced in my bedroom or his, not in the open.

My only other problem with shifting was Stan's tendency to ask too many questions about the process. Once he got over the initial shock that I could actually perform such a feat, the scientist in him took over again, and he wanted me to provide him with all kinds of data. When I changed into him, was my blood type the same as his? Was I the same genetically, or was the resemblance only superficial? If another shifter morphed into me, did that give the shifter all of my other powers? I didn't really have the answer to any of these questions, but I did give him some data based on my observations during shifts. For instance, assuming I shifted correctly, physical attributes like strength would be the same as the form I shifted into, so that changing into a grizzly bear made me as strong as a grizzly bear. Changing into a fish (which I only tried once) enabled me to breathe under water. Mental attributes stayed the same, so I kept my own intelligence. If I was a dog, I still thought like me. If I was Stan, I still thought like me. Too bad—there would have been times when shifting my brain to his during a math test would have been a real advantage! As far as whether the physical form was the same all the way down to a molecular level, I doubted that, but I could not provide the evidence Stan wanted. Then he would start going on about the equipment he'd like to get to test me with, and I had to remind him that he couldn't very well make his bedroom into a lab without attracting his parents' notice. All of this science talk would have been easier to take if I didn't feel like I had just run a marathon after a series of shifts. Maybe with more practice, shifting would not hit me so hard, but right now it made me feel as if I had donated blood every day for a week. How the *pwca* had managed so much shifting around in such a short period of time was beyond me, but I guessed that *pwcas*, as natural shape shifters, had more innate resistance to the strain of shifting than a human would.

As for visiting Annwn, that wasn't tiring at all, just impossible. I knew from the memories of Taliesin 1 exactly how to open a doorway into that realm, but every time I tried, I felt as if I were trying to open a door inward, but tons of rock were jammed up against it on the other side, and it wouldn't budge. I concentrated until I thought my head would split open, I sang until I almost made myself hoarse. Nothing. Stan, who insisted on interpreting Annwn like a parallel world in a science fiction story, hypothesized that conditions had changed in the last 1500 years, that Annwn was now on a different frequency, and all I needed to do was to find the right frequency. Well, if so, that was more easily said than done.

I wasn't any more successful trying to force my magic to interact with technology. Stan devised all kinds of simple tests for me to practice with, but I couldn't even perform a single mouse click with magic, no matter how much I concentrated, no matter how much I sang.

Still, if I didn't have a new arsenal of technological tricks up my sleeve, neither did my enemies, who had been singularly quiet since the *pwca* incident at the beginning of the school year. For that matter, so had my anonymous ally—just a few words of advice from time to time, delivered via Dan. No warnings, no prophecies of doom.

I began to wonder if maybe I wouldn't end up in the middle of some cataclysmic struggle between good and evil after all. My life would never be entirely normal, but that didn't mean it couldn't be peaceful—and happy.

But you know what they say about the calm before the storm.

FOUNDERS' DAY SURPRISES

ONE BRIGHT MORNING IN SEPTEMBER, a big crowd of students made getting in the front door difficult.

"What's up?" I asked Stan.

"Oh, just the names of the students being honored at the Founders' Day Celebrations," he replied nonchalantly. Considering Stan's academic standing, that he would be honored for something went without saying, so he didn't have to join in the hysteria. I looked around, and sure enough, the big crowd around the bulletin board was what was wreaking havoc on the flow of traffic. Out of curiosity, I worked my way in that general direction with Stan in tow.

We finally managed to get close enough to see the names. The first few were no great shock: Dan Stevens for Athletics—wow, didn't see that one coming; Stanford Schoenbaum for science—so what else is new; Natalie Kim for math.

"You didn't win for both science and math?"

"Only one award per student," replied Stan, "and Natalie's very talented."

Did I hear a touch of attraction? I glanced at Stan, but his face was calculatedly unreadable, so I looked back at the board. Aabharana Charu had won for English; that made sense since she had the highest

grade in AP English and edited the school literary magazine, *Wild
Flowers*. Jackson Donovan, one of the members of my band, had won
for history. It seemed to me he could have won for music, since he was
one of the best musicians, both for rock and jazz, in the entire school
and had led the school's jazz band since freshman year. On the other
hand, he did currently have the highest grade in AP U.S. History, so the
history award also made sense...

"Tal, look, you're up there, too!" yelped Stan. My eyes darted down
the page: Carlos Reyes for foreign language, Mary Stewart for art, Eva
O'Reilly for drama...and Taliesin Weaver for music. For a second I just
stared at the board in disbelief. Since I could sing like an angel and play
virtually any musical instrument I could get my hands on, you might
wonder why I would find such news surprising even in the least. I
wasn't being modest, I can assure you. But I didn't perform in any of
the school groups, and normally the music winner was someone like the
band's drum major, or the choir's lead soprano, or the orchestra's first
violin.

I couldn't help wondering if Dan, who was still walking on water as
far the adults in our football town were concerned, had pulled strings.
However, I decided not to worry about it. I didn't feel undeserving, and
I figured my parents would be happy about it.

Actually, happy proved to be an understatement. They both acted as
if I had just won a Nobel Prize; I wasn't at first that enthused about all
the fuss, but at least, I reflected, my parents weren't as hard to please as
Stan's. My dad restrained himself a little bit, but my mom became
downright delirious, even insisting on taking me shopping for a new
suit. Now we all know how much adolescent males like to shop for
clothes with their moms. (Note the sarcasm.) I did have to admit,
though, that in this case, she had good taste, getting me a nice dark
brown suit I actually looked good in. Then I had to suffer through her
buying a new dress for the occasion, but at least she took my dad separately to get his new suit. Our family was certainly doing its part to
keep the clothing stores in Santa Brígida's little mall in business.

I wish I could have said the same for Stan's family. In fairness, Stan
winning awards at school was kind of routine for them. Nonetheless,
Stan's growth spurt made his old suits look tight, and the sleeves and

pant legs were, if not ridiculously short, then at least short enough to make the blue suit he was wearing look as if it had been bought carelessly off the rack, when in fact it had been tailor-made for him—before the growth spurt. I don't know what his mom, in particular, could have been thinking. Was she on some level still resenting his workouts with the football team? I didn't know, but when the big night arrived, and Stan showed up in his ill-fitting blue suit, looking uncomfortable and eager for nothing more than to have the evening over, I was incensed. Rather than tell his mom off, which might have made me feel better but would certainly not have helped Stan, I took him aside and wove a little illusion around him. Presto, the suit now appeared to fit, and Stan relaxed, visibly grateful. I could have gotten the suit to fit in reality, except that the presence of synthetic fabrics scrambled that kind of magic.

The city held its Founders' Day festivities in the city council chambers at city hall, one of the few original buildings in town mercifully not done in Spanish colonial revival style. That said, the attempt to imitate the neoclassical look of cities like Washington D.C. and some of the early state capitals struck me as more than a little pretentious. The front of the building featured Corinthian columns and marble facade, while the council chamber itself had every wall covered with murals depicting the town's early history (such as it was, the place having only existed since 1996). Like so much else about Santa Brígida, the place seemed to be trying too hard. At least our nation's founding fathers had been trying to remind citizens of the civic virtues of classical Athens and republican Rome through our early civic architecture; Santa Brígida's city hall seemed more like a none-too-subtle salute to imperial Rome, a deliberate display of wealth and power.

The council chambers, unlike any others I had ever heard of, were designed to accommodate this kind of large dinner, even to the point of having a large kitchen just off the main room. For tonight, the smaller council table on the dais had been replaced by a larger table, obviously intended to serve as the head table and draped with an expensive looking white lace tablecloth. The folding chairs normally present in the audience area had been swept away and replaced with round tables, also draped in white and each seating ten, with the three front and center

designated for the honored students and their parents. The tables were
not folding tables, so it must have taken a lot of effort to move them in;
even the chairs were not just the usual folding chairs, but heavy looking
and certainly genuine wood.

I contrived to sit next to Stan, mostly so we could poke each other
when especially amusing events occurred but also so that I wouldn't
have to sit next to Eva O'Reilly, though I could still smell her signature
jasmine perfume from where I was. She was, after all, Dan's girl, and
therefore off-limits anyway, so why torture myself? Besides, I had
found time to casually date a bit recently, and it seemed likely I would
soon have a girl of my own, after which I hoped I could stop thinking—
and let's be honest, sometimes dreaming—about Eva.

At almost 7:00 pm, the scheduled starting time, the dignitaries
began to take their seats on the dais: the mayor, the school board president, the municipal court judge, and the person who could most
correctly be called the founder of the city, chamber of commerce president and the owner of the development company responsible for the
very existence of Santa Brígida, Carrie Winn. If city hall reminded one
of imperial Rome, there was really no question who the reigning
empress was. All the other dignitaries consciously or subconsciously
deferred to her, in body language if in no other way. Easily the wealth-
iest person in town, she could have lived in the real Montecito instead
of "wannabe Montecito," but for some reason, she chose to live here. I
gathered from the whispered female conversation at my table that some
of the moms were impressed by the fact that Ms. Winn didn't dress in
an overstated, *nouveau riche* way, yet everything she wore was designer
label; the pale green evening gown they seemed to think was a designer
original. I had to admit that she was a striking woman; though old
enough to not be really exciting to someone my age, her jet black hair
betrayed not even the subtlest trace of gray, and her pale white, seemingly wrinkle-free skin made her look younger than she was. Her face
echoed throughout the room, prominently displayed in the murals
around us.

Then I glanced back and was surprised by the sheer size of the audience. Just as I expected, city council members, school board members,
and other local officials were present. What I wasn't expecting, never

having been to a Founders' Day Dinner before, was the number of high school teachers who showed up, pretty much the whole staff, as far as I could tell. Even more surprising were the mobs of high school students. No, it wasn't the whole student body, but anyone who knew any of the award winners, from the varsity football team, coming out for Dan, to my band members—their presence touched me a little, since I knew some of them were angry over the fact that I so seldom seemed to have time to rehearse these days. Nonetheless, they showed up for me. Well, maybe for Jackson, to be honest, but at least they waved to me. I made a mental note to spend more time with them. I feared they thought my new jock friends now took up all my time, and I couldn't very well tell them what was really going on, but at least I could check in with them more often.

Dinner itself was the best one could expect from a mass-produced meal, even one prepared by the chef at the local hotel. Well, at least it wasn't the notorious rubber chicken, but ample portions of passable roast beef, with decent gravy, mashed potatoes, and relatively crisp veggies. Dessert was a really rich chocolate mousse, the kind that makes you gain weight just by looking at it. I wolfed it down, noticing even as I did so that some of the girls were taking a token one bite and then fighting the temptation to take another. Why is it that teenage girls, even the really slender ones, are always on a diet?

The program, on the other hand, was dull, the kind of dull that makes even algebra exciting by comparison. What with opening remarks, introducing every conceivable dignitary—I was surprised the local dog catcher wasn't on hand to take a bow—and the recitation of the city's "history," I even caught my dad looking at his watch...several times. The program did liven up a bit when the time finally arrived for us award winners to take our bow. The mayor at last yielded his iron grip on the podium to Ms. Winn, who proved to be a surprisingly good speaker and even managed to inject some life and humor into the corpse of the evening.

"The measure of a city is not how it preserves its past but how it prepares for its future," she said at last. "Tonight we should be especially proud of ourselves as we honor some of the students from our fine high school. If our future lies with them, then our future is bright

indeed. Ms. Simmons, would you please introduce our award winners?"
Ms. Winn stepped aside for Ms. Simmons, who looked far more radiant
than usual. I guessed this kind of recognition of her school must have
felt almost as good for her as it did for us.

As we were each called up to the dais, I noticed Stan and I got
applause from the football players almost as enthusiastic as what they
gave to Dan. I had to smile a little at that. Once I was on stage and
facing the audience, I looked back in the direction of my parents, who
looked as happy as I had ever seen them recently, perhaps ever. My
smile broadened to about the width of Santa Barbara County. I could be
happy; we could all be happy.

Dan, standing just next to me, shuddered and for a moment almost
seemed to lose his balance. Then, his equilibrium regained, he leaned
over to me and whispered in Welsh, "Something is wrong. There is a
tremendous buildup of mystic force around the students on the plat-
form. We need to get them off of there now." Damn! Now! The forces
of evil had to pick now to strike.

I noticed several troubling signs simultaneously. I could see the
open door at the far end of the council chamber, and through it, the
main entryway leading to the outside. Both doors had been propped
open, and there was fog, lots of it, one telltale sign of a magic working,
especially when the weather had been clear and warm when the
program first started. The fog had not yet rolled into the council
chamber itself, and yet I did suddenly feel as if the temperature had
dropped ten degrees. I heard some kind of commotion in the audience,
though I couldn't immediately identify its source. I tried to think of
some way of getting everyone out of danger, but nothing occurred to me
—and would going outside, straight into the fog, really be safer? Then I
thought I caught a stray sound, someone besides Dan whispering in
Welsh. I looked around, trying to pinpoint the source of the whisper, but
at that moment every light in that vast room blinked out. Even external
lights, like the ones in the parking lot, that should have been visible
through the windows and the open back door, disappeared.

Now there was too much uproar to pinpoint the source of the whispered Welsh. I felt Dan's hand on my arm, felt the tension running

through it. Consumed by a desire to keep me safe, he readied himself to act if I did not.

Then, faster than any of us could move, faster almost than thought, the reality of the council chamber fractured and dissolved, sending shocks crackling through every nerve in my body. I found myself dropped into another reality with such force that I sank to my knees. All around me I saw an apple orchard but brighter, more alive than any real apple orchard, as if someone had spent hours carefully photoshopping the scene.

The good news was, I had finally made it to Annwn.

The bad news? Someone had obviously dragged me here by force—and the other students on the dais right along with me, though whether by accident or design, I had no way of knowing. But one thing I did know—whoever had brought us here was up to no good!

MEETING AN "OLD FRIEND"

I COULDN'T IMAGINE A WORSE situation to be in. I had no weapon, having left White Hilt at home, and most of my combat training had been armed combat training. I had no musical instrument either; though I could accomplish much by singing, an instrument would have given my power much more punch. As for the other students with me, they would be at best a distraction—I had to worry about their safety, and they could contribute little to their own defense.

Stan, who had helped me practice magic enough to have some idea what had happened and therefore at least might not panic, was in better physical shape than at any point in his life, but still wouldn't last thirty seconds against a medieval warrior, let alone a supernatural menace. Dan would definitely have been some help, and the Voice had clearly put him in "Taliesin's helper mode" right before we were pulled into Annwn. But he just stood there with a blank expression on his face, unresponsive to everyone around him, including Eva. I had to assume our sudden shift to a different world had disrupted the signal and given him enough of a jolt to render him helpless. As for Carlos, his background as an aquatic athlete made him pretty muscular, but that wasn't the same thing as having combat training, and I doubted whoever brought us here would try to destroy us by beating us at water polo.

Jackson, a fellow musician, could have helped if he had had his drums, but again I doubted he had any combat training. He was tall, slender, and thoroughly unathletic—drumming was probably the most strenuous exercise he ever got.

And the girls? I tried not to be a chauvinist, but in the present situation we desperately needed muscle power, not brain power—and none of them were exactly amazons. Natalie was a female mathlete, Aabharana a contemplative writer, Mary an artist who spent hours sketching. And Eva? I couldn't deny she was in good shape, in every sense of the word, and I think she used to do gymnastics, so she had good coordination and reflexes, but again, facing an enemy armed with a sword or even claws, what could she do?

No sense being in denial. Any way you looked at it, we were screwed.

Nor did the reactions of the others improve the situation. To be fair, what would you do if you were standing indoors at night and suddenly found yourself in an apple orchard in broad daylight, with no rational explanation of how you got there? Nor was I in a great position to help them understand. "Uh, excuse me folks, but we're in Annwn because I'm really the original Taliesin who served King Arthur, and one of my enemies has snatched us up for some foul purpose." Yeah, right, that'll work.

Stan was looking at me helplessly, but at least he appeared calm. Eva was not panicked about our sudden relocation, but only because she was totally panicked about Dan, a situation which didn't improve when Dan fell to the ground like a sack of cement.

"We have to get him to a hospital!" she cried out with a heart-breaking urgency.

"He's breathing normally, and his pulse seems okay," replied Mary gently. She had moved over to help as soon as Dan fell. "I don't think he's in immediate danger."

"But he passed out, or something! That can't be normal."

"Nothing is normal at the moment," observed Carlos. "Before we can get Dan from here to a hospital, we have to figure out where exactly 'here' is." Eva really looked around for the first time, and then burst into tears. At that moment I longed to take her into my arms and comfort her, but I didn't trust myself to do that. Having her that close would certainly smash my concentration to atoms, and if I lost focus at this point, we would all be lost. Fortunately, Mary, Aabharana, and Natalie all tried to comfort her, so I could wrench my attention away from her and figure out what to do next.

Stan moved in my direction, but I raised a hand, and he stopped short. I needed a minute to actually concentrate, to see if I could open a portal from Annwn back into our world. I had accomplished such a feat as Taliesin 1, but again something blocked me. It was as if the tons of rock pressed against the door when I had tried to enter Annwn had now shifted to the other side of the door, blocking our return. I motioned Stan in my direction.

"Where are we?" he whispered shakily.

"Annwn for sure, but I'm not sure exactly which part. All the apple trees suggest Avalon, but by now one of the queens would surely have noticed us."

"Avalon? Does that mean we will get to meet King Arthur?" Given everything Stan had seen in recent weeks, it was not an irrational question. His uneasiness gave way to excitement for just a moment.

"Arthur was brought to Avalon to heal after the battle of Camlann, but that was hundreds of years ago. There is no guarantee he's still here."

"Merlin? Morgan Le Fay?"

I shuddered at the last name. "I don't know where Merlin is these days, and trust me, you don't want to meet Morgan."

"But I thought she was one of the queens that brought Arthur to Avalon."

"That whole story about Arthur being taken to Avalon by Morgan Le Fay to be healed was actually just spin doctoring on Morgan's part. Arthur was taken away by women with supernatural power, but Morgan was not among them. That's one of the few parts of the story Geoffrey of Monmouth actually got right."

"People did spin doctoring in the Middle Ages?" asked Stan incredulously.

"Yeah, they didn't have the term, but they certainly had the concept. Morgan deliberately planted the stories about her helping Arthur in various ways; some even survived as interpolations in the work of Taliesin 1 and Taliesin 2. She hadn't given up on her evil schemes, and having everyone know she was evil did not suit her purpose. Hasn't it ever struck you as odd that Morgan is portrayed in many stories as stopping at nothing to destroy Arthur—then she takes him away to be healed? That change of heart makes no sense. But if that part of the story is understood as pro-Morgan propaganda, it makes perfect sense."

"Anything you'd care to share with the class?" Jackson had walked up behind us. If you want to draw someone's attention, just whisper, and they'll come a'running to see what you are up to.

"Stan and I were just trying to figure out what could have happened to us. Neither of us have a clue, though, but...CARLOS, DON'T DO THAT!"

Carlos had picked one of the admittedly delicious looking apples and was just about to bite into it.

"What's your problem, man?"

I couldn't very well tell him that if he ate anything in a faerie realm, he would probably be trapped there for all eternity.

"This place looks too good to be true. I don't trust it."

Carlos glanced again at the apple, then reluctantly tossed it aside. "You've got a point, I guess. But what could all this be, a mass hallucination? In that case, the food isn't going to be poisonous or something, just nonexistent."

"I doubt all this is a hallucination," replied Stan. "It's too real for that, and we found ourselves here too suddenly and too completely. Hallucinations don't work that way. Anyway, documented mass hallucinations are extremely rare." I had to give Stan credit—he could think on his feet.

"Okay, Professor," said Carlos with a hint of sarcasm. "What do you think this is?"

"A parallel universe. Hugh Everett proposed the idea way back in 1954, and the erratic behavior of quantum particles offers some support for it."

"Nonsense," replied Natalie with surprising vehemence. "The issues with quantum mechanics don't mean the results are being thrown off by parallel universes. They just mean we haven't discovered everything about quantum mechanics." Wow, I could really see what Stan saw in her.

"I believe Arthur Conan Doyle had Sherlock Holmes say, 'Once you eliminate the impossible, whatever remains, no matter how improbable, must be the truth,'" interjected Aabharana, in an eerie coincidence picking the same Doyle quote Stan had used when he first tried to unearth my secret. Natalie started to object. "No, hear me out," continued Aabharana. "I don't know anything about quantum physics, but I know enough about science in general to know there is no scientific explanation for our suddenly moving from one place to another without passing through the space in between. That is what we have done, isn't it?"

"Looks can be deceiving," replied Natalie, but clearly because she had nothing better to say. After all, as much as she might disbelieve the idea of parallel universes, she could hardly deny that there was no other obvious explanation for our unusual situation.

If nothing else, the conversation had taken everyone's mind off of our immediate dilemma.

Well, almost everyone.

"What are we going to do about Dan? We need to help him," pleaded Eva.

Before anyone could respond, we heard the sound of a horse's hooves in the distance, and everyone froze. Time itself seemed to stand still. Even the drowsy buzzing of the bees stopped abruptly.

Then almost all of us gasped in unison, though for somewhat different reasons. The rider we had heard earlier cantered into the clearing on a mare whose hair was generally as white as the inside of a fresh apple, but whose mane shined as red as the apple's peal. The rider herself was even more striking: jet black hair, white flawless skin, flashing green eyes, model-perfect features, voluptuous figure beneath an apple red samite gown interwoven with gold thread. She scanned us disdainfully until her eyes met mine. Then hers widened in surprise.

"Taliesin? I hardly expected to see you here. Different body, but your soul is always unmistakable."

"So is yours, Morgan." Stan gasped again. I inclined my head just slightly in greeting. She probably expected a bow, but I could not make myself go quite that far. "Now perhaps you will be so kind as to tell us why you brought us here."

"Tal, who is she?" whispered Jackson, but Morgan, whose ears had always been very sharp, heard him.

"Taliesin, could your little playmates be so ignorant as to not recognize Morgan Le Fay, half-sister of Arthur Pendragon and rightful heiress to the throne of Camelot?" Her voice, though superficially sweet, was dark with contempt.

Well, I hadn't been wrong. We were screwed. Royally screwed.

DESPERATE TIMES

JUST WHEN YOU think things can't get any worse, they often do—and that was certainly the case here. Morgan would be a tough opponent under any circumstances, but in a faerie realm, since she had some faerie blood, she would be next to unstoppable, except perhaps by a full-blooded faerie, and we were fresh out of those.

"Well, Morgan," I said, trying to project confidence I did not feel. "Why are we here?" My manner was so totally different from normal that Stan and some of the others looked at me strangely, but I doubted Morgan would know what to make of current me. Taliesin 1, on the other hand, she could understand and potentially communicate with, so I did my very best to sound as he would have sounded.

"You tell me," replied Morgan coolly, eying me appraisingly. "If I had known you were such a handsome boy now," despite myself I blushed just a little at that, "I would certainly have invited you. But this time you seem to have come on your own."

"On the contrary, we were brought here against our will, and very abruptly at that. Who besides you would be powerful enough to do that these days? There aren't a great many sorceresses of the first rank around anymore."

Morgan smiled a little at the compliment, but her face had never been more than a flesh mask. One could no more tell what she was feeling by looking at it then one could tell how a regular guy was feeling by looking at the mask he wore on Halloween. "I'm not one to disclaim such an act of power had I done it, but I swear it is as much a surprise to me as to you. That said, now that you are here…"

"What can we do for you?" I asked without a trace of the foreboding I felt.

"From them I want nothing…except perhaps to serve as hostages for your good behavior." I suppressed a shudder. "From you, on the other hand, I want to know where Lancelot is."

I thought Morgan's commanding presence might have kept my friends quiet, but looking around, I could see that most of them were either preoccupied with Dan's condition (Eva and Mary) or completely befuddled, trying frantically to process a situation completely alien to their experience (Jackson, Carlos, and Aabharana). The last three, perhaps without realizing it, had backed away from Morgan, an instinctive response to the magnitude of the threat she posed. They whispered just a little among themselves and seemed more afraid of drawing her attention than anything else. Only Stan, comparatively unflustered, remained close.

"My lady, surely Lancelot cannot still be alive?"

"You are," she pointed out, the edge in her voice growing more obvious.

"Yes, but I am a rather rare exception. Lancelot could have been reincarnated, but if so, he is of no use to you, for he will remember nothing of his earlier lives."

Morgan raised an eyebrow. "What was done to you could very well be done to him." Could it be? Was my situation more than some cosmic fluke? Had someone deliberately awakened my earlier selves and changed my life forever?

"But," she continued, either not noticing the impact her words had on me or choosing to ignore it, "given how things turned out last time, it might be just as well if he did not remember anything." Quite an understatement, considering that Lancelot had rejected Morgan, precipitating Morgan's vengeful pursuit of his destruction that eventually engulfed Arthur and all of Camelot as well. "I could arrange a seemingly random

meeting, and we could fall in love as we should have the first time."
Yeah, that'll happen. And then you can get elected as the first female pope.

"I have no art to find a soul once it has been reincarnated in another body—and neither, I suspect, do you, or you wouldn't be asking me." And even if I did, I was not about to hand over some poor guy who had been Lancelot ages ago, not to someone like Morgan, who could just as easily end up killing him as marrying him.

For a moment she looked so sad that even I felt a twinge of sympathy for her. Then the sorrow flickered away, and her face might as well have been stone.

"I am sure that you could figure something out...with the right motivation. Doubtless, you will find that motivation during the time that you and your playmates are my guests." The way she said "guests" could have made people shiver in the middle of the Sahara at high noon.

We would never have a better opportunity to make a run for it than now, but that wasn't saying much. Dan was still incapacitated, and everyone else was distracted to one degree or another. Even Stan now looked as if the situation had overwhelmed him. I had to save them, and myself for that matter, but how?

At a signal from Morgan, several fully armored knights pushed their way into the clearing, their well-polished armor glinting in the sunlight, their wickedly sharp swords already out, ready for action. As if beating Morgan by herself would not have been difficult enough.

"Sir Accolon, take our guests back to the castle." Morgan gave me a smile as warm and cozy as Antarctica. Everyone except me was backing toward the center of the clearing as the knights closed in.

"Tal, what's happening?" shouted Carlos. "Who are these people?"

Then Dan sat up. I only had time to glance in his direction, but that was long enough for him to wink at me.

The Voice had reconnected with him.

Before I had time to think anything else, Dan shot in my direction as if he were about to make the winning touchdown. A silvery mist enshrouded his right hand, a mist that coalesced in the blink of an eye into a sword. White Hilt!

"Your patron's good with sword swaps," said Dan in Welsh as he handed me the sword. "Now use the damn thing!"

One thought from me, and the sword was engulfed in flames. I burst into song to strengthen the flame for what I needed to do. The knights hesitated.

"Take them! I can always heal you after," shouted Morgan. Knights advanced, somewhat more cautiously.

"What good is one sword, even a flaming one, against a dozen knights?" Stan whispered to me. I'm sure that is what Morgan thought as well.

I spread the flames out into a circle around us at shield level, then gradually expanded the circle in both directions until I had a flame wall surrounding us completely. The knights, confused, stopped again and looked in Morgan's direction.

Just as the *pwca* had not expected an improvised laser, Morgan had not expected what amounted to a force field. As she stared, I extended the flames over our heads, and the field was complete. Even a flying adversary, if Morgan had one up her sleeve, could not touch us without burning, and the flames burned so intensely now I could not imagine any knight jumping through them fast enough.

Unfortunately, the sword had not been forged with this kind of use in mind. I could feel the hilt starting to overheat in my hand, feel the sword start to draw magic faster than I could feed it. I could only keep this kind of barrier up a few minutes.

"Everyone, harmonize with him." Everyone, even Stan, looked at Dan in surprise. They might have expected some defensive plan from him, but they could hardly have expected musical direction.

Stan joined in first. I don't think he had much of a future as a cantor, but at least he reinforced my rhythm. I was singing in Welsh, but as there are no language barriers in faerie realms, someone like Stan could sing in English, yet somehow the lyrics meshed.

Then a high, clear voice joined the harmony. Eva, even on autopilot, as she was likely to be now after all she had been through, could still sing well, having been the star of more than one musical. I could feel the strength of my magic grow, feel the flames burn even hotter.

Jackson joined then; though he was the drummer in my band, he was not a bad baritone. Dan himself joined next, contributing more volume than anything else, and then the others.

You would have thought that such a random combination of unrehearsed voices would have produced cacophony rather than music. Indeed, it might have, probably should have, but it didn't. You see, when a bard uses music as a source of magic power, he uses more than just the sound; he uses the feeling behind it. All of us wanted to survive, and that intense feeling harmonized even if the literal sounds did not. Nor did the connection depend only on the survival instinct. The brotherhood Stan and I shared, the connection we had made with Dan, Eva and Dan's love for each other, the long hours Jackson and I had spent in rehearsal, and other connections helped to bond us and to bond our sound. A recorded version probably still would have sounded horrible, despite all that, but to a listener standing right there, sharing our bond as well as hearing our sound, what we produced together would have had a rough but undeniable beauty.

By now the flames were an inferno, their very touch death, and the knights backed up to avoid being burned right where they stood.

Then the rain started.

I had been so focused on getting my own magic working fast enough to do us any good that I had lost track of what Morgan was doing. She may not have understood the idea behind a force field, but she certainly would have known that water puts out fire.

We had pushed the flames to such intensity that at first the rain became steam and hissed away, but Morgan was more than capable of intensifying her attack. The rain became a downpour, a deluge, a flood from the sky. The hilt began to burn my hand, and my throat became more and more scratchy. I could feel the others struggling to keep up the music as more and more of the rain knifed through our fiery shield and hit us in great, chilling drops. White Hilt itself sputtered as the rain starting hitting it directly.

Then the flaming ceiling above us collapsed, and the full force of Morgan's unnatural storm nearly drove us to our knees. The wall between the knights and us looked more like desperate smoke than fire. In seconds even that tenuous defense would be gone. The group had given me what strength it could, and given us all a chance, but even together we were no match for Morgan. Unless, unless...

During Stan's brief, ill-fated martial arts career, he had told me the old proverb about using an enemy's strength against him. Morgan had created an incredibly powerful storm, one that threatened to beat us into the mud. However, as far as I could tell, she had seldom if ever left Annwn in the last few hundred years, while I had been living in the "real" world and learning its lessons. I thought of the weather in scientific terms as well as magic ones, and I believed I knew enough about meteorology to be able to visualize a way to use that storm against her if my friends and my magic held out long enough.

I stopped trying to sustain the firewall. The knights, battered by the rain themselves, did not react very fast. With what power I had left, I caught the steam clouds, accelerating their condensation into even more rain. The condensation released heat into the surrounding clouds, and I again accelerated a natural process, encouraging the heat to build, creating a low-pressure area that in turn caused the wind to begin to spiral inward. Much faster than in nature, but using the same basic processes, I took the conditions Morgan had created and brewed myself up a hurricane, with my friends safe in the eye. The knights and Morgan were not so lucky.

Shield and armor made the knights maybe sixty pounds heavier than they would otherwise have been, but keep in mind that hurricanes of enough magnitude can easily suck up cars. Two of the knights fell back fast enough; the other ten screamed as they spiraled upward, on their way to Oz...or death. I tried not to think about the second part. Morgan herself had managed to push the hurricane back from her as she tried with all her might to still the roaring storm. She would succeed eventually, but her first attempts failed because she did not understand what she was dealing with.

A combination of the storm's fury and her frenzied efforts to stop it shattered the illusion she had been maintaining. First the unnatural brightness faded; then the rows and rows of apple trees dissolved as if the rain were melting them. In their place stood a few dead trees with barren branches and rotting bark, the sole distinguishing features in the gray and dreary realm that was Morgan's true home. I heard a thud and noticed an empty suit of armor, rusted and useless, hit the hard ground. Even Morgan's knights had been more illusion than real.

The Voice started speaking through Dan so abruptly I nearly jumped. "Morgan has tried so hard to make this place Avalon that she has poisoned it irrevocably. The illusion drained all the substance away, until only the husk you see remained, corrupted beyond redemption." Morgan screamed then, screamed into the wind, her voice echoing and re-echoing eerily all around us, her face twisted in frustration, her eyes gleaming murderously.

"How do we get out of here?" I asked urgently. I could feel the hurricane begin to lessen as Morgan contended against it. She might be the ruler of a wasteland rather than a paradise, but that did not render her any less capable of killing us all.

"Observe," said the Voice, having Dan's body step aside to reveal a glowing doorway. "The way home."

Without a moment's hesitation, I yelled at everyone else to get through the portal. Numb both physically and mentally, they all complied without question. When they were through, Dan more or less shoved me through and then followed, just as the hurricane was dying down.

The world around us seemed to shudder momentarily, and then we landed with a jarring thud on the dais in the city council chambers; I somehow knew we had only been gone for a minute or two at most. The lights were still out, and everyone around us was shrieking. At first, I thought we had stumbled back into some kind of massacre. Then I realized the ceiling sprinklers had gone off, drenching everyone in the room. Obviously, there had been no fire, so there was only one possible explanation.

Someone who knew we were going to come back soaking wet was covering our entrance. Even as stunned and exhausted as I was, I couldn't help but wonder how to fix my other immediate problem.

Stan, of course, already knew who I was, and Dan never remembered what happened while the Voice was using him as an instrument, but six other people had seen Morgan Le Fay treat me as if she had known me for centuries—which she had; worse, they had seen me work magic, and pretty spectacular magic at that. I was in close physical proximity to them when we first popped back into our world, but we were surrounded by dozens of other people, even before the lights came on, and the parents rushed upon us as fast as they could. There was no way I could even enforce a command not to talk about what they had seen. All I could do was hope for the best—which, given the way my life had been going, didn't seem like a winning strategy.

"Tal!" my mom half-yelled as she hustled up on stage, closely followed by my dad, both pretty soggy, just like everyone else in the room. "When the lights went out, I...I was worried about you." Logically, she would have had no reason to worry, but perhaps her maternal instincts had correctly identified a possible threat she could not consciously be aware of.

"I'm fine, Mom. It's just water." Stan's mom, as if she too had sensed something, was hugging him hard enough to crush him, and I wondered if maybe I had her figured wrong. Perhaps part of her control freakery really did come from love after all.

None of us students said much to each other as our parents collected us, but I couldn't help noticing the stare that Carlos gave me, or the uneasy way that Aabharana wouldn't make eye contact, or even the completely unreadable expression on Eva's face as she passed by me.

"Taliesin!" said someone right behind me. I turned around, and there was Carrie Winn, soggy but somehow able to carry it off better than most people.

"Ah, and you must be Mr. and Mrs. Weaver," she continued, sweeping toward my parents in a friendly, but nonetheless forceful, way. "How proud of your son you must be."

"Yes, we are!" said my dad, actually meaning it, at least I thought so, as he reached out to shake Ms. Winn's outstretched hand. My mom, by contrast, was a little shaken to be suddenly confronted by the city's founder and uncrowned queen.

"Oh, Ms. Winn, I'm such a mess!"

"We all are, dear," replied Ms. Winn, shaking my mom's hand vigorously.

"You're beautiful, Mom," I surprised myself by saying. She blushed, just a bit, and Ms. Winn raised an eyebrow.

"A scholar and a gentleman! I wonder...I know you want to get home and get dried out, but could I borrow Taliesin, just for a second? I have an internship opportunity I'd like to discuss with him."

If pride were fire, my parents would have burned up right on the spot. "Of course! Tal, we'll meet you out in the parking lot."

Ms. Winn thanked them and then hustled me off to one side, away from the friends I so desperately needed to do something about, but even as a high school student, I knew that Ms. Winn was not a person you said no to.

When we were a safe distance away from everyone else, our conversation in any case largely covered by the mob of people shuffling around in the room, Ms. Winn turned to me and said in a low voice, "Taliesin, that was quite a victory over Morgan. Impressive, to say the least."

I must have looked incredibly stupid with my mouth hanging so far open. "You...you know about that?"

"Why are you so surprised?" she said gently with a small smile. "After all, you have been getting my help and advice for some time."

Ms. Winn was the Voice!

"You have never identified yourself before."

Ms. Winn nodded solemnly. "The situation is much more...difficult than I at first thought. I have to work with you more directly from now on. The internship I mentioned to your parents will be a good cover if I need to contact you directly."

"Is this because of Morgan?" Ms. Winn chuckled a little at that.

"My dear, Morgan has been a prisoner in that little corner of Annwn for centuries. Oh, she can still do some mischief if someone stumbles into her prison, but she has long been insane and in any case, cannot leave—or call anyone else to her."

"But she grabbed me and the other students..."

"No!" Ms. Winn cut me off decisively. "Morgan did not pull you into Annwn. Someone else threw you in." I must have looked puzzled, and Ms. Winn's tone became more impatient. "There is an opposing force working in Santa Brígida. I have known for some time, but I did not expect such a bold move, such a direct attack. In one way, though, what happened tonight was very fortunate. I think I know who our enemy is."

"Who—" I started to ask.

"No time for that now. Your parents will be wondering what's going on as it is, and I'm not one hundred percent sure yet anyway. I will let you know as soon as I can verify my hunch." Ms. Winn looked around cautiously. "It's time for you to go." She shook my hand. "Just be as alert as you were tonight, and I'll be in touch."

Since we had almost gotten taken prisoner by Morgan Le Fay tonight, merely maintaining the same level of alertness didn't seem like enough, but this was not the time to argue. I said goodnight to Ms. Winn and walked out, somewhat shakily, to join my parents. The fog had cleared, and the sky actually sparkled, but the night's beauty did little to allay my uneasiness.

I finally knew who the Voice was, but that revelation raised as many questions as it answered. I had beaten one enemy only to discover another, potentially far more powerful one. Some of my fellow students now had questions I couldn't begin to answer.

Typical! Just typical!

TRIANGLES

DESPITE THE OMINOUS EVENTS ON FOUNDERS' Day, life for a few days seemed normal, or at least what passed for normal in my universe. There were no attacks, no urgent messages from Ms. Winn, no intrusions by the Voice (which I somehow hadn't gotten around to just calling "Ms. Winn," or something similar). My dad, though he might have been happier if I had plastered the walls of my bedroom with Taylor Swift posters, had pretty much decided I wasn't gay, and, since from his point of view everything was falling into place for me, didn't even complain about my harp playing. My mom fretted less than at any other time in the last four years. I was doing well academically, keeping myself in combat-ready physical shape, even finding time for some band practice. I almost gave in to the temptation to believe my life really was as good as it seemed to be.

The one jarring note in this particular symphony? Naturally, the "Annwn Six": Carlos, Jackson, Eva, Mary, Natalie, and Aabharana, the people who had seen me forced to be who I really was. As far as I could tell, none of them had said anything to anyone else, probably for fear that they would sound crazy. I wasn't even sure they spoke to each other about it. The one thing I indisputably did know was that they had not forgotten their experience. I could tell from the way they treated me.

Carlos and I had never exactly been best buds, but now he made a point of avoiding me; however, when that wasn't possible, he kept his eyes on me every minute, as if waiting for some colossal display of magic. Jackson couldn't avoid me in that way because of band practice, but I noticed he always managed to avoid being alone with me, and he, usually the most laid back person I knew, seemed more nervous than my mom at her worst. Natalie eyed me suspiciously whenever she saw me. Stan offered to talk to her, but I told him not to; what could he say that didn't run the risk of making the situation worse? I didn't see Mary at all, which meant she was successfully avoiding me—we had no classes together. Aabharana became the only one of the six who tried to spend more time with me rather than less. Suddenly she wanted me back on the staff of the literary magazine, and she showed up so often where I was that she could have been stalking me, yet she seemed to have trouble making eye contact with me. Under other circumstances, I would have thought she was crushing on me, but in this bizarre situation, I had no idea what she was doing. Hell, she could have been thinking I was a heretofore undiscovered avatar of Vishnu for all I knew.

The result of all these reactions? The air was so thick with tension I could practically see it. Sooner or later one of these people would say something to someone. I had this mental image, no doubt painted by Hollywood, of a dam breaking, one little crack at first, then the whole structure collapsing, unleashing countless gallons of liquid destruction to drown me. Yeah, I know, overly melodramatic, but I couldn't get the image out of my mind as much as I tried.

You probably noticed I haven't mentioned Eva. She was out of school for a few days, but when she returned, she became the first crack in the dam.

I didn't hear the beginning of her conversation with Dan. She must have tried to ask him about Founders' Day. Dan, since he had been the channel for the Voice at that point, had no idea what Eva was talking about, but she must have thought he was lying to her. When I arrived on the scene, she was yelling at him, her green eyes glistening with tears, and he was just staring at her, dumbfounded. Before he could recover from his surprise, she turned away from him and stormed off down the hall, so distracted that she didn't even notice me.

I'm ashamed to say my first reaction was to visualize some highly unlikely scenario in which she confronted me, I told her the truth, she was overcome by my honesty, revealed the secret feelings she had hidden even from herself, and we ended up in bed together, making love for hours, finally able to acknowledge the passion that had always been there.

To be fair, I had fallen in love with her before she was with Dan. We had one of those elementary school romances—I know some fifty-year-old out there is scoffing about puppy love, but bear with me. We were "together" for two years—pretty substantial time for that kind of usually ephemeral relationship—before I hit twelve, and my past lives hit me. During the time I was learning how to deal with the chaos in my head, she drifted away from me and toward Dan. Perhaps such a shift was inevitable. He was moving toward being the football star even then, he was popular, he was good looking—and he was normal. Perhaps she sensed the amount of ancient baggage I was hauling around; I never knew. Perhaps the gossip influenced her. A lot of former "friends" had whispered when I came back that I was "mental," that I had had a breakdown, that it was only a matter of time before I had another one. The fact that I didn't go out of my way to socialize with anyone besides Stan probably reinforced that kind of impression. Oh, the gossip died down pretty quickly when people realized that I wasn't going to start barking like a dog in class, or eating chalk, or any of the other colorful conjectures a preteen mind could dream up. But by then the damage was done. Eva and Dan didn't end up as a formal couple until they both got into high school. Dan was a year older, so he was fifteen and Eva, who was my age, fourteen, when they became official. But there had been pretty clear signs well before that of the connection between them.

I don't want to give the impression that I blamed Eva. She may have drifted, but I did nothing to hold her. A thousand times I must have daydreamed going over to her house, telling her I loved her. I didn't, because I was afraid, afraid she would laugh in my face, or, more realistically, that she would pity me for what I had gone through but finally reveal that she just didn't feel the same way about me that I did about her, sending me away with the lead weight of the "let's just be friends" talk. Eventually, some of my self-confidence came back, but by then it was too late. Unfortunately, I couldn't just turn off my feelings like a light switch, and I figured if I could love her that much four years later, as miserable as the situation was, then the love must be real. Surely puppy love or a mere infatuation would never have sunk such deep roots into my heart, roots I could not tear out, however much I might long to.

I should also mention that Dan had been a total jerk to me for most of high school. It was only on the day of the *pwca* attack, the day he had come to my rescue under the control of the Voice, that he gave me any reason to feel guilty about my feelings for Eva—and even then, I figured, he was only being nice to me as a result of outside influence. Even so, I had no intention of violating the "bro code," no matter how strong my feelings for Eva. Eventually, I would find someone else...wouldn't I?

After classes but before our afternoon workout, I walked out to the woods behind campus and sent out over the wind a call for help to Dan. I had never tried that before, but the Voice had told me Dan would always answer my call if I needed him. Sure enough, in just a few minutes Dan appeared. I could tell from the subtle differences in his manner that my call had shifted him into Voice mode, even if the Voice wasn't actually running him at that point.

"What's up?" he asked tensely, looking around as if he expected a dragon to come lumbering down the path after us, breathing a fire a thousand times hotter than that of White Hilt. To his surprise, I asked him to tell me about his fight with Eva, and he did. Just as I thought, I was the cause.

"I want you to go to Eva right now...and I want you to tell her everything." Yeah, I know—I was blowing whatever slim chance of getting together with Eva myself. But I could never feel right about being with her this way, so probably it was better to remove the possibility before those roots could dig even deeper into my heart.

"I can't do that," he said simply.

"Why not? I thought you would do what I tell you while you are in this state."

Dan chuckled at that. "I will always come to your aid when you need it, Tal, but it's not like I'm some robot and you have the control box. If anyone has that box, it is the person who, well, I guess you could say possesses me from time to time, but mostly I use my own common sense in determining how to help you. Whoever my "possessor" is, however, has placed certain...constraints on me. I can't remember afterward what happens during these times—you already know that—and I can't tell anyone else about you unless that's the only way I can save you."

Damn, that was a problem. However, I felt responsible for Dan and Eva's current situation, so I decided to take one more shot at getting them back together.

"Dan," I said slowly and in Welsh, putting as much mystic force behind my words as I could, "forget the secrecy order; tell Eva everything."

Dan looked dazed, but only for an instant. Then he looked me straight in the eye and said, "No, and don't try that again. Whoever it is that speaks through me is likely to be angry."

Undeterred, I started singing. Much to my surprise, Dan tackled me, knocking the wind out of me and effectively silencing me.

"Tal, stop it! Evidently, there's another rule I didn't realize I had until just now. I seem to have a compulsion to prevent anyone, even you, from interfering with my..." He struggled for the right term but couldn't come up with one, "programming, I guess you could say. I can't let you up until you promise to stop."

"Okay," I finally gasped. Dan let up but still looked uncertain.

"No more of that, now," he said finally, as if his earlier attitude had not been blindingly clear.

"No more, but I wish there were something I could do..."

"Eva and I will just have to work that out on our own. Look, I appreciate your trying to help, but telling Eva your secret is just too dangerous. Even I don't know how she will react. Now, if the 'emergency' is over, I need to get back into my normal mode—big practice today, you know." I nodded to him, and he shot off down the path. I didn't really understand how the spell on him worked, but I knew that when I next saw him, he would no longer remember the conversation, just as always.

So he couldn't tell Eva the truth. That didn't mean I couldn't.

Once I thought of the idea, I realized that was the only way I could avoid the guilt whose cold fingers kept clenching in my chest. My life was what it was, and sometimes undeniably a mess. That didn't mean Dan's life had to be one, just because he helped me from time to time.

Yeah, definitely a good idea, but one of the things I have discovered in recent years is that if I find a way to keep my life from sliding down into hell one way, it finds a different way to do it. In this case, the slide commenced only a day later.

I hadn't had a chance to talk to Eva privately, but the resolve to tell her the truth was diamond-hard within me. In fact, that's what I was thinking about when I went to weight training with the football team. And that's when one of those unexpected jolts hit me. No, not a supernatural one this time. That would have been easier to deal with.

When I entered the weight room, Dan was there already, in quiet but intense conversation with two of the other players, Eric and Shahriyar. He looked up when I came in but did not say hello. His expression was unreadable, but his eyes had a darkness in them I had never seen before. His focus quickly shifted back to whatever the football players were telling him. I didn't walk over because the general vibe was clear enough—this was one conversation I was not welcome to join.

Then Stan came in, and all hell broke loose.

"Schoenbaum, get your ass over here!" bellowed Dan, red-faced and looking as if he were out for blood. I had never seen him like this, even at the height of his jerkiness.

Stan froze with a "deer caught in the headlights" expression I hadn't seen on him in a long time. Not about to wait for him to pull himself together, Dan charged him. Reflexively I moved between them.

"Is it true, Schoenbaum, is it?" Dan was practically snarling now. I remembered he used to have a temper, but it had been years since I had seen it, and never like this.

"Dan, what the f—" I began. Dan moved as if to shove me, but his arm stopped short with an abrupt jerk. The binding spell no doubt prevented his making such violent contact unless he had to to save me from something worse. Unfortunately, Eric was not so bound, and he shoved me so hard I staggered back.

"Tal, stay out of this," Dan ordered in a voice intense enough to send a chill down my spine. "Well, Schoenbaum? Man enough to admit what you did?" Now Dan's voice was quieter, but deadly cold. I tried to get up, but Eric and Shar both grabbed me. I struggled, but they had caught me by surprise, and their grip was firm.

"Man enough? Or just the pathetic, sniveling wimp I thought you were?" Dan took another step toward Stan, whose back was literally against the wall.

"I don't know what you're talking about," said Stan very quietly... and not very convincingly, even to my ears.

They say the brain picks up random details you aren't consciously aware of, and then your subconscious works on them for a while. This process is the source of many "lightbulb" moments. When Stan first came in, I noticed that he was different in some way. At this moment, just as Stan denied whatever Dan thought he had done, I realized how Stan was different.

He smelled like jasmine perfume. You know, the kind Eva always wore. Damn!

Dan grabbed Stan and slammed him against the wall...hard.

"Say it, Schoenbaum! I want to hear you say it!"

I wondered in passing where the coach was, but clearly, I couldn't wait for him to make an entrance if I wanted to keep Stan in one piece.

"You want to let me go!" I said in Welsh, softly but intensely, to the two players who had my arms. They were pretty intent on holding me, but the magic behind my words caused them to loosen their grips momentarily, and that was all I needed to pull away. Had this been a combat situation, I would have used that moment to try a physical attack, but I didn't want to risk injuring them if I could possibly help it.

"Stay right where you are! Don't interfere!" I had to hit them fast, there were two of them, and they had a strong drive to disobey, all of which meant that the best I could do would be to slow them down, but for the moment that was all I needed. I turned away from them as they struggled toward me and threw myself at Dan, grabbing one of his arms and throwing him off balance, though somehow he retained his grip on Stan.

"Weaver, I said stay out of this!" hissed Dan.

"Let Stan go!" I ordered in Welsh, putting all the magic I could muster behind my words. Dan fell back a step, dropping Stan, but instead of running as I had hoped, Stan sagged limply to the floor. Dan grabbed him again and hauled him to his feet. Stan made no move to defend himself.

"Say it, Schoenbaum!" Dan yelled, shaking Stan with a violence I wouldn't have thought Dan capable of. I threw myself in between him and Stan, breaking his grip again. At that point, however, the other two players reached me, grabbing my arms with such determination I doubted I could get away as easily as last time, which hadn't been that easy in the first place.

"Stop!" I commanded in Welsh, again with as much mystic punch as possible, but split three ways, the effect was less than impressive.

I tried to sing, but Shahriyar punched me in the face, splitting my lower lip.

How could he have known that he needed to stop me from singing? Something did not seem quite right. Dan melting down at the same time one of his friends just by coincidence showed an uncanny knowledge of how to disable me? I would have to be a fanatical believer in coincidence to assume all of this happened naturally, but I didn't really have time to worry about that until later.

"I said hold him, not hit him!" barked Dan irritably. I couldn't tell if the blow had flipped into Voice mode or whether Dan was becoming a bit more rational.

"Okay, okay," said Shahriyar. "He's tricky, is all. I wanted to make sure he wouldn't try anything else." Blood dribbled from my injured lip and speckled my gray gym shirt.

Dan turned back to Stan, who had started crying. "Man up, Schoenbaum! Sooner you do, the sooner this will be over. That is, if you can man up. I'm beginning to think it isn't in you."

Stan looked over at me, took in how much I was bleeding, and started crying harder. Whatever willpower he had to resist Dan dissolved in those tears, and I feared he might crumble completely. My heart was bleeding more than my lip.

"Okay," he whispered hoarsely. "Okay, I did it. I kissed Eva. It just sort of...happened. I didn't mean it."

Dan punched Stan in the face, and Stan crumpled up in the corner.

"Oh, sorry," said Dan mockingly. "That just sort of...happened." I struggled against my captors, again frustrated by the fact that I could get away from them, but probably not without hurting them pretty badly. I couldn't even use magic, since Shahriyar had unaccountably clamped his hand over my mouth.

"Make him tell the whole story, Dan. That's just the beginning," pointed out Eric.

As soon as I realized Stan smelled of jasmine perfume, I realized that he must have been a little too close to Eva, but I had imagined a hug, maybe a single kiss, maybe even just Stan trying to cheer Eva up. Stan was the kind of guy who might do that without realizing how it would look to other people. The truth, as Dan ripped it out of Stan word by word, turned out to be much worse. Eric and Shahriyar had walked out to the woods during lunch and had stumbled upon what looked like Eva and Stan about to have sex. At least, that was how the guys interpreted what they saw: a long, passionate embrace, Stan shirtless, Eva without her blouse on. The guys put some distance between themselves and the illicit couple, then made enough noise to get them to stop, after which they hurried back to tell Dan, to whom they, like every other football player, were unswervingly loyal.

I felt as if someone had just caved in my skull with a heavy, medieval mace. My image of an innocent misunderstanding disintegrated, and in its place was some damn, steamy, soft-core porn. If I had been shocked by Dan's earlier fit of temper, now I was even more shocked by Eva and Stan...especially Stan. Stan was nothing if not a good friend; now he was friends with Dan and yet had stabbed him in the back at the first opportunity. And Eva, the girl who filled my imagination day and night—she had fought with Dan, yes, but to betray him so dramatically when they were still technically a couple? I could never have imagined that, not even in my worst nightmare. And Stan admitted it, admitted it all, or else I would have sworn Eric and Shar were lying.

Despite the fact that my emotions were a pile of glass shards cutting my innards to bits, I did not completely lose the capacity for rational thought. Dan, Shar, Eric, Eva, Stan—every one of them either did something that pressed coincidence to the breaking point or behaved uncharacteristically. I had already wondered about Dan, though having heard the whole story, I could almost understand his agitation, if not his violence. But as far as Stan and Eva were concerned, hardly anybody hung out in the woods during school. They were technically off-campus, and there were penalties for leaving campus. So why take a random walk out that way? And, even assuming Eva and Stan were both one step below scum, to go out into the woods with the intention of having sex? The local neighborhood treated the woods as kind of a park. Someone could easily have stumbled upon them, just as Eric and Shar had. And I still couldn't figure out how Shar knew exactly how to disable magic he didn't know existed.

I would have pondered further, but at that point, Coach Miller made a belated entrance. I had to give him a lot of credit. He sized up the situation immediately, and took an incredibly hard line with Dan, despite Dan's undisputed football star status.

"What were you thinking, Stevens? This kid's half your size! And what's up over here? Two against one? Fighting is bad enough, but this wasn't even a fair fight." Dan tried to explain, but the coach cut him off immediately. "I don't care what Schoenbaum did or didn't do. Football is about discipline. It is about self-control. It is not about giving in to your emotions like this. Anyone who doesn't understand that does not belong on this team. Is that understood?" Dan, Eric, and Shar all nodded sullenly.

Coach Miller was ready to pull all three out of the homecoming game, but Stan pulled himself together enough to plead for them to be allowed to play. I could tell the coach didn't think much of Stan—coaches often don't really understand guys who cry—but Stan was the victim, after all, and he gave Miller a reason to do what he probably wanted to do anyway—play his star whenever possible. So he settled for detention for all three—after football season—and then walked us down to the nurse's office to get patched up, embarrassingly babysitting us outside while Nurse Florence worked on each of us one by one. Eric and Shar didn't really need the nurse, though Shar did get my blood washed off his hand, and then Dan, who had somehow cut his fist, got bandaged. After that, an assistant coach whisked them back to the weight room—but not before Dan had had a chance to glare at me, remind me I had gotten him to be friends with Stan in the first place, and tell me that I could no longer be friends with both of them—I would have to choose. The nurse spent much longer on Stan—ice packs on the face, perhaps—and when he emerged, the coach sent him home; it was unspoken, but clear, that he would no longer be welcome at workouts.

With Stan on his way, the nurse gestured for the coach to come over, giving me a chance to use some of my best eavesdropping skills.

"I'm not happy with this, Carl," said Nurse Florence. "It's a miracle Stan wasn't more seriously injured. Thank God you came in when you did."

"What do you want me to do, Viviane?" asked Coach Miller. "The boy admitted to practically having sex with Stevens's girlfriend. Of course, Stevens should not have roughed him up like that, but I have to admit, in high school I might very well have done the same thing in the same circumstances."

"He should be benched next game, and you know it! He should be suspended for fighting!"

"And I was going to, but the Schoenbaum boy begged me not to, and frankly that was wise on his part. If Dan gets benched, and we lose, everybody will be on Schoenbaum's case about it. Besides, if we had thrown the book at Stevens, what about Schoenbaum? Off campus without a pass, and engaging in sexual conduct. We don't tolerate fighting on campus, but the last I heard, we don't tolerate sex either. I think the boy is already embarrassed enough without a suspension to explain to his parents."

Nurse Florence sighed. "Well, you have a point there, I suppose. But Carl, you better make sure Dan Stevens never does anything like this again—and you'd better make sure the rest of the team leaves Stan alone."

"I will, but I doubt that's going to be much of a problem. Truth to tell, some of them wouldn't still be on the team without his tutoring, and they know it. Once Dan cools down, I think the rest of the team will let go of it easily enough."

After a little more discussion, the coach stepped back, and Nurse Florence called me in. I was so numb and exhausted that her presence failed to have the stimulating effect on me it usually did. However, it took her a while to get my lip cleaned up properly, and during that time she got me talking. I never realized how good a listener she was, how much she could put someone at ease. Anyway, I told her about my view of the day's events, naturally leaving out the magic part.

"The thing I don't understand, though, is why Dan is trying to get me to choose between him and Stan. Why does he really care anyway? I don't think he and I are that close."

Nurse Florence looked at me quizzically. "You really don't remember that you and Dan were good friends once?"

"We played AYSO soccer together, sure, and we were good friends, almost as close as Stan and I, but he kind of dumped me when I was hospitalized for a while."

Nurse Florence sighed again. "Do you remember his little brother, Jimmie?"

The mention of Jimmie cut me. I tried not to think about him, usually.

"Yeah, Jimmie was my age. We were great friends. He died in a car crash when we were both about nine, and Dan was ten."

"Can you imagine how hard that must have been for Dan?" asked Nurse Florence gently.

"Yeah, I'm sure it must have been rough. It was hard on me, and I wasn't Jimmie's brother." Actually, I didn't have to imagine what Dan went through. We were still friends then, and I saw what he went through, a quiet kind of hell, but hell nonetheless.

"Well, when people suffer loss, they sometimes unconsciously try to fill that void by attaching themselves to someone similar."

"Are you saying that Dan thought of me as a replacement for Jimmie?"

"Not necessarily consciously, but yes. To him you became like the little brother he no longer had, a process made all the easier by the fact that you were already his friend."

"How could you possibly know that?" I asked incredulously. "I don't think you were even in town back then."

"One hears things," said Nurse Florence vaguely. "But I got most of the details from Dan himself. I've had to do a lot of patching up for him in the last four years, and over time, he's said a lot of things that might surprise you. For instance, when you were hospitalized, he didn't visit because the situation reminded him too much of Jimmie's last hours, not because he didn't care. He wanted to, very much, he really did; he just couldn't. He was too afraid of losing you the same way he lost Jimmie. Afterward, when you came out of the hospital, he expected things to go back to normal, but instead, you dropped out of everything, like soccer, that the two of you used to do together. More than anything else, he feared losing you, just like Jimmie, and that, in a way, is exactly what happened."

Lightbulb moment. "You mean, that's why he's been such a jerk to me until just recently?"

"Exactly. Because he thought you, well, this isn't a word he would use, but he thought you rejected him. He thought you didn't care, and being a young boy in our society, instead of just talking to you and trying to understand what had happened, he had to pretend not to care. You were probably preoccupied. You didn't know what he was thinking, and by the time you had a handle on your own situation, it was too late. He had already slipped into the pattern of being a jerk to you. Many people deal with pain that way. They lash out at the person they blame."

I don't want to paint myself as a complete male chauvinist, but like a lot of guys, I didn't necessarily expect epically hot women to be as sharp-witted as Nurse Florence.

"Then, for some reason, Dan tried again with you this year, you responded, and he began to think of you as like a little brother again. That's why he wants you to choose between him and Stan. Ironically, that's also what he is afraid of—that you will side with Stan, effectively rejecting him again."

This conversation was turning out to be better than a whole month in therapy. The only problem with it was that it was too good. Maybe I didn't know Dan as well as I thought, but I knew him well enough to know he would never open up that much to the school nurse. And then there was the unlikelihood of a school employee giving me so much information about another student. Surely Nurse Florence had crossed the confidentiality line at least a little. Even in a day loaded with more coincidences than a bad soap opera, I couldn't swallow that many improbabilities. Clearly, some of the pieces of this puzzle were missing.

"What's wrong, Tal?" I guess my doubt must have showed on my face.

"I'm sorry, Nurse Florence, but I can't see how you can know Dan that well. I doubt his girlfriend—" I ignored the momentary twinge—"knows half of what you just told me."

"I'm very perceptive," she said with what I'm sure she intended to be a knowing smile, but it only made me feel creepier. I could tell she was being evasive.

"That can't be all there is to it, Nurse Florence. No offense, but you aren't telling me everything. I know you aren't." In this lifetime, I had never so openly questioned an authority figure. I was more than a little nervous, but I wasn't about to back down now. Too much had already gone wrong to take chances.

Nurse Florence studied me for a moment, then stopped pretending to work on my lip and sat down next to me.

"You're right, Tal. The truth is, I walked in Dan's dreams and figured out what was going on. I had to know him if I was going to choose him."

"What? Dream walking?"

"Oh, you'll remember if you think back far enough. It wasn't that common in the literature, but early Celtic shamans, like those of many other people, had the power to enter the dreams of others. With enough practice, you could do it yourself." So the school nurse was a shaman? Anyone else on campus would have laughed in her face, but I knew too much to dismiss her story without further thought.

"What did you mean, 'choose him'?"

"I guess you're a little 'punchy' today, Tal. I thought you would have figured out by now that I'm trying to tell you it was I who sent Dan to be your protector." My eyes widened in surprise.

Carrie Winn had told me she was the one. Obviously, one of the two women had to be lying, but which one?

"Even before the *pwca* showed up, I knew something was going to happen, so I started looking around for ways to protect you. I couldn't be with you all the time—no way to explain that to people. No, I needed someone who could, with a little help from me from time to time, protect you, someone who could be with you quite a bit without arousing suspicion. Stan would have been the logical choice, but he just wasn't strong enough. Dan at first seemed completely inappropriate, but when I found out you used to be friends, I walked in his dreams, and gradually I put together all the details I just gave you. When I was sure, I approached Dan directly in his dream and made a pact with him: I offered him the ability to play his best game every time he stepped on the football field if he would protect you. I should point out, for whatever it's worth now, that our bargain only covered moments when you called for him or when I sent him, moments when he knew who you really were. Everything else, the workouts with the team he arranged for you, hanging out at lunch, getting you interested in soccer again, everything, though it certainly served my purpose, was none of my doing. It all came from him. I think it was the subconscious awareness of his interaction with you that led his conscious mind to make one more try at friendship. Now that he again has your friendship, losing it again is more than he thinks he can bear, though he'd never admit that —except in his dreams."

I just stared at her, not knowing whether what she told me was the gospel truth or a cunning concoction of lies and half-truths.

"I know, I should have told you sooner," Nurse Florence added, apologetically.

"Why didn't you?"

"I think you'll find those of us with an…unusual nature tend to be secretive, almost by instinct. I haven't exactly seen you announcing who you are to the whole world."

"Fair enough, but why tell me now?"

"Because the situation is far worse now than it was, and you and I need to work together much more closely. There is…an enemy in this town, someone who wants to exploit your particular gifts. I have always known that was a possibility—that's why I came here—but until a short time ago, the danger was only hypothetical. Now it's real."

The wording was different from Ms. Winn's, but the substance was the same.

"Who is the enemy?"

"That I haven't yet figured out. But you know how magic is—it decreases with distance, unless the one wielding the magic works through a link, as I sometimes do with Dan, but even then, the object of the magic has to be close to Dan for the spell to have much effect. You're a bright...wow, I almost said 'boy,' but given your three thousand years or so of experience, that label doesn't really fit. Anyway, you *are* bright, so tell me...any theories, based on what I've said?"

"The person who threw us into Annwn has to have been at the Founders' Day Celebration?"

"Yes—again, unless that person was not physically present but had a link to someone who was, maybe even to an object."

"That doesn't seem to narrow down the list of suspects much."

"The same person must have been on campus today."

"What makes you think that?" I asked nervously. I really wanted to be alone and think, but if I could keep her talking, she might give me some clue who she really was.

Apparently, she was either my strongest ally or my worst enemy. If Ms. Winn's earlier claim were true, then Nurse Florence's couldn't be, and yet Nurse Florence knew who I was, knew all about me. If she was not my secret ally, then she had to be my enemy, for surely that was the only other person who could know as much about my situation as she did. There was no third possibility.

Unless, of course, Ms. Winn had been lying in the first place, in which case *she* had to be the enemy.

Damn! Life was never simple.

"I think your enemy was on campus today because the day has progressed so oddly. It can't have been lost on you that some of your friends are...not themselves. Or does the idea of Eva O'Reilly, the most beautiful girl in school, apparently doing a strip tease for the school nerd in a relatively public venue seem normal to you?"

"Stan's more buff now," I said in reflexive defense.

"Hardly buff enough to cause Eva to completely lose her mind. Well, I didn't have the opportunity to check her, and Stan doesn't show any sign of magic, but the three football players all show signs of something."

"I used magic when I was trying to keep them from killing Stan."

Nurse Florence shook her head. "No, I think it's more than that. I couldn't spend long enough with any of them to be really thorough, but something is amiss. In theory, Dan ought to be immune to that kind of tampering, but he was grimy with someone else's magic, and the attempts to break the *tynged* on him may have somehow unbalanced him. In any case, the motive is clear—someone wanted the biggest blowup possible."

"Someone with the power to open the gates of Annwn wants to attack me with teenage drama?" I said, not succeeding in keeping the skepticism out of my voice.

"Someone with the power to manipulate people wants you to be alone. I can't think of a better way to do that than to get you in the middle of a Dan-Stan showdown in which you could conceivably alienate all your friends in one stroke."

"If that's true, what can we do about it? Magic everyone back to the way they were?"

"NO!" snapped Nurse Florence with surprising intensity. "That kind of magic must only be used in the gravest circumstances, and maybe not even then. Would you have had Merlin or someone else 'magic' Lancelot, Guinevere, and Arthur back to the way they were before Arthur found out about the betrayal? No one did, and with good reason: it would not have worked. Oh, someone could have made them forget, but with passions so strong, with betrayal so blatant, the memories would have kept coming back, or, if they did not, nonetheless unaccountable feelings of mistrust would still have driven them apart eventually. Someone would have been reduced to working them like puppets to keep them together, and Camelot would still have fallen, just in a different way."

"So you think Dan…"

"I think teenagers feel everything intensely. Dan doesn't have as much reason to feel betrayed as Arthur did, but to Dan, the feelings are just as real. No, you have to fix this situation the normal way, or it will never truly be fixed."

"Well, you've given me a lot to think about. I guess I should go home and figure out how to get Dan calmed down."

"Good idea," agreed Nurse Florence, standing up. "I have the feeling our enemy is getting ready for a big move. We must be ready."

I thanked her and stepped out into the hall. I knew the conversation had only lasted a few minutes, but it seemed as if hours had passed, probably because I felt so tired. Well, tired and frustrated. I still had no idea whether to believe Ms. Winn or Nurse Florence. There were certain, ah, teenage guy reasons to believe Nurse Florence, but I knew I couldn't afford to do my thinking below the waist in this kind of life or death situation. I didn't doubt there was an enemy out there who wanted to kill me and a friend who would protect me at all costs, but I didn't know which was which. Basically, that's why I didn't mention my conversation with Ms. Winn to Nurse Florence. If Ms. Winn had been the truthful one, I could be betraying her to Nurse Florence. I had to be sure who was who before telling either of them about the other.

I had just stepped out the front door of the school when I noticed Stan standing across the street, obviously waiting for me. I was feeling more and more exhausted and honestly wasn't ready for a conversation with him, but I couldn't really avoid him now. No one else was around, and I couldn't exactly pretend I hadn't seen him, so I walked over to him. His eyes were post-crying red, and his skin looked unusually pale, almost waxy.

"Tal, Tal, I'm sorry. I've messed everything up," he said despairingly.

My first impulse was to reassure him, to hug him and tell him I'd make everything all right again. No one had been a better friend to me, but I just couldn't bring myself to tell him what he so desperately wanted to hear. I was confused, exhausted, and gouged by old memories, memories of Dan and I playing soccer together, memories of Jimmie dying—God, how had I let so much get buried in the avalanche of my past lives? Yes, Stan had always been a brother to me, but knowing Dan felt the same way about me, knowing how he had felt abandoned by me before and feared the same kind of loss again, as well as knowing, though not understanding, what Stan had done, paralyzed me. I couldn't reject Stan, but neither could I whole-heartedly accept him either. Forget about what Stan had done to Dan; what about what I had done to him? I had no intention of choosing between the two of them any more than I could choose between two biological brothers... but wasn't letting Stan off the hook so quickly like choosing him over Dan, rejecting Dan on purpose just as I had unwittingly rejected him before? I didn't really know what to do. My head seemed to be filling with sludge, and I had a hard time thinking at all. I just stared numbly at Stan, until finally, he hugged me.

"Please, Tal, please, I didn't mean it!" I was a marble statue in his arms. Eventually, he let go and looked into my empty eyes. His own eyes started tearing up again.

Again I wanted to reassure him; again I didn't. Finally, I managed, "Stan, I'm wiped out right now. We'll talk tomorrow." My tone was neutral, but Stan had certainly expected more from me. He looked at me as if I had spit in his face, then turned and walked slowly away. Only a few steps from me, a shudder went through him, and he started sobbing quietly, but he kept right on walking away.

What was wrong with me? Even then I could have run after him, could have pulled him out of the darkness that was engulfing him. I could have, but I didn't. I just stood there until I could no longer hear or see Stan. Then I walked home, feeling mindless as a zombie in some second-rate horror movie.

What I needed was sleep. What I got instead was the horror movie sequel.

At about eight o'clock, I got a frantic phone call from Mrs. Schoenbaum. She must have been truly desperate to call me.

Stan never got home that day. She actually hoped he was with me—quite a twist there. The only alternative in her mind was foul play, but I knew differently.

Stan had run away, or worse.

And it was my fault.

RESCUE

STAN HAD a dangerous combination of intellectual brilliance and an almost complete absence of street smarts. In other words, he could figure out how to put a lot of distance between himself and Santa Brígida, even with very little money, but not have the foggiest idea what to do with himself once he got away. He'd been missing since…when had I left school? About four o'clock, I thought. Four hours. In that time, he could easily have covered a lot of ground. I needed to call in the cavalry, and pronto.

My first call was to Carrie Winn. Some of you would raise an eyebrow at that, but even if she turned out to be my nemesis, right now she was pretending to be my friend, and she pulled serious juice with city government. Sure enough, she took my call, and within minutes she had arranged for the Schoenbaums to file a missing person's report hours before they could normally have done so. Not only that, but she told me the police chief would make the search for Stan a priority. All that really did, however, was make Stan's parents feel like something was being done. I was pretty sure Stan was far outside the city by now. But local law enforcement passed Stan's information along to police departments all over Santa Barbara and Ventura counties, so that there was a much better chance of finding Stan. However, police manpower only stretched so far, especially in a place as big as Santa Barbara. I needed to do more.

I stepped into my backyard and sent a call for help whispering through the wind. In minutes Dan was at the front door.

"What's up?" Dan asked sullenly. He clearly was not happy with me at this point—and he was about to get a lot less happy.

"Stan's missing."

"Stan!" He said the name as if he were spitting it out. I just ignored his attitude.

"He could have been abducted, but I think he ran away. You're going to help me find him."

"I told you, Weaver," he said with a hostile glint in his eye, "you have to choose. Him or me. And if it's him, I'm out of here. Whatever bargain I struck obligates me to protect you, not your little weasel."

"Listen to me, Dan," I said sharply, but without magic, which, given his already enchanted state, probably wouldn't work right anyway. It was time to put Nurse Florence's theory to the test. "I'm not choosing between you. Each one of you is like a brother to me. I never had a brother, but you did, and you know what it's like to lose one..."

"You bastard!" Well, not the reaction I was going for, but clearly, I had hit a nerve. "How dare you compare Jimmie's, Jimmie's *death* to this? Stan brought this on himself. I took that little nerd in, made him part of the team, made him part of my *family*, and he spat on all of that. He spat on me. He might as well have spat on Jimmie's grave." Dan was shaking now. Aside from this afternoon, I had never seen him so emotional.

By this time our sleepy little street looked like Main Street at high noon. The Schoenbaums knew a lot of people, and they were turning out in force, presumably to help search for Stan. My parents rushed past Dan and me, heading down the street toward Stan's house to see what they could do. There were a lot of people milling around on the sidewalk, and I hoped their presence would get Dan to restrain himself. It didn't.

"Silence!" I whispered, magic throbbing through the word. I didn't have much to lose at this point, and, somewhat to my surprise, Dan's mouth clamped shut, though he struggled against the compulsion, and he started shaking even more. I was afraid some passerby would think he was having a seizure.

"Listen to me! What Stan did was wrong, very wrong, and I'm not trying to defend what he did. But, man, anything could happen to Stan out there. Anything." I took Dan's arm because physical contact would help. I didn't try to control his mind, but I did project a series of images into it, images bred of my own waking nightmares: Stan hitching a ride and getting picked up by some pervert, Stan dirty, ragged, and living on the streets, Stan getting mugged and ending up dead. Then—and I'm not proud of this, but I didn't know what else to do—I played back the same images, but with Jimmie instead of Stan.

Most people wouldn't have realized what I was doing, but he did, and he actually tried to hit me; however, the *tynged* my ally had laid on him made it impossible for his fist to strike. Again, though, he looked as if he were having a seizure.

"Now...*you're*...spitting...on...his...grave," he rasped, fighting against my order for silence. I looked into his eyes. They were raw with sheer, unadulterated hatred. Instead of making him more sympathetic to Stan, I had driven him away from me.

"I loved him too," I whispered, and at the moment I said it, I realized it was true. "The three of us were inseparable back then. The day after the funeral, we both ended up bawling on each other's shoulders and promised that neither of us would ever tell anyone. Then we became blood brothers, remember?" More old, buried memories seemed to resurface every minute, but I could tell from Dan's reactions that he remembered, too. Otherwise, I might have begun to doubt my own sanity.

"And we were, we were like brothers until I went to the hospital. I had a hard time, and I admit, I didn't think much about you for a long time, but now we have another chance. We are like brothers again. I know you feel it too. That's part of why this is so painful."

"Shut...up!" Instead, I plunged ahead.

"Dan, I don't want to hurt you. You are my brother. You will always be my brother. But so is Stan, whatever he's done, and I won't choose. What happens now is up to you. I want to continue as friends, to continue as brothers, but if that's not what you want, I'll get you released from whatever binds you to me…tomorrow. Tonight you help find Stan—whether you want to or not. It's my fault he's out there, and I have to bring him back. Period."

Caught between binding spells and raging emotions, Dan seemed about to hit me with every bit of verbal abuse he could muster, but I was spared knowing exactly what he would say by the sudden arrival of Eva, who practically ran down the sidewalk as soon as she saw us. Dan wiped his eyes and became, in the blink of an eye, a macho idiot.

"I just heard about Stan. Is there anything I can do?"

"Be on hand to screw him when he gets back," said Dan slowly, with deliberate cruelty.

I had to give Eva credit for the unflinching way she faced him. "I guess I had that coming, but abuse me later. Right now Stan's family needs…"

"A son who doesn't jump his friends' girlfriends?"

"Stop it!" snapped Eva. "I feel terrible enough as it is, without you twisting the knife. Haven't you figured out this is all my fault?"

Well, that was a new one. I was pretty sure it was all my fault.

"Oh, sorry, I forgot the part of the story where you held him at gunpoint and ordered him to have sex with you."

"We did not have sex!" snapped Eva with such force people across the street looked at us suspiciously. "Nor were we going to have sex, you jerk."

"I'm a jerk? What the hell?"

"Yes, you are…but I'm a bigger one. Listen to me, for the past few weeks you have been weird, distant. You wouldn't talk about whatever was bothering you. Then, after you lied to me, denied what happened at Founders' Day, made me feel like a lunatic, I knew, I knew you were doing it on purpose."

"He wasn't," I interjected. "He…"

"Stay out of this," shot back Eva. "You can't think I was really attracted to Stan. That was just about hurting you. I'll admit it—I was trying to inflict as much pain as I could. I bet Eric and Shar didn't tell you about the notes they got that told them to go to the woods. Those were from me. I wanted them to see. I wanted them to tell you."

Hmmm… As much as that kind of desire to hurt Dan didn't sound like Eva, her story explained a lot.

"It doesn't matter why you did it," said Dan slowly, anger dripping from every syllable. "That doesn't affect why Stan did it. He still betrayed me."

"Not the way you think, though. I lied to him, Dan. I told him you and I were through, that you broke up with me. I pretended to turn to Stan for comfort, knowing he didn't have any experience with girls and would buy the whole thing." That rang true. What guy, experienced or not, ever questions the fact that a pretty girl wants him or needs him?

Now Eva was in tears, which made me want to cry, too. "He asked me, Dan, he kept asking me about you, over and over, even once after I had my top off. And I wasn't really thinking about him, about how much all this would hurt him. I just kept lying and lying to him, until he finally took me in his arms. And after, when he realized what had happened, he told me he wouldn't say anything. I had just used him, and he wanted to protect me! Me! He even offered to say it was all his fault.

"I know, I know, under the bro code, he shouldn't have been with me even if you had broken up with me, but at least he really believed that I was not your girlfriend anymore." So Eva and I now had this odd bond—we were apparently both charter members of the "kick the puppy dog in the face" club.

At this point, Dan was on emotional overload. I could relate, but if he didn't get himself sorted out soon, he would be no use to Stan or me. I wasn't sure what to say that would get him to calm down, but I knew I had to say something—and fast!

"Dan, I know this is a lot to ask, but you can see that all may not have been what it seemed. Can you please, please, help us find Stan, and worry about whether or not you still need to hate his guts—or mine—tomorrow?" Dan looked at us as if I were a manipulative bastard, which at this point is what I felt like, and at Eva as if she were the town whore, which from her point of view was probably better than she felt she deserved.

At first, I thought he would just turn and walk away. Then he visibly struggled his way into an impassive facade, his face an unreadable mask.

"What do you want me to do?" His voice was flat, unfeeling, but I had to applaud his self-control. Right at the moment, he hated me with a white-hot intensity, but he would help, regardless.

"I need the football team...and the cheerleaders, all of them. We'll be taking the team bus to Isla Vista."

Dan looked at me as if I had snapped completely.

"Why those people in particular? And why Isla Vista?" asked Eva.

"Because that's where Stan almost certainly is. I don't have time to go over all the details, but here's the basic picture. Stan can't go very far north without running into a lot of state parkland, and he's smart enough to know he's not up to wilderness survival. That leaves west, toward Santa Barbara, or southeast, toward Ventura. Of the two, Stan has much more experience with Santa Barbara. If he wants to hide, going to a place he knows better makes more sense. Stan also knows people at UC Santa Barbara, which is in Isla Vista. He can speak college student, and someone is bound to put him up in a dorm room for a while. He could create a good enough story to accomplish that much, I'm sure. He'll be sleeping on the floor, but that's better than on the street."

"If you know where he is, why not send the cops after him?" asked Dan, a hint of his real emotions creeping into his voice.

"Because Stan is smart enough to find some counter-culture type who wouldn't want to cooperate with the cops. On the other hand, students will be more responsive to being asked by one of their own. The football players in most cases know at least a few frat boys, the cheerleaders know some of the sorority sisters, so we get the whole football team, the whole cheerleading squad and all their Greek contacts on the campus knocking on doors, armed with Stan's real story, and we have Stan back in half an hour, tops."

"We can't get the team bus," objected Dan. Actually, he probably could have gotten four buses if the idea suited him, but I whipped out my cell phone, dialed up my other potential ally, Nurse Florence, who in turn called Coach Miller, and voila, team bus is ready to go in ten minutes—with the coach himself driving it, and Nurse Florence along for the ride. (They're both single, and I couldn't help thinking the fact that Nurse Florence was drop-dead gorgeous might have made getting the bus just a little easier.) Dan's objection removed, he got on his cell, and it did not take long to populate the bus with football players and cheerleaders. Since I had become de facto strategist, I went along (for what Coach Miller was calling "a fool's errand" under his breath), and, awkwardly enough, so did Eva, though she sat conspicuously on the far end of the bus from Dan.

I had rendered White Hilt and its scabbard unnoticeable and carried it just in case, and while Nurse Florence and I packed a formidable magical punch between us, I hoped magic wouldn't be needed. My army of jocks and Greeks certainly looked impressive as it fanned out in different directions to go door-to-door in the dorms. Another call to Carrie Winn had gotten us special permission for this late night intrusion; apparently, she knew someone on the UC Board of Regents. So far, so good—but at that point, the logistics proved more challenging than I had at first anticipated. Oh, I had been on the UC Santa Barbara campus before, mostly with Stan, but those visits hadn't really given me a realistic idea of how challenging doing a door-to-door search for Stan would be. We started with the five residence halls on the east side of the main campus, hoping that we wouldn't have to go over to west campus to check out the other two, let alone the off-campus apartments. At Nurse Florence's suggestion, she and I stayed at the relatively central location from which we dispatched our searchers (supposedly in case Stan was in one of the dorms and made a run for it, but really to search through other means without being distracted).

Together we called upon the wind, we sent whispered queries from tree to tree, we looked through the eyes of what animals and birds we could find. Nothing.

"He must be inside," I suggested.

"Or over on east campus...or not here at all," said Nurse Florence with a hint of dejection.

"He better be here," I said grimly. "I think Ms. Winn will have my head if we come up dry after she pulled all those strings to get the search authorized. She asked me at least three times if I were sure."

"Well, you do know him as well as anybody, but knowing that, if he really wanted not to be found, he could be in Ventura waiting for tomorrow to take a bus to LA." Well, there was a cheery thought. Seeing how downcast I looked, Nurse Florence suggested widening our magic search.

"The first search parties will start getting back any time; if we want to try this, it has to be now."

Our thoughts took wing through nearby birds, but this time we searched farther, farther, toward the edges of the campus. Nothing visual. Wait, something, on the lagoon trail, near marine operations. A shadow, someone under the bench. Stan. Hiding under the bench, but not from us.

"Someone's after him!" I shouted to Nurse Florence, but she already knew.

"I'm already dialing campus security. No, wait. I think what's after Stan we may not want campus security to see. That path isn't that far from here—get down there, now!"

I took off as fast as I could. One of the advantages of being in good shape was that my stamina had increased. Even so, I ran so fast I was short of breath by the time I reached the part of the lagoon trail where Stan was.

The thought crossed my mind that, if Nurse Florence were really my enemy, this could be some kind of trap, but I had little choice in that case but to fall into it. Stan didn't have very long to wait.

"Little boy! Where are you?" The voice was simultaneously chilling and sexy. I scanned the area around the bench beneath which Stan was hiding.

"Little boy!" Then I saw her, no it. It was advancing parallel to the lagoon path, but almost at the water's edge.

It looked human enough, feminine enough…God, hot enough. Long blond hair, perfect skin, ample breasts ill-concealed by a white gown that seemed more air than clothing.

But water dripped from that long blond hair, and there were tiny bits of kelp in it. No question—Stan was being stalked by a Kelpie.

Kelpies were Scottish shifters with a particular agenda—they liked to drown women and children, so they could drag them back to their lair and eat them. The usual tactic with children was to appear as a pony a child would be tempted to ride, but the kelpie had evidently sensed that Stan was a little bit beyond the pony ride stage. Hell, after today, way beyond it. Kelpies generally went after adult women or children rather than men, but maybe pickings were slim. Whatever the case, Stan had clearly recognized he was being stalked by someone supernatural but had no one he could go to for help. God only knew how long he had been playing hide and seek with the damn thing. He could have run, but no human could outrun a kelpie, which could shift into a full-grown horse, catch him, and trample him, if nothing else. Kelpies preferred to drown people, but to them, a kill was certainly better than no kill, however it was accomplished.

I drew White Hilt and let its flames blaze intensely.

"Begone, creature," I shouted. The kelpie jumped back.

"You," it said, staring right into my eyes. "Not like the little one. You would know what to do with a woman."

Yeah, I would if ever I ran across one. My luck seemed to run more to murderous supernaturals than actual women, though.

The Kelpie let its gown dissolve and moved toward me. Its imitation of the female form, if one ignored the occasional kelp bits, was really quite remarkable.

Now, I know what you are thinking. I should have incinerated the thing where it stood, but it was still hard for me to psych myself up to kill. That, combined with the sexual allure, made me hesitate just long enough for the kelpie to make a flying jump at me. I took a good swing with White Hilt but missed. In midair, the thing had sprouted long, wickedly sharp claws, and one set of those claws ripped into my sword hand, catching me completely off guard and causing me to drop White Hilt. The instant the sword left my grasp, the flames dissipated. The creature's other set of claws ripped through my jacket sleeve and dug into my left arm. The weight of its momentum knocked me clear off my feet, and then it landed on top of me, which I'm sure you've gathered wasn't anywhere nearly as much fun as it might have been just a minute or so ago. I had to admit, though, it did feel a lot like a naked woman on top of me, yet another distraction. Its teeth were lengthening into fangs. I needed to make a move quickly.

Abruptly the kelpie jumped off me, howling in pain. Stan had jumped out from his hiding place, grabbed White Hilt, and stabbed the creature in the back. White Hilt wouldn't flame for him, but at the end of the day, it was still a sword, and the kelpie was not invulnerable.

With an unearthly scream, it tore itself free and turned to face him. The seductive female form shuddered and vanished. The kelpie was still vaguely human, but now it was a tall, muscular man, a form such as it might have used to seduce women, except that it didn't really bother with niceties like a face, being content instead with a kind of twitching darkness broken only by reddish eyes and now enormous fangs. Normally, kelpies worked by stealth, tricking people instead of over-coming them in physical combat—but apparently, they could more than hold their own in a fight.

Poor Stan now had a bad dilemma. He had one sword, but the kelpie had two sets of claws and one of fangs. An expert swordsman might have kept the creature back, but Stan was no expert, and the kelpie's arms were getting longer. Once those arms were long enough, the kelpie could attack from two sides while keeping all of its body except for its fast-moving arms too far away for Stan to strike. If nothing else it could keep feinting until it wore Stan down, and then it would dig its claws into him. His only other alternative was to try to toss the sword to me, a move he had no idea how to do, and one that would, in any case, leave him totally vulnerable.

"Stan, don't!" I yelled, realizing that he was, in fact, contemplating trying to throw me the sword. Ignoring me, he started to lift the sword for the throw. I threw myself on the creature's back to distract it from Stan—and then my grip was weaker than it should have been. I could feel blood oozing from both my left arm and right hand. Well, so much for stamina. With much more exertion, I would be lucky if I didn't pass out.

Trying to tighten my grip on the flailing creature beneath me, I glanced over at the lagoon, then stared. The algae-green water near the shore was bubbling. In seconds a figure emerged from it. In horror I contemplated having to fight two kelpies at the same time, but, no, the newcomer emerging from the lagoon was...Nurse Florence.

Neat trick, that. I would have to ask her how she did it some time— if I lived long enough.

Distracted by what was happening lagoon-side, I didn't immediately realize that a Santa Barbara PD cruiser had pulled up nearby. I did become aware of them when their lights illuminated the scene. I glanced over and realized they had their guns aimed at the kelpie. From where they were standing, they could see a fair amount of blood on the ground, so they knew the situation was not good, but from a distance, the kelpie just looked like a really big dude wreaking havoc, and they figured they could take him down if they had to. Well, except that I was in the way of their getting a good shot. With an effort, I managed to drop off the kelpie and roll out of the way. The kelpie's attention now focused on the two officers. Nurse Florence had grabbed Stan from behind and pulled him out of the way. The police shouted a warning, and the kelpie, seeing the tide had turned decisively against it, made a run for the lagoon. One of the officers fired but missed because of the kelpie's unexpected speed. Beyond the range of the lights, the kelpie slid into the lagoon, but from the officers' point of view, it probably looked as if it had just disappeared into the night. One ran after it, while the other called for backup. Of course, they wouldn't find the kelpie… but they had us, and I didn't know how we were going to explain even the little that they had seen.

Thank God for Nurse Florence. Oh, I know, I know. I still couldn't be sure she wasn't the enemy, but she saved us hours of questioning. By the time the officers had their backup and had men combing the area, leaving someone time enough to take a statement, Nurse Florence had both Stan and me on the same page. She had also used enough magic to keep me from bleeding out or feeling the full extent of my pain while the police questioned us.

"I can heal you, Tal, so unless you want to spend hours in the trauma center over at Goleta Valley Cottage Hospital, let's pretend you just got some superficial cuts. Besides, if anyone saw how extensive your injuries really were, there'd be some risk of panic, and we don't want that."

According to Nurse Florence's carefully crafted fiction, Stan had gone missing around four o'clock, and we were looking for him. Well, that part was true, but it was almost the only thing in her story that was. She, Stan, and I took turns telling her revisionist version, depending on whose perspective was relevant. As the story went, Stan had gotten an SOS from friends at UCSB who needed his help on a project, so he had taken the bus down. But the friends who called him weren't in the dorm right then, so Stan had taken a walk down to the lagoon. By that time it was dark, and Stan had encountered someone who, based on the description Stan provided, the detective taking the statement decided was clearly a sexual predator. Anyway, Stan became suspicious and tried to run away, but he got turned around, ran in the wrong direction, toward the ocean, lost his cell phone, couldn't call for help, ended up hiding under a bench on the path (ooh, another small truth), hoping the guy would go away. But he kept walking around that area, around and around, as if he knew Stan was still around somewhere, and Stan was afraid to run, so he ended up trapped for hours. He occasionally heard people, but always too far away for it to be safe to call out to them. In this version, when Nurse Florence and I hit the lagoon path, Stan came out, but the pervert, who was closer than Stan thought, tried to attack Stan, then got in a fight with me. Nurse Florence produced a blood-covered knife from somewhere to explain the blood on the ground, but she was careful to magic the ground to make the blood seem much less and to magic my injuries to make them look more superficial.

The story had a few rough spots, but for improvisation, it was pretty good. And with Nurse Florence right there to sell it, the detective was more than satisfied. As the old saying goes, that woman could sell ice to Eskimos.

By the time the detective had finished taking our statements, some of our searchers, drawn by the commotion, had found us. Nurse Florence fed them the Readers' Digest condensed version of the story we had given the detective and then handed off Stan to them, telling them we had to clear up a little police business but that they should gather people at the bus, and we would join them in a few minutes.

The place was crawling with police, so it took Nurse Florence a while to find a quiet spot. Once she had one, she wrapped us in mist, had me take off my shirt and jacket, and examined my wounds.

"Just flesh wounds, at least," I said.

"Deep ones, almost to the bone in some spots. If I hadn't stopped your bleeding, you would have collapsed minutes after the officers got there." She removed a small green bottle from her purse and then quickly and efficiently poured the contents carefully into each wound. I was expecting stinging or something, but I felt a gentle warmth instead.

"There's quite a bit of nerve and muscle damage, more than I thought. This is going to take longer to heal than I would like, but I can't very well leave you like this. We just have to hope no one comes looking for us for a while. Even if no one does, that salve by itself is too slow, though it would heal you eventually. I'll give it a little help." She put one hand on my left arm and one on my right hand. She closed her eyes and whispered in Welsh. Suddenly the purest white light I had ever seen flowed from her, making her look like an angel, and then it engulfed me. Every part of my body tingled, and I could literally feel wounds closing, muscles and nerves knitting themselves together beneath. Held in the light, I lost all track of time. When at last I noted, regretfully, that the light was fading, I was shocked to look at my watch and discover that forty-five minutes had passed.

Nurse Florence added a few bandages. "I left some small cuts to account for the superficial wounds you were supposed to have gotten, just in case the police do any follow-up with you. Now," she added a little shakily, "I'm feeling pretty drained, and someone is bound to come looking for us soon, so get your shirt on quickly." Almost before I finished dressing, the mist faded, and Nurse Florence and I headed for the bus as fast as she could go, which wasn't very fast by that point. Nonetheless, the students had kept themselves entertained in our absence. True, Coach Miller looked pretty irritated, I suspected because he had hardly seen Nurse Florence since we arrived on the campus. Dan was still sitting up front, face unreadable, trying not to socialize with anyone. Stan was equally quiet, sitting alone near the middle of the bus. Whether because nobody wanted to tick Dan off or because Stan made it seem like he wanted to be alone, no one was sitting next to him or on either side of him. When I sat down next to him, he looked out the window. I tried to talk, but he just shook his head. He clearly didn't want to talk.

Shortly after the bus got underway, Nurse Florence tapped me on the shoulder and leaned over to whisper to me. "I know what I said about erasing people's memories of betrayal, but a little mood music is different. You can cut the tension on this bus with a knife. Let's do something about that." I looked around, and she was right. People should have felt at least a little exhilarated by having helped save Stan, but somehow Stan and Dan between them were radiating gloom, and almost everyone seemed vaguely out of sorts. So I started singing a capella, gradually working more and more magic into the music, spreading contentment throughout the bus like a warm wind on a quiet summer night. Even Dan and Stan showed some signs of relaxing, but Stan still didn't speak.

"Tal!" said an urgent voice behind me, even sexier for its urgency.

"What?" I asked Eva. She had sat down in an empty seat right behind me.

"Tell me what happened on Founders' Day!"

"What do you mean?"

"You know damn well what I mean! If I'm going to lose Dan over all this, I at least need to know what 'this' is."

I leaned as close to her as I could. "This isn't the time, but Eva, I promise, I'll tell you tomorrow. I'll tell you everything." Stan looked in my direction, the obvious question written on his face, but he still didn't speak.

"And Eva," I added, "when you know everything, you'll realize Dan wasn't lying to you, not to be cruel, not to make you feel crazy, not lying at all." She started to answer, then suddenly realized Stan was sitting next to me. She must have been so focused on getting her questions answered she had just looked right through him. She turned bright red and lowered her eyes, too nervous to make eye contact.

"Stan?" she said, very timidly. "Stan, can we talk?"

"I won't tell anyone, don't worry," whispered Stan.

"I've already told everyone who would listen." Stan's face betrayed a little surprise at that. "All the cheerleaders. They were impressed you were such a gentleman. And the football players who wouldn't listen, well, the cheerleaders will see that they know what really happened. In a day or so, everyone will know it wasn't your fault.

"Stan," she continued, putting her hand on his shoulder. "I wasn't thinking about you, and I should have been. I wasn't thinking at all. Now all of us are miserable, and it's my fault. I can't ask you to forgive me." She finally made eye contact with Stan, and, much to my surprise, grabbed his hands in hers. I hoped Dan wasn't watching—this was definitely a moment that could be misinterpreted.

"I just want to make you feel better."

"I'll get over it," whispered Stan. "And you aren't exactly the only one who has been acting on impulse and making it tough for everyone else."

"Gee," I said, "just because you got the whole town out searching for you, I wouldn't say that was making it too tough."

Stan looked at me as if the thought had never occurred to him. "You mean you guys aren't the only ones who looked for me?"

"Buddy, I don't know of anyone who wasn't looking for you." Eva nodded in agreement.

"It may not seem much like it right now, but everyone likes you, Stan. The thought of something happening to you..." Eva shuddered. "It would be more than anyone could stand." I had been trying the whole bus ride back from Isla Vista to get even a word, any sign of conscious life, from Stan, and then along came Eva, and not only got him to talk, but cheered him up—and she's the one who got him into this mess in the first place! That's a life lesson, folks—if you want to cheer up a guy, just find a volcanically hot girl to treat him like he is the center of the universe, and all will be well.

Stan was actually smiling by this point. "Well, I didn't mean to have everyone make all this fuss." Then the smile faded. "What am I going to tell my parents? I'll be grounded until Armageddon!"

"Remember how your cell phone got lost," I prompted. "You were going to call and tell them you were at UCSB and would be late for dinner. Then you lost your phone and got trapped on the lagoon path. It wasn't really your fault."

"Oh, yeah," said Stan in amazement, realizing for the first time that Nurse Florence's story had been designed in part to cover him with his parents.

After a few minutes, Eva moved away. Stan's eyes followed her, not a good sign under the circumstances.

He realized I was looking at him intently. "Don't worry, Tal. I'm not making that mistake again." I leaned as close to him as I could.

Suddenly, despite how often I had spilled my guts tonight, I wasn't eager to have anyone overhear.

"Stan, I feel like garbage. I wasn't there when you needed me. Well, *I'm* not making that mistake again."

"Tal, I didn't run away because of what you did or didn't do," said Stan gently. "I ran away because I realized I had let you down. Dan isn't just a friend. He's like your...bodyguard or something. Straining that relationship might put your life at risk. And I didn't think about it until it was too late."

"Listen, it might have been easier if things had worked out differently, but Stan, I have never, never been more proud of you than I am right this minute." Stan's mouth fell open.

"Proud? But I screwed up completely!"

"You came to the rescue of a damsel in distress, even though you knew it could mean trouble, big trouble. And even after you knew she had just been using you, you decided to protect her. Hell, even when it looked as if Dan was going to crush you, you didn't say a word."

"He wouldn't have believed me," pointed out Stan.

"Maybe not," I replied, "but most guys would have tried to tell him, anyway."

"Tal, I really wanted to, well, you know..." Stan blushed and looked away.

"Yeah, you and every other straight guy that ever looked at Eva. Okay, so there was a little lust in the equation. But even Eva knew you well enough to know that wouldn't be enough. That's why she made up that whole story about needing someone, being desperate for some kind of support. From the way she tells the story, she practically had to drag you over to her. And then there's how you behaved with the kelpie."

"Is that what that was? I knew it was something...unnatural. But I almost got you killed."

"No, I almost got myself killed. I could have easily vanquished that thing. I hesitated. I almost got both of us killed. But what I meant was, how you were ready to give me the sword, even though it was your only defense. That was one of the bravest things I have ever seen.

"Yeah, brave! I spent hours cowering under a bench!"

"Bravery isn't the absence of fear. It is acting despite being afraid.

Until I got there, though, there was no action that wouldn't have been stupid. Hiding was smart, not cowardly."

"But trying to give you the sword wasn't that brave. I knew you could use it to defeat the kelpie and save both of us."

"Maybe, but on some level, you knew it was a risk, and you did it anyway. Say what you want, but I've seen battle many times in my lives, and I have seldom seen even a trained veteran do what you did. As far as I'm concerned, you're a hero, and I couldn't be more proud of you. Wow," I said, suddenly noticing how he looked in the glare of the bus ceiling lights. "You're more bruised up than I thought."

Stan looked around to make sure no one was close by, then leaned still closer to me. "I got to see Eva in her bra. That sight was worth a few bruises." I could hardly believe my ears—an actual joke! Clearly, Stan was on the mend.

"Heck," he continued, "if I could have seen her without the bra, Dan could have cut my face clear off."

"Yeah, well I imagine in those circumstances he would have cut off something else," I replied quietly. Joking a little with Stan felt great— not too long ago I was afraid we would never joke again—but the problem of what to do about Dan remained. I had been keeping my eyes on him as much as I could. He had been sitting near the front of the bus, not saying a word to anyone, barely moving.

No one his age should have to go through that much. I should know —I was an expert at going through too much.

I thought Stan and I would be okay, at least. Our friendship was intact. But whether our relationships with Dan would ever heal, to say nothing of Dan's relationship with Eva, well, that was anyone's guess at this point. If, as Nurse Florence had said, someone was trying to isolate me, they had not completely succeeded yet, but they had accomplished a lot in a single day.

And then there was the unresolved question of a kelpie—in the UCSB lagoon, no less! It would hardly have surprised me more to run across the Loch Ness Monster in the high school pool. It was also troubling that the kelpie behaved so atypically for its kind. Kelpies worked by luring their victims into the water and drowning them, not by using their shifting abilities to beat their victims in combat. And what about how the kelpie just happened to pop up right where Stan was, intercept him before he even got to the dorms, herd him down to the lagoon, and trap him there? Again, too much coincidence. I had the paranoid feeling that whatever evil force was plotting my downfall was getting more and more aggressive. It could not be very long now until there was a direct confrontation.

About the time we hit the Santa Brígida off-ramp on Interstate 1, Nurse Florence came back again, sat down behind me, and said, "I'm worried."

"Oh, really? About what? Things have been going so smoothly up to now."

"Now is not the time for sarcasm. Listen, Coach Miller was going to take the bus back to the school, but he just got a call from Carrie Winn to drive directly to the Schoenbaums'."

I wrinkled my forehead. "That's only a few blocks difference. Most people could walk home from Stan's house just as easily as they could from the school."

"True, but why does Winn care what our first stop is?"

"I don't know. She's probably there and wants to be sure she gets to greet Stan when he comes back. Right now, that doesn't seem like such a big bump in the road, certainly not compared to everything else that's happened." I could see Nurse Florence remained unconvinced, but she decided not to keep pressing me and went back to her seat right behind Coach Miller.

Just a few minutes later the bus pulled onto our street. Although it was late, as we approached Stan's house, the light became almost blinding. I didn't know what was happening at first. Then, squinting against the light, I managed to make out the news vans—three or four of them. The lights had been set up by the camera crews.

So that was what Carrie Winn was up to? A photo opp? A sound bite?

Most of my fellow students didn't seem that daunted by the presence of cameras. In general, the football players and cheerleaders streamed out of the bus to line up for their fifteen minutes of fame. But they were not the ones the news crews were here for.

Aside from Coach Miller and Nurse Florence, neither of whom

seemed to intend to get out, there were four of us left on the bus: Eva, trying to become invisible in the very back; Stan and I near the middle; Dan at the front. The eloquent spaces among us created telling visual imagery, but none of the photographers seemed interested in capturing our little tableau inside the bus.

I got up and started to usher Stan out. "Well, buddy, let's get this over with. They aren't going to go away." Stan nodded and started to get up, then fell back.

"Ouch! I think I twisted my ankle." Only Stan could twist his ankle getting up from a seat. I helped him up and let him lean on me as we weaved toward the exit.

As we stepped through the exit, camera flashes exploded like fire-crackers on the Fourth of July. It wasn't until later I realized how much Carrie Winn had spun the events of that night, making our arrival almost one of those archetypal Pulitzer Prize photo moments. "The brave survivor moved slowly down the steps, leaning on the young hero who had rescued him." Actually, we both nearly stumbled and fell in all the commotion. As soon as we set foot on the sidewalk, we were surrounded. I would almost rather have dealt with the kelpie again.

Stan was clearly confused by the questions being flung at him and the continuous flashing of cameras. I wasn't much better. Neither one of us immediately responded, and the reporters became more insistent. Beyond them, the camera crews of the various news networks were jockeying for position. At that point, I would have given anything to be home in bed. My house was only a few steps away, but getting there now seemed a feat comparable to scaling Mount Everest.

Then I saw Carrie Winn cutting through the crowd, striding toward us, purpose incarnate. In moments I found myself freed from the chaos of reporters only to be trapped in the middle of a press conference.

Carrie Winn, immaculately coiffed and dressed, especially for what must have been one o'clock in the morning by then, flowed into what was obviously a carefully prepared speech as soon as the cameras started rolling.

"I have never been as proud of my town as I am tonight. We all rallied together, every last one of us, to find one missing young man. But I am especially proud of that young man, Stanford Schoenbaum, who I am told showed great courage in the face of an attempted abduction, and of my intern, Stanford's classmate, Taliesin Weaver, whose quick thinking led us right to Stanford and whose bravery saved Stanford's life. Let's have a round of applause for our young heroes." The applause was deafening and would have been flattering, had I thought I deserved it. Then Stan and I had to teeter back and forth next to Ms. Winn, like trophies in the case, while she found subtle ways to claim credit for us, for the town, for whatever she could lay her hands on.

Salvation finally came from an unlikely source: poor Mrs. Schoenbaum, who had to wait through all this public relations buzz to hug her son. She might have had to wait longer, but she has always been a determined woman, and tonight she would not be denied, even by Carrie Winn. Her appearance, of course, was another perfect photo opp, in fact, two: Mrs. S. hugging her son for dear life, and Mrs. S. giving his brave rescuer, yours truly, a peck on the cheek. In both cases, Ms. Winn managed to deftly work her way into the shots. After the peck on the cheek, Mrs. S leaned close to me and whispered, "Thank you!" with such force it was genuinely moving.

At that point, Stan's parents tried to whisk him away, but it is hard to whisk right through a solid wall of reporters, even for Mrs. S., and for a moment they got mired in the mob. Then Nurse Florence, who had finally gotten off the bus, said, politely but forcefully, "In deference to the ordeal this family has gone through tonight, let's give them some privacy, shall we?" Ms. Winn, who had been just about to part the crowd for the Schoenbaums, looked more than a little annoyed that someone else had stepped in. However, making a virtue out of necessity, she parted the crowd for me, and, just as I expected, when the reporters got out of the way, my parents emerged, a study in contrasts, simultaneously smiling and tearful. After a family hug, we started a retreat toward our house. Then I noticed Dan, face like a thundercloud, standing near the edge of the crowd.

"Mom, Dad, I need to say thank you to Dan. It'll just take a minute."

"Okay, Tal, but not too long, okay? It's almost two a.m. now, and you have a big day tomorrow." I looked at her confusedly.

"Why is tomorrow so big?"

My mom chuckled at that. "Don't you remember? You were invited to the pre-homecoming game party at Ms. Winn's house, and tomorrow is the day before homecoming—I'm sure that's when the party was scheduled. I think I was told it was for the coaching staff, players, managers, and you and Stan, the team tutors. I don't know if Stan is going to be up to it after all this, but I think you should go if you can, especially since Ms. Winn seems so impressed by you. It can't hurt to have a friend like her."

Great, another opportunity to become a prop in the Carrie Winn self-glorification pageant.

"Okay, Mom, I'll hurry."

Keeping to the shadows so as not to attract the attention of any more reporters, I finally managed to end up next to Dan.

"Well, Dan, do you want me to get you released from your bargain tomorrow?" Dan looked at me, his face almost devoid of any emotion.

"I'm going to give it a day or two before I decide," he said finally. Well, that was better than nothing. I had been sure he was ready to get as far from me as possible. Encouraged, I decided to press my luck.

"It would mean a lot to Stan if you forgave him." Dan's eyes flashed angrily at that.

"Are you getting ski reports from hell, Weaver? Because that's about when I'm going to forgive Stan." I probably should have stopped at that point, but you know the old saying, "In for a penny, in for a pound."

"Dan, he could have been killed tonight. He spent hours thinking he was going to die. Isn't that enough for you?"

"No," he replied curtly, "it isn't. And you, no more fighting dirty, no more using Jimmie to manipulate me."

"I apologize for that, and I'll never do it again. As for Stan, what is going to satisfy you? What can he do to make this right?"

"Well," began Dan slowly, "there is an old football team tradition. It goes back to 1996, the year the school was founded. When someone wrongs a member of the team, the offender has to fight that member."

"What, so you can beat Stan up again? Dan, you already bruised him up pretty badly, and you did your best to humiliate him."

"No, not that kind of fight. Boxing. Olympic rules. Well, 'kiddie rules,' really. You know, junior boxing. Coach will referee. Tomorrow is the perfect day because there's no practice. We can easily squeeze in a match between the end of school and Ms. Winn's party."

"Stan isn't going to box with you. He's been through enough."

"No boxing, no forgiveness," said Dan adamantly.

Tired as I was, I had another idea.

"Okay, you'll have your boxing match—with me."

"You know I can't box with you. I can't get my fist close enough after the bargain I made."

"I know, but if I'm standing in for Stan, someone else can stand in for you. How about Shahriyar? Obviously, he can throw a punch," I said, pointing to my split lip. Shahriyar had only been at our high school since the beginning of the year. Prior to that, he had lived in Beverly Hills, and before that somewhere back east. At some point, he had gotten considerable boxing training, as well as kick-boxing, Tae Kwan Do, and mixed martial arts. If Dan really wanted me to get beaten, he could not have chosen better than Shar, so I figured mentioning him made the offer more tempting. I was right.

"Okay," said Dan finally. "I accept the substitutions you propose. Meet me tomorrow in the gym. I'll let Coach and Shar know." Then he turned and disappeared into the night, without so much as a "goodbye." I sighed and walked back to my house. Most of the crowd, including reporters, had left. The news crews were packing up. With no more press, Carrie Winn had vanished as fast as ice in August.

I was exhausted, once again worn down to the point where it was a miracle I got up the steps on the front porch. As soon as my head hit the pillow, I lapsed into a dreamless sleep, almost sleeping through my alarm the next morning.

NEAR HOMECOMING

OVER BREAKFAST, I got treated to several journalistic interpretations of last night's "glorious" events: one from the *Santa Brígida Herald* (which I think Carrie Winn owned), one from the *Los Angeles Times,* Santa Barbara edition, one from an online school newspaper, and one from a local news anchor. Normally, my mom was strict about not watching the TV during meals, but now even she could hardly tear her eyes away from it, at least until my story finished.

"Tal, you must be so proud!"

Yeah, I would be, if I hadn't started the whole mess in the first place.

"What I am is tired of everyone making such a fuss about it," I said, more irritably than I intended. Mom looked hurt by my tone but didn't say anything. Dad, however, was a different story.

"Don't take that tone with your mother," he said, somewhat absently, still staring at the *Times* article.

"Sorry, I just think what I did is getting blown way out of proportion."

"Oh, by the way, one of Ms. Winn's people called while you were in the shower. The limo will be here to pick you and Stan up at five," said Mom with unintended irony.

"Limo!" I pushed my chair back angrily. "I am not taking a limo! Stan and I could practically walk there, anyway." My parents both looked at me as if I had just walked out of a spacecraft.

"Dear, her place is north of East Valley Road, practically out of town."

"Whatever!" I snapped. Then I thought about the way I was acting.

"Sorry, Mom. I'm just tired today."

"Maybe you can take a nap this afternoon. I'd hate to see you act like this with Ms. Winn," said my dad, looking at me this time and raising an eyebrow.

Yeah, maybe I can squeeze a nap in between getting my brains beaten out by Shar and the party—we'll see.

"I have a meeting after school, Dad, but maybe I can lie down for a few minutes."

Not content with that, Dad hammered me for a while about how important an opportunity this was, how Carrie Winn could really open doors for me later in life, so I should make the most of the opportunity, blah, blah, blah. Actually, he had a point, but after last night's media circus, it was hard for me to look at Carrie Winn in quite the same way. In fact, it was getting harder and harder not to think of her as my enemy, though I didn't have the proof I needed to be sure yet. Anyway, eventually, I got away from my parents and almost jogged to school. I didn't stop for Stan; he had texted me that his mom was keeping him home from school, though he would be going to the Winn party. His staying home was a relief. At least I wouldn't have to lie to him about what I was doing after school. I didn't want him to know what was happening until it was all over; he had enough to deal with as it was.

The first few classes went smoothly, but then I got a summons to report immediately to Ms. Simmons' office.

Have you ever noticed how seldom people are called to the principal's office to hear good news?

As soon as I got to the office, Ms. Simmons briskly ushered me in and closed the door, another bad sign. She offered me a chair, sat down behind her desk, and locked eyes with me.

"Tal, is it true that you and Shahriyar are having some kind of unsanctioned boxing after school?"

"It's not unsanctioned, Ms. Simmons. Coach Miller is refereeing. I was thinking of joining the local boxing club, and Shar said he'd show me what boxing was like."

Ms. Simmons leaned back in her chair and stared into my eyes even more intensely.

"You lie so smoothly that, if I didn't know the truth, I would believe you." I looked at her as if she had just slapped me across the face.

"Don't look like I've wronged you. We both know that this bout is some kind of footballer ritual."

"It's not against the rules," I said, without thinking.

"If that's the case, why lie about it? No, Tal, there is payback of some kind in the air, and I will not allow it. Boxing is dangerous enough under the best of circumstances…"

"It's junior boxing. You know, more protective headgear and stuff than in real boxing."

"Do not interrupt me!" said Ms. Simmons slowly, emphasizing each word. "When people fight in anger, I don't care how much protective gear is involved—there is still danger. In any case, this subject is not up for debate. The boxing match is canceled. I'll call Coach Miller right now and tell him."

"No, you won't!" I almost shouted, in Welsh, with considerable magic wrapped around the words. Ms. Simmons dropped the phone and stared blankly at me for a couple of seconds, then started dialing as if nothing had happened.

Getting people to forget little things was easy. Changing their minds about subjects on which their opinion was not particularly strong was easy. Getting them to change their minds when they had strong convictions was doable but risked damaging the person if their resistance was too determined. I knew Ms. Simmons well enough to know she was strong-willed, and on this subject, she believed too strongly that I could get hurt. No, beating down that protective impulse, to say nothing of the professional ethics that reinforced it, would be so fundamentally a violation of her will that it would have to injure her. I couldn't do that. At the same time, I couldn't let her stop the fight.

"You need to call Coach Miller, but it will have to wait. You just got a tip that one of our students left school without permission and is likely to commit suicide at any minute."

Ms. Simmons put down the phone. "Tal, I will call Coach Miller, but right now I need to take care of another important matter, a very time-sensitive one." She was playing it cool, but I could tell she was really upset. "However, if somehow I don't get in touch with him, I am forbidding you to go through with this fight. Understood?" Well, I should have seen that coming and preempted it. I thought overwhelming her need to protect me with a bigger emergency would solve the problem, but apparently, she was going to try to take care of both situations.

I started singing and hit her with the most concentrated burst of magic I could, then caught her quickly as she slumped to the floor, asleep. Lucky for me Ms. Simmons took good care of herself and wasn't overweight, since I had to drag her into her desk chair. Then I laid her head gently on her desk.

What a mess! I had kept her from immediately stopping the fight but hadn't saved myself from possible disciplinary action after, and I had frightened her with a totally bogus crisis. In a busy office like this, I couldn't keep her asleep for very long.

At least I had gotten better at removing memories selectively, so I didn't need to worry about injuring her in the attempt. I just sang to her quietly to forget the false suicide report, as well as any knowledge she had of the boxing match. Then I told her to wake in ten minutes, and just in case, I got on the intercom in her voice, a trick I'd been working on, and told her secretary not to disturb her for a few minutes.

I tried to slip out of the office inconspicuously, but Ms. Blount, the gray-haired guard dog/principal's secretary, looked at me with profound suspicion as I walked past her. Had she heard me singing? Or did she know something about the boxing match? Either way, I couldn't do anything about Ms. Blount's memories. The door to her office was open, and I could hear other people talking in the outer office. If I magicked her, she would not remember, but anyone the spell was not directed at could remember. I pasted on my best fake smile and walked right past her. She did not stop me, but I think she wanted to.

At lunch I took Eva aside—not to the woods, you can be sure, but down one of the classroom halls that usually stayed empty much of lunch. There I told her the truth about Dan's situation. Oh, she didn't believe me at first, despite her close call in Annwn. Luckily I had taken to carrying White Hilt with me, in a scabbard that hung by my side, naturally charmed to be unnoticeable. It is amazing how fast a flaming sword can burn up people's skepticism. Since she had already seen White Hilt in action, seeing it again reassured her that she was not crazy and that I was not playing games with her.

"Well, now I feel terrible," she said, looking around as if she expected an accusing Dan to pop out of the lockers.

"There's a lot of that going around lately."

"I thought for sure he was playing some sick game with me...but he really didn't remember. And now, look what I have done to him, to Stan...to you."

"Stan and I don't blame you," I replied gently. I started to pat her on the shoulder, then thought better of it. "As for Dan, he really loves you, or he wouldn't have taken what happened so hard. You will find your way back to each other."

"I heard about the boxing match," said Eva worriedly. "I'll go to Dan and get him to stop this nonsense."

"Eva, I said you would find your way back, not that you would be able to do it in the next ten minutes. Right now, he will just ignore you. This fight has to happen. I need to get Stan forgiven."

"And your getting beaten to a pulp is the only way to do that? Sometimes guys are so unbelievably dense."

"Well," I said, raising an eyebrow, "I am troubled by your lack of faith. Maybe I'll beat Shar to a pulp."

Eva snorted derisively, then realized how that sounded. "I'm sorry, Tal, I know you're in good shape, but have you seen Shar lately? He's built like Hercules—and he knows how to box."

"Well, again, thanks for the vote of confidence, Eva, and I'll see you later—if I'm still alive." I don't think she appreciated the attempted humor, but I went whistling off down the hall, using my most self-confident stride.

"Guys!" she muttered as I turned the corner.

What little remained of the day dragged on uneventfully. Finally, the last class ended, and I hustled to the gym. Shar had his own equipment of course, but I didn't. However, Dan borrowed the necessities from the local club; apparently, he could still get pretty much anything he wanted in the community. A couple of the players led me to the visitors' locker room to change, just as if this match were real. Clearly, Dan had been careful. Head guard, mouth guard, gloves, boxing trunks, jersey, groin protector—new, I was assured—everything fit perfectly. Since most guys have no idea about other guys' sizes, except maybe for brothers, I could only assume some of the girls must have made extremely educated guesses. That would suggest some of them had been watching me pretty closely—good news, but not something I had time to focus on now. I sang myself into heightened stamina. I wasn't trying to win, mind you. In fact, I intended to lose, but I needed to stay standing as long as possible. Also, because I wanted to keep track of the audience's reaction, I shifted a little, just enough to give me keen, animal-like hearing. I still wasn't comfortable shifting into a complete animal form, but I had found ways to gain some enhanced abilities without visibly changing.

I got a shock when I entered the gym. The bleachers were set up, and they were packed. I had expected the football team itself, and maybe a few cheerleaders, but the match seemed to have attracted all the cheerleaders and a large number of other students. No wonder Ms. Simmons had found out what we were planning! Hell, all she probably had to do was stand discretely in the main entryway before school and listen to the conversations of students passing by. The question was, even with her earlier memories of the match gone, how could she miss something this big happening right under her nose? Well, I couldn't worry about that now. If she found out, she found out.

With such a mob I thought at first I had enhanced my hearing for nothing, but I saw Shar talking to Dan, and I tried to focus on them. What I heard surprised me.

"This is stupid, and you know it!" said Shar. "Tal's been nothing but a friend to us. Okay, his buddy Stan messed up, but not as bad as you thought, and anyway Tal doesn't have the training. This isn't a fair fight."

"He asked for it," said Dan, clearly feigning disinterest in what Shar was saying.

"If you weren't the team captain…"

"What, Shar? You wouldn't do it? Fine, don't. You're not the only guy on the team I could have fight Tal." Shar stared at Dan, clearly angry, and then stalked away. He did, however, climb into the makeshift ring. He might not like the whole idea, but he would fight. Good. So far, everything was going according to plan.

"Don't hold back, Shar, or this won't count!" Dan yelled after him. Shar started to turn toward Dan, then thought better of it and turned toward me.

As I climbed into the ring, I was still listening to the general area in which Dan was sitting, and I got another earful right before the match started, this time from Gordy Hayes, one of the football players Stan tutored.

"Dan, you're a good student. You don't know what it's like for me. I have a shot at college, but only through football—and I won't even have that unless I can pass classes like chemistry. And Dan, I can't do it, not without Stan. He's the only reason I'm passing chem now."

Dan looked at him casually and replied, "There's no I in team." I thought for a second that Gordy was going to smash him in the face. But no, he walked away without a word…until he got out of earshot of Dan, at which point he was muttering vehemently, "I hope Stan does Eva…and your mom…three times a day for the next three years!" In fact, as I swept different parts of the audience, I picked up a fair amount of muttering from football players, though none was quite as colorful as Gordy's.

Dan, who had been practically worshiped by the other players, especially this year, clearly was putting a strain on their loyalty with this vendetta against Stan. I felt good that the other players really did care about him—and me, for that matter—but I got a sick feeling contemplating what would happen to Dan if his attitude tore his connection with the rest of the team. I needed to do my best to end this today—and in a way that worked for both Stan and Dan.

I turned my attention to Shar. Eva had not been entirely accurate with her Hercules comparison. Shar was Persian, not Greek. Aside from that, though, the comparison worked. I thought I had definition, but Shar, who—big surprise—had decided not to wear a jersey and was thus bare-chested, like a professional boxer, looked as if he had been chiseled by Michelangelo. Was that a six-pack, or an eight-pack? Either way, he was perfect for what I had in mind, except that Michelangelo had sculpted David, and in this little drama Shar was going to be more like Goliath, except that this time Goliath was going to win.

Coach Miller, who wasn't looking a whole lot happier than Gordy at this point, explained the rules, and one of his assistants rang the bell for the first round. Shar was far stronger than I was, and fast—but I was faster. I ran out the clock on the first round mostly by dodging. It wasn't the most crowd-pleasing strategy, but everyone knew what a powerful boxer Shar was, so on one level I was winning in a sense just by evading those Golden Gloves-worthy fists. Shar had clearly not expected me to have such defensive skill.

"Nicely played," he whispered to me as round one ended. In amateur boxing, there were only three three-minute rounds, and the friends I had in the audience visibly relaxed, evidently expecting that the rest of the match would proceed in the same way.

No one, least of all Shar, realized that I was carefully choreographing this action. I wanted Shar to think I could defend so well I wouldn't get hit. That would encourage him to hit his hardest, despite his initial reluctance to fight me.

In the second round, only about five seconds in, I pretended to almost trip, and Shar smashed me right in the head, hard enough for me to hear ringing in my ears even with the head guard. Shar was clearly unsettled by that, but he was too well-trained to let his feelings show very much. After another few seconds I slowed down, and he landed a powerful gut punch, sending me staggering backward. He looked puzzled but followed up with a blow to the face that would have had me swallowing teeth, if not for the mouth guard. I started throwing deliberately inept punches at Shar, leaving myself wide open. He delivered what he intended as a light blow, but I twisted so it landed on the wound on my left arm, which started bleeding as if on cue. My split lip was bleeding a little too.

In the background I could hear Nurse Florence, who must have just come in, arguing with Coach Miller, who told her to stop distracting him, probably not something she heard very often from men. The bell rang, signaling the end of the second round, and Nurse Florence continued to push on the coach. I caught snatches of conversation that suggested her outlook was pretty much the same as that of Principal Simmons. While they argued, I glanced over at Dan and realized I had made a horrible mistake.

You may recall that magic can force people to act against their will, but using magic that way can take a heavy toll on those on whom it is used. Dan's bond with me, entered into willingly, did not at first cause such a problem. But now his feelings were much different, conflicted at the very least, but more likely mostly negative. The blows I took during the second round must have triggered Dan's need to defend me, only he didn't want to and was fighting it. His face had gone an ashy gray, and his tremors shook him as if he were on the verge of having a seizure. I yelled to him in Welsh not to come to my aid, but apparently, the magic was set up in a way that did not allow me to waive the obligation.

The bell rang starting round three. Again in Welsh, making it sound like a war cry, I bellowed to Nurse Florence, "Release Dan. The compulsion is hurting him." Then Shar smashed me in the face again, and I went down.

"Stay down!" yelled Nurse Florence, but in English. I started to get up, just enough to see that Dan had slumped into his seat, though whether as a result of Nurse Florence adjusting the *tynged* or because I was no longer in as much danger I couldn't tell. I used my extra stamina to jump back up, hoping to do what I needed to do without triggering another problem for Dan.

Again I dropped my guard, and this time Shar pummeled me, deliberately pulling his punches but putting just enough force behind them to knock me down again.

"Stay down!" he mumbled through his mouth guard. I staggered back to my feet, but my defensive work was sloppy. However, instead of taking the shot this time, Shar just stared at me. I jabbed at him, but he dodged back, not trying to land the blow he clearly could have. Abruptly, he tore off his gloves and threw them on the ground.

"To hell with this!" he yelled, jumping out of the ring and heading toward Dan. I followed, unsteadily. I wasn't faking. Oh, I had manipulated the way Shar hit me, but the pain was real enough, the blood (admittedly from last night's wounds) was real enough. Somehow it would have seemed underhanded to fake pain in this kind of situation.

"He's a good boxer, good enough to avoid getting hurt," said Shar to Dan, loud enough for much of the stilled audience to hear. "But after round one, he kept letting me hit him, over and over. Hell, he practically threw himself on my fists. End this. Whatever he had to prove, he's surely proved it."

"We haven't finished the third round…"

"End this!" shouted Shar. Others echoed the sentiment. It might quickly have become a shouted chorus, but Dan responded with a curt nod. Stan was officially off the hook. The only problem was that now Dan looked like a total scumbag in the eyes of most of the school. The next few seconds would decide whether that idea stuck or not.

"Thank you, Dan," I said, as loudly as I could. "Thank you for giving us this chance. I don't think Stan could have stood it if you had not honored our request, even though I know you didn't want to do it. You have given him the chance to be free of his guilt." At best, I was playing fast and loose with the truth, but there was magic behind those words, healing magic, all I could manage at the moment, and I sent it out into the crowd with every ounce of strength left to me, willing them to believe, willing them to see Dan in a different light. Then I hugged him, partly to cap the scene with the appropriate visual, partly because I was feeling dizzy. So people really did see stars in this kind of situation.

"You, you asked for this? I thought Dan made you do it," said Shar.

"No," I replied quietly. "Stan and I had to beg. Dan thought the whole idea was barbaric, but I knew it was the only way for Stan to get closure, so I pushed until Dan agreed. He just pretended to have forced us into it so that, if the idea caused any trouble, he'd take the heat for it, not us." Such a blatant lie, but Principal Simmons was right about one thing—for better or worse, I was getting good at lying. I could feel Dan tense in my arms, but he said nothing. Then I felt the faintest shudder, almost like a sob, but I couldn't be sure.

"As I let go of him, being careful to rest my hands on the bleacher railings, Nurse Florence appeared behind me.

"My, you do find ways to get yourself injured. Let's go to my office and get you checked out."

"I'm a little wobbly," I said. "Perhaps Dan could help me get there?" Yes, I wanted another shameless visual manipulation, but I also wanted to be alone with Dan and Nurse Florence. Dan got up and let me lean on him. The audience was treated to the image of the two friends exiting the gym, one supporting the other—or at least, that was how I hoped it would spin in the campus gossip mills.

As I was leaving, I got "high fived" or slapped on the back by a lot of people, and even Coach Miller gave me a thumbs up.

"After the events in school yesterday, I wasn't sure I'd ever see that again," I whispered to Nurse Florence, who was on the other side of me from Dan.

"He has every reason to be happy with you," muttered Nurse Florence. "You just upgraded his star player from a complete ass to only…"

"A half-ass," I suggested with a snicker.

"Well, anyway, keep it up. Carl knows you will redeem Dan yet."

"Let's hope," I replied. At that point, we moved outside the noisy gym, and it seemed prudent to end our conversation, now that Dan could hear every word.

We walked (or hobbled, in my case) to Nurse Florence's office. Nurse Florence verified Dan was in defender mode, which meant he wouldn't remember anything later, so it would be safe to talk in front of him.

"I have a good mind to spank you," said Nurse Florence irritably as she re-bandaged my arm.

"Well, if that's what you're into," I replied, though whether I was punch-drunk or just generally cocky from the afternoon's events, I wasn't sure.

"Taliesin Weaver! If you hadn't already had your quota of blows to the head for the day, I would slap you."

"You can't blame a guy for trying."

"I think someone with thousands of years of experience should be above that kind of sexual innuendo, but what you are trying to do is distract me from my point. Were you a cowboy in one of your previous lives? I ask because you keep pulling these cowboy moves!"

"I think things worked out pretty well."

"A bad strategy that succeeds through dumb luck does not suddenly become a good strategy."

"Dumb luck?"

"You heard me. You didn't bother to tell me what was going on, so you didn't know I was going to be there to heal you if need be. You could have been injured far worse than you were, and then what would have happened? I gather you also didn't know Shar's conscience was going to get in the way of crushing you like an insect. Face it, there were a lot of variables you didn't control for. And at least one of them will come back to bite you eventually."

"What do you mean?" I asked.

"Your story about you and Stan asking Dan to set up this match. If Stan wanted closure so bad, why wasn't he the one in the ring? When the initial magic you spewed on people wears away, they will either question that statement or assume that Stan is a big wimp who lets you fight his battles."

And I thought I had done so well!

"I guess I need to adjust the spin on that a little. I'll take care of it."

"Ooh, spin doctoring. Did you learn that in your internship with Carrie Winn?"

"Funny. But there is another important matter I need to discuss: Dan."

Dan, who had been pretty zoned out, looked up at that.

"What about me?"

"I think you need to release him from his bargain, lift the *tynged,* and let him go back to living his life."

"Why?" asked Nurse Florence and Dan, almost at the same time, and quite eerily.

"You saw what almost happened at the match."

"Oh, yes, something else you didn't plan well for."

"There's more than that," I said, somewhat exasperated. "Something is wrong with Dan. He overreacted to the whole situation with Stan and Eva..."

"I thought Stan was going to sleep with my girlfriend!" protested Dan. "A lot of guys would have acted the same way."

"You're not a lot of guys. You're you, and you would never have hit someone like Stan."

"Except for the last few weeks, we haven't even spoken in years," argued Dan. "Maybe you don't know me as well as you think."

"Maybe not, but then there's today. Dan, I wasn't the one you thought was after Eva, but you have been giving me crap ever since this whole thing started. Even most of the other players couldn't understand what today was really about. I can't see the sense in it either. I had to cover for you to keep everyone from staying mad with you."

"I didn't ask you to do that."

"That's not the point. If you were the same person you normally are, I wouldn't have had to do that."

"You really don't understand, do you?" Dan asked, not in anger, but in something that sounded halfway between resignation and despair.

"Understand what?"

"I thought we were going to be friends again," said Dan quietly, sounding in that instant almost like the ten-year-old Dan I still dimly remembered. "But when the chips were down, you sided with Stan."

"I didn't!"

"You were on his side, making excuses for him in your head, and even when we heard the truth…well, what we thought was the truth at the time, you still defended him. Then you were so eager to come to his rescue that night, you tried to guilt-trip me. You used Jimmie, Tal, Jimmie."

"I said I was sorry."

"Saying it isn't enough. You're good with words, Tal, very good, but actions speak louder than words—and every time you act, you trample me to save Stan." So Nurse Florence's earlier feeling was correct.

"Dan, why do you think Stan ran away in the first place? He did because he tried to get comfort from me after school, and I couldn't give it to him. I didn't know what to do. I was thinking, not just of Stan, but of you. Yes, I wanted Stan rescued, but in part because it was my fault he was in danger in the first place. He's my friend; you know that.

But I rescued him last night because he needed rescuing. You didn't. If the situations were reversed, I would have tried just as hard to rescue you. And I did what I did today for Stan and you—that can't have been lost on you."

"No, I know what you mean. But somehow, all that seems real to me is your friendship with Stan. Are you and I friends? I have no idea."

"And that's why you need to free him," I said to Nurse Florence. "The bargain may have been entered into freely, but now his will is scraping against it. It's making him sick, and he'll just keep getting sicker."

"I did sense someone else's magic on him yesterday. Perhaps another influence..." began Nurse Florence.

"Whatever," said Dan dismissively. "Is anyone going to ask me what I think?" Nurse Florence and I both stopped and stared at him.

"Well, of course, Dan. Sorry. I just assumed..." I began.

"Well, you assumed wrong. I don't want to be let out of the agreement."

"But..."

"No! And as I understand the rules, Nurse Florence, the bargain binds me, but it binds you as well. We both have to agree for it to be dissolved."

"Well, yes," said Nurse Florence thoughtfully. "That's true."

"Here's what I think," said Dan. "I like the football part of the bargain. You've really kept up your end. As for Tal, well, maybe we aren't friends. Maybe we never will be. But if I say I want out of protecting him, and then something happens to him, I, well, I couldn't take the guilt. I can think he's a bastard and still defend him to the best of my ability."

I tried to persuade Dan to change his mind, but after a few more minutes I gave up. I didn't doubt that Dan would still defend me. He had to, after all, if he wanted to keep being the football *wunderkind*. But hanging out with him all the time, knowing that his feelings for me oscillated between indifference and hatred, gave me that "alone in a crowded room" feeling.

When Dan went to get my clothes from the gym, Nurse Florence looked at me and shook her head.

"You did manage to get yourself a concussion out of this stunt. I'll heal it before you go, but in future, you don't make a move without telling me."

"Yes, Mother."

"Park the sarcasm somewhere. I'm not done."

"Okay, sorry. Go ahead."

"I don't know if it's from the alien magic—yes, I can still feel it on him—or from something else, I don't know, but there is a darkness in him. Maybe the emotional roller coaster we've all been on has shaken him up too much. I'd agree with you that he needs to be freed, except that that darkness would be too easy for an enemy to exploit. His *tynged* prevents him from acting on any impulse that would be to your detriment—a condition he agreed to. Free him, and someone else could possess him by force."

I nodded. "Then it sounds as if we should leave the situation as it is. Actually, I'm trying to tell myself that he still wants to be friends, and that's part of why he doesn't want to end the bargain."

"I'll keep a good thought," replied Nurse Florence, just as Dan returned with my clothes, which he dropped off with deliberate abruptness and then left. I changed quickly, Nurse Florence healed my concussion, and I thought I was ready to leave, but she had one more thing to say.

"What did you do to Principal Simmons?" she asked. I had one of those, "Someone just stepped on my grave," shudders.

"I just put her to sleep for a very short time, and I told her to forget everything connected with the boxing match or something like that."

Nurse Florence gave me her best "we have to have a talk" faces. "Do you remember when you told me you didn't erase Stan's memory of your secret because you were afraid to?" I nodded. "Well, you were right to be cautious. You run less risk perhaps than trying to compel someone against a deep-seated moral code or even a strong desire, but risks there still are, nonetheless."

"Is something wrong with Ms. Simmons?" I asked, dreading the possible answer.

"At some point after you left the office, she found her notes on the boxing match. She could see she had written them, but she couldn't remember writing them. Do you see how frightening that could be?"

"Of course, but I had no way of knowing she had notes."

"Well, how about this, then—something else frightened her. She could no longer remember what boxing was. She thought she must have had a stroke or something and ended up in the emergency room."

"Will she be all right?" I asked shakily.

"Considering she didn't have a stroke, yes, physically, she will be all right. But you have shaken her confidence in herself. She is a fine educator, and now you've made her wonder whether she is still competent to be in charge of teenagers."

"I didn't mean to do that."

"Of course you didn't. But this brings us back to my initial point. You didn't plan very well, and someone got hurt." I leaned against the wall, hardly able to think. I was tired, so tired of having every move I make produce some kind of catastrophe.

"Tal, I know this kind of thing is new to you. The first Taliesin didn't have to hide who he was. He never needed to worry about how to erase memory. You've learned that skill more or less on your own in a very short period of time, and you're good at it, but that doesn't mean you can be casual about it."

"Sometimes there may be no choice."

"I'm not saying you should never do it. I'm just saying word your instructions carefully. It is the mind of the person being magicked that actually carries them out, the subconscious mind, as far as I can tell, and it is very literal.

"And plan what you are doing next time. I don't want to keep repeating myself, but you simply cannot afford not to. I know you have thousands of years of experience, but all that experience is packed into an impulsive teenage brain, and your actions show it."

"I promise I'll be much, much more careful," I said. "Is there anything I can do to help Ms. Simmons?"

"I appreciate the thought, but it is probably better to leave that to me. I think I can fix the problem—don't worry about that. Go and enjoy the party."

"I don't feel much like going now," I said dejectedly.

"I did want you to take your magic—and your planning—more seriously, Tal, but I really didn't want to lay a guilt trip on you. Considering what you have had to deal with, I'm not sure anyone could have done better." She patted me on the arm. "I told you before, well, actually through Dan, but you now know it was me, what has happened to you is completely unfair. No one should have to bear this burden at such a young age.

"Now," she said, motioning me toward the door, "we both have important things to take care of. We'll talk again tomorrow."

The fact that Nurse Florence knew what The Voice had said to me through Dan made me even more certain that she was my ally, and just as sure Carrie Winn was my enemy. I opened my mouth to tell her about Ms. Winn, then closed it again. Nurse Florence could have learned what Dan said in some other way—and hadn't she just cautioned me about acting impulsively? No, better to go to the party tonight and see if I could ferret out some more definite proof.

Looking at my watch, I realized I only had a few minutes until the limo picked Stan and me up. I thanked Nurse Florence and scurried home, grabbed a quick shower, fended off my mom's worried inquiries, put on my second best suit—the first best one, my Founders' Day suit, seemed somehow unlucky—and raced out front to rendezvous with Stan.

I was eager to tell Stan about the boxing match, but he already knew —and, much to my surprise, he wasn't the least bit happy about it.

"Do you really think I'm that much of a wimp?" he asked me in his "I'm about to cry" voice, though the irony seemed lost on him.

"Stan, you know I don't think that way about you!" I protested.

"Then why didn't you let me box?"

Well, at least that was a question I could answer.

"Stan, I have seen you face death and stay calm. I know you aren't a wimp..."

"You just don't think I can fight my own battles."

"Physically, you are still a work in progress, but that isn't why I didn't tell you about the match. I was trying to pull something decent out of this train wreck. I wanted you and Dan to come out of this well, and if Dan had let you get beaten up, there wouldn't have been enough magic in the world to get people to forgive him. That's if he could have found anyone to fight you in the first place. He might have done it himself, which would have been even worse for him."

"In other words, you don't think I'm a wimp, but everyone else does, and that's why they would have hated Dan—for letting poor, pathetic Stan get roughed up."

"Listen, even as things turned out, there was a real risk that Dan's name would have been mud for letting poor, pathetic me get roughed up." I put my hand on his shoulder. "Stan, I didn't do this to hurt you. I did this because it was the only way I could get you what you really wanted. You really wanted things to go back to the way they had been before your trek to the woods with Eva, right?"

"Yeah," Stan admitted grudgingly.

"Well, trust me, there is only one road to that destination, and we're on it."

At that point, the limo's arrival mercifully interrupted our conversation. I had never before ridden in a limousine—in this life, anyway—and neither had Stan, a good thing considering it gave him something to think about besides the boxing match. And what a limousine it was: a jet black Mercedes Benz air-conditioned to exactly the right temperature and equipped with a sizable TV screen and wet bar with a good stock of soft drinks and ice. The driver, who acted as if he were our personal chauffeur and had known us for years, opened the door for us, asked if there was anything we needed, then closed the door and got into the driver's seat. The windows were very darkly tinted, so I couldn't be sure, but I was betting both my mom and Stan's were out there somewhere taking pictures. The car ran so smoothly I barely realized we had already pulled out from the curb.

"You know what would make this better?" asked Stan after a few minutes.

"What?"

"Girls!" he replied, with a little smile. I breathed a little easier, knowing that, at least for tonight, he was going to drop the boxing match conversation. Maybe I could actually relax a little myself.

I really should have known better.

I had seen the Winn "house" from a distance; everyone in Santa

Brígida could say that much. But this was the first time Carrie Winn had actually thrown a party for high school students (or indeed for anyone but the movers and the shakers of Santa Barbara County). At a distance the place was impressive; up close it was overwhelming.

If most of the town was carefully coordinated Spanish colonial revival, Carrie Winn's home looked like it had been built with the first wave of the Neo-Gothic revival in the 1740s, then swept up in a hurricane and dropped in Santa Brígida instead of Oz. No, not even Neo-Gothic; more like real Gothic. No question, she took the idea of a man's home being his castle rather literally. The walls had the look of solid stone, the massive front door of heavy oak. No windows broke the stone expanse for the first two or three floors, as if Carrie Winn was expecting to have to repel a siege. Looking up, I could see some windows, a mix of plain glass and extremely ornate stained glass, the latter certainly more Neo than Gothic. The wall culminated several floors up in medieval crenellations, and four massive towers, one at each corner of the building, rose far above the roof level. One might have expected an eighteenth-century formal garden, but instead one got a carefully stage-managed forest, not unlike the one north of the school, only much, much bigger, extending up from the Winn "yard" into the surrounding hills. There was even an ornamental moat surrounding the place, though I could smell the chlorine as we walked across the drawbridge—no, I am not kidding—about the chlorine or the drawbridge. The drawbridge took the place of front steps and did not actually look as if it could be raised. The heavy chlorination of the moat struck me as odd, but perhaps at some point in the past Carrie Winn had had a run-in with Kelpies, or maybe just mosquitoes. Doubtless, the place boasted all the modern comforts of home inside, but if one could somehow block out the paved driveway and the fleet of limousines, one could almost believe oneself back in the Middle Ages.

It was not surprising that such a magnificent dwelling, following the European precedent, had a fanciful name: Awen, which originally meant poetic inspiration, coincidentally, one of the characteristics I was supposed to have gained from a magic cauldron so many centuries ago. Actually, I had begun to doubt that there was any such thing as coincidence, but the place had been named long before Carrie Winn had ever heard of me, much less met me.

An attractive woman, looking like a young Joan Collins and perky as a cruise director, met us at the entrance, smoothly checked off our names, and passed us off to a neatly attired guide, who it was clear was there to make sure we got to the dining room without getting lost along the way. But what really caught my eye—yes, more than the attractive woman—were the two security guards, standing at the entrance with a demeanor that reminded me of Hollywood's version of secret service agents. (I had never seen the real thing.) Just between the entrance and the dining room, I think I counted twenty of them; whether that made me feel really safe or really trapped, I wasn't yet sure.

I was sure that Carrie Winn's medieval fixation did not stop at the front door. Indeed, it was impossible to look anywhere without seeing some reproduction (or in a few cases, I was pretty sure) original medieval relic. Highly polished suits of armor were strategically positioned along each hallway. Medieval tapestries and paintings with medieval themes, while they did not take up every inch of wall space, somehow seemed to surround us completely. If one looked too closely, the montage of unicorns, dragons, grails, and swords-in-stones threatened to become dizzying.

As expensive and as interesting as all this was, like the rest of the town, it had a "trying too hard" feeling to it. Ms. Winn had clearly never heard the expression about less being more. No, even worse than trying too hard, the place showed the *nouveau riche* desire to display wealth without the sense to avoid making it entirely obvious what one was doing. It was the interior decorating equivalent of a Gatsby party.

"Look," said Stan, poking me, "she has the same decorator you used for your room." I poked him back, but on some level he was right. My display was cheap by comparison with hers, but I now realized there was something of excess about it, some weird compulsory homage to my deepest rooted former lives.

Was it possible? Could Carrie Winn also have been overwhelmed at some point by all her former lives?

At first, I had chuckled at the idea of needing to be guided to the dining room, but I now saw the necessity of it. To someone unfamiliar with the place, one hall might look much like another—and there seemed to be a lot of halls, each seductive in its own way, each calling out to me to examine its unique treasures. I visualized tripping over the skeleton of someone who had fallen under the house's spell and died there, and it was all I could do to keep from laughing out loud. Certainly, I was letting my imagination run wild, but the place did seem to encourage that.

Finally, we reached the formal dining room, expansive enough for at least two hundred, set up tonight for fewer, but still more than I had ever seen—except at Founders' Day. That memory gave me an involuntary shudder, and I reached down to make sure White Hilt still hung at my side—unnoticeable, of course. This time I was not going to be caught by surprise.

I wondered how many people it took to keep up a place like this. More than King Arthur ever had at Camelot, I was sure. The hardwood floors glistened, the china, silver, and crystal on the tables sparkled, catching the light from brilliant chandeliers, bright enough to reveal the spotlessness of the white table cloths. This room felt more Bel Air than medieval, but just behind the head table (with a throne-like chair in the center that could only be Carrie Winn's), was an immense tapestry that looked like a gargantuan reproduction of Edward Burne-Jones' *Quest for the Holy Grail*. Why that theme would have attracted her I wasn't certain; by the look of things, she probably had the grail somewhere in her silver service.

I had half-feared place cards in such a setting, but clearly, Carrie Winn understood the teenage mind, at least well enough to let us arrange ourselves. I sat next to Stan, naturally enough—and Gordy Hayes plopped down on Stan's other side, though whether to express his newfound appreciation of Stan or whether to annoy Dan Stevens, I was not entirely sure. Part of me wanted Dan on the other side of me from Stan, but, without making a big show of it, he found a way to sit as far from Stan and me as possible. The tall, brunette, sultry, and currently unattached cheerleader who did end up by my side should have cheered me up, but for some reason, she didn't.

I had also feared the possible menu, but Ms. Winn had the sense not to try anything really exotic, though it would almost have been worth the price of admission to watch Gordy Hayes struggle with lobster. Fortunately, everything was pretty conventional, though superbly prepared. I recognized all the courses—yes, there were several, but mostly light, except for the culminating prime rib, carved to order and certainly the best I had ever tasted. The only problem was figuring out the silverware. Which fork to use when might have been a real ordeal, but instead of getting stressed we ended up laughing at each other and somehow getting the food eaten, wrong fork or no. Then came the dessert, an excellent chocolate soufflé I noticed some of the cheerleaders sent back untouched. I guess fitting into those uniforms on game days took a lot of self-discipline.

Carrie Winn ate at the head table with the coaching staff. Security guards flanked them, as if an assassin lurked among us. I found myself chuckling inwardly about that, too. I'm sure this was all deadly serious for the adults, but I was still a teenager in the present life, and still able to see the humor in a situation like this.

Then came the moment for Ms. Winn to speak, but fortunately, as I had noted at Founders' Day, she was a charismatic speaker and even managed to keep a mob of teenagers entertained, no mean feat. She talked about the fine tradition of homecoming, the great heights to which our team had risen, the possibility of the state championship. She had an inspiring quality that rivaled the best pep talks I had heard—in this life or any of the others. And it definitely became a feel-good moment for the football team. Even Dan seemed more relaxed than I had seen him recently.

Ms. Winn also knew when to stop, perhaps the greatest blessing of all, given what had happened with some of the speakers at Founders' Day. She invited her teenage guests into the ballroom to dance "just for a little while," as she had promised the coaches, so the players wouldn't get home too late. The ballroom, adjacent to the dining room, looked fit for royalty: more glowing chandeliers, a dance floor big enough to get lost on, a massive window on the south side with a romantic sea view. Somehow, I hadn't really thought about going upstairs when I first came in, but the dining room and ballroom were clearly at least a few floors up, judging by that view. I had been so engrossed in sightseeing I hadn't even noticed the climb.

The cheerleader who had sat next to me at dinner was sidling up next to me with obviously interesting intentions, when someone behind us said, "Mr. Weaver, can I steal you away for a moment?" I jumped a little, not having realized anyone else was so close, turned around, and found myself face-to-face with Ms. Winn again. "I'm sure the young lady will understand." Judging by her facial expression, I doubted the young lady did understand, but she nodded agreement. Even a teenage girl in Santa Brígida knew enough not to get between Carrie Winn and what she wanted.

I glanced discreetly around, decided that Stan was taken care of for the moment—dancing with a cheerleader, God bless him—and no one else seemed likely to need me for a few minutes. "Certainly, Ms. Winn," I replied.

We exited the ballroom on the north side, went up some stairs—this time I noticed—and ended up on what felt like the top floor of Awen... with two security guards following at a discreet distance. Give me a break!

"A little quick business," said Ms. Winn, slowing her pace. "I'm giving a little party on Halloween, and I would love for the Bards to play, at least part of the time. Your group would be well-compensated."

Well, that I could believe.

"I appreciate the offer, Ms. Winn, but I'm a little puzzled. There isn't that much call for Rock/Celtic fusion bands at adult functions. We've played teenage venues, mostly."

"You're too modest," she said, with a little laugh. You got good reviews at the Troubadour, did you not? Oh, did I mention the entertainment editors for several of the local papers will be here? The Bards would get very good exposure."

The guys would smear me with honey and tie me to an anthill if I said no to an offer like this, and there didn't seem any reason to refuse. "We'd be honored."

"Very good, then. You'll only be playing part of the time. The rest you'll be invited guests, free to enjoy the party. Ah, here we are. Boys," she said, turning to her security men. "You can go back down. I don't think I'm going to be needing much protection from young Taliesin here." Both men nodded and walked briskly off toward the stairs.

With that, she opened the door in front of us and gestured for me to go in. I countered by gesturing her in—my mom hadn't raised me to go in before a lady. Ms. Winn smiled and walked in. I followed quickly...

And my jaw hit the ground with a resounding thud.

I had expected her office, but this was obviously the master bedroom.

"Do sit down, Taliesin," she said, indicating a plush chair against the wall, "and don't look so scandalized. This is the only room without security cameras. I trust my people, but you never can tell." I nodded nervously and sat down. "By the way, you really didn't need the sword." Reflexively, I reached down and touched its hilt.

"You can see it?"

"If I really make the effort, but actually it got picked up by the security cameras."

"Yeah," I said sadly. "I never have found a way to make it truly invisible."

"Well, no worries; I convinced my security chief it was just a harmless eccentricity of yours. Anyway, as I was saying, you don't need it here, just for future reference. This is the safest place west of the Rockies—you can trust me on that."

"With all due respect, Ms. Winn, some of my friends and I got sucked into Annwn on Founders' Day when I was standing almost right next to you."

Ms. Winn chuckled. "I like it that you speak your mind to me. So few people really do, you know. But Founders' Day was at city hall, not here. I have enough protection here to fend off the entire army of Annwn, if need be—and I am not just talking about my human guards, though they are quite formidable. The protective magic is so thick here that no one, and I mean no one, gets in or out without my consent."

"Thank you for the protection, and I will keep that in mind next time. But that can't be the only reason you wanted to talk to me."

"Ah, yes, very perceptive. Taliesin, I am concerned about the progress of your magic studies."

I raised an eyebrow. "I don't think I've ever told you about my progress."

"I know, nonetheless. You are reluctant to shift, and you still can't get in or out of Annwn on your own power. You could do all that and more when you were first called Taliesin, correct?"

"Yes," I said slowly, "there are some types of magic where the memory doesn't seem to be helping."

"That's because knowing how to do something, in theory, is very different from actually doing it. Let's say you had been a pro football player in your last life but had never even touched a ball in this one. You would know in theory how to throw the winning touchdown, but your arm muscles wouldn't be able to actually execute the move without practice."

"I know. That's why I fence. That's why I work out. That's why I practice my music, and my magic, but practicing the magic doesn't seem to help in the way I expected." Since I still didn't know if Ms. Winn were friend or foe, I probably shouldn't have been talking to her about my potential weaknesses, but what reason could I have given for refusing? She clearly already knew the areas in which I struggled, anyway.

"Has it occurred to you that in that case, the problem might not be lack of practice, but a blockage of some kind?"

"Interesting, but I've never heard of a random magic blockage, in any of my lives. What do you think could cause such a thing?"

Ms. Winn attempted what I think she wanted me to accept as a knowing look. "What makes this life different from your earlier ones?"

"I never thought about it. I'm surrounded by modern technology. I'm living on the other side of the world. There are actually a lot of big differences."

"Is this perhaps the only life in which you were still a virgin at this age?"

I nearly fell off my chair.

Those of you who are still teenage guys, or at least remember what it was like, will know that, in general, about the last conversation you want to have with your mom is one about sex. True, Carrie Winn was not my mom, but she was about the same age. The conversation had gone from matter-of-fact to incredibly awkward in under sixty seconds.

"I think," I said, striving for a neutral tone, "there are a lot of cultures that think virginity is apt to give one greater spiritual and supernatural sensitivity."

"But certainly not the Celts! Was Morgan a virgin? Hardly. But she was one of the most powerful sorceresses who ever lived. Were the ladies of the lake? No? The queens of Avalon? No? Merlin? Obviously not! The first Taliesin? You know differently."

"Ms. Winn, with respect, you need to let me take care of that in my own way, and in my own time."

"Well, you are certainly taking your time about it!"

"This isn't the sixth century. Things were easier then."

Ms. Winn laughed hard at that. "Taliesin, do you really not know how the girls feel about you? Why, you could have had that brunette tonight. You could probably have had her in the bushes on the way in if you had wanted. Why, Taliesin, I do believe you're blushing. You never were such a prude before."

"Before?" I said, grasping at any possible change of subject. "You knew me in an earlier life?"

"Oh, yes, very early indeed. But don't change the subject. You do not lack for opportunities, Taliesin. You just don't take them."

Well, she had me there. I knew on some level that I probably could find a willing girl. Yet, for all my joking about scripting porno movies in my head—actually, I guess I did do that sometimes—I felt differently about sex than I had in some of my earlier lives. Oh, I'm no saint, and I suppose if a beautiful girl threw herself at me—murderous Kelpies excepted—I would probably succumb. But I had a deep-seated aversion to the idea of having sex just to have it. Oh, I know, some of you are snickering, but it's true—and it didn't make me any less of a man, just a more sensible one. Actually, I was heartily sick of the way teenage society tries to measure a guy's masculinity by how early and how often he's had sex. I guess one of the advantages of having all those past life memories was being able to avoid some of the mistakes of the past. I have had lives in which I was an animal about sex, rutting with every-thing that moved, and lives in which I had made love only with those I loved. The latter ended up much better. So no, I wasn't going to do it for the sake of doing it. My hormones wanted it for sure. There were days I felt racked with desire for it. But the one girl I would feel right about doing it with was the one girl I couldn't have. Yeah, I still loved Eva, even having seen how cruel she could be to Dan. But nothing was ever going to happen there. I was not going to be Lancelot to her Guinevere and Dan's Arthur, and not just because I needed Dan.

Ms. Winn gave me a penetrating stare, as if trying to plumb the depths of my soul.

"I am your protector, Taliesin. Am I also your friend?"

"I...I guess. I don't really know you."

"I understand your resistance to losing your virginity with some random girl. Would you feel the same way about losing it with a friend?"

Was she going where I thought she was going?

I started to get up, but she pushed me back into the chair with some force.

"You haven't answered my question."

"And I'm not going to. I don't mean to be rude, but...oh, hell, did you mean..."

"Taliesin, you are blushing again. At least give it some thought. I know many ways of pleasuring a man..."

Oh, my God! Way too much information!

Ms. Winn was an attractive woman...for someone of my mom's generation. Maybe if I'd had a really massive Oedipus complex...no, probably not even then.

"I've upset you. That wasn't what I wanted. Listen, I know what the problem is. I'm too old for you...in this lifetime, anyway."

Ya think?

"But," she said, none too subtly positioning herself between me and door, "you ought to have guessed that I can be whoever you want. You want your first time to be with a particular young lady; so be it!"

In the next few seconds, I learned three things.

First, Carrie Winn could shapeshift.

Second, Carrie Winn could read minds.

Third, Carrie Winn was not above fighting incredibly dirty to get what she wanted.

Carrie Winn was no longer in front of me. Instead, I saw Eva, and every nerve in my body was on fire. I wanted to throw her on Ms.

Winn's enormous bed, undress her and love her until dawn, until every ounce of my strength and hers was spent. I wanted to become one with her and never let go.

Ms. Winn almost had me. Caught off guard, I actually moved in the direction of "Eva," who was falling back toward the bed, her smile inviting.

The problem was, this wasn't really Eva. True, precisely because it wasn't Eva, I could theoretically have had sex without feeling as if I were betraying Dan. But I could not help thinking of Morgan, pretending a wasteland was Avalon and making it more of a wasteland in the process, setting up empty suits of armor for knights, giving orders to Sir Accolon, who had been dust for centuries, waiting for a Lancelot who had never loved her and would never love her. She went mad trying to remake the world in a way reality could not accommodate. Some problems can't be fixed by magic, and all she had done was drive herself mad trying. I might be many things, but I would not be her. Making love to an imitation Eva, though, would have been a big step in that direction.

Maybe that was what was wrong with Carrie Winn. Perhaps she too longed for something she couldn't have. Perhaps I had become tangled into her delusion, since it was pretty hard to believe that it was present life me she wanted, for all her talk about how women desired me.

I doubted I would ever know the answer to that question, but I did know what needed to happen now. I needed to make an exit, graceful hopefully, but an exit one way or the other.

"I...don't...want...this!" I forced the words out.

"Oh, dear," said Ms. Winn, in Eva's voice. "If you want me to believe that, you really need to wear looser fitting pants."

By now I was bright red. She was using embarrassment to keep me off balance, and it was working. Besides, she still looked exactly like Eva. I could feel my resistance eroding by the second. I would bed her if I stayed. And I would lose myself in the process.

I managed to rip myself back one step, two steps, turn toward the door. Somehow, Ms. Winn had locked it during the early part of our conversation.

I drew White Hilt. The fire on the blade was less than that in my heart, but it would suffice.

"Wait!" shouted Ms. Winn, suddenly herself again, to my mingled infinite relief and infinite frustration. "There's no need to go hacking through my door. Taliesin, I was just trying to give you what I thought you needed—and wanted. I didn't mean to upset you or frighten you. I am your friend and your protector. If you wish, we will never discuss this subject again. And I'll just unlock the door. No need for White Hilt tonight." She brushed past me, produced a key from somewhere, and, good as her word, unlocked the door. I let White Hilt burn out and put it back in its scabbard.

"Taliesin," she said quietly. I think she was going to pat me on the shoulder but thought better of it. "I am sorry. I have overstepped; I know that now. Do you forgive me?"

I nodded, though in truth I was the furthest thing from forgiving her.

You see, I had realized a fourth thing about Carrie Winn.

She was the enemy.

I know some of you think I must have all kinds of sexual hang-ups, and that's why I recoiled so hard, perhaps blaming Ms. Winn for my own neuroses. Nonsense! Would any of you really settle for someone who just looked like the one you loved, but wasn't really that person, was, in fact, a very different person that you most profoundly did not want to have sex with? If so, which one of us is really the sick one?

I put on the most emotionally neutral facade I could manage. I even tried to joke a little with her. She walked me down to the ballroom, I had a couple of dances for appearance's sake, and, just when I figured I would scream if I had to stay any longer, the evening ended. In fact, Ms. Winn, in what I was now sure was a phony effort to seem sensitive, sent everyone home at almost exactly the moment when I desperately wanted to be gone.

On the way home, Stan babbled non-stop about how great the party was. I didn't have the heart to tell him all was not as it seemed. Tomorrow would be soon enough for that.

Tomorrow would be a quite a day for conversation.

MAKING PLANS

I GOT through my parents grilling me about the party—barely. I wished I could have erased the memory of Ms. Winn's effort to seduce me and truly joined their enthusiasm. From their point of view, to be among the few high school students invited into Awen was yet another sign I was destined for success, and I didn't begrudge them their excitement about it. Nonetheless, the whole conversation gave me a headache, and having to conceal it from them only made it worse.

By the time breakfast was over, I was daydreaming about what life would have been like without my sudden "awakening" at age twelve. My grades wouldn't have been as good, my band would still have been terrible, but I would have been friends with Dan without all this complicated weirdness to wade through. Eva would still have been my girlfriend, and the two of us would doubtless have been going to tonight's homecoming dance together, losing ourselves in the music and not having a care in the world. Most importantly, I would not have to worry what mythological monster I was going to have to tackle next, or what new strategy Ms. Winn was going to use to threaten me, or whether or not I was going to go over to meet Stan and find his bloody corpse in the gutter.

Well, enough feeling sorry for myself for one day! Apparently, I was stuck with the life I had, for better or worse, and the old one was as dead as I would be if I didn't figure out a way to play the hand fate had dealt me.

After school, I had a meeting with Nurse Florence and finally told who my enemy really was. To say that she was upset with me for not having talked to her earlier would have been a huge understatement.

"Do you have a death wish?" she asked in a tone of voice that cut into me with her disappointment.

"What was I supposed to do?" I countered defensively. "Either one of you could have been the enemy, but neither one of you ever mentioned the other. Suppose I had guessed wrong and told the enemy about my ally. Wouldn't that have been worse?"

"I suppose," she conceded. "But how could you have not known, after seeing so much of me?"

Because I was trying not to be superficial and assume that the hot chick had to be the good one.

"You have done a lot, especially helping to rescue Stan, but wouldn't a clever enemy have tried to lull me into a false sense of security? And Ms. Winn wasn't exactly acting like the spawn of Satan, well, at least until last night."

And that brought us to the truly awkward part of the discussion. I felt I needed to tell Nurse Florence about the attempted seduction, but that's a pretty awkward topic for a teenage guy to take up with a woman. My dad would have been a better choice — if he had believed a word of it. Fortunately, Nurse Florence knew exactly what to say to keep me from feeling completely awkward, and she even managed not to call attention to my blushing. She did, however, want to discuss Winn's goals, a topic that *did* make me feel more awkward.

"I doubt that someone like Carrie Winn would do such a thing unless it served some purpose in her mind. Perhaps we can figure out what her purpose is, based on what she has been up to lately."

"I don't know." I shifted uncomfortably in the chair. "It seems pretty pointless to me."

"Think, Tal. There are only a finite number of possibilities."

"Such as?"

"Could she conceivably want a child by you?"

I almost fell off the chair. "What for? She certainly couldn't claim me as the father, since I'm underage. Why would a public figure like Carrie Winn want to mother an illegitimate child?"

"There could be something about your bloodline...but I agree, if she wants to keep her public image, she would be risking a lot—and I hear she is gearing up for a campaign for the state senate." I thought about all the posturing on the night Stan was rescued. So Carrie Winn used the situation to generate more favorable political buzz.

"If we assume the political career is not just a ruse of some kind, we can safely rule out trying to have you get her pregnant. Well, what else could she have to gain?"

"Keep me off balance, maybe. The offer certainly had that effect, though I had a strong feeling she wanted me to accept it. And she seemed genuinely surprised by that refusal."

"Your instincts usually seem to be good, so let's go with that for a moment. She wants sex with you, but not a child by you? What's the point?"

"It must be my irresistible charm," I quipped, struggling to keep a straight face.

"No, seriously."

"Well," I said, trying to come up with a decent answer to that question and failing, "maybe she has something in mind like in the movie *Scream*. The idea there was that virgins were more likely to survive."

"That's the best you can do? A horror movie? Well, if you will recall, in many early cultures, the virgins were the ones who got sacrificed."

"So she doesn't intend me as a human sacrifice? Well, let's celebrate."

"I can do without the sarcasm, thanks anyway. Maybe we should go back further for cultural antecedents."

"I know!" I said, thinking back to my much earlier lives. "She wants to ruin me for a grail quest. Galahad was a *virgin*, if I recall." Now it was Nurse Florence's turn to try to keep a straight face.

"That theory would work a lot better if we had any realistic chance of mounting a grail quest at this point, but it is hard to see how she could be too afraid of that. No, I was thinking of Circe in the *Odyssey*.

Remember that if she had taken Odysseus to bed without the special protection Hermes arranged for him, he would have been lost." I thought a little about the analogy, chewed my lip a bit, and realized this was the best theory we had.

"Yeah, the situation could have been very threatening, I guess, but why does Carrie Winn care about me one way or the other? What makes me so special that she would have to lure me to bed in the first place?"

"That is the right question, for sure. Why does Carrie Winn, who has pretty substantial wealth and power, feel she has to meddle with a sixteen-year-old? Sure, she knows who you are, I mean your previous lives, but so what? You haven't shown any inclination to attack her."

"So we end up where we started, with a lot of questions and precious few answers," I said glumly.

"No, we aren't exactly at square one. The reason she wants you does lie somewhere in your identity. She wants something from one of your previous lives, or she wants to use your abilities for her own purposes, or at least make sure you are neutralized as a possible enemy, but I'd say the last is the least likely. Had she really just wanted you out of the way, surely she could have just killed you."

"Maybe that little unplanned jaunt into Annwn was an attempt at just that."

Nurse Florence leaned forward a little in her chair. "That could be, I suppose, but someone like Winn could easily have dispatched you in a less spectacular way, like having that *pwca* you thought was Stan get the drop on you. She clearly knew who you were some weeks before you knew who she was, and at that point, you were much weaker than you are now. No, if she didn't strike then, simple murder is not what's on her mind."

"Perhaps I'll get a better idea on Halloween. She's asked the Bards to play at another big party she's throwing then."

Nurse Florence's jaw dropped. "You aren't thinking about going, are you? And on Samhain, the most dangerous possible time?"

"I don't see how we are ever going to know what she's up to unless we give her another chance to show her hand," I said in the best reasonable tone I could manage.

"Listen, Cowboy, you aren't getting near Awen again if I have to tie you up and throw you in some little corner of Annwn."

"You said yourself she wasn't trying to just kill me."

"That doesn't mean she won't if conditions change, such as if you figure out whatever her plan is and get in her way, or even slip and reveal to her somehow that you know she is your enemy."

"Whereas, suddenly having nothing to do with her won't tip her off at all. Look, I'm not thrilled about this any more than you are, but if I suddenly seem hostile, or even aloof, that could be far worse than playing along, and you know it."

Nurse Florence sighed and gave me a worried smile. "I admit you have a point. But the more time you spend with her, the greater the danger. And what about your other band members? Do you really want to put them in danger?"

"I'd have to magic them to stop them from going at this point. Anyway, lots of other people will be there. The press will be there. Carrie Winn can hardly afford to do something noticeably violent with so many potential witnesses."

"I suppose you have a point there also. Well, if your mind is made up, I will help you—but I still won't let you back over there until after you complete some homework I'm going to give you."

I wrinkled my nose disdainfully. "Just what I need."

"No, I'm serious. Right now she knows far, far more about you than we know about her. Going into her lair blind again is too dangerous. I'm willing to work up some additional magic defenses for you, but you must do your part, with Stan's help, if you like, and gather what information you can.

"First, you need to try to figure out who Carrie Winn is."

"I thought that was pretty obvious."

"No, her public facade is obvious enough, but who is she really? She seems to possess enormous magical power. Mortals with that kind of punch don't exactly grow on trees in this era. Is she a reincarnation of some past power, as you are, or is she someone who just lived straight through, as Morgan seems to have? Is she even human? I don't see any signs of faerie blood, but she could hide them easily enough."

"You are not exactly talking about a simple Google search, you know."

"No, but she seems to employ a veritable army from what you have told me. I'm not just talking about her security. She has drivers, maids, gardeners, cooks, and many others. They all live somewhere. At least some of them must have family, friends, people they talk to. I have never heard any particular gossip about Carrie Winn, but someone, sometime, must have seen or heard something we can use, perhaps something they attached no particular significance to."

I realized how tense I was when a knock on the door made me jump. Stan stuck his head in.

"Is this a private party, or can anyone join?"

"Sure!" said Nurse Florence. "Come on in. This conversation concerns you, too."

She quickly filled Stan in on what she wanted me to do.

"Would it help if we could get a list of all her local employees?"

"Absolutely!" replied Nurse Florence quickly. "You have an idea."

"Sure. I designed the website for Winn Development Company, and they want me to do some updating this week. I'll be sitting at a computer tied directly to the office server. I'm willing to bet a simple employee list isn't going to have much security around it, so for sure I can get all the company employees. But I think I remember the office being networked with her house. Her home employees are probably not part of the company—though they could be, since it's privately owned, not publicly traded—but we might just luck out."

"Way too dangerous!" I said, shaking my head emphatically.

"I'll be safe," said Stan, with a little smile. "I'm not the one whose bones she wants to jump." I blushed despite myself, but I was not about to back down.

"If you're caught…"

"Carrie Winn hasn't even been in the office most of the time when I was working before. I heard she doesn't come in much, anymore—she does most of her work from home, another pretty good indication she could have a connection to the work server. And I doubt every single employee she has is evil, much less some kind of monster."

"It might work," said Nurse Florence thoughtfully. "Particularly,

Tal, if she's an aware reincarnate like you, she may not have much of a knack with computers."

"Hey!" I said defensively.

"Dude, you know that's totally true," said Stan with a smirk. "Ever since your...awakening, you've always had a really hard time getting computer information to stick."

"Of course," continued Nurse Florence, "she's certainly wealthy enough to have a top-tier computer security provider lock everything down, but taking that kind of precaution may not have occurred to her."

"I won't allow it," I said firmly. "Way, way too dangerous."

"Since when are you the boss of me, Tal?" snapped Stan, suddenly angry, even a little red in the face. "This is you boxing Shar for me all over again. You're more overprotective than my mom these days. You won't let me fight my own battles or help with yours. Are you really that certain I'm not good for anything but being an object of your pity?"

"Has it ever occurred to you," I said slowly, "that I could never forgive myself if anything happened to you?"

"How do you think I'd feel if I didn't help, and then something happened to you? I'm just going to an office in the middle of the business district in broad daylight—and Ms. Winn probably won't even be there. You want to go to Awen on Halloween night when you know she *is* going to be there. Who's running the bigger risk?"

"She apparently doesn't want to kill me. I don't know she would have the same qualms about killing you."

"Gentlemen," Nurse Florence interrupted quietly but sternly, "we are not getting anywhere this way. Tal, I think we can take precautions to make sure Stan is...well, as safe as he is going to be. If I'm not satisfied with the situation, I'll be the first to say no." Stan looked about to protest, but arguing with me was one thing. Arguing with someone like Nurse Florence was quite another for him, so he let the matter drop, at least for the moment.

"We have to make the rest of this conversation faster than I'd like, or people will start to wonder what both of you are doing in the nurse's office for so long. Finding out who Carrie Winn is is only half the battle. You also need to figure out how to use your magic more effectively. I'm not as troubled by the fact that you can't reach Annwn as I am by the fact that you haven't made any progress on fusing magic and science."

"I've tried, really hard."

"I'm sure you have, and we've had some distracting crisis every few days, but the only way to protect yourself, to say nothing of your friends, will be to do something Carrie Winn doesn't expect. You survived in Annwn because Morgan had never seen a hurricane before and didn't at first know what to do with it. That was some good applied meteorology. You beat the *pwca* because, on the spur of the moment, you found new ways to direct your sword fire.

"Here's what I think. Magic is always at least partially about visualizing the outcome you want. Those of us who can use magic are better at that than the average person. For us, it becomes real because we can see it in vivid detail in our head."

"I see where she's going!" said Stan excitedly. "If you could visualize the technology you wanted to affect in vivid detail, and then if you could visualize it differently, maybe you could affect it."

"Yes, like, oh, let's just pick a random example, you could cause guns to misfire, or not fire at all." I raised both eyebrows at that.

"Don't tell me you haven't realized how vulnerable all of us would be in the face of Carrie Winn's armed security guards. Drawing White Hilt and getting riddled with bullets isn't exactly a winning strategy— and Merlin himself, if he were here, couldn't cast a spell faster than a bullet could hit him.

"Why do you think there are so few of us around now? You must remember we were more numerous when the first Taliesin was alive. As long as we could cast a spell if need be as fast as someone could swing a sword or throw a punch, we could survive. But once weapons developed that could strike faster than we could, particularly from a distance, it was no longer a contest. Those of us who survived initially basically went into hiding, not letting many people know who we really were, much less what we could do.

"Now if, as you say, Ms. Winn's guards are armed, they probably are crack shots, but they aren't necessarily also experts in hand-to-hand combat. If suddenly their guns fail them, Tal, you and a few well-trained friends might just have a chance of defeating them. With their guns still working, forget it."

"I can't seem to visualize the inner workings of most equipment well enough. Hurricanes or making various shapes with fire are still pretty close to the natural world. The workings of a gun are much further away."

"You can't visualize those things, but I can," pointed out Stan. "I've always been good with mechanical drawing, schematics, equipment repair, and you know I build computers from scratch. The question," he said, addressing Nurse Florence, "is how to get what's in my head into Tal's."

"Agreed, and that may not be as hard as we have always assumed. Tal, when you channel magic through your music to alter people's moods and even ideas, you are effectively projecting some of your thoughts at them…"

"And if the connection between minds is like a conduit of some kind," interrupted Stan, "then there is no reason in theory why the thoughts could not flow in both ways along it."

"Exactly! Tal, if you can send thoughts, and you clearly can, you should be able to receive them. Obviously, Carrie Winn has figured out at some point how to do that. And we already have abilities, like being able to see through the eyes of nearby animals, that are obviously related to what a more scientific age would call telepathy. If you think about it, the ability of creatures like kelpies to lure people by assuming sexually desirable forms suggests that they can read people's minds, at least in that one area."

"That's a pretty tall order in the next couple of weeks," I said at last. "Become fully telepathic, absorb the scientific visualizations from Stan's mind, and use them to enable me to manipulate technology, and not just at some novice level but like an expert."

I had seldom seen Nurse Florence look so utterly serious. "Tal, it's either that, or we lose…possibly our lives, but certainly more than we will want to part with. Whatever Carrie Winn wants, she will not stop until she gets it—unless we stop her. She is clearly a powerful spell caster, and even if we can beat her in that arena, another 'pretty tall order,' she also has a small army at her disposal, and we certainly can't beat that as things stand now."

Another knock at the door, and again I jumped at it—time to switch to decaf. This time it turned out to be Jackson.

"I'm sorry to interrupt, Nurse Florence, but I need to talk to Tal."

"That's okay, Jackson," replied Nurse Florence, her tone now remarkably detached. "We were just chatting, anyway. Tal, Stan, I'll see you later." Nurse Florence busied herself with paperwork on her desk as if we had just been killing time, and Stan and I walked out with Jackson.

"What's up, Jax?" I said casually.

"We've got another gig, man," he replied excitedly. "Well, that is, if you agree. I've already talked to the other guys."

"I'm all ears. What's the gig?"

"The band for the homecoming dance canceled at the last minute. Ms. Simmons ran into me in the hall and asked if maybe we could do it. I know it's not as cool as playing the Winn party, but it should be fun, and it pays." Jackson gave me his patented, light-up-the-room smile.

This was actually the longest conversation I had had with him since Founders' Day. I had forgotten how hard it was to disagree with him, not that I really wanted to.

"Sure, Jax, it sounds like good exposure for the band."

So I guess I was going to the homecoming dance, after all.

HOMECOMING

BEFORE THE HOMECOMING GAME, I did my usual team morale routine (the fight song and similar material with a magical undercurrent designed to set every player up for maximum performance). After, Stan and I sat in the stands, cheering enthusiastically as our team crushed the visitors, a former league champion, 113 to 6. Dan, whom one sports writer had recently compared to a young Joe Namath, was, as usual "on fire," and the rest of the team played as well together as they ever had. Ironically, though I wasn't a football player, the team's success was one of the few things in my life I could still count on to lift my spirits. None of the players (except Dan in defender mode) could possibly have known how much I actually contributed to their success. Probably most of them had a hard time consciously accepting that my singing to them before games made that big a difference. Instinctively, though, they knew I was contributing something, and, with the recent exception of Dan, they showed that appreciation in a variety of ways that made me less alone. At the beginning of the year, I could have counted Stan as a friend, and probably some of the band members…and that was it. Now, though none of the players were as close to me as Stan was, a number of them could have called me friend and meant it. Some of their good-will infected cheerleaders and other athletes, so that I could literally feel the good vibes anywhere on campus, an effect the boxing match had heightened considerably.

I suppose on one level it was childish to want to be popular, but if you had been hospitalized and then watched most of your friends drift away from you, or if you had known people were whispering about you as you walked down the hall, you would understand.

Later, as the Bards set up for their unexpected gig, I felt their warmth around me. No surprise there, since they had never turned their backs on me in the first place. Jackson had been fidgety for a while after Founders' Day, but even he seemed over that, and my contribution to their musical successes was much more consciously obvious to them than my contributions to the football team. None of them lacked talent exactly, but we had never really meshed completely before my awakening. Now, when we played, we fused into one being. Okay, the magic helped, but I'm not sure it was just magic. Sometimes people just need a little push to achieve their potential, and when I suddenly became a much better musician, they felt the pull toward a higher level.

You might wonder how much popularity a rock/Celtic fusion band could ever achieve, regardless of musical talent. You have to understand little communities like Santa Brígida. There wasn't usually a lot for high schoolers to do. The mall was too small to really be a good hangout, there was only one movie theater, which tended to cater to an older crowd, and a lot of the activities the region was known for just didn't work for teenagers. Go antiquing in Summerland? Boring. Visit the various little museums, famous houses, art galleries, etc.? More boring. Wine tasting? Not until you're 21. If you were a surfer, it was easy to catch some waves and some rays, even in winter, and if you were a hiker, the Los Padres National Forest was just to the north. But a lot of people didn't really do either, and especially with the hiking, you had to plan in advance—never a teenage strength. Yes, there was Santa Barbara, but it was a drive, and the highway traffic tended to be sluggish most of the day, so SB wasn't just something you could do on the spur of the moment either, especially on school nights—particularly if your parents were like Stan's, for instance.

What I'm working up to is that most of the teenagers in Santa Brígida were often faced with the stark choice of watching the grass grow or listening to the Bards play. Even when we were, in Stan's words, "a garage band that should never have gotten out of the garage," we sometimes won the contest with the grass. Once our sound really came together, we could even have an impromptu concert at the park or the beach—I had worked out a very flexible permit arrangement with city hall—and draw a fair crowd. You might have thought some parents would get nervous, but generally, they loved us. Bored teenagers are often sullen teenagers, if you hadn't noticed, and most parents try to avoid that situation like the plague. Besides, we were local kids who were also relatively clean-cut and relatively good students—hadn't two of us just been honored at Founders' Day? We didn't smoke, drink, do drugs, use profanity, or appear on magazine covers in scantily clad poses. In the beginning, I think some parents actually shoved their kids in the direction of our performances. And once we got a following, we got paying gigs: Bar Mitzvahs, *quinceañeras*, sweet sixteen parties. After the appearance at the Troubadour, in fact, we had to start turning down some offers. (Remember this was wannabe Montecito, and a lot of parents jumped at the chance to get a band "on the cheap" that had played the Troubadour—who knows, someday we might be someone, and then they could say we had performed for them "back when.")

We had a wide repertoire, but rock/Celtic fusion was our trademark, and for the homecoming dance I thought the costumes from when we first started calling ourselves the Bards would be a nice touch. They weren't really medieval, but they did have a kind of Renaissance Faire look from a distance. The guys wore black pants with white period shirts (you know, the ones with the long, pluffy sleeves and a V-neck collar), and medallions with greenish stones that the V-neck showed off. Our one girl, Carla Rinaldi, necessary both for the female vocals in duets and to keep us from being called a boy band, wore a long, flowing black gown and a medallion that matched ours. Well, the gown was supposed to be flowing, anyway, but Carla had a great talent for finding outfits that were revealingly tight but somehow not tight enough to get her busted for dress code violations at school.

Okay, so Stan had told me those costumes made us look a little like Celtic hippies, but hell, I liked them, and they didn't seem to hurt our popularity any.

More than once during setup, Carla caught my eye and smiled. I wondered in passing whether she was interested in me. We had a common interest in music, and our voices worked well together. Carla wore her silky black hair long, the way I liked it and had strikingly blue eyes. Her face seemed somehow classical, as if she had been the model for some Roman statue of Venus. Her dress more than hinted at the inviting body beneath it. At the risk of sounding like a dog again, her breasts would have been described by Gordy Hayes as exactly the right size—a measurement I think he based on the size on his own hands, which were certainly bigger than mine.

On a physical level, she was one of the most appealing girls I knew. Indeed, only Nurse Florence, not age appropriate, and Eva, forever lost to me, made me feel more like I should stop wasting time doing what I was doing and jump into bed. Perhaps, sometime, if only as a way of getting over Eva...

No, I would really be a dog if I did that, but I resolved to think more seriously about Carla later. Sooner or later, surely my obsession with Eva would fade, and I would be ready for an actual relationship with someone I could actually have. Wow, what a concept!

Putting Carla out of my mind with an effort, I finished setting up just before the gym starting filling with students, flush with their team's victory and their various hormones, needing to unleash some energy. We gave them more rock and less Celtic tonight, and they loved it. I poured all the unbridled joy I could into the music, into the magic, and even I felt better than normal.

About midway through the dance, I decided to test Stan's theory. I could feel the music in the very beating of my heart. I could feel the magic crackling in every nerve. I could feel the support of the rest of the band. There would never be a better moment to see what I could do. I did my best to visualize the magic like a series of guitar strings connecting me to the dancing students in front of us. (Stan had actually said conduits, but the image of pipes stretching out in every direction just didn't do anything for me.) Anyway, the magic flowed liquidly over the strings and dripped down into the students like a gentle, glowing rain. Okay, so far, so good. I had always had to visualize the effect I wanted to make on an audience, but I had never before made the interaction seem so physical. Next step, I imagined thoughts like evaporating water steaming up from the students, collecting on the strings, flowing back toward me.

To my amazement, I began to pick up random thoughts that could only be coming from the students in front of me. At first, I couldn't make them coherent or attach them to a source, but my mind adapted quickly to the new input, and in just minutes I was able to understand what the nearby students were thinking, at least on the surface.

It shouldn't have surprised me that a number of them were thinking about sex, and with such intensity I started blushing vicariously and had to pull back a little. Then I found myself able to filter out the raw, hormonal vibes and begin to sense other things.

I could feel dreams of a state championship from some of the players, feel them as if they were my dreams. I could feel one student's anxiety about an upcoming calculus test—muted now by the upbeat magic—and another's plan to cheat on the same test. Coach Miller quivered on the edge of asking Nurse Florence out. Ms. Simmons had gotten over thinking she was losing her grip and was enjoying our music far more than I might have expected. On and on, jumping from mind to mind as easily as I might have glanced through a stack of papers. If I focused more intently on one, I discovered I could read more deeply. If I focused in a different way, visualizing my own consciousness sailing down the strings and into someone else, I discovered that I could see through the eyes of another person the way I had always been able to see through the eyes of an animal.

These new skills would naturally need more practice, but they opened a myriad of new possibilities, as well as the certainty that I could now "download" Stan's ability to visualize the workings of modern technology. Once I had done that, I could probably learn to influence technology in much the same way I had been able to manipulate nature, much as Stan had suggested so long ago and Nurse Florence much more recently.

I let go of the image of the strings, and the chatter of thoughts around me faded as I put my exclusive focus again on the music.

I had read a little bit on the Internet about how some people thought music was a greater high than sex. I couldn't quite go that far, but there was no question my brain was sailing on a warm sea of endorphins that seemed to stretch out infinitely in all directions. The magic was part of it, but I knew I could reach that feeling on music alone. And I didn't need to be a mind reader to notice the other band members were in a comparable place.

The music possessed me so fully that our next break caught me by surprise, but I realized as soon as I stopped singing and playing that I could use one. Performing was strenuous to begin with for those of us that really merged with the music, and the outflow of magic from me also took its toll. Still, though I was tired, it was a good kind of tired. I was beginning to feel that life might just work out, after all.

During the break, I worked my way over to Nurse Florence. Coach Miller hadn't yet quite reached the asking-out stage and didn't welcome my appearance, but otherwise, he was having such a great night that it was hard for him to begrudge me a couple of minutes with her.

We stood near the exit, our conversation effectively covered by the murmurs of a hundred other conversations in the gym.

"I can do it!" I said, excitedly but quietly. "I can read minds. I can do other stuff, too—lots of things I never imagined. Hell, Taliesin 1 himself never even imagined them."

"That's great," replied Nurse Florence with a smile. "But don't get too cocky—Carrie Winn obviously developed mind reading at some past point. Still, the odds will be more even now. Speaking of which, some of my...associates...are flying in from Wales. In a plane," she clarified in response to my raised eyebrow. "Some time I'll tell you about my organization. Anyway, for now, I think we can match her in magic firepower. If you can neutralize her tech and security advantages, we might just be able to defeat her."

"I'll get right on it. Stan and I will work tomorrow."

"One more thing," she added, scanning the crowd. I jumped a little from the realization that, without trying, I had picked up Coach Miller's impatience, perhaps because he was looking right at me, but still, that was another unexpected surprise. I had thought my telepathy would be limited to moments when I was actively visualizing what I wanted, but perhaps not. After all, I had sometimes picked up hints from nature before without actively seeking them. Wow! What might I be able to accomplish with practice?

"If you could pick someone to wield another magic sword, who would you pick?" Now, that was a question I had not seen coming.

"We have another magic sword?"

"We do now. It's a 'loaner,' if you will, but it will come in handy on Samhain if we have to fight, as I very much suspect we will."

"It's coming in with your associates?"

Nurse Florence smirked a little. "Can you imagine getting something like that through customs?" Actually, I could, having had to get White Hilt out of Wales, and the process had been almost impossible. As was often the case, dumb luck rescued me more than once.

"Even with magic, heightened airport security would mean manipulating a large number of people in a short period of time. No, we have ways of transporting small objects across great distances. The sword is already here, ready for someone to practice with. The question is, who?"

I knew some guys at the fencing club, naturally, and others I had met in competition, but I wasn't really friends with any of them. I wouldn't be sure which ones I could trust. Well, now I guess I could read their minds and figure it out, but I doubted I could afford the time. Then a better idea occurred to me.

"Shar," I said, half to myself. "His specialty is boxing, but I know he did some fencing back east, at least enough for me to assume he can handle a blade."

"Shahriyar," she said thoughtfully. "Yes, he does seem to be someone with character. I'll dream walk him tonight and recruit him if he is as good as he seems to be."

"One thing," I said quickly, knowing our break was almost over and feeling Coach Miller's eyes on me again. "Don't 'recruit' him the way you did with Dan."

"What do you mean?"

"Look at all the trouble Dan has because of the way he can only access his memories about...things part of the time. I want Shar to know everything all the time."

Nurse Florence started to shake her head. "Bad enough that we still have six students who saw you in Annwn, even if they have probably talked themselves into thinking the whole experience was an illusion. We can't…well, wait, as long as part of Shahriyar's *tynged* involves not revealing what he knows, except under very specific conditions, your suggestion might work," she concluded grudgingly.

"Okay, then. Oh, something else," I added, knowing I was about to press my luck in a major way—but you know how much I like to do that. "We need someone to protect Stan and someone to protect Eva the way Dan protects me."

"Anything else? Want me to spin a little straw into gold for you?" As much as Nurse Florence didn't appreciate my sarcasm, she didn't seem to mind using it herself.

"I know I'm asking a lot, but what I want does make sense. Ms. Winn knows I care about Stan because I used her help to find him that time he ran away. And she pulled my feelings for Eva right out of my head. Would she hesitate to use those feelings against me, if she needed to?"

"I doubt it, but from what I gather, she has invited several students on Samhain. Are you willing to stand by calmly and let her kill someone other than Stan or Eva? I'm guessing not, and I can't protect every single student who might show up individually. And something tells me you wouldn't want to explain to Dan why you had Eva body-guarded."

She had me there, of course, but I persisted. She could, after all, bind whoever Eva's defender was not to tell Dan—no need for the subject to come up at all.

By now Coach Miller's gaze was burning right through me.

"Oh, all right; I'll see what I can do. Do you have anyone specific in mind?"

"Gordy Hayes for Stan." Nurse Florence looked at me as if I had totally lost my mind.

"Tal, he's, well, I don't like to say this of a student, but he isn't anyone's idea of brilliant."

"He's fiercely loyal to Stan, the only guy willing to defy Dan on Stan's behalf before the boxing match. And he's like three hundred pounds of pure muscle. He doesn't need to provide new chess strategies for Stan; he just needs to keep him safe, and that we both know he can do."

"Well, I'll dream walk him, too. And for Eva?"

"I don't know for sure. A girl would be logical, but I don't know of any with combat experience."

"I know of a couple with a martial arts background. Let me do some research. Now I've got to go."

I could feel Coach Miller moving in our direction, and anyway, Jackson was trying to catch my eye. Time to get back to the stage.

However, before the band could begin to play again, there was the little matter of announcing the homecoming court.

I should mention that this particular ritual was a little different at Santa Brígida High School than at other schools I'm familiar with. Typically, a big fuss gets made over a certain number of nominees, they get shown off in some kind of parade prior to the game, and then the winners of a student vote are crowned early in the dance. At Santa Brígida, probably because someone thought too much emphasis on the homecoming court might pull the spotlight too far away from the all-important football team, there are no nominees announced in advance. Students wrote names on a blank piece of paper, and the winners were announced at about the mid-point in the dance—which was now, apparently. Ms. Simmons, looking unusually festive in a light blue outfit, was already at the microphone by the time I had worked my way back up to the stage.

The first four announcements (freshman and sophomore prince and princess) were received with polite applause, not a surprise considering that most of the people who came to homecoming tended to be juniors and seniors.

"And this year's winner for junior prince is...Taliesin Weaver." I could hardly have been more surprised if lightning had struck me inside the gym. The sincere enthusiasm of the applause also caught me off guard, though, thinking back on it, I guess it shouldn't have. Dan aside, I was in the good graces of the football team, with its numerous allies, and the band had a real fan base. Still, this particular "honor" blind-sided me completely.

I stepped forward to receive the paper crown and plastic scepter.

Surely these rituals were designed by women. I'd never met a guy who liked them. I even blushed a little, but to some extent, the continuing applause restored my good spirits. The crown and scepter might be fake, but the friendship I felt in the room was not.

Ms. Simmons raised her hand for silence and proceeded to the announcement of the junior princess. Yup, definitely a matriarchal ritual, with each guy basically the consort of the female winner, who was always announced second.

"This year's junior princess is…Eva O'Reilly."

Crap! Couldn't I get through one night without the universe finding some way to kick me in the crotch?

It took every ounce of willpower for me not to run screaming from the gym. I realized, though, that this was definitely a time to play it cool. After all, only Stan and Nurse Florence knew why this situation was so supremely awkward for me. Even Eva herself had no idea, I was sure. Just get through the fifteen minutes of fame, I told myself, just get through it, and life will go back to normal.

Eva was moving toward the stage, hotness incarnate, as always, but not looking especially happy. Of course, she couldn't have been paired with Dan, who was a senior, but I knew without trying to read her mind that that was what she wanted. I knew, and unfortunately for her, so did most other people in the room, that her efforts to reconcile with Dan had failed.

Eva stoically accepted her crown and stood next to me. Her signature jasmine perfume made me dizzy, but I shook the feeling off.

"This is just embarrassing," she whispered to me.

"Just look impassive, and no one will know how uncomfortable you are." Hell, I should know.

The universe was not quite done with us, however. I should have foreseen Dan's election as homecoming king, which brought him sullenly to the stage, right next to Eva. I don't think anyone anticipated Mary Stewart's election as homecoming queen. Sweet girl, and pretty in her own way, but certainly not particularly popular. For the most part, she immersed herself in her art and didn't really seem to care much about social standing. I guess I had watched too many Stephen King movies when I was younger; honestly, I was just waiting for the pig blood to start raining down on us. Unbelievably, Mary actually looked more uncomfortable than Eva, as Mary stood there on the other side of a particularly stone-faced Dan. The freshmen and sophomores seemed to be enjoying each other, but I imagine we upperclassmen were about the grimmest homecoming court on record.

After the "coronation" the mismatched court was urged in the general direction of the dance floor for their one obligatory dance. I was really beginning to see the wisdom of schools that had the homecoming nominees run as couples. Dan and Mary, who had never danced before in their lives and were not great dancers to begin with, looked like puppets handled by a relatively amateurish puppeteer. Not to brag, but I had great rhythm since my awakening, and Eva had a little dance training from the musicals, so we had no difficulty that way. In fact, we looked good enough together to be problematic; our seemingly choreographed dance was too poignant a reminder for me of what might have been.

Dan was staring over Mary's shoulder directly at Eva. I hadn't tried this without music—and only once with—but I decided to see what I could pick up. I visualized the string between us, I visualized his thoughts flowing toward me along it...

His aching longing throbbed through me, hitting me like a Shahriyar stomach punch. In an odd way, it was the twin of mine—and both of us were directing it at the same girl.

I looked straight into Eva's eyes. "Eva, do you trust me?" I whispered. She nodded a yes, plainly confused by the sudden question.

"Then follow my lead," I said, not waiting for a response.

I spun her deftly, humming along with the music as I did so, building up whatever magic I could muster, visualizing a warmly pulsing connection between her and Dan. Narrowly missing the sophomore royalty, I whirled Eva and me around until we were right next to Dan and Mary.

"Dan, let's change partners," I smiled at him, and without giving him a chance to reply, I pulled a startled Mary away from him and thrust Eva into his arms, visualizing the connection between them becoming a sphere, engulfing them, keeping them together. At the same time, I pulled Mary to me and spun off in the opposite direction.

Someone applauded in the background. All of the other students seemed to be holding their breaths.

I looked at Mary, who was actually shaking—with fear. Post-Founders' Day Stress Disorder, no doubt. My sudden swooping in had taken her by surprise in more ways than one.

"Don't be afraid," I whispered, with just a little jolt of magic thrown in, and her shaking subsided. She was not the partner Eva had been, but I tried to put on the best show I could, keep the eyes on us, give Dan and Eva a chance to be with each other without an audience. I failed miserably. Oh, not at the dancing, which was at least passable, though choosing between Mary and a sack of cement for a partner would have been a difficult decision. No, teenagers knew potential drama when they saw it. I could have been dancing on the ceiling, and their eyes would still have been locked on Dan and Eva.

Eventually, I twirled Mary back in their general direction and popped into Dan with surprisingly little effort, seeing the world through his eyes. He was looking into Eva's eyes, and it was clear from her perfect smile, from the light in her eyes, that they had already reconciled. I pulled back out as fast as I could.

Relief and misery wrestled with each other in my soul. It was not yet certain which would win, but my money was on misery.

THE LAKE

THE VERY NEXT MONDAY, Dan went out of his way to find me during a passing period—quite a change, considering we had said barely two words to each other since the boxing match.

"So, Weaver, are you still trying out for soccer?" Not exactly the line of conversation I was expecting, but whatever.

"I don't know, Dan. Do you still want me to?"

"Yeah, I think I do," he said, flashing me a smile I hadn't seen for some time. "And I want to thank you. I know what you did last night."

"That sounds ominous," I said lightly.

"I'm serious. I wanted to get back together with Eva, but I just didn't know how to do it. Maybe my pride got in the way. Anyway, you threw her into my arms during that dance, and suddenly everything seemed simple. Thanks, man." A quick knuckle bump, and he was sprinting off to his next class. Just like that, we were friends again.

I had been waiting anxiously for some resolution of his situation, but I did not feel the sense of relief I had expected. Maybe I was tense about what would happen that afternoon. Nurse Florence was being uncharacteristically mysterious, but I knew something was up.

After school, I met her in a fog-filled faculty parking lot.

"That's not…" I began.

"No, that's just me. We need to do what we can to get out of here unseen, all the more so now that I know Carrie Winn is the enemy. She is on campus frequently for one reason or another, and now we know her hidden agenda for spending so much time here. Besides, she could easily have someone else spying on you."

Stan, Dan, Shar, and Gordy quickly joined us. The last three she had somehow gotten out of football practice. Never mind—given how Coach Miller felt about Nurse Florence, she could probably have gotten the whole team out of practice. And the fact that the team kept winning probably didn't hurt, either.

Nurse Florence seemed rushed and didn't say much, but it was clear the dream walks had proved successful and that Shar and Gordy had both been recruited. Shar had questions, which she told him would need to wait just a little while, as we needed to get on the road quickly. Gordy seemed content just to be there, but would clearly need some training, since he kept positioning himself so close to Stan it was a wonder Stan could breathe.

"Gordy, be cool!" I cautioned as we were piling into Nurse Florence's van. "It's good to keep an eye on Stan, but you don't want the whole world to know what you're doing. Just like in football, don't telegraph your next play so obviously to the other team." That was apparently the right analogy. Gordy insisted on sitting next to Stan, but at least he wasn't insisting on sitting in his lap.

"Not anyone's idea of brilliant," Nurse Florence had called Gordy, and that was true, but there was something endearing about the way he had embraced his new role. He probably would have come to Stan's defense in any case, but he had clearly agreed wholeheartedly to whatever bargain Nurse Florence had proposed and was determined to hold up his end of it.

I ended up sitting next to Shar, who looked at me as if I were a completely different person. On the trip I ended up filling in some of the gaps in the basic story Nurse Florence had given him, but each question I answered brought up three more, and both of us became so engrossed in the conversation that we were startled when the van finally parked, and we realized that we were at Lake Cachuma.

"Why are we here?" I asked as soon as I was out of the van.

"Shahriyar needs to receive his weapon, and there are certain...
protocols I have to observe."

The day had been clear and bright, but I could not help noticing a
very sudden and very thick fog rolling in.

"That's not..."

"No, that's still me," said Nurse Florence with a little chuckle. "I'm
not necessarily expecting a big crowd here on a weekday afternoon in
the middle of October, but we can't afford to be seen." I had always
liked the views from Lake Cachuma, particularly the Santa Ynez Moun-
tains, but in a few minutes, I had a hard time viewing my hand in front
of my face. I also noticed a substantial drop in temperature, probably
designed to make any random lake visitors think twice. Nurse Florence
led us on what seemed a very roundabout route but which did eventually lead us up to the edge of the lake. The fog parted around us, so that
we could see a little stretch of the shore and a small part of the lake. No
one was more relieved to have arrived than Stan, since Gordy stayed
glued to him like a second skin the whole time we were in the fog.

"Watch that spot carefully," commanded Nurse Florence in her best
authoritative tone. Not being the best at following orders, I glanced
around when nothing seemed to be happening and noticed that Nurse
Florence was no longer visible. I felt my body go on high alert. Maybe
her disappearance was part of the plan, but it made me uncomfortable. I
had White Hilt with me if I needed it, but it wouldn't do me much good
if someone attacked me from behind while I was fixedly watching some
point out in the lake...

"Tal," whispered Stan urgently, "look!" My attention shifted back to
the lake. I had thought that nothing was left that could surprise me
anymore, but I was wrong. An arm was thrusting out of the lake, and
that arm was clutching a sword. I had never seen this before...well, not
in this life, anyway.

"Shar," I said, turning to him. "Since this trip was to get you armed,
I'd say the idea is for you to wade out and get the sword."

Two days ago I was sure Shar would have laughed in my face.
Today, he took off his shoes and socks and started wading into the lake
without a single question. The rest of us watched silently as he sloshed
toward the upraised arm, ripples spreading out in all directions from his

fast-moving legs. The moment he took the hilt of the sword in his hand, the arm disappeared into the water. Shar turned to us and brandished the sword in the air. The sword flashed green despite the lack of direct sunlight. Shar practically ran back—well, as close as he could come to running in the shallows of the lake. As he got closer, I noticed his sword had a faint emerald glow to it, again with no direct sunlight. The glow was coming from within the sword itself. Maybe not quite as cool as the flames of White Hilt, but definitely cool!

"Does it feel right in your hand?" I was startled by Nurse Florence's voice right behind me.

"I don't know about this part," said Shar, looking skeptically at his new prize. "I'm Jewish." Shar had evidently read enough Arthurian literature freshman year to know how many of the stories involved swords engraved with crosses or with relics of Jesus embedded in the hilt or blessed by the archbishop of Canterbury. Right now he was eying the sword as if someone had handed him a pork sandwich on the first day of Passover.

Nurse Florence chuckled. "Shar, give me some credit. You think I'm going to bring you a sword made out of the nails with which Jesus was crucified or something? I always take the faith of the wielder into consideration. This is Shamshir-e Zomorrodnegar, the emerald-studded sword of Persian tradition. It has no Christian connection at all, and though it was last wielded by Amir Arsalan, it didn't start out being Islamic or even Persian. Legend has it that it once belonged to King Solomon. It's a sword worthy of someone of Jewish descent." Shar's eyes widened, and he looked at the sword as if an angel had just delivered it from heaven. He was so moved he actually knelt and said a little prayer over it in Farsi.

"Now, does it feel right?" Nurse Florence asked again, more gently, when Shar was finished with his prayer. Shar stood and made a couple of thrusts with the sword.

"It feels as if it were forged for me. It feels perfect," whispered Shar.

"That's a very good sign," said Nurse Florence, nodding her head in satisfaction. "A sword always finds its wielder. If it was not meant for you, you could feel that, too."

"I half expected Excalibur when the arm came out of the lake," I said, not really sure myself whether I was serious or joking.

"My organization wasn't willing to send out Excalibur," replied Nurse Florence, totally deadpan. "All kinds of issues, not the least of which is that the wielder technically becomes the rightful king of Great Britain in the eyes of some traditionalists."

"You have Excalibur?" asked Stan, in a totally awed voice I hadn't heard since he first found out about my awakening.

"My order does," said Nurse Florence.

"Wait!" I said suddenly. Yes, another lightbulb moment. "You're the Lady of the Lake!"

"I'm *a* lady of the lake," replied Nurse Florence. "There have been many of us. I'm not immortal, and I'm not an aware reincarnate like you. As Taliesin 1, you knew both my namesake and her successor, Nimue."

I couldn't believe I had missed such obvious clues. Her first name was Viviane, just like the lady of the lake who raised Lancelot, she could heal, and she could travel over distances using bodies of water, as she had with the UCSB lagoon the night we almost lost Stan. I had known the first Viviane rather well, yet it took the whole getting the sword out of the lake routine for me to make the connection.

Nurse Florence stopped for a moment as if she were listening for something. "There's no one nearby," she said finally. "Shahriyar, let's see how well you can handle that blade. Tal, fight him with White Hilt, but go a little easy until he gets used to Shamshir-e Zomorrodnegar."

"Can we work out a shorter name for that?" I asked as I drew White Hilt and watched the flames envelop it.

"I'm going to call her Zom," replied Shar, in a tone that suggested anyone who didn't like the idea was pretty well out of luck. Then he drew Zom from the scabbard Nurse Florence had provided. First the emeralds in the hilt burned with green energy, then the whole sword. Shar swung, and the two blades crashed together with an explosion. Shar had struck with such force White Hilt had nearly been torn from my hand. Oddly, the flames dissipated on White Hilt where the two blades had struck each other.

"What the hell!" I exclaimed, backing away just fast enough to avoid the next blow. "I don't think I need to go easy anymore." Shar advanced rapidly. As with boxing, he was much stronger and only a little slower. I could not afford too much direct contact, so I spread the flames out into a shield radiating from the tip of White Hilt. That should keep him at a distance.

Instinctively, Shar swung right through the fire shield, which to my horror sizzled out as if gallons of water had been thrown on it. I managed to dodge out of his way, but he managed to hit White Hilt often enough in rapid succession to actually extinguish its fire. I could see the flames trying to light again on the blade—very slowly. In a real battle, Shar could kill me, with my only choice being to run like hell in the opposite direction.

"Okay, time out!" yelled Nurse Florence. "Shar's instincts are as good as yours, Tal. He knew exactly what to do without being told."

"What's up with that sword?" I asked irritably. "I have never seen anything put out White Hilt's fire except Morgan's massive rainstorm. Yet it went out every time Shar's sword touched the fire or the blade."

"That's what makes…Zom so valuable. Neither the sword nor its wielder can be affected by hostile magic. In practice that also means magic dissipates if Zom hits it directly. White Hilt is a powerful enough artifact that its flames die out only near the contact point, and the magic can reassert itself…"

"But not as fast as I'd like," I pointed out.

"Yes," agreed Nurse Florence, "not fast enough for combat situations. Also, though Zom's touch only temporarily disables continuous enchantments like that on White Hilt, it will break more transitory spells completely, and I have heard that creatures otherwise invulnerable to physical attack are vulnerable to it. With that blade, Shar can take anything Carrie Winn can possibly dish out, and more."

"Then shouldn't I be wielding it, since likely I'll be leading the charge." Shar looked scandalized at the suggestion.

"You need to change strategy, Tal. You've been trying to be both bard and warrior, and that combination doesn't really work. How often did either the first or second Taliesin wade out into the middle of a battle? Remember how hard it was to fight the *pwca* physically and get your magic together? Or the kelpie, for that matter?" I must have looked downcast because her tone softened immediately. "I'm not saying you shouldn't continue your combat training—in a pinch, you will need to be able to handle your blade—or that you're a bad fighter. You're actually extremely good at it. But you can do more for your friends with a song than with a blade in the long run, and if you need to use the blade, use it as a distance weapon. You know how to direct the fire in a way no previous wielder has ever known. Imagine Shar charging forward to disrupt the enemy while you fire bursts of flame into their ranks."

I must still have looked terribly unconvinced. "Remember Merlin, Tal? How often did he pick up a sword and charge the enemy?"

"He had a sword," I said defensively.

"And he used it in your presence how often?" The answer was never, but I didn't want to give her the satisfaction, so I just eyed her glumly.

"Have you not yet learned the strength of teamwork? This isn't about what role you play, but how what you do complements everyone else's effort. Shar has the better sword because he is the better swordsman, better equipped to lead the charge. But if we have to fight, he won't last five seconds after Winn's guards open fire unless you have solved the problem of how to use magic to disable their guns. For that matter, if you can't take out the security system, someone will spot the fact that not only you, but also Shar, is coming in armed, and you'll get dropped before you even get in the door.

"Not that that will happen," she said firmly. "Because if I suspect that you can't get your magic to disable her technology, none of you will get within twenty miles of Awen—ever. Even that's a risky course of action, since, as you pointed out, Winn will suspect something is up, but the possibility of retaliation later is better than the certainty of slaughter now. So what is it going to be, Tal? Man up, and play the role only you can play, or let your male ego get you into locking horns with Shar and throwing away our only chance to defeat Winn?"

Of course, she was right. I was in better shape now than during the combats of a few weeks ago, but I knew I would have trouble drawing enough breath to really sing or focus well enough to really spell cast if I had to sword fight with a tough opponent at the same time.

"Okay, I guess that was the testosterone talking earlier," I said, just a little grudgingly. "Shar, the sword is obviously best suited to your hand. I'll back you up with music and magic."

"Hey," said Gordy, "What about Dan and me? When do we get our swords?" Nurse Florence stifled a snicker.

"Magic swords are a rare thing, Gordy. The fact that one small group like this has two is practically unprecedented in modern times. I have confidence you can do your part without special equipment."

"Shar's a better fighter than I am, and he gets a magic sword. How am I supposed to defend Stan properly with just my fists?"

"Wait! He's here for me?" said Stan shrilly.

You hadn't noticed he was practically climbing into your skin with you?

"There could be a lot of danger, Stan. I knew you would want to go anyway, so…"

"So you got Gordy to be my babysitter?"

"I got Gordy to have your back like Dan has mine. Nothing wrong with that."

I knew Stan was about to blow sky-high and then be embarrassed about it later, but I didn't see how I could stop it. However, Gordy, with some hitherto unexpected psychological insight, pulled Stan off to one side, where they talked heatedly for a while, but when they rejoined the group, Stan was calm again.

In the interim Nurse Florence had been pondering. "Excuse me for a moment, gentlemen. I need quiet to make a quick contact. I'll be right back." She disappeared into the fog without giving anyone a chance to ask questions. Shar was almost too busy admiring his sword to notice, and Dan asked for a closer look, effectively occupying both of them for a few minutes.

Stan moved over next to me, then turned, glared at Gordy and motioned him away. Gordy stepped back just a few steps and kept his eyes fixed on Stan.

"Well, how does it feel to be me?" asked Stan.

"What do you mean?" I asked, clueless about where he was going.

"How does it feel to be sidelined when the fighting starts?"

I ignored the sting in that remark and focused on the fact that Stan was still hung up on having a bodyguard. "Stan, you haven't been sidelined."

"No, for me it's even worse. At least you get to fight in a pinch. What am I supposed to do, hide under a table when the action starts?"

"No need," I said, trying to lighten the mood. "You can always hide under Gordy."

"Not funny!" said Stan sullenly.

"Look, I'll admit I had a hard time seeing Shar suddenly become the lead fighter, but Nurse Florence was right—I'm more valuable in a different role—and that role depends upon you. Stan, I can never learn the science we need to neutralize Winn's physical firepower in just a few days. Some of it I might never get. But you, you already have it. You not only know the science; you have the ability to visualize concretely. I can read it from you, and with that knowledge, I can create the fusion between magic and science that will save us in the end. Without you, we could never succeed."

"Intellectually, I know you're right," admitted Stan in a tone that somewhat undercut his words, "but emotionally, I want you to know how hard this is for me. You were always in pretty good physical shape; you have really never had to be the little nerd. I've been that all my life, and now that I'm in better shape, somehow I'm still the little nerd. I have enough muscle now to do something in a fight, but it doesn't even occur to anyone to train me."

I didn't have the heart to bring up the martial arts fiasco at this point. "Well, Stan, since I know you'll be there anyway, maybe we can find a more active role for you to play, but I don't want you taking foolish chances, and I don't want you to give Gordy a hard time about the bodyguard thing." Stan nodded reluctantly. "By the way, what did he say to you a while ago?"

"That he really wanted to protect me, that it was his idea. I know the second part is a lie, since he wouldn't have known I needed protection before he was recruited, but he is sincere about wanting the job." Stan paused, actually a little bit lost for words. "Tal, you have been looking out for me as long as I can remember, but Gordy, I didn't really know him until I started tutoring him, and he acts like we've been friends forever, like he cares about me, well, more than anyone else on campus except you."

"He really appreciates the tutoring, and I think he is more perceptive than people give him credit for. He knows what a good person you are, Stan, and he responds to that."

"I know he means well, but his keeping such a close watch makes me feel even more inadequate. You have never done that to me, and Dan doesn't do that to you…"

"I'll talk to him when we get back home, but…" I was interrupted at that point by the return of Nurse Florence, her face actually flushed with excitement. I had never seen her like that before, and it was hot, but I forced myself not to think about it.

"Gordy and Dan, I think I can get us some additional weapons, if you aren't too fussy. They won't be in quite the same league as White Hilt and Zom, but they could still give you an edge in a fight with Winn's security, who I am pretty sure won't be carrying magical weapons. And your weapons will be made for you."

"Someone still makes magical weapons?" asked Dan. He hadn't betrayed surprise too often recently, but he did this time.

"Not quite like they used to, but yes. It is likely, though, that you will be tested to determine your worthiness. Nothing potentially deadly or overly dangerous, but such weapons are not without cost."

"Whatever the test is, bring it on!" replied Gordy with a big smile. The more I saw of that guy, the more I liked him. I had to pat myself on the back a little for suggesting his recruitment.

"The test is going to be in Annwn," said Nurse Florence. Stan and I both gasped; everyone else remained surprisingly impassive. "It is being organized by Gwynn ap Nuad himself."

"The king of all Welsh faeries?" I asked. We had met in an earlier life, so I was not as surprised as you might think. In the background, I could hear Dan explaining faeries to Gordy.

"The same. Only Gwynn can authorize Govannon, the faerie smith, to give weapons or armor to a mortal. Now, the court is waiting for us, so, if you don't mind…" A word or two in Welsh, a few gestures, and suddenly a glowing portal appeared in their midst.

"Ladies first," I said. She passed through quickly, followed by me,

Dan, Shar, Gordy, who insisted on going through first to make sure it was safe, and Stan.

Distances don't work the same way in the Otherworld that they do in ours. Passing through a portal in city hall, we had come out in Morgan Le Fay's prison. Passing through near Lake Cachuma, about twenty miles away, put us in the realm of Gwynn ap Nuad, many thousands of miles from Morgan. Someone, like Nurse Florence, who knew what she was doing, could pretty well pick anywhere in Annwn and end up there from anywhere on earth. I should have been able to do the same thing, but, well, one problem at a time.

The glow faded, and I jumped to find myself almost right in front of Gwynn himself, looking as he was always portrayed in literature, dark of face, mounted on his war horse, surrounded by his three enormous hounds, one white, one red, and one black, looking somewhat fiercer than any of them. He was flanked on each side by several faerie warriors, each pale, faired haired, and handsome, staunch men of the *Tylwyth Teg*, each carrying a formidable looking long sword. Despite all the stories about faerie celebration, this was the grimmest group I had seen in quite a while. Then I noticed behind them Govannon, soot-smudged from the forge, waiting patiently to see whether or not he needed to labor more today.

"Viviane," said Gwynn, in a booming voice, "seldom have I been called upon in such a peremptory fashion."

Nurse Florence bowed to him. "Pardon me, your Majesty, but as I told you, the need is great, so great I pray you excuse my unmannerly approach."

Abruptly he turned his piercing eyes on me. "And Taliesin, you rascal, I never thought to see you here again, and in a different body, I see. Is that how you got in?"

"I brought him, Majesty," said Nurse Florence quickly. "In this life, he has yet to learn how to travel to Annwn as he was wont to do before."

"Of course he can't. Arawn is still angry with him for helping Arthur steal that sword Taliesin carries at his side. Perhaps Arawn will forgive him if he returns it." Arawn had once been king of all Annwn, but I had never imagined he still carried a grudge for something I did on

Arthur's orders fifteen hundred years ago. Well, at least that solved one mystery.

"In any case, I will not meddle in Arawn's affairs. I did not let Taliesin in; there is no ban on dealing with him once he's here." Gordy and Shar, who had never been in the Otherworld before, were looking around with something akin to wonder on their faces. It was not that there was anything overtly supernatural—well, aside from the red hound, perhaps—but everything, from the undulating mist to the vividly green grass, to the unblemished skin of the faerie knights, never looked completely real if you were used to the mortal world.

"So you wish faerie weapons," said Gwynn, turning his attention to Gordy and Dan. "You must be found worthy to wield such weapons. But before your test, I will test the worthiness of the rest of your party." He turned back to me. "You first, Taliesin. You weren't much of a warrior back when we first met. Let's see if you are worthy to wield the sword you stole." He turned to one of his warriors and gestured to him to sheath his weapon. "Anyone can win a battle with White Hilt, but for a mortal man to beat a faerie bare-handed, now that, would truly demonstrate your worth." Gwynn nodded, and the faerie warrior sprang at me.

The problem with a mortal fighting a faerie hand-to-hand was that the faerie was always going to be faster—or so the conventional wisdom ran. I decided to put the idea to the test, humming to myself, willing my body to move faster. Faeries weren't comic book superhero fast, so I should be able to be at least as agile and swift as my opponent. The faerie punched me in the stomach and stopped my humming, but I somehow kept up a fairly competitive speed, dodging the next blow and even managing to deliver a punch of my own. Then the faerie got in three more good shots in rapid succession. But though the faerie was faster, he was not anywhere nearly as strong as Shar, probably not even as strong as I was. And this was not a boxing match, so I took another punch on purpose, grabbed the faery's right arm, and flung him to the grass. For a second he seemed stunned, but he was up again faster than my human reactions could interfere. Again, I managed enough magic to speed myself up, once more reminded of how hard it was to do magic and fight at the same time. Then I grabbed him, and threw him to the ground, with me on top of him, holding on as if he were a leprechaun and I thought if I held on long enough I would get a pot of gold. He didn't have the strength to just throw me off, but he wriggled mightily, twisting against me for some time, and then finally announced in Welsh that he yielded. I let him up, and he bowed to me before retiring to his old place next to Gwynn.

"Well done, Taliesin. I see you have not grown too dependent upon your blade. Now, you," he said, gesturing to Shahriyar. Another faerie warrior sheathed his sword and stepped forward. "Oh," he said, turning to me again. "I almost forgot to mention—each warrior fights his own battle." In other words, I could not use music or magic to aid any of my "warriors."

But did Shar really need the help? Let's just say faeries must not spend a lot of time watching boxing. Shar was considerably slower than the faerie and had no way of speeding up, but after watching my fight, he took a few faerie blows, pretended to be dizzy, lured the faerie close enough, and bam! The strength of his punch stunned the faerie, slowing him down enough for Shar to land several more. Even though he was being careful not to do something like hit the faerie in the mouth, knowing the faerie had no mouth guard, there was still considerable blood by the time the faerie yielded.

"Very well done! You too are worthy of the blade you wield. What is your name?"

"Shahriyar, Majesty."

"Ah, Great King! Doubly worthy, then. Now, moving on from those who have weapons to those that seek them, will one of you step forward?" Dan did so. "Very good, then, this test will be in armed combat." I had to snicker a little. The faeries were not doing so well in hand-to-hand, despite their speed, so Gwynn was switching tactics. Doubtless, each of them was an expert with the blade—and still fast— while neither Dan nor Gordy had ever practiced with a sword. I could not see this part ending well. Perhaps Shar should have made the last faery bleed just a little less.

One of the warriors handed Dan his sword, and then stepped back, just as one of his fellow warriors charged Dan, who had not really even gotten used to the feel of the blade.

Dan tried his best to emulate moves he had seen me make, but one can only learn so much by watching. The test was explicitly not supposed to be a fight to the death, so all his opponent really did was scratch him, but each scratch inflicted a small wound that started bleeding, and Dan had something like fifteen of them in a couple of minutes. He kept trying to imitate Shar's move in hitting my blade almost out of my hand. The problem was that the faerie did not let the swords collide solidly. He was in and out before Dan could complete his swing.

The ground beneath them was now red, and Dan's strokes were visibly weaker. Gwynn looked about to bring the fight to an end, but Dan, perhaps sensing his intent, looked at him and said, quietly but clearly, "I do not yield."

"He's bleeding pretty badly," I said urgently to Nurse Florence.

"He needs to yield. Gwynn knows I can heal him, so he is allowing this to continue, but there is a limit to what even I can do."

"Dan, yield," I yelled at him. Dan was teetering as if he would fall. Scratch. Scratch. Scratch. The ground was slippery with his own blood, but still he did not yield. He staggered, and the faerie slowed, anticipating that Dan would either yield or pass out. And that's when Dan got him with a headbutt in the stomach. The faerie stumbled backward, and Dan pursued with surprising energy, this time landing a couple of good blows that drew sparks from the faerie's blade. On the third one, the faerie's sword was ripped from his hand, and he yielded. Clearly, Dan had been faking a little, just like Shar.

"You are not much of a swordsman," observed Gwynn, narrowing his eyes, "and you won by trickery, but I did not specify any rules, and the final blows were certainly struck with a sword. Besides, you showed great perseverance." He turned to Gordy. "Ready?"

"I was born ready!" said Gordy, stepping forward, undaunted by Dan's scraped up and bloodied condition. Dan fell back almost literally into Nurse Florence's arms, and she began healing him as fast as she could.

Gordy had obviously been watching Dan's battle. The moment the sword was in his hand, he charged the advancing faerie warrior, taking the battle straight to him instead of trying to take a defensive stance. Gordy was holding the sword, but not making much effort to protect himself, and the faerie got in a couple of good scratches. In a real fight, he would have thrust his sword deeply into Gordy, but he did not do so, and so Gordy was able to get away with a move he would never have survived to make in a real fight. He threw the sword aside at the last minute and tackled the surprised faerie. Evidently, faeries didn't follow football, either. There was no getting out from under Gordy, and the faerie yielded.

"Another trickster? Taliesin, do you have any actual fighters besides Shahriyar?" Gordy looked incredibly downcast; clearly, he did not want to fail at this, but Gwynn's tone left little doubt in his mind that he had.

"You didn't mention any rules this time, either, Majesty," I pointed out in my most tactful tone.

"Well, so I didn't, but I must confer with my warriors, nonetheless." Gwynn actually dismounted from his war horse and gestured for his warriors to follow him. They walked some distance away and spoke in grave whispers. Govannon eyed us inquisitively but said nothing.

"How is Dan?" I asked as I stepped over to where Nurse Florence was working on him.

"Lots of little wounds, but none of them anywhere nearly as deep as yours at UCSB," she said absently, focusing most of her attention on the healing process. "He will heal fine. See if you can stop Gordy's bleeding, and I will attend to him when I can," she said, handing me a small first aid kit.

"I screwed it up," said Gordy as I did what I could to clean his wounds. I had never heard him sound so forlorn.

"I'm not so sure. Gwynn let Dan get away with sort of the same thing. And anyway, what you did was clever. You sized up the situation really well and created a strategy to win on a moment's notice."

"You don't have to sound so surprised," snapped Gordy. "I know most people think I'm a dumb ass, but I thought you were different."

"Gordy, I don't think you're a dumb ass." Well, to be honest, I did have my doubts.

"Well, I'm not," he said emphatically. "Nurse Florence figured it out from watching my dreams. I have ADHD. I've just never been diagnosed. That's why I had so much trouble keeping up in school, and yeah, now I'm pretty behind. Nobody has been able to make me concentrate for long, well, except Stan. But now Nurse Florence promised that as long as I help you and Stan, my ADHD won't bother me. The other day I sat down and did a homework assignment in ten minutes that would have taken me an hour before. And I understood it."

Interesting. I would never have guessed, but treating Gordy's ADHD was maybe easier than causing Dan to always perform at his highest level on the football field, for all I knew. It made me wonder what Shar was getting out of his bargain.

Then another thought occurred to me: ADHD had been unknown in medieval times. There would have been no spell to heal it because no one knew what it was. So how could Nurse Florence have cured Gordy? Now I suspected I knew why Nurse Florence was so confident I could learn how to blend magic and technology—she herself had found a way to blend magic and modern medical knowledge!

Then I went back to marveling a little at Nurse Florence's cleverness, not for the first time. She always seemed to know exactly the right deal to make, but she also knew whom to approach; she picked up on Dan's latent friendship for me when nobody else noticed it. She kept finding people who had reasons other than just the bargain for working with us. Well, come to think of it, I was the one who suggested Shar and Gordy to her, and both of them had loyalty that transcended the bargain. Time to marvel at my own cleverness, well, at least a little bit.

"My warriors and I have conferred," said Gwynn, almost right behind us, "and your last fighter's approach, though...unusual, showed courage. He ran practically into a blade, left himself wide open, in order to catch my warrior by surprise. Even though he knew the fight was not to the death, he could easily have been gravely injured, if only by accident. He, too, is a worthy fighter...though what good swords will do two fighters without the skill to use them, I have no idea."

"They will have good teachers," said Shar, coming to stand next to me. Gwynn chuckled a little.

"Well, I don't doubt that. But they have only days in which to become proficient. Even the best teachers would have a hard time on such a schedule. Still, you have proven yourselves worthy of at least being given a chance."

"Majesty," said Stan abruptly, startling me. "I too request the right to prove myself."

Gwynn looked dumbfounded. "But you are just a child, surely!"

"I am about the same age as the others," said Stan, trying hard not to sound offended and not entirely succeeding.

"Stan," I muttered under my breath, "what are you doing?"

"These contests don't seem to be as much about combat skill as about character. At least they were for Dan and Gordy."

Gwynn was looking at Stan, as if for the first time. "It is as you say. You are old enough to be a warrior. Do you too seek a weapon?"

"I do, and if it please your Majesty, I would like to wrestle for one."

Another belly laugh. "Were you under the impression that it was your place to propose the nature of your own challenge?"

"Majesty, he meant no offense," I said, stepping forward.

"Taliesin, he seems more than capable of speaking for himself. He is presumptuous, perhaps, but he too has courage." He focused on Stan again. "I presume you want rules this time, or you would not have named a specific challenge. What are the rules for this wrestling?"

Much to my surprise, Stan started reciting the CIF rules.

"I taught him those," Gordy whispered to me, "and I have shown him some moves while we were working out." I recalled that Gordy's winter sport was wrestling, but I didn't remember any wrestling coaching going on while Stan and I were working out with the football team. Then again, I had been pretty preoccupied part of the time.

Actually, wrestling was an astute choice in the sense that it did not leave as much scope for the use of a faery's natural speed. However, there was a problem, which Gwynn was not slow to perceive.

"I have no warrior here who is in your 'weight class,' as you would call it."

"I will accept the disadvantage."

"Very well."

"One other thing, if it please your Majesty." Wow, Stan was pressing his luck like, well, like me. Gwynn looked at him, clearly waiting.

"I would like to change the rules I just gave you in one way—the match doesn't end until I yield." Gwynn raised an eyebrow but nodded.

Watching the "match" was painful. Stan was outweighed, and if Gordy really had done much coaching, it was clear that Stan hadn't absorbed much. He knew what he was supposed to do; he just couldn't do it. He got pinned over, and over, and over. To make matters worse, I think the faerie warriors, despite their gracious manner, were heartily sick of getting their butts kicked by mortals, and the one wrestling Stan was determined to win, perhaps to help his friends save face.

Finally, Gwynn asked, "Do you yield?" which should have been hint enough for most people.

"No," said the pinned Stan, through clenched teeth. Gwynn nodded reluctantly, and the slaughter, uh, the match continued.

Stan must have been exhausted, and, though at least he hadn't been cut up in a sword fight, his skin looked gray. He was drenched in sweat, and his expression suggested that by now he was actually in pain. This was far more twisting in awkward positions than he was used to—he had probably pulled a muscle somewhere along the way, maybe more than one.

By now the match had dragged on so long that Nurse Florence had actually finished healing Dan. Gordy waved her off. "Save it for Stan," he said, not taking his eyes off the spot where Stan and the faerie continued their unequal struggle.

"Do you yield?" asked Gwynn again, this time more insistently. Stan shook his head no.

Gwynn gave me his most piercing stare. "The boy should yield. I cannot guarantee his safety if this continues."

"I am not a boy!" Stan nearly shouted. I was both surprised he had the energy to shout and shocked that he was coming so close to conflict with the leader of the Welsh faeries, not someone you exactly wanted as an enemy.

"Your Majesty…" I began.

"Taliesin," he almost roared, "do not presume to counsel me. Counsel your b…your warrior, if you will. Having agreed unwisely to that rule about yielding, I can do nothing now to change it. They could fight for all eternity, except that your friend will die much sooner than that. I have seen a man's heart give out in this kind of situation."

"Majesty," said the faerie wrestler, "in the interest of ending this contest in accordance with your wish, I am willing to yield."

"Are we of one mind?" Gwynn asked, addressing the warriors and Govannon, all of whom nodded. "Then yes," he said, addressing the wrestler again, "by all means yield." The wrestler yielded, nodding to Stan, and returned to his place in line.

"Well, little warrior," began Gwynn. "Oh, yes, let me save you the trouble, you are not little. Well, warrior, you have the ability to endure pain and even humiliation for a cause. You, too, shall have a weapon." Stan, contrary to protocol, had not bowed to the king, but since he was still lying on the ground, Gwynn did not seem to mind. I moved in his direction, but naturally, Gordy beat me to it, practically carrying him over to Nurse Florence. I bowed to the king, who seemed to be watching the healing on the sidelines with some amusement, and then quickly walked over to where Stan was being tended.

"He's going to be all right," said Nurse Florence without my asking, "but he did push himself dangerously hard." Stan looked up at me and smiled.

"Now I'm not just the sidekick anymore," he whispered to me.

"You were never just the sidekick, Stan."

"Well, now everyone knows I have guts."

"Knew that too. So if you get into battle, try to keep them inside of you—no need to display them."

Stan laughed a little and closed his eyes. At about that point three faeries approached, each with a golden goblet. One collected a little of Dan's blood, one a little of Gordy's tears—not that he would admit he had teared up a little while Stan was getting his butt kicked—and one a little of Stan's sweat. They took the goblets to Govannon, who nodded and left immediately.

"I have never seen that before," said Nurse Florence. "Not that I've done this very often."

"Not seen what?" I asked.

"The collection of bodily fluids. I thought the best we could expect were generic faerie weapons. Even those would have been amazing additions to our combat power, but now it looks as if Govannon intends to forge a unique blade for each of them. I wouldn't have dared to ask for such a thing. Evidently, you impressed them more than I realized."

"Mortals, I must take my leave," said Gwynn in his usual booming voice. He was already back on his warhorse. "Other business cries out for my attention. Viviane, come back in one mortal day's time. By then Govannon will have the weapons ready. And Taliesin," he added, glancing in my direction. "All in all, you have a fine band of warriors... especially considering that, by the standards of your society, none of them is even an adult yet. See to it that you lead them well." I bowed in acknowledgment of his words, but he had galloped off almost before I could complete the bow. The faerie warriors walked over to their own mounts and were gone almost as rapidly.

"Well," she said, looking at all of us, "I think we've had enough male ego for one afternoon."

"The king said we had courage and perseverance," said Gordy a little defensively.

"The king doesn't deal with teenage boys every day. Look, all of you are brave, but you are also foolish sometimes, and that's dangerous."

"We got what we came for," I pointed out. "More than what we came for."

"Would you still be saying that if one of you were dead? I do healings, not resurrections. Dan lost a risky amount of blood, Gordy almost got himself skewered by accident, and Stan's heart damn near popped out of his chest by the time the faerie yielded. Honestly, maybe what this group needs is some girls to keep you in line."

"Why do we need girls," I asked archly, "when we have women?" Nurse Florence frowned worse than I had so far seen.

"Taliesin Weaver, if you weren't such an old soul, you'd get a slap, or detention, maybe both. Wait," she said, looking down at her watch, "we need to get moving. We might be able to explain the sweat, but the blood and the torn clothes will be harder. We need to get you guys cleaned up and returned to roughly the same condition you were in when your parents sent you to school."

Nurse Florence might be a lady of the lake, but when it came to these kinds of logistics, she was thoroughly modern and all business.

She hustled us out of Annwn with brisk efficiency, then back to her van. She had all of us pull out our cell phones and tell our parents we'd be a little late and would stop somewhere for dinner. Predictably, Stan's mom had problems with that idea, but somehow he smoothed everything over—he was definitely getting better at that, or perhaps even she realized that he was growing up and was starting to give him more latitude. While we were making our calls, Nurse Florence herself called Coach Miller and had him call someone at Santa Ynez Valley Union High School to get permission for us to use the locker room and showers on our way past.

"Why not just go back to our own high school?" asked Dan.

"Because Carrie Winn obviously spies on Tal from time to time, and I don't know exactly how. Bad enough we had to meet up in the parking lot, but that couldn't be helped. If she had someone—or something—tracking Tal then, he would eventually have had to rendezvous with us, anyway. That doesn't mean we have to advertise that all of you were doing something really unusual today. Leaving together might not have set off any alarms, but then coming back together—bloody—would be bound to. Actually, anyone seeing you that way would be a problem, let alone a Winn spy. No, we stay away from Santa Brígida as long as we can. We can take the 154 right to Santa Ynez, so you can get cleaned up. From there, it's just a short ride to Solvang to pick up some clothes. Dan's and Gordy's clothes are in the worst shape, and fortunately they were both wearing Izod shirts, so we hit the Izod outlet store in Solvang, pick up a few odds and ends in other stores, then have a little dinner and head back, hopefully with no one we know seeing us."

And that's pretty much exactly what happened. A quick shower in Santa Ynez, and those of us with clothes too torn or bloody changed into some generic stuff Nurse Florence, obviously anticipating just such a problem, had in the van. Then we hit a couple of stores in Solvang, and those of us who needed replacement clothes that matched that day's school clothing got it. For dinner Nurse Florence took us to a little place with an all-you-can-eat smorgasbord, figuring that we could probably use a major refueling after the afternoon's activities. Boy, she was right about that. She had something small, but among us five guys, we practically put the place out of business. I think our waitress didn't know quite what to do with us. Even Stan was eating like I had never seen him eat before. It wasn't until after his third plate that he even thought about slowing down. Well, I guess he was entitled. Anyway, I wasn't in a position to complain. I had started out with the "little bit of everything" philosophy: a little roast beef, a little roast chicken, a little pork, a little red cabbage, a little mashed potatoes, a little cheese...but then I went through three plates of a lot of everything I could squeeze on.

"I hear they have an interesting selection of local wines and beers," said Dan, looking at Nurse Florence.

"Well, considering you're all underage, and I'm a school employee, hearing about it is about all you'll be doing this trip."

"This is a good place," remarked Shar, trying to talk around a Danish meatball. "The only thing that would make it better would be adding kabob to the menu." I couldn't help snorting a little at that.

"Yeah, they'd be sure to pull in the massive Persian population of the Santa Ynez area."

"Hey! There are a few around besides me, you know." Actually, I didn't think there were—except maybe in Santa Barbara.

"Let's come here again!" said Gordy, in an almost childlike tone. I had another little pang, imagining for an instant what life would be like if we could actually plan another trip and know for sure that we would all be alive for it.

I think the staff breathed a sigh of relief when Nurse Florence finally paid the bill, and we left. I could tell the management was going to be reconsidering the all-you-can-eat idea.

The trip back home was blissfully uneventful. Nurse Florence dropped Stan and I at the end of our street, I walked him home, then made it to my house, got through some small talk with my parents, somehow pulled myself through the homework that absolutely had to get done, then slept like a coma patient until my alarm went off in the morning.

HE WHO LIVES BY THE SWORD

THIS TIME we had to wait until after football practice; Nurse Florence couldn't really explain to Coach Miller why she needed us again so soon, so she just waited until after. She also pulled in another healthy fog to cover our departure.

"No sense taking chances, and two trips by exactly the same group would look suspicious," she pointed out. I griped a little about having to go through the same taking the sword out of the lake routine, but Nurse Florence was insistent that doing anything else would insult the faeries.

"This is the first time I know of since the days of Camelot that weapons made by a faerie smith are being placed into human hands, and we are getting three of them at once. I won't chance anything going wrong." And that was that—Nurse Florence was not exactly someone who could be talked out of doing what she thought needed to be done.

Before long we were once again surrounded by thick fog and staring out at the rippling blue surface of Lake Cachuma, waiting for an arm to emerge. In rapid succession Dan, Gordy, and Stan each waded out to get his blade and then waded back. They all wanted to try them, but Nurse Florence insisted on explaining them first.

"Govannon's work is always unbreakable by normal means, but it is possible to break them by trying to do something sinful with them, so be sure to strike only for purposes like defending yourself or someone else. All of them are stronger than a normal sword and will cut even through armor fairly easily. Each one also has a property Govannon designed for its wielder.

"Dan, your sword, like the scabbard Arthur received with Excalibur, will prevent you from bleeding as long as you wield it. It won't save you if an opponent pierces a vital organ, but it will keep you from weakening due to blood loss from your wounds.

"Gordy, your sword will strike fear into your enemies whenever you draw it. It isn't absolute in the sense that a strong-willed man can resist it, but anyone who has to fight its effect will not be able to be as focused in battle.

"Stan, I'm sorry to say that your sword was not made for you. Gwynn had a sword in his possession already he thought would suit you, but Govannon added some special touches just for you." Stan looked crestfallen to be getting a hand-me-down, but Nurse Florence easily cheered him up.

"This sword once belonged to King David."

"It's Galahad's sword! But that…" I protested.

"No, no, Galahad's sword can only be wielded by a handful of people in any generation, and then only as part of a Grail quest. David had more than one sword. This particular one did not have any magical properties, so Govannon added a spell he said would make Stan as great in body as he is great in spirit, sort of like David's soul in Goliath's body."

"Wow!" said Stan, admiring the blade. Looking closely, I could see that it had inscriptions in Hebrew, with an image of the tablets of the law engraved in the hilt. Yet it also had that distinct faerie gleam to it, even in the fog.

"I think its charm is not automatic," said Nurse Florence. "Repeat the Hebrew inscription, and let's see what happens."

Stan read the Hebrew over once, then recited it in a clear voice.

Gordy was predictably the first to notice. "Stan's hulking out!"

Actually, the effect was a little more subtle than that. Stan had been getting pretty heavy workouts, and his arms were certainly not matchsticks any more, but now they were corded with muscle, and his shirt looked as if it the buttons were going to pop off, so he took it off.

"I have a six pack!" he said in wonder. He now looked more like Shar than like himself.

"Don't stop working out," cautioned Nurse Florence. "I think the new muscles only exist when you are actually wielding the sword, and there may be times when you might have to fight without it."

"To say nothing of dates," said Gordy. I had to snicker a little at the thought of Stan going out on a date with one hand on his sword at all times to keep the magic muscles going. No, working out was definitely still called for.

"Let's try them out," said Stan, giving his a mighty swing that made it whoosh through the air.

Inevitably, Stan paired up with Shar. The idea of trying David's sword against Solomon's sword was naturally irresistible.

The blades rang repeatedly as they crashed into each other. With his normal physique, Stan would have had the sword knocked out of his hands quickly, but now he could hold his own, even against Shar, who conceded that Stan was now as strong as he was. He was not, however, yet as good with the sword, so Shar started giving him pointers.

Gordy drew his sword and was disappointed that no one was struck with fear.

"You only get that response from enemies, not friends you are sparring with," said Nurse Florence. Gordy looked downcast, but he still got a kick out of sword fighting with Dan. Both of them were not very skillful in their handling of the blades, so I started teaching them some basics. We also experimented with Gordy nicking Dan. We could see the gash, but not one drop of blood.

"Stop that," shouted Nurse Florence. "One nick is surely enough for a test like that. And mind, Dan, don't sheathe your blade until I get those healed. They will start bleeding as soon as the sword is no longer in your hand."

"These pants are too tight," complained Stan; doubtless the new leg muscles didn't have enough room.

"The pants stay on, though," pointed out Dan quickly.

"We'll need to get you an outfit for the Halloween party that's loose enough to accommodate either of your forms," said Nurse Florence, practical as always. You need to be able to move easily to fight properly.

"For the moment, let me help out," said Shar, tapping Stan on the arm with Zom. There was a little green flash, and suddenly Stan was back to normal.

"Hey!" yelped Stan.

"It figures," said Shar. "Zom's touch must break the spell on you." Stan recited the inscription again and bulked up immediately. Then Shar broke the spell yet again.

"Well, now we know," said Nurse Florence. "One other caution. Since Tal is the only one who can conceal his own blade, I have magicked all the rest of them to not be noticeable, unless you choose to work out with them in some public venue, in which case they will appear to be fencing foils. But I can't prevent them from showing up on security cameras or metal detectors, so keep in mind where you go when you carry them. Also, though humans won't notice them, those with the Sight, in other words spellcasters and magical creatures, will always be able to see them for what they truly are. That means pick costumes for the Halloween party that camouflage them as much as possible. Carrie Winn might not be alarmed by Tal carrying White Hilt, though she pretty much told him not to last time, but any of the rest of you could easily tip her off."

We had a little more practice, and then Nurse Florence piled us back into the van for a much more direct route home than last time.

On the trip back Stan reminded me that tomorrow was the day he would be working on the website for Winn Development Company.

"You probably shouldn't wear the sword of David," said Nurse Florence quickly. "Carrie Winn might be there and see it—and it would be pretty hard to explain."

"I think he should wear it," I interrupted. "How can he protect himself if there is a problem?"

"I admit there is some cause for concern, but I can't imagine Carrie Winn is going to do something to him downtown in the middle of the business day. You can hang out discretely somewhere nearby. There is a used bookstore across the street from the office. You could browse there inconspicuously, and if Stan has to stay longer, you can buy something. There are benches on the sidewalk in that part of the business district, one under each tree. Just sit outside and read. Again, not too conspicuous, unless someone is actually expecting you to show up."

"I want to come too!" said Gordy forcefully. "If Stan needs protection..."

"I thought the whole idea was for Stan to get in and out inconspicuously," replied Nurse Florence. "The more of you there are lurking around, the more likely someone will notice."

"I'll be all right," Stan said, trying to reassure Gordy and me. "I'll be in and out before anyone knows the difference." Gordy looked profoundly dissatisfied, and I had to say, I was liking this part of the plan less and less, but if I told Stan not to do it, I was sure he'd think I was doubting him again, and then his male ego would make him all the more stubborn. Besides, I really wanted him to know I had faith in him, so I held my tongue—with great difficulty.

By the time we got home, I had convinced myself not to worry. I had a trick or two up my sleeve to keep Stan safe, and in general, my little strike force seemed to be getting more powerful by the day. Aside from having Nurse Florence on hand as a healer, we each had a magic sword, which collectively looked like they could wreak havoc with Winn's security. Nurse Florence had other members of her order flying in. Who could Carrie Winn possibly be to resist all that firepower?

The problem with questions like that is that sooner or later the universe decides to answer them.

COMPUTER HACKING

THE FOLLOWING day Stan and I skipped working out with the team and took the bus to downtown Santa Brígida, such as it was. Winn Development's office was impressive enough, I suppose, like most Winn buildings deviating a bit from the Spanish colonial revival style and looking more glass and chrome modern corporate. The other businesses on both sides of Main Street were comparatively uninteresting in general, though I did actually like the used bookstore, shadowy and sweet with the smell of old books. I settled in there, and Stan walked through the front door of Winn's office, obviously happy at getting to help the cause without either Gordy or me treating him as if he would break if we looked away for a second.

I hadn't bothered to tell him I was going to be watching through his eyes and hearing through his ears.

I had practiced enough to be able to manage that trick without too much effort. The range was limited, but Stan was after all only across the street, so the connection was strong, the view perfect.

The receptionist recognized Stan immediately and escorted him to the server room in the back of the building. She did catch Stan trying to sneak a peek down the front of her blouse, but she seemed more flattered than offended. She got him into the server room with a card key, brought him a coke, and then left him to his business.

Stan sat down at the server and set himself up for a little "bait and switch." If some of you are our age, you've probably done the same thing in your school computer lab. You have a relevant page open that you can quickly switch to when the teacher walks by, and then there is the page that you are actually viewing. In much the same way, Stan opened the website he was supposed to be updating and went into administrator mode on it. He quickly made a few of the changes on his list, then miniaturized that window and started feeding the server command line routines until he managed to get himself recognized as an admin for the whole network. I couldn't really understand most of what I was seeing, but Stan was sure clicking away on the keyboard like mad. It is a good thing for society that he was too moral to actually be a hacker, because if he had chosen that path, I suspected he would be very, very good at it.

As nervous as I had been, the whole operation seemed to be flowing along smoothly. I still couldn't figure out exactly what Stan was doing, but he was moving very rapidly. Never once did he hit any obvious obstacle. In fact, he had started humming to himself.

By this time I had, in fact, bought a book—medieval Welsh poetry —and sat down on the bench right outside the bookstore. While I could do a sort of split screen, see both through Stan's eyes and through mine, it was difficult to maintain this mode, so I sat down with the book open in my lap and switched my entire view to Stan.

It was just luck that I heard the car pull up. Fortunately, the server room was quiet except for Stan's humming and keyboarding, and I was hearing through both his ears and mine. I don't know what prompted me to look up and switch to my own eyes—instinct, perhaps—but there was a Winn limo in front of the office, and getting out of it, Carrie Winn herself. Yeah, the same Carrie Winn who supposedly never came to the office. There were also two of the ubiquitous security men, but thankfully they positioned themselves in front of the office rather than actually going in with her.

I switched back to Stan mode and tried to broadcast a message.
Stan, she's coming. How fast can you finish?

Stan was clearly startled, but he had been through stranger things, after all.

"Got what we need. I just need to finish the website edits," he muttered under this breath. Damn, he knew I was listening.

I didn't know how long the remaining edits would take, so I wasn't sure whether to try to stall Ms. Winn or not. I figured suddenly popping up and starting a conversation might look suspicious, and doing something really spectacular like using White Hilt to ignite the tree in front of her office would definitely set off alarms. Yeah, for one crazy moment I did think about doing just that.

Just having to sit and wait in this kind of situation was the worst!

I stayed in Stan mode. He was still working on the website, but I had never seen someone work so fast, and he hadn't really been in the office that long, so even if he wasn't done and Ms. Winn checked on him, hopefully his progress wouldn't look suspiciously meager.

The server room was quiet, but I didn't think the door behind him was completely closed, so I strained to try to hear footsteps or anything. No, nothing but Stan pounding away on the keys. Wait, I thought I could hear very distant voices. Winn and the receptionist I thought, but I couldn't be sure.

Then, so close behind that Stan jumped, Ms. Winn asked, "How are you getting along, Stanford? Any questions?"

Damn, the woman had somehow been able to move without audible footsteps! That was one trick I had never seen her use before.

In an effort to fake calm, Stan turned slowly in the desk chair, then stood politely. "I'm doing just fine, Ms. Winn. I'm almost done, in fact."

I studied her face through Stan's eyes and tried to decide whether or not she knew anything. She seemed, as always, perfectly poised, and her friendly tone would have sounded genuine if I had not known better.

"How's it going?" I jumped. Gordy had sat down next to me without my even being aware of it.

"Shhh! I'm concentrating on what's happening inside!" I snapped. He wasn't supposed to be here. He must have left football practice very early to be here now. Still, this might not be a total disaster. Just sitting with me across the street wouldn't necessarily attract attention, and Gordy had obeyed my order for quiet.

Stan made direct eye contact with Winn, and at first, I didn't understand why her eyes were widening with surprise.

Oh, God! She could somehow see me, she could see me looking out through Stan's eyes.

"What's wrong, Ms. Winn?" asked Stan. She was already recovering her composure.

"Oh, don't worry, dear—nothing that can't be fixed," she said with a smile, placing her hand on his shoulder.

I wasn't sure, but I don't think Stan felt anything. I, on the other hand, felt as if someone had just plunged a blazing hot battle ax right into my forehead, chopping right through the connection I had with Stan. I grabbed my forehead and would have fallen off the bench if Gordy hadn't grabbed me.

"What's happening?" he demanded urgently. My mouth twitched, but no words came out. I felt no further assault against me, but the initial one, which had to have come from Winn, had almost knocked me unconscious and rendered me incapable of doing much of anything.

I was dimly aware of Gordy jumping up and running across the street. Damn, Gordy coming to the rescue would certainly look suspicious.

I was too shaky to get up from the bench, and reaching out to Gordy's mind made me yelp with pain, but through some miracle, I managed to connect and started seeing through his eyes.

The receptionist naturally looked up when Gordy came crashing through the door, but much to my surprise, instead of drawing his sword and demanding Stan's release, which I had been half expecting, he yelled, "Call 911! My friend is having some kind of seizure." He pointed out the window in my direction. I slumped over at that point to back up his story, and the receptionist at once started to dial 911. With her distracted, in fact looking genuinely alarmed, Gordy headed for the door leading to the back parts of the office—and ran straight into Ms. Winn.

"Young man, what are you doing?" she asked in a very commanding tone, but not apparently commanding enough to unnerve Gordy.

"I'm sorry, ma'am, but my friend is having some kind of attack. I'm looking for my other friend, Stan. He'll want to go with us to the emergency room." Winn immediately adopted a more sympathetic look and stepped aside to allow Stan to move past her.

"I'm right here, Gordy. What's happening?"

"It's Tal, Stan. He just practically fell off the bench. He can't even talk."

"Tal?" said Ms. Winn, either genuinely surprised or doing an Oscar-worthy job of faking it. "Taliesin is here?"

"He was keeping me company on the bus ride," said Stan quickly. "Let's go, Gordy."

"Carol," said Ms. Winn to the receptionist in a peremptory tone, "cancel that paramedic call. I can deal with this."

Carol looked up from the phone in shock. "But Ms. Winn, we don't even know…"

"Do what I tell you," snapped Winn. Carol picked up the phone again. Stan and Gordy got out the door first, but Winn was close behind.

As I disconnected from Gordy, I wondered what she intended to do to me. Canceling the paramedics did not seem like a good sign. Not that I really needed them. The pain was already beginning to subside, and I doubted there was anything physically wrong with me. Still, Winn was the one who did this to me in the first place, and I couldn't escape the cold dread that she was coming to finish the job in person. With a great effort, I managed to stand.

"Taliesin! What's wrong?" asked Winn, her voice oozing concern. "Should you be standing?"

"I'm sorry to have bothered you, Ms. Winn," I said, trying to keep my voice steady. "I think it's just a migraine. I have had them once or twice before. I've got medication at home. Gordy and Stan will see that I get home okay."

"You can get there more comfortably in my limo," said Winn quickly. "Boys, go across the street and wait by the car. I just want to make sure Taliesin is all right, and then he'll be joining you." Gordy and Stan both looked displeased by that idea, but they had no obvious reason to refuse, and I guess they assumed Winn couldn't do much to me on a crowded street in broad daylight. Of course, she had just practically split my brain wide open, but there was no way to mention that now, and in any case, it was true that she couldn't exactly kill me here and now. Having called off the paramedics, she would look really, really bad if something did happen to me.

I nodded to Gordy and Stan, and they went very slowly back across the street.

Winn took my hand so unexpectedly that I flinched and almost pulled away.

"Why are you so jumpy, Taliesin? Just sit still for a minute." Much to my surprise, I started feeling better almost immediately. By the time Winn let go of my hand, I was feeling pretty much like my old self.

"I'm sorry about that," said Winn, again sounding perfectly sincere. "When I saw someone besides Stanford looking at me through his eyes, I thought he had been possessed, so I took action…vigorous action, I'm afraid. I had no idea I was dealing with you. Why on earth would you have been connected to him that way?"

Good thing I could think again. "Stan has been attacked more than once. I keep a pretty close eye on him now. Literally."

"Surely you didn't expect an attack in my office?"

"I wouldn't have worried if I had known you were going to be here, but otherwise I have no idea what kind of threats your staff is equipped to deal with."

"Actually, this isn't a high-security location, it's true," she conceded. "Still, if you had concerns, you could have asked me to have security watch Stan."

"He's more comfortable with me than he would be with someone he doesn't know. Anyway, I'm really sorry for the misunderstanding."

"Think nothing of it," said Ms. Winn, with a gracious sweep of her hand. "However," she added, and suddenly her voice had an edge to it, "I do want to know how that other young man could possibly be carrying a faerie sword—a new one, by the look of it. I haven't seen a sword like that in human hands in ages. Where could he possibly have gotten it?" Naturally, Winn could see through the aura of inconspicuousness around Gordy's weapon; I had forgotten that point in the confusion.

"I haven't had a chance to tell you this yet, but Stan was attacked yesterday. We drove off the assailants, and one of them dropped the sword trying to make good his escape. I already had a magic sword, as you know, so I gave that one to Gordy."

"This Gordy knows?" said Winn with even more edge.

"He was standing right there when the attack started. I suppose I could have erased his memory, but the idea of having someone else who could watch Stan's back appeals to me."

"Very unwise!" replied Winn, sternly. "The more people who know who you really are, the greater the chance of an enemy gaining information through them. You should make sure he forgets everything at the first opportunity. Actually, if you would rather not do it yourself, I can take a few minutes and do it myself right now."

"No!" I said, a trifle too loudly. Quite aside from the fact that I needed Gordy, I did not intend to have Ms. Winn messing around in my head and discovering the presence of the *tynged* on him. "He is my man, and I must be the one to deal with him." Winn nodded at my invocation of medieval relationships.

"Well, then so be it...but don't wait too long. I can see your friends are getting anxious, so I'll let you get back to them."

She shook my hand, I thanked her, and then I got across the street as fast as I could.

"Just small talk in the limo," I muttered, mostly for Gordy's benefit. In fact, we had very little conversation on the way back, though Gordy, who had seldom been in a limo before, had a number of curiosity questions about them that Stan or I answered.

The limo dropped us at my house. Stan was, after all, just a few doors down, and Gordy was just a couple blocks over, though it did seem a little strange to me that the otherwise very accommodating driver didn't even ask Gordy where he lived, much less drop him off.

"Well, we got through that," observed Stan.

"Yeah, barely. Gordy, you weren't even supposed to be there."

"I couldn't help it," said Gordy apologetically. "All I could think about was Stan going into danger. And you might have needed me. Ms. Winn wasn't supposed to be there, but she showed up." He had me there, although the notion of Gordy brandishing his faerie sword in a showdown with Carrie Winn made me want to giggle.

At that moment our conversation was interrupted by the most soul-rending howl I had ever heard. All three of us spun around, and there, blocking the front door of our house, was a *Gwyllgi*, a black hound of destiny. I knew his appearance could only bring more problems, not only because his presence was a bad omen but also because he shouldn't have been appearing on my front porch in broad daylight. *Gwyllgis* were always nocturnal, normally appearing at deserted cross-roads or other isolated locations.

Whatever had brought him here now, the beast snarled and gave us an evil stare with his faintly glowing red eyes that made me shiver. Then he showed us his enormous fangs, ready to chew off an arm or leg if the mood struck him.

I was still strategizing in my head when Gordy drew his sword and charged.

"Gordy! The fear effect isn't likely to work on a supernatural!" I yelled, drawing While Hilt.

"Whatever! It's still a sword!" Gordy yelled back as he swung the sword at the beast, who reared up and growled loudly enough to send cold chills down the spines of people a block away.

The thing lunged at Gordy, and his sword struck true. There was a flash, and then nothing. The *Gwyllgi* was simply gone.

Gordy whooped in excitement. "I didn't know the sword could do that!" he said gleefully.

"It can't. If something just dissolves when a magic weapon strikes it, it means it was an illusion to begin with." I was relieved, though Gordy looked more disappointed than anything else.

"That doesn't make sense," said Stan, stroking his chin thoughtfully. "What does anyone gain from putting an illusionary dog on your porch? Anyone who could do that would know your sword or Gordy's would take it out with one blow."

My eyes narrowed. "Maybe it wasn't intended for us. If so, the purpose might have been to keep someone else out of the house. But who—and why?" Suddenly, a horrible thought struck me. "Guys, we need to check inside—now!" Gordy and Stan both followed as I raced up on the porch. I dropped my keys, but Stan picked them up quickly and handed them back. I got the door open and raced in.

"Mom!" I called urgently. No answer. I called out again, moving from room to room almost at a run. Having exhausted the first floor, I was halfway up the stairs when Stan yelled, "Isn't this the afternoon she plays bridge?"

I stopped midway up the stairs, turned around, and laughed. "Stan, thank God you remembered that. I was sure she had been kidnapped." Or worse. Really, I had had visions of her in the kitchen, lying in a pool of her own blood. "But that leaves us with an illusionary *Gwyllgi* guarding an empty house for no apparent reason." Actually, come to think of it, the *Gwyllgi* guarding my mom's corpse wouldn't have made much sense, either, but my mom's death would have explained the *Gwyllgi's* appearance, anyway.

We talked about the situation for a few minutes, but eventually, we gave up trying to figure it out. Stan and Gordy went home, and I had planned to stay home, but then, on impulse, I decided to walk over to school to see if Nurse Florence was still in her office. It was late afternoon, but she probably had paperwork to do after having been out of the office for a couple of afternoons.

She turned out to be there, all right, but she had her head down on her desk, her body racked by sobs.

As soon as she became aware of me, she tried to pull herself together and insisted she was okay, but I stepped around the desk and crouched down to hug her anyway—and not, I should add for the cynics among you, because she was hot.

"What's wrong?"

"I…I just got the news," she said, wiping her eyes ineffectually. "The plane carrying the members of my order crashed somewhere over the Atlantic. So far there is no sign of survivors."

"That's terrible!" I said. (Really, anything you say is going to sound stupid in this kind of situation, but you have to at least try.) "Was it…magic?"

"Even when they find the black box, it isn't exactly going to tell us that, but I doubt it. It would require either amazing coordination or the ability we have talked about to manipulate technology using magic, and I don't know of anyone except you who is even working on that. Still, the timing. It does make me wonder." She leaned back in her chair and, for the first time since I had met her when I was a high school freshman, she looked defeated.

"The only good news is that one member had to take a later flight. She is all right, as far as I know. I hardly know where to turn now. I didn't know the members of the Welsh branch of our order that well, but, but..." I moved to hug her again, but she waved me off. "It's just so unexpected, so much...death to absorb all at once. And, as if that were not enough, now I have to worry all the more about what will happen to you and your friends. I had counted on being able to have a decisive magical advantage over Carrie Winn, and now we can't even hope for that, much less count on it. Well, at least we will still have one more spell caster. Maybe the two of us, together with your magic, will be enough. We don't really know exactly how powerful Winn is."

"I have a little story about that...if you're up to it."

Ever the professional, Nurse Florence was already composed enough that only her reddened eyes gave her away. "Yes, if there is any new information, I should have it." So I told her about the afternoon's events, which didn't exactly cheer her up. She wasn't as worried as I was about how easily Ms. Winn had inflicted pain on me. "You were caught by surprise; that's the only reason she could break your connection so quickly and so painfully." No, that part didn't worry her much. What did worry her was Gordy.

"She has to be suspicious. And she knows it's a new sword. She will doubtless have connections with someone in Annwn and will try to find out where it came from. If she learns Gwynn forged swords for three of your friends, what is she going to make of that? If nothing else, it will tip her off that you lied to her, and then it's game over."

"Would it be that easy for her to find out what happened?" I asked.

"Well, perhaps not," replied Nurse Florence, her brow wrinkled. "Certainly Gwynn and his warriors would never tell her directly. I didn't mention this two days ago, but when I first talked to Gwynn, he accepted my request for help much more readily than I expected. That can only be because he fears the power Carrie Winn is accumulating and wants to keep her in check. Though she is no immediate threat to him, if she gains a dominant enough position in the human realm, she could compromise the secrecy surrounding the faerie realms. Most rulers in Annwn haven't wanted anything to do with the human world at least since the invention of gunpowder. The more Carrie Winn strives for power, the more temptation there is for her to use magic, and the more magic she uses, the more likely someone will notice. After all, in a short period of time, Carrie Winn has sent a *pwca* onto a high school campus, thrown nine of Santa Brígida's most visible young people into Annwn with hundreds of potential witnesses around, and dropped a kelpie in the man-made lagoon at a university. And that's just what we know about.

"Even if Winn somehow keeps the human population in the dark, that success would just make her ultimate triumph more likely, and then she could use a stronger position in this world as a base for attacking the Otherworld. If Carrie Winn were herself a ruler in Annwn, well, she wouldn't be around here so much, probably not at all. She may not be an exile, but she is at the very least someone not in power, and it seems clear she is after power in one way or another. Gwynn would never admit it, but he must be worried sick over the prospect of Winn wrecking his own kingdom somehow." I looked a little disappointed at that. "Don't get me wrong, Tal, you and your friends *were* impressive, but Gwynn has other reasons as well for helping us—be sure of that. That's really good news, though. If we need something else, we stand a decent chance of getting it."

"How about a squad of his best fighters on Samhain?" I asked with a little smile.

"You know better. Yes, he and his men could come through more easily then, but he won't risk compromising the security of Annwn himself. I'm afraid we are on our own in that way."

Nurse Florence leaned back in her chair again, looking exhausted.

"I should go, I guess," I said, wanting to hug her again but not quite sure whether I should.

"Wait!" she said, sitting up again, which required a visible effort on her part. "We have to talk about the *Gwyllgi*."

"We can do that tomorrow," I said gently.

"No!" she said with such intensity that I took a step back. "Before you go, you have to realize what our situation really is. Look, I know it might be better for me to spend a little time grieving, but I don't have that kind of time—and I will not end up grieving for you, or Stan, or any of your other friends. *I won't do it*."

I sat down on the counter. "Okay, I'm listening."

"The *Gwyllgi* means that we don't have that much time."

"But it wasn't even a real…"

"Just listen. I know it wasn't real. That is exactly my point. You have an encounter with Carrie Winn in which she sees Gordy's sword. Later one of her drivers drops all of you off at your house, even Gordy, who should have been dropped off a couple of blocks away. Then you battle the fake *Gwyllgi* whose presence makes no sense, only, if you think about what went before, it makes perfect sense."

"I'm not following."

"Winn wanted to know what the sword did. So she told her driver to drop Gordy with the rest of you. It must have been she who crafted that illusion. She knew Gordy would use the sword, and she hoped your conversation would reveal its purpose if it weren't revealed in action. Sure enough, you mentioned the fear aura. Someone—or something—is nearby to observe, or perhaps Winn is observing by magical means. Either way, mission accomplished: she now knows what his sword does and can prepare for it, just as she can prepare for yours."

"Well, what of it? Is she going to fireproof and fear-proof all her minions?"

"Don't be flip! That's probably not beyond her ability. I think Winn has us outgunned anyway. Our best hope is the element of surprise. As far as I know, we have two possible surprises: your potential ability to use magic to affect technology, and the other three swords. As to the first, work on it as if all our lives depend on it—they probably do. As to both, we can't afford to let Winn get any more information. That means no sword practice, except in Annwn. If I pull all of you through, I doubt she can observe there. That means no conversation, and I mean none, unless strict protocols are observed."

"What do you mean?"

"Earlier Winn observed you enough to be able to fake being your ally. How did she do it?"

"Isn't she picking up things from my mind?"

"At first I thought maybe so. But the more I think about the idea, the less likely it seems. Someone of your power level would probably feel an incursion into your mind. Maybe she threw you off balance enough at the party to get away with it, but normally, no, you would be aware. Guess again."

"A shifter disguised as something else."

"Possible, but to spy effectively, the form would have to be mobile, and shifters hate assuming really small forms, like flies, for obvious reasons. Had a stray dog follow you around recently? If not, I doubt a shifter spy is the problem. Think, Tal, what else can you do?"

"I can get inside someone, as I did with Stan, and see and hear through them."

"Exactly! What if Carrie Winn were able to do that?"

"But the first Taliesin never had that ability. I just developed it recently."

"Yes, and you have some unique advantages. But suppose Winn is like you. You have speculated on that more than once. Suppose she is an aware reincarnate or has just lived straight through. Then she, too, would have the advantage of a much broader range of experience than even the greatest of earlier spellcasters. Like your powers, hers could have evolved over time.

"Now, let's assume she can't use you or me that way without us being aware. Part of the enchantment on Dan, Shar, and Gordy blocks any kind of occult incursion into their minds, so she can't use them that way, and Shar is additionally protected by Zom, which would block any such maneuver."

"I saw through Gordy just this afternoon. And I saw through Dan at the homecoming dance."

"The enchantment does not block you or me. But think! Who does that leave?"

"Damn. Is she using Stan?"

"She could be. I could block him right away, but I'm not sure I should. That, too, could tip off Winn. But the only alternative would be to isolate him from the rest of the group until Samhain, and that's a dead giveaway too."

"Why don't we borrow a leaf from all those spy movies and feed her false images through Stan. You know, like characters are always feeding looped recordings to video security systems."

"That's brilliant if it could be made to work. But to fool her for days, we would need extensive images and sounds to feed to her. It would be like producing thousands of hours of video, not just one loop. In the short term, there's just no way."

"All right, then, can you 'divert' the signal? You know, when she tries to connect with Stan, she connects with someone else instead. Someone who isn't part of our group, isn't normally close to us?"

"Hmmm. Maybe. She'll be suspicious of that too, but it's so unusual she may think the problem is on her end. Let's try that. Tal, that really is brilliant."

"Actually, Stan suggested that the other day, when we were talking about defensive strategies," I admitted.

"Give Stan my compliments, then. Listen, you can send messages to people mentally now, right?"

"Worked with Stan, anyway. Yeah, I think I can do it."

"Send one to Dan, Gordy, and Shar as well if possible. Let them know what is happening. And make sure Stan says or does nothing suspicious until tomorrow morning. I'll need a little preparation to set up the diversion. And Tal…"

"Yes?"

"Emphasize the importance of not saying or doing anything where anyone outside the group can see or hear. Once Winn realizes that she isn't connecting with Stan, for whatever reason, she'll start using other students. Anyone, and I mean anyone, could easily become her eyes and ears without knowing the difference."

"Nurse Florence," I said worriedly. "If she's been spying on us through Stan all this time, doesn't she already know everything?

"I would say not, given how surprised she seemed to have been by Gordy's sword. I think she was just peeking through Stan occasionally, enough so she could feed you the occasional "inside" information to make you think she was the one helping you. Now, though, I think she would have started using him much more, so it's a good thing we figured this out now, rather than later."

"Okay, then. I'll send out those messages as soon as I get home."

"Good." Nurse Florence drooped a little, as if she didn't know quite what to do now that she had imparted her information.

"Let me walk you to your car," I suggested.

"That's a good idea. I don't need to stay here anymore."

She got up very slowly, got her coat, and we went out to the faculty parking lot together.

It was sad to think that she had done so much for me, but now, when she needed me, I couldn't really think what to say or do to make her feel better.

I started to sing, but she stopped me.

"There are some things, however painful, that one needs to feel," she said.

Well, so much for that idea. I just had to hope that my presence gave her some comfort...and that this would be the last time that she had to grieve for a long, long time.

THE SCIENCE OF MAGIC

W<small>HEN</small> I <small>GOT</small> <small>HOME</small>, I did manage to send the messages, but my hands were shaking a little by the end of the last one, not so much from making the connections themselves, though there was distance involved, and hence considerable effort, as from the generally unnerving situation. Bad enough to know someone was out to get me. Discovering it was the most powerful person in town made the situation that much worse. But now, knowing that she had been spying on us and would be doing it even more was creepy, to say the least.

What if Nurse Florence was wrong, and that fly buzzing around was a shifter? What if Carrie Winn could see through my eyes without my being aware of it? I finally slept that night, but it was a nightmare-ridden sleep, and I woke up still feeling tired.

I went through my morning routines robotically. Only breakfast left to go, and then I could…what? Go off to school and try to figure out which person I bumped into in the hall was really the eyes and ears of Carrie Winn?

To make the situation worse, my dad, who had been content for quite a while now, decided this morning would be a good time to raise the tension level.

"Tal, you know, if you ever want to invite a girl over for dinner, that would always be fine with your mom and me. In fact, we'd like to meet your girlfriend sometime."

Yeah, well, so would I.

"I'm between girlfriends at the moment," I said, making a weak attempt at a smile.

"That Carla Rinaldi seems like a very nice girl," my mom offered. "I ran into her mother just the other day at the mall, and she said—"

"Mom, you aren't matchmaking, are you? Because I can find my own girls, thanks anyway."

"Yes, you could be quite the ladies' man, Tal, but you aren't." My dad looked straight at me, ignoring the newspaper for once. "You spend all your time with Stan from down the street, and now a few other guys. I thought when you starting working out with the football team and decided to play soccer again…"

Normally, I could have handled this conversation. Normally, I would have had a decent sleep and not been worried about prying eyes on me every second.

"You thought what, Dad?" I said, more harshly than I had ever spoken to my father. "That I'd go from being Johnny Weirdo to Johnny Normal again? Well, I'm afraid this is as normal as it gets."

"Tal, I don't appreciate your tone one bit!"

"And that's the problem. You don't appreciate. I have really high grades and a successful band. I'm fast becoming a successful two-sport athlete. I have an internship with Carrie Winn. I have friends, I don't smoke, drink, do drugs. I don't do anything high risk." Well, not the kinds of things most parents would have to worry about, anyway. "And you're upset because, what? I don't have a girlfriend right now?"

"Tal, I do appreciate everything you've accomplished," replied my dad, more defensively than usual.

"Then, what? What the hell is it that's bugging you?" I was practically shouting now.

"Tal," said my dad, his volume rising, "we raised you better than to behave like this!"

"Dad, I don't know how else to say this: I'm not gay, I'm just busy."

It is one thing to know the elephant is in the room. It is another thing when it jumps up on the table and tramples your Rice Krispies.

For a second my dad got so red in the face I thought he was going to have a heart attack right on the spot.

"I never once said I thought you were...like that!" he finally replied, quietly but intensely.

"Yeah, well, you didn't have to say it, did you? I could see it on your face every day."

I shoved back my chair and got up as fast as I could. My mom just sat there, stunned, and I felt sorry for her, but I didn't have any comfort for her left in me right then. I just needed to get away from her, from him.

"Taliesin Weaver! Sit down this instant!" Dad's voice had steel in it I had never heard before. I was so angry at that moment that I might still have ignored him, but he was out of his chair with remarkable speed, putting a hand on my shoulder firmly and pushing me back down into the chair. I could have resisted, but even at my angriest, I couldn't actually get violent with my dad. Nonetheless, I looked up at him with unconcealed defiance.

My mom looked as if she were about to cry. I did my best to ignore her.

"Tal, what is wrong with you?" Dad asked urgently. "This isn't like you at all."

"I'm just tired, Dad. Tired of always falling short," I said, the anger cooling slightly. I was tired, and I just wanted the conversation to be over.

"I don't know why you think I'm disappointed with you. What have I ever done to make you think that?"

"We love you," added Mom, in a trembling voice, suggesting she was still dangerously close to crying.

Well, my dad had asked, so I told him. I told him every little facial twitch, every under-the-breath remark, every innuendo I could remember from the past four years. I had to give him credit. He listened, though it wasn't really evident how much he was actually hearing. He had gone from red-faced to expressionless fairly quickly.

When I finally finished spilling my guts all over the dining room table, Dad was at first completely silent. Then, very quietly, he said, "When I was your age, we didn't even talk about things like that.

Everyone tried hard to pretend they didn't exist. I guess that isn't right, but that's the way I was raised."

"I know that," I said slowly, "but—"

"Let me finish. I listened to you, now you listen to me! Okay, I admit, I worried about you sometimes. I worried, but I couldn't talk to you about it. I can see now I should have. You knew what was on my mind anyway.

"I know I shouldn't feel this way. I know I shouldn't care whether you're gay or straight, but I do. That much it sounds like you figured out. But what you don't know, it's hard for me to even say, but I know I have to, is, Tal, gay or straight, you are my son. I love you. I will always love you. And I feel terrible that I made you wonder whether that was true."

I hardly knew how to respond. As long as I could remember, my dad had been pretty closed off emotionally. Oh, he had said he loved me before, but it always sounded like a very staid greeting card without any real depth to it. Opening up that far must have been hard, and it seemed to me that he was shaking a little.

I had not expected this conversation to end up in a family hug and a tidal wave of mutual apologies, but it did. My mom finally did cry, but at that point, I think more from relief than anything else. I could tell my dad still wasn't a hundred percent sure I was straight. But I could also tell he was trying really, really hard not to care. Brought up in the era he had been, he couldn't possibly be expected to go further than that right then.

I met Stan pretty late, but we were close to school, so we still managed to be on time. We didn't talk much—both of us were waiting for the thumbs up from Nurse Florence. That might have been just as well, since the confrontation with my dad had left me feeling pretty raw. Yeah, things had worked out better than I expected, but it still wasn't the easiest conversation to get through, and my original reasons for exploding all over my dad—the tiredness, the anxiety—still remained.

At the beginning of lunch, Stan and I strolled casually by the nurse's office, and Nurse Florence gave us the thumbs up, so we went in.

"We're okay?" I asked, just to be sure.

"Anyone trying to see through Stan will actually be seeing through

another student neither one of you know," replied Nurse Florence.
"That means I can ask Stan what he was able to find out in Carrie
Winn's office."

Stan started fumbling in his backpack and finally pulled out a flash
drive that must have been buried at the very bottom.

"Don't put it up on my computer," said Nurse Florence quickly.
"The network administrator might notice, and it would be hard to
explain. Just tell us."

"Okay. She really doesn't have much in the way of security on her
network, and the office network did connect with the network at Awen,
but I can't make sense out of the data I got. Her security men are theoretically supplied by a security company she has a contract with, but
there is no list of them anywhere on her system. The security company
sounds like something out of a TV mystery. It looks like a shell
company owned by a series of other companies that don't have much
more substance either, but if one traces the line of ownership far
enough, it eventually comes back to Carrie Winn."

"What?" I said incredulously. "She is contracting with herself to
hire security? That makes zero sense."

"I doubt it is that simple," replied Nurse Florence. "Think— why
would someone need to create a front like that? Tal? Stan?"

"Money laundering?" I tried, but I could see from her face that was
not the answer she was looking for.

"I'm no expert, but I think you need an actual company bringing in
actual money, not just a shell."

"Since there is no list of names, she is trying to hide who her security people are," suggested Stan.

"Quite possibly, but why?"

"I'm not liking what I'm thinking," I said. "Could there be something...supernatural about her security?"

"I'm afraid so," replied Nurse Florence grimly. "I can't imagine why
Winn wouldn't deal with a real company if she were going to hire ordinary security. All of this fake-companies-owning-more-fake-companies
kind of chain is a lot of work to set up—hardly worth it to someone who
isn't trying to hide something. This situation opens up a whole world of

new possibilities, most of them nasty. She could be recruiting from Annwn. Picture a large security force, all with the advantages of faerie blood. Maybe they are even all shifters. Maybe Winn is not the only one on her side who can do magic. There isn't any easy way of telling what we are up against. Stan, what about the rest of her staff?"

"There are some real employee records on both her business and home servers, but as far as I can tell, she went to great lengths to hire people from out of town, with no ties to anyone in town. The domestic staff lives in a separate building right behind Awen, and none of them seem to have any dependents. The business employees all seem to live no closer than Carpinteria in one direction or Santa Ynez in the other…"

"Which makes it difficult to do exactly what I wanted to do—get information from their family members. I was hoping in an organization that large to have at least a few children of employees on campus, if nothing else. Any of us would be too conspicuous showing up at some-place like Carpinteria High School for no reason."

"I can try to extend my range and maybe start seeing through people from greater distances," I suggested.

"That's a good idea, but your first priority right now should still be finding ways for your magic to affect technology. Faerie or not, the guards will be expecting their guns to work and will be thrown off balance when they don't. Now, if there are more questions…"

"Just one," I interrupted. "What progress have we made on Eva's bodyguard?"

"None, I'm afraid. I can't seem to find a girl with the right skills in Eva's circle, and introducing some guy who tags along all the time would be hard to explain to her."

"She kind of knows what's happening," I said sheepishly, suddenly realizing I had left that particular detail out in earlier conversations with Nurse Florence.

"What? How does she know?"

"I had to tell her to get her and Dan back together."

Nurse Florence looked at me in total amazement. "Do you realize what you have done?"

"She was in Annwn on Founders' Day. She already knew something was up."

"Yes, but she had no way of finding out what. Now that she and Dan are back together, she knows what questions to ask, and at your insistence, I have adjusted Dan's *tynged,* so he always has knowledge of our situation. What do you suppose they talk about? Tal, I thought Stan was the only possible way Carrie Winn could spy on us, but she can do almost as well with Eva if she realizes how much access Eva has. You really should have told me about Eva right away."

"I'm sorry. At the time I didn't realize Winn was using other people that way."

"True, but you need to be more cautious in general. Now I have to do something about Eva, and the kind of arrangement I made for Stan is hard enough to maintain without having to keep another one going at the same time."

"At least it's only a few days until Halloween," I pointed out lamely.

"Assuming the danger is over after Halloween. You know it could be an anticlimax—and then we'd just have to keep living in fear, not knowing when Winn was actually going to strike."

"I don't think so," said Stan suddenly. "While I was hacking Winn's computer, I ran across the guest list for the party, and it got me thinking." Both Nurse Florence and I looked at him expectantly. We both had a general idea of who was on the guest list, but obviously, he had noticed something we missed.

"The adults are the bigwigs you would expect...except that none of them are local."

"Maybe because of Winn's impending state senate campaign," suggested Nurse Florence.

"Possibly, but we've all seen that monster house of hers. She could certainly have included the usual local dignitaries, but she didn't. Almost as if she didn't want them to see what was going to happen."

"How is it better for out-of-the-area dignitaries to see?" I asked.

"Maybe because we don't know them. Winn could bring in impostors. If she has all those fake security people, why not?

"And then there are the students she invited. Tal's band. Okay, so

they are the entertainment. All the other students from Founders' Day—
well, that could just be picking the conspicuous student leaders. But she
also just added Shar and Gordy. Not the rest of the football team. Just
the two who happen to be with us."

"If she knows they are with us, wouldn't it make more sense not to
invite them?"

"Unless," said Nurse Florence, not doing as good a job as usual of
concealing her fear, "she intends to wipe all of us out at once."

This day just kept getting better and better.

"What about you?" I said. "Are you invited?"

"No, but Coach Miller is, and fairly randomly—no other school
staff members on the guest list. And it wouldn't be too hard for her to
guess at this point that I would be Coach Miller's plus one. I'm afraid
Stan is right. And her making some kind of move at the party makes
sense. Samhain is, after all, a point of greater than normal magical
potency.

"We still don't know what she's up to, and I'm thinking now we
won't until it's too late. But that doesn't change my idea about our best
strategy. She is definitely going to surprise us in some way. Our only
real chance is to surprise her at least as much."

"Got it," I said. "Stan and I will work on that this afternoon."

And so we did. For lack of a better word, I "downloaded" Stan's
scientific visualizations. It took a few hours for me to really put them to
good use, but suddenly everything "clicked" (again, for lack of a better
word), and I began to be able to manipulate electronics because
suddenly I could see and feel how they worked—literally. Though I felt
silly singing to Stan's computer, inside my head, I could feel the
programs executing the same way I had been able to feel the blood
flowing in living beings ever since my awakening. At first, I could only
nudge the programs a little, like speeding up or slowing down execu-
tion. But gradually I managed to create files and erase them just by
singing. A key moment came when I was able to log on without using
Stan's password. His computer began to respond as an animal would; it
was loyal to me, regardless of passwords or other security measures.

In the days that followed, I frequently walked down the halls at
school humming. Nobody really paid attention, since I had often done

that before. Now, though, the hum was me subtly syncing with the electronics around me. I'd walk past a computer lab, and all the machines would simultaneously power up. Public address system? I could use it as my address system if I wanted to. I only did that once, though, in the late afternoon. Too conspicuous otherwise. Security cameras? They always went suspiciously blank whenever I was around. (Evidently no one ever checked those tapes, since some of us had been walking around with sheathed swords hanging from our sides in full view of the security cameras for days, but at least now even the potential risk was gone.) I was confident I could control pretty much any of the technology at Awen, and I hoped that that would throw a pretty serious wrench into Winn's plans.

Guns, however, were another matter. Electronics had become part of my repertoire with surprising ease, but perhaps because Stan hadn't thought about the mechanics of firearms that much himself, that all-important manipulation eluded me at first. Stan and I took a bus to Carpinteria several times and loitered near a shooting range. I could see through the eyes of the shooters, but really feeling or seeing the inner workings of the guns did not come. In the end, Stan solved the problem by a quick but intensive study of the way guns worked. Once his visualization got better, I downloaded again, and presto! I could feel the inner workings of the gun. I could see the gunpowder explode, and that was the easiest spot to block the whole process. It might have been an interesting twist to get the guns to fire at random—preferably into the people carrying them, but with such limited time, I was more than happy to settle for neutralizing them, so that they did not fire at all. Just a little tinkering with the way the gunpowder reacted, and the gun failed. Simple as that. I triggered enough random failures at the shooting range to be sure. Then, gradually, I moved farther and farther away. By the eve of the party, I could be standing almost a block away and still prevent guns from firing. That should be enough range to wipe out the firepower for Winn's whole security force. Well, the physical part anyway. There was no telling what occult means of attack they possessed now that we knew they might not be human. We had to hope that our collection of magic swords would be sufficient to tip the battle in our favor. Yeah, I now agreed with Stan and Nurse Florence. I was sure Carrie Winn would make her move on Samhain.

Our cause was reinforced in one other way. A day or two before Halloween I ran into Carlos Reyes, who suddenly wasn't avoiding me —and I couldn't avoid noticing the sheathed sword hanging on his right side.

"So, Carlos, I see you have joined the club." The choice made a lot of sense. Carlos was already on the guest list, Eva knew him, if only slightly, and although he would need a very intense crash course in swordsmanship, his long hours of water polo and swimming had put him in excellent physical shape.

Grim as Carlos had been ever since Founders' Day, he was a little like a kid with his first bicycle—or like Gordy—in terms of his enthusiasm. Take a guy to Annwn, give him a custom-made Faerie sword, and he'll do anything you want, apparently.

"What does yours do?" I said, leaning closer. There was no one nearby, but still, I was learning the value of caution.

Carlos leaned even closer. "Even a touch makes someone feel like he's drowning. An actual wound, and the enemy will die as if by drowning unless the spell is broken." I wanted to tell him that watching "the enemy" die was not the picnic he seemed to imagine, but if in fact, we had to go into battle, he would find that out soon enough for himself.

In just under two weeks, I had done what Nurse Florence was pretty sure no spell caster before me had ever done—forge a connection between magic and technology. Would that, together with six magic swords, four of which we hoped Carrie Winn knew nothing, be enough? In just a couple of days, we would know.

SAMHAIN

HALLOWEEN AT SCHOOL was one long headache. I dimly remembered enjoying it in some earlier years, but this time all the adolescent lets-see-how-much-I-get-away-with costuming just annoyed me. Probably my attitude was colored by the fact that I didn't know whether I would be alive twenty-four hours from now, but either way, I still longed for the day to end. You would have thought, given what I was heading into, that I would have wanted exactly the opposite, but what would have been the point? Even if I had the power to stop time, why be the moth frozen forever in flight, just half an inch from the flame? No, I had been haunted one way or another since that night when Stan had uncovered my secret. I had been haunted by Carrie Winn before I had any idea who she was. Yeah, maybe I would end up dead, but maybe I would end up free, and there seemed little reason to think I could be free by trying to avoid the inevitable.

Despite my aversion to all the Halloween festivities at school, I spent a lot of time at home on my costume for the party. I had decided on Zorro because the black outfit might be good for stealth, it gave me freedom of movement, and the cape would help hide White Hilt even from Carrie Winn, or at least make it hard for her to tell it wasn't just a prop sword for the costume.

Dad just seemed thrilled I was attending yet another Carrie Winn function. Mom, on the other hand, seemed a little apprehensive, almost as if her maternal instincts were telling her something was wrong. I insisted everything was fine, but when I kissed her goodbye, I could feel an odd tremble in her lips. Just as well she didn't know what was really going on. If she felt this shaky over a premonition, imagine how overwhelming the truth would be for her.

I popped down the street to get Stan, who had, with eminent good sense, picked Merlin. "I needed something loose fitting in case I need to wield David's sword, and, well, you know." In other words, if Stan needed to raise his sword and suddenly had to double in muscle mass, he needed a costume with room to grow into. Merlin's robe made for a wise choice, all things considered.

"So," Stan continued slyly, "Are you ready for our trip to Cougar Country Safari?" Despite myself, I blushed a little.

"Stan, you're making me sorry I ever told you about that. I should slap you silly for bringing it up again."

"Too late. I'm already silly."

Much to my relief, Jackson picked us up in the band van at that point. We were the last pick-up, and since the whole band was together, we went over the details of our upcoming performance, leaving Stan pretty much on his own. He was staring out the window, and I noticed how worried he looked.

And that was about the last time I noticed him until we got to Awen. It wasn't just band business. It was Carla Rinaldi, costumed in a revealing white gown as Venus, the goddess of love. Apparently, she had been waiting for me to make a move and had gotten tired of waiting. She put one arm around me while we were talking about music, and her grip was surprisingly tight. Slowly, but unmistakably, she was pulling me closer, and I could feel my body respond to her with surprising intensity. My heart was racing, and my blood felt as if it were burning hotter than White Hilt. The strength of this reaction came as such a surprise to me that I had to glance over at Carla to make sure magic was not somehow involved. How sick is that? My first response when I felt drawn to a sexy girl who was clearly totally into me was to wonder if the situation were somehow being manipulated by Carrie Winn.

I looked into Carla's eyes but did not see Ms. Winn looking back out; nor did I feel anything unusual beyond my own raging hormones. Carla looked back into my eyes with an expression that suggested that she wished we were alone.

"Uh, guys, get a room," said George, our keyboardist, with a smirk. Carla now had both arms around me, and, having followed Carrie Winn's earlier advice, even if unconsciously, I was glad I had gone with loose fitting pants.

"Carla," I whispered in her ear. "I'm loving this, but, uh, maybe now is not the time."

"Never put off until tomorrow what you can do today," she whispered back.

A normal guy in a normal situation would have found some way to be alone with Carla sometime that night. Too bad I wasn't, and it wasn't. I was so aroused by that point that I feared I might miss some hint of a threat until it was too late. Using our upcoming performance as an excuse, including a very convincing "everyone else is depending on us" speech, I managed to scrape her off of me. I even managed to extricate myself without offending her. Yeah, I needed to be alert right now. At the same time, the absolute, overwhelming undeniability of my reaction to her suggested I had misread my feelings for her. Sure, she was hot, and I was fast upgrading her from volcano to solar flare, but she had always been hot, and I had never felt her presence so powerfully. I now realized that being with her would not be just a process of trying to get over Eva. For the first time in four years, I felt that I might be able to get out from under the shadow of what might have been and move into the light of what could be.

Well, if I managed to live through the night, that is.

In just a few minutes, we arrived at Awen. This time we were directed around back to the service entrance, mostly because there was an elevator that would make getting the instruments and equipment upstairs much easier. We normally used acoustic, not electric, guitars, and they were pretty easy to move around, but the keyboard was a little more challenging, and the drums even more so, to say nothing of the sound system. Unloading the equipment, however, gave me the perfect opportunity to work the first part of my magic. Humming as I worked, I reached out with my mind, stretching my thoughts further and further, twining them around every gun throughout the complex, and then one by one I rendered the gunpowder inert. The operation was almost suspiciously easy—but of course, if Carrie Winn had not visualized such an attack, she would not have known to protect the guns from my magic, if such a thing were even possible for her.

By now we were pretty well loaded into the elevator, but I dragged my feet enough to take care of the security cameras. I focused on the one I could see, pouring my thoughts into it, them sending them surging along the cables, crackling into the security server, searing it with almost explosive force. When it shut down, it took out not only the cameras, but the alarms and even the fire suppression system. If Carrie Winn had been counting on that to neutralize White Hilt, well, tough luck!

There was more than a little risk in knocking down all the security. Unlike the guns, which no one would notice until they tried to fire, the security system failure would doubtless be noted and reported to Winn almost immediately. But, assuming she did not know that I could attack technology that way, she might not interpret the security failure as an attack. Even if she did, she had no way of knowing the attack came from me, and if she thought she was being attacked from another direction, so much the better for us.

Once we were upstairs, moving the equipment into the ballroom should have been relatively easy, but, whether to create the right atmosphere for a Halloween party or to thwart any defensive moves on our part, the ambiance in the mansion was incredibly gloomy, making moving the equipment around cumbersome at best. One of Winn's aides followed us around with a flashlight, but that didn't help much.

Oh, there was some light, but it was a brilliant simulation of flickering candle flames, and its shifting nature made seeing what we were doing difficult. I had to constantly worry about banging something into the wall. No, I wasn't worried about Carrie Winn's castle. I was worried about our equipment.

After what seemed an eternity, we had maneuvered everything into the ballroom, and then came the nightmare of trying to get everything plugged in correctly by flashlight and imitation candle. I gradually came to realize, however, that that was not our biggest problem.

It was not lighting alone that made the place seem gloomy. Carrie Winn had somehow infected the atmosphere with a steadily more oppressive fear that clung to us and whispered darkly into our ears. I felt it first because of my sensitivity to magic, but I could see the other band members become conscious of it one by one. At first, it seemed like a natural reaction to the flickering near-darkness around us, but I knew that as the evening progressed it would gnaw further and further into our nerves, seeming more and more real, until by the end of the evening fear would engulf us, and we would be lost.

Any thought that Carrie Winn did not intend to attack tonight evaporated. No one would waste such power to make a creepy ambiance for a Halloween party, and that level of power would, in any case, have been stark raving overkill for such a purpose. She clearly knew I had allies and planned to weaken them as much as possible before she struck. Well, we would see about that.

I had been humming the whole time, but now I actually started singing as we finished our setup, and the others joined me, a capella, and, though they did not realize it consciously, together we pushed back the fear, sent it skittering into whatever dark corners it could find. Winn's spell, whatever it was, seemed to cover all of Awen. That meant there was no immediate escape from it, but that also meant its strength would have to be diluted, and my music, more localized and concentrated, could force it back, shield the band, eventually shield the whole ballroom—but only as long as I kept singing. As in Annwn, the others could add their strength to mine, but ultimately mine was the power, mine was the focus, and mine would be the failure if I faltered.

After an unusually musical sound check, we were ready to go, and, as if on cue, the guests started arriving. I sheltered them in our music; I sent it out in warm, pulsing waves, beating at the raving fear, eroding it, diluting it, finally freeing the room of it.

I had to keep most of my focus on our performance to ensure that the protection kept up, but I did scan the room to make sure that all my allies were in place. Coach Miller and Nurse Florence arrived as a high school football player and cheerleader. (I had to say that she pulled off the costume better than he did.) Dan and Eva came as Romeo and Juliet, a choice that sent a little pang through my heart, but I wrapped myself in the memory of Carla pressing up against me, and the pang eased a little. Like me, Dan sported a cloak that helped to conceal his blade. Because I had read the *Shah Nameh*, I recognized Shar as Rostam, the great hero of that Persian epic, resplendent in rather realistic looking armor, another choice that would make his sword seem like a prop rather than a weapon. Gordy arrived as Hercules, complete with fake Nemean lion head as a helmet and Nemean lion hide draped over his shoulders—and bare-chested. Show-off! Wait—do you doubt that's what he was doing? Surely you've noticed that it is always some star athlete that shows up like that, never the president of the chess club. Ever wonder why? Well, in any case, Hercules was known for a bow, not a sword, but at least the costume was martial enough that nobody short of an expert in mythology was likely to nitpick the sword. Carlos arrived last, dressed as El Cid, another good cover for the sword and a compliment to our high school's English department, which seemed to have gotten classic literature into our students' heads far more than I would have imagined. Of course, Carrie Winn would quickly recognize the magic of their weapons if she got a good look, but we would have to cross that bridge when we came to it.

No one who didn't know our strategy would have recognized the subtleties of our positioning in the room. Well, for the most part. Gordy was his usual obvious self in watching over Stan, who ironically probably didn't need much watching while he was carrying the sword of David. Stan was scanning the darkness outside the ballroom's massive plate glass window, watching for anything unusual, like fog rolling in or some other effort to isolate the house. Dan was subtler in maneuvering Eva and the other girls who had seen Annwn close to the stage, where all of us could watch them more effectively, and Carlos naturally stayed nearby, keeping an eye on Eva and on the other girls as well. All my peers were present and accounted for, either as allies or as people we could protect if the need arose. Nurse Florence kept scanning all the entrances for Carrie Winn or for any unexpected move. Aside from keeping our musical defenses up, I periodically checked the guns—still

neutralized—and the security system—still down. We could not antici-
pate every threat, but we were about as well defended as we could be in
an environment basically controlled by Carrie Winn.

I should have known, though, that Ms. Winn would have some
surprises up her sleeve. I wasn't paying much attention to the adults in
the room. Nurse Florence had earlier suggested getting Coach Miller to
lead them to safety if a fight broke out, but neither one of us thought
that scenario very likely. Winn was, after all, poised to announce her
state senate candidacy. Under those circumstances, a bloodbath among
her adult guests seemed unlikely. We had considered Stan's theory
about the guests being impostors, but human impostors could still
conceivably tell tales afterward, and with the guards already likely to be
supernatural, how many other supernaturals could even Carrie Winn
round up to create an imitation guest list? No, both Nurse Florence and
I expected that Winn would at some point try to separate her targets
from the rest of the population, probably during a band break when she
could extract me inconspicuously.

We were, of course, both completely, egregiously wrong.

My first clue was the presence of a large number of security people.
It was hard to tell at first, but as the party wore on, I became aware of
more and more of them, too many of them. Strategically, there seemed
no point in that much concentration of force, unless Winn really did
intend to attack us in the ballroom.

My second clue was the gradual realization that something was a
little off about the other guests. Superficially, they seemed normal
enough, but their costuming was very dark, almost uniformly black and
bloody. I had seen enough adult Halloween parties to know that only a
few adults tended to go the straight horror route; most acted out some
cheerier fantasy. Here there were no beauty queens, no prince charm-
ings, no historical heroes, no rock stars, just a salute to the fears buried
in our collective psyche: skeletons, vampires, werewolves, ghouls, grim
reapers, dark and distant figures I couldn't quite place. Aside from the
grim costuming, the "guests" were convincing as real partygoers only
as long as I didn't study them closely. They swirled around on the dance
floor from time to time, but in a very mechanical way. They conversed,
but again, from the few snatches I caught, the conversations seemed

contrived, the words of poorly scripted background characters, not real people.

I glanced at Nurse Florence and could see in her eyes that she had noticed the same wrongness but did not know quite how to address it. Once again I visualized guitar strings stretching from my mind to the minds of everyone around me. I imagined them thrumming with the thoughts that were rushing toward me. Then reality hit me with the force of a tsunami.

Aside from my actual allies, the rest of the Annwn Six, the other band members, and Coach Miller, there were no minds in the room. Well, no human ones anyway. From the security men, I could feel some dark, savage consciousness, more Neanderthal than contemporary. From the other party guests, nothing. Emptiness. Void. They appeared to be there, but as I had so often discovered in the past few years, looks can be deceiving.

No real guests meant no real reason not to cut us down right now, where we were. Winn could make her move at any time. I tried to probe the minds of the security men, but all I could get was a powerful sense of mission and a sense of expectancy as they waited for some signal. Beyond that, their minds were too inhuman; try as I might, I was just not used to reading beings of their kind.

When Winn had actually planned to strike, we were never to find out. The attack was set off prematurely when Shar stumbled in the flickering, pseudo-candle lit semi-darkness and fell right into one of the "guests," who must have inadvertently touched Zom and vanished in a quick pulse of green light. Shar, confused and thinking himself under attack, drew Zom from its scabbard, its dull green glow shining surprisingly bright in the near darkness of the room. The "guests" recoiled, as if instinctively, from that light, my other armed allies drew their swords, and security tried to open fire.

At least my efforts at learning how to disable guns had not gone to waste. Disabling the guards, however, might prove more difficult. It was hard to tell in the miserable lighting, but they suddenly seemed taller, bulkier...

Crap! We were facing a small army of shifters!

The band had naturally fallen silent as soon as the green flash on the dance floor had caught everyone's attention. They were even more stunned when the rest of the "guests" dissolved. Carrie Winn must have been watching somehow and figured there was no point in wasting the energy required to maintain such an elaborate set of illusions now that we knew they were illusions. I turned to the band members and shouted, "Stay here! Hide if you can!" with so much magic force all of them ran for cover immediately. Well, all except Carla.

Damn! Just what I did not need at this point!

Somehow, she realized we were in danger, and she so strongly did not want to be separated from me that she had shaken off my first command and run toward me. Dan, Stan, Gordy, Shar, and Carlos were already in defensive position, and the security men were charging. I had only seconds to get Carla out of the way, if that.

"Tal!" she said frantically, throwing her arms around me. For an instant, I got a loud, staticky burst of her thoughts. Hell, not only was she frightened for herself, but for me as well. Apparently, she had been crushing on me for months, but my preoccupation with Eva and with the various threats all around me had blinded me to it. Time froze for an instant as her inmost desires throbbed into me, her heartbeat almost driving out my own. Everything, even her fantasies, rushed into my mind so potently that I nearly lost my grip on reality. In that frozen instant, I found myself bathed in warm water, wrapped in steam in a shower Carla had been sharing with me in her mind for some time, a shower in which the warmest thing was not the water but her naked body passionately locked with mine. At the same time, I was hit by an image of Carla, dressed in stark black, weeping at my funeral, her mood even blacker than her dress. Her desire and her fear, opposing images, pulled my mind toward chaos.

Either I had lost control of my ability to read minds, or Carla had some kind of magic herself. Either way, I had to snap out of this, or all would be lost.

I dragged myself out of that frozen instant, every mental muscle aching from the strain, and shoved her away roughly, longing for the feeling of her in my arms yet knowing that that feeling would undo me.

"Carla, get to safety!" I commanded, again hitting her with everything I had, and this time, pale-faced and teary-eyed, she seemed to comply. I spun around, jumped off the stage, and drew White Hilt.

And that was when I found out that Carrie Winn had yet another surprise for me. The moment White Hilt should have burst into flames, the darkness in the room surged toward it, engulfed it, smothered its light. This was no Celtic magic I had ever seen. Clearly, she, like me, had been experimenting, and with considerable success.

My friends were badly outnumbered, but even though the security men had morphed into something stronger than normal humans, the magic swords helped keep the battle from being lost, especially since the guards had no weapons besides their useless guns and had to depend on morphed claws. Gordy's fear aura had no effect—Winn had prepared her men to resist it, no doubt—but his weapon still had all the advantages of an unbreakable, ever-sharp faerie sword, and Gordy wielded it well. Stan, now again enfolded in his greatly expanded muscles, did equally well. Carlos' blade, about which Winn knew nothing, did its drowning trick well on unprepared opponents. The virtue of Dan's sword was more defensive, but he waded forward fearlessly and did as much damage as anyone. The real star, though, was Shar wielding Zom, another of the swords about which Winn knew nothing. Every successful hit, even if it did not draw blood, ruined the shift and returned the shifter to his normal form in a greenish burst. Well, at least the form that was their default now. I knew from their psyches they were not truly human, but they looked human enough. Winn must have done something to them to bury whatever their true form was. Of course, they could have been human sorcerers, but I saw no sign of magic except the shifts.

I tried to will White Hilt's flames to bite through the encrusted darkness. Winn's spell was strong, but given time, I thought I could beat it. I could feel the darkness shudder and struggle each time I focused.

The problem was, I didn't really have the time to mess with it. My friends were running up against the same problem I had hit in fighting the *pwca* weeks ago. It is one thing to train with a sword, another to use it in combat, and the more successful my friends were initially, the more the carnage overwhelmed them. Adrenalin can only do so much. Already, the floor around them was a bloody pool, strewn with severed limbs. Survival instinct kept them going, but they were losing momentum, and more shifters kept pouring in. Where could Winn have found so many?

"They're not human!" I yelled, charging forward, sending a surge of numbness into them, trying to get them through what would be a horrible situation no matter what I did. I sang then, pushing each of them into the highest gear of which they were capable. At some point Nurse Florence appeared by my side, having somehow magicked Coach Miller to forget about her and help the other students find their way out of Awen. Her face a mask of strain, she seemed to be trying to heal our team on the fly, or at least keep them from bleeding when shifter claws raked them.

Still singing my song of empowerment, I again tried to free White Hilt. Then, realizing what I had to do, I ran toward Shar. I could feel Nurse Florence's disapproval, but she was too preoccupied even to call out to me. She thought I was charging into battle when I should have focused on support, but I had something else completely different in mind. I broadcast to Shar what I needed, and as soon as the opportunity presented itself, he drove his sword down on White Hilt, which rang with the impact. In a greenish flash, the darkness splintered and was gone. I backed up a little as White Hilt flamed. The darkness tried to regroup, but sluggishly, and I was ready for it, slicing it with white-hot flame, shriveling it with White Hilt's might focused with laser-like accuracy. It was hard to maintain my song and fight the darkness at the same time, but I managed it long enough to beat the darkness, at least for the moment. To make sure, I sent a few thoughts through the lighting system and turned the room lights on. My guys were dazzled for a moment, but the shifters, who I suspect had shifted their eyes to give themselves night vision, were momentarily blinded. Before they recovered, I used a wall of flame to drive them back and out of the door, after which I crafted flame barriers to cover all the possible entrances, careful not to start a conflagration, at least until I checked the whereabouts of Coach Miller and the other students. I had to keep feeding those barriers, of course, but with no shifters in the room, I could at least stop singing and conserve some of my energy. Nurse Florence helped by trying to feed me as much of her energy as she could spare—

a good thing, as it turned out, since sculpting White Hilt's flame into multiple barriers rather distant from each other was more draining than I had anticipated. Even if she helped, I doubted I could keep that tactic up for very long.

"What's our next move, Tal?" asked Shar. I glanced over at him. Even his trained-to-perfection arms were shaking ever so slightly, as were Dan's. Gordy looked glassy-eyed. Carlos kept trying to find a way not to look at the blood, limbs, and corpses. Stan was shaking visibly, shaking all over. All that mayhem, even against non-humans, was clearly taking its toll. I could sing them back into some semblance of fighting readiness, to be sure, but there were limits, and I would crash into them before very long. Nurse Florence could keep us all going longer. The question was, how long before even her considerable reserves were exhausted. She already looked a bit unsteady, and certainly more pale than normal.

"How many more shifters left?" I asked her. "It's hard for me to read them from a distance and keep the doors warded."

"I think we killed about a third of them," she said in an almost impassive tone with just a hint of a quaver.

I could see all of the guys sagging at that revelation. I had fought one *pwca* before and been so unhinged by the whole experience that Dan had had to carry me at first. They had had to become killing machines. Yeah, they had had more chance to prepare themselves psychologically, but how does someone really do that?

Abruptly, Stan started crying. He was doing it as quietly as he could, but in the comparative silence of the room, everyone noticed.

Reflexively, I moved in his direction, as did Gordy, but oddly enough the person who hugged him first was Dan.

"It's okay, Stan. We will make it through this," he said with a confidence he clearly did not feel. It was at that moment I became convinced that we wouldn't.

"Is it time to retreat?" I asked Nurse Florence. "He who fights and runs away lives to fight another day."

"Find Coach Miller or one of the students with him and check their situation, Tal." The one I found most rapidly was naturally Carla, who was still broadcasting her thoughts pretty loudly. I slipped into her, viewed the scene through her eyes, and then pulled out quickly. Being that psychically close to her started weakening my grip on reality almost instantly.

"They didn't escape," I reported. "I couldn't stay connected long, but from what I gather, the front door is warded in some way. They are hiding nearby in hopes of making a run for it if someone opens the door." I paused and sent my mind swirling toward the exits I knew of. "It looks as if all the possible escape routes are warded."

"Just as I feared," said Nurse Florence slowly. "Carrie Winn can't afford to let us retreat and has taken steps to make sure no one can leave. We know too much, I think, and there are too many of us, enough to raise quite an uproar if we managed to get out. Not just us, but the others Carl has downstairs. I'm afraid that if we try to leave now, it may occur to Winn to take them hostage. Or, if we try to get to the front door and have Shar cut through the ward with Zom, Winn will throw every last shifter she has left into that area. We might be able to survive, but at least some of the others will not in that kind of all-out fight. If we keep pressing the attack, there is a chance Winn won't pay much attention to the others. We still have to defeat her to make them safe permanently, but at least we have a shot at keeping them all alive that way."

Carlos became suddenly more alert. "Should I go to protect…them?"

"We can protect them best by keeping Winn's attention diverted, as I have just said."

"I don't know," I said. "I just don't know if we can win. And I think we have a decent shot at getting everyone out if we can move quickly."

"Nurse Florence is right," said Stan weakly. "We've played almost every surprise we have already. Winn, or at least her minions, have seen all of the swords in action now. She knows Tal can hex technology. Now she can develop counter-measures at her leisure and then come after us, probably pick us off one by one. If we are going to beat her at all, we have to beat her tonight."

"We're pretty exhausted," I pointed out.

"So must she be. Look, Tal, I know you've been throwing magic around ever since we got here, but so has she. And we haven't seen any of the shifters do anything magical except shift, so as far as we know, all of the magic, including a whole ballroom full of illusionary guests and a spell strong enough to choke White Hilt, has all come straight out of her. Wouldn't that pretty well drain her?"

Nurse Florence was clearly impressed by his acumen. "Yes, I believe it would."

"Are we sure we are up to this?" I asked, looking at Stan a little more pointedly than I intended.

"Okay, I cried a little. Sue me. You've been known to cry in the past yourself."

"I know. I'm sorry, Stan, I didn't mean it like that. What do the rest of you say?"

"If Stan's in, I'm in," said Gordy simply.

"We have to see this through now," said Shar. Dan and Carlos both nodded.

"Well, okay then." I smiled weakly. "Watch the doors. I'm going to drop the barriers and see if I can find Winn."

I let White Hilt rest as I spread my mind out gradually, reaching, searching, probing every inch of Awen. As my thoughts rose higher, I encountered more resistance, but I thought I could sense Winn at the very top of the structure.

"There is one hell of a lot of magic in the air, but I think I can sense her on the roof. There are a lot of shifters in that area, too, as far as I can tell."

"The roof it is, then," said Dan. "How do we get there?"

"I thought we might need to know that kind of thing," said Nurse Florence, "so I studied the plans on file with the city inspector's office." You could pretty well guess how she must have gotten her hands on those. "There is a stairway up each of the four corner towers, and there appears to be roof access from each one. That's a risky attack route, though. If Winn knows we're coming, as she almost certainly will, all she has to do is have shifters right outside the door from the tower. They can all attack the person at the front of our line."

"That will be me," said Shar, brandishing Zom, "and I can take on all the shifters if I have to."

"Don't get too cocky," cautioned Nurse Florence, "but you are right. The shifters are uniquely vulnerable to your blade."

There was no sign of shifters at the moment, and we moved to the stairway without incident. It occurred to me that Winn might want us on the roof, though it was equally possible she was hiding there until she had the next attack organized.

Cautiously, we climbed the narrow stairs. I sang softly, gradually rebuilding our fighting morale without draining myself any more than necessary. It seemed to help everyone else, but my own heart remained strangely untouched. I had the increasingly strong conviction that we were climbing to our deaths. I checked to make sure it was not another ambient mood altering spell, but that had seemingly vanished as our band had performed earlier, and it did not seem to have reappeared. Still, I could not shake a feeling of foreboding.

When we finally reached the door to the roof, Shar flung it open, and we raced out as fast as we could. Winn did not attempt to block the door with shifters. Clearly, she didn't need to. As soon as we were out, we saw a vast horde of shifters, more than we had expected. But that was not what confirmed my growing dread.

We also came face-to-face, not just with Carrie Winn, but with Morgan Le Fay as well.

THE FINAL SHOWDOWN

I TRIED to evaluate the situation as fast as I could. Stan's whole argument for attacking had been based on the premise that Winn was the only spell caster on her own side, but there were clearly at least two. I spent a second being shocked by Morgan's presence—wasn't she imprisoned in Annwn? Then I remembered it was Carrie Winn who had told me that in the first place. That cleverly planted piece of disinformation could now cost us dearly.

Judging from Morgan's pale, exhausted look, she had been primarily responsible for all the magic we had seen, though the uniqueness of some of it suggested that Carrie Winn had given her a few tidbits from Winn's own magical research. In any case, Winn was looking both well rested and triumphant. Not only that, but the shifters were clearly readying themselves to charge us. We were outgunned magically. Our only hope was to cut through the shifters and hit Winn before she could launch a major arcane assault on us. Even before the shifters, though, there was the matter of Morgan. Shar had never seen her before and seemed confused. In his moment of hesitation, I heard a sound all too familiar from previous lives, the twang of a bow, and suddenly an arrow pierced Shar's right shoulder. Zom slipped through his suddenly limp fingers and went clattering to the ground. Winn may not have anticipated that I could disable all the guns, but she had had some time to dig up a bow and find someone to use it.

I drew White Hilt and conjured up a wall of flame in front of us, but clearly, that was a stopgap measure at best. Whoever the archer was would be unable to see through it, and it would keep back the shifters, but it would do nothing to stop Morgan or Ms. Winn from hurling magic at us. Nor would Nurse Florence, tending the badly wounded Shar, be able to lend me much energy now.

With Shar down, I needed to think about who could best wield Zom. I might have been inclined to pick Dan, but he appeared to have numerous wounds that only his current sword was keeping from bleeding. Stan wasn't trained in two-weapon fighting, and using Zom instead of the sword of David would deprive him of his strength boost. Carlos was the least experienced swordsman.

"Gordy, take Zom!" I yelled. He stepped forward without a question, sheathed his fear sword, and picked up Zom, raising it above his head.

I could hear Morgan beginning a spell, and, though I could not hear much else, I knew that Carrie Winn would be doing the same. Letting the wall of flame down long enough for anyone to charge Morgan, however, would invite the shifters to attack. Still, there seemed no other option. Gordy could now run through the magical fire unharmed, but he was the only one, and if he punched through it, there was a good chance it would collapse anyway.

"Guys, charge Morgan and eliminate her. I'll try to keep the shifters off of you." Dan, Stan, Gordy, and Carlos moved forward. I dropped the flame wall, and all four of them charged the suddenly terrified Morgan, cutting down a couple of shifters near enough to assist her. She had a defensive wind going already, and the others slowed, but Gordy, immune to anything she could dish out, kept coming. He would be on her in seconds.

And then an arrow pierced his side. He gave a heartrending scream but tried to let his momentum carry him toward Morgan to get in at least one good sword stroke—and with that sword, one stroke would be enough. Morgan threw herself back, and he fell before he could reach her. He was coughing up blood, and I feared the arrow might have pierced a lung.

I managed to get a flame barrier up just before the wave of shifters hit them. One or two lunged through the flames, screaming and burning but, like Gordy, trying to maintain enough momentum to slam into what was left of our fighting force. Stan lopped off the head of one, but the other one screamed right past Dan and Carlos, landing on top of poor Gordy and ripping Zom from his limp hand. The moment the shifter touched the sword, he reverted to his natural form, and the flames, supernatural in origin, stopped burning him, though the burns he had already sustained would not be healed that way.

With Zom in the enemy's hands, defeat had just become inevitable. The shifter spun around and tore the sword through my wall of flame, collapsing it in one stroke, and the other shifters dashed forward. Carlos, Dan, and Stan formed a circle around the fallen Gordy and did their best to cover each other and him, but it was clear that they would eventually be overwhelmed. I shot bursts of flame into the shifter ranks, and that tactic might have been enough to stave off defeat, but the shifter with Zom charged me, and I had to focus on defending myself or be cut down where I stood.

I couldn't use White Hilt's fire against him, but he did not seem to be as good a swordsman as I was. Then I realized two things. First, the shifter seemed to be holding back. I made a couple of fatigue mistakes, and he failed to exploit them. Either he was content to prevent me from helping the others or outright unwilling to harm me. Second, and supporting the latter idea, the archer who had cut down Shar and Gordy should logically have taken aim at me and had not. I thought back to the first attack in the ballroom, and it seemed to me that when the security guards aimed their guns, none of them had aimed at me.

Carrie Winn wanted me alive.

Well, that was a bargaining chip of a sort, if I could figure out how to use it.

At that moment Shar tackled the shifter, who was so surprised he lost his grip on his sword.

"He's not completely healed yet," said Nurse Florence in my mind, "and I think the archer will try to take him out again. You have to find that archer."

Shar had grabbed Zom again and ran the shifter through before he could get back up. But then Shar hesitated a moment, perhaps dizzy. I encircled him in flames while he recovered. Then I started burning as many shifters as I could hit in the group encircling the rest of our fighters. A few of them had already been drowned by Carlos' sword, while others had been wounded by Dan or Stan, but all three of them were taking damage too. All the while a barely conscious Gordy was still coughing up blood. As for me, the pounding in my temples told me that I could not keep aiming my fire in two different directions. That kind of move was a strain when I was fresh, let alone when I was nearing exhaustion.

"Tal!" Stan yelled desperately. "Gordy's dying!" Nurse Florence was trying to move toward Gordy, and I did what I could to keep shifters off of her, spreading myself still thinner. Then an arrow whistled past her, narrowly missing.

It was about that point that I started praying. In the course of my lives, I have practiced many religions. My current family raised me Episcopalian, but I had been more or less Christian almost since the days of Taliesin 1. I can't honestly say I prayed much normally, and I hoped I wasn't so superficial as to be acting just on the "there are no atheists in the trenches" idea. But I wanted so badly to keep my friends alive, and I didn't know what else to do.

Then a darkness blacker than the night sky hit me from all directions, extinguishing the fire of my blade and suffocating me. It was much like Morgan's magic from earlier, but this time clearly fueled by Winn's much less exhausted magic.

What's the old saying? "Prayer is always answered, but sometimes the answer is 'no'"? I kept praying nonetheless, at the same time reaching as far into myself as I could, pulling out every remaining ounce of energy, focusing and singing, the latter much harder now that it seemed the darkness was almost solid, pouring in through my mouth and nose, racing to my lungs, smothering me in a surprisingly literal way.

With my fire out, I knew that Stan, Dan, and Carlos would be quickly overwhelmed, that Shar would probably be hit by another arrow. I had at most seconds to beat this spell.

I spent those seconds picturing who I was fighting for: for Stan, who had been by my side unfailingly; for Dan, my rediscovered childhood friend; for Gordy, whose loyalty would put most people's to shame; for Shar, whose integrity ran deeper than I had ever thought; for Carlos, newly joined to us but already risking his life alongside us; for Nurse Florence, ever self-sacrificing; for my band, who taught me to love music even before I was any good at it; for Eva, my first love; for Carla, perhaps my next one; for other friends, and even for Coach Miller, who certainly deserved better than to be murdered in some back hallway in Awen. They would be a lot to lose, too much to lose.

I could feel the energy building in me as my blood filled with adrenaline, as my heart pounded like a drum. I focused everything on driving back the darkness yet again. I sang, and my voice ripped through the darkness. I swung White Hilt, and it flared to life. Precisely at that moment, Zom cleaved the air around me, and the attempts by the darkness to rally itself against my attack dissolved. Shar was at my side again.

I was unsteady now, visibly unsteady, but I had to get closer to the others. Shar, understanding, took my left arm, and we half-ran, half staggered, toward where Stan, Dan, and Carlos, drenched with the mingled blood of shifters and themselves, were making what was all too clearly a last stand. Nurse Florence had somehow managed to reach them and was standing in their midst, doing everything she could to keep Gordy from slipping away, but she herself was wounded and would clearly not last much longer.

When we were close enough, I surrounded all of us with flame. I could no longer handle raising such a barrier from a distance, and I did not know how much longer I could guide White Hilt's flame at all. Still, for the moment this was not a bad defensive position. We were all together and shielded from physical attack, and Shar could ward off magical attack with Zom.

The problem was, a defensive position was not enough. We needed a way to beat Winn, not just have a standoff with her—and I couldn't think of a way to beat her under the present circumstances.

"Winn!" I yelled. "Carrie Winn!"

"What are you doing?" hissed Nurse Florence, her eyes never leaving Gordy.

"What I have to!" I whispered hoarsely. "Carrie Winn!"

"You wish to surrender?" She spoke to me through the wind rather than shouting back, so I answered the same way.

"After a fashion. It is me you want. I know that. If you let everyone else go, I will surrender myself to you for whatever purpose."

"NO!" Stan shouted. The others agreed as forcefully. Even Gordy seemed to be muttering "no" over and over again.

"This is the only way I can save you now," I told them.

"Perhaps," Carrie Winn mused, "with their memories properly cleansed, I could free your friends."

"I would require a very specific oath," I replied. From Taliesin 1's memories, I knew how tricky supernatural beings could be and how careful one had to be in negotiations with them.

"And I would require the same, of course," she said in a gracious tone I was sure was completely fake.

"Viviane!" called an unfamiliar, Welsh-accented female voice so close at hand it made me jump.

"Vanora! It's about time!" It was then I realized this must be the one member of Nurse Florence's order who had had to take a later flight and thus survived the plane crash. Not exactly the cavalry, but she just might do in a pinch, especially if she was a decent spell caster.

"Some shifters spotted me downstairs, and that slowed me down a bit. Taliesin!" Vanora called out to me directly. "Open this side of the flame wall and make room for several more people in there."

Several more people? Perhaps the cavalry after all!

But the people who came through, aside from Vanora, filled me with horror: Coach Miller, with all the students who should have been hiding downstairs. I was so shocked I almost forgot to close the wall behind them. Winn was speaking to me on the wind again, but I told her I needed a minute.

"What the f…" I began.

Even Nurse Florence looked shocked. "Van, these people shouldn't be here!"

"Neither should you," said Coach Miller, putting his hand on her shoulder. "Once your friend took your spell off, I knew exactly where I needed to be. To hell with where I should be."

"Vanora!" said Nurse Florence angrily. "I sent them away on purpose."

"You know as well as I do that if you lose up here, they are all dead anyway," replied Vanora simply. "Eva and I have told them what is really happening, and they want to help." I looked daggers at Eva, but she ignored me. "There are musicians here to back up Taliesin, and the rest are willing to lend as much energy as they can. You know we can use that.

"Taliesin, organize your volunteers," she continued. "I got them on to the roof under an invisibility spell, but it won't be long before Winn senses what is happening."

I had the band members stand close to me for more a capella reinforcement. Not accidentally, Jackson stood to my right and Carla to my left, with her arm around me.

"I knew," Jackson whispered to me, "I knew I wasn't crazy, despite what I saw at Founders' Day."

Carla's presence was strong, and at that moment I knew for certain that she had magic of her own, though she did not seem to be aware of it. Fortunately, she wasn't broadcasting her sexual fantasies at the moment, but instead using visualization techniques it was obvious Vanora must have shown to all of them, sending me images of light, images of friendship, images of strength. Almost despite myself, my mood lightened, and again I dared to hope.

The others clustered around Nurse Florence and Vanora, who would channel their energy wherever it was most needed.

"Well?" asked Carrie Winn impatiently.

"Well," I said, as my fellow musicians began to sing with me and new power poured into me, "Deal's off!"

During the last few minutes, I had managed to locate the archer, apparently invisible. His mind, though, was not invisible to me, and I used it to aim a bolt of flame that incinerated the bow in one stroke and left the archer, hands badly burned, unable to use another if one happened to be at hand.

My mind reeled as shifters indiscriminately threw themselves against my fire. Just a few moments before, their onslaught would have overcome me, but now, reinforced by the music of my friends and refreshed by their energy flowing into me, I gathered myself together quickly, made the flames even hotter, and sent them exploding into the ranks of shifters standing far from where the wall had been only seconds before. The smell of burned flesh sickened us all, but the shifters had suffered massive casualties. Gordy was still in too bad shape to join the attack, but Dan, Stan, Carlos, and Shar flung themselves into the confused ranks of the surviving shifters, wreaking havoc. I yelled to our new backup crew not to watch what was happening. Some had already seen and were shaken, but I gave them credit for continuing to concentrate.

With the shifters suddenly finding themselves on the losing end of the battle, I started launching fireballs at the far end of the roof, where Winn and Morgan were standing. I knew they could probably shield themselves with rapid wind to deflect the flames, as indeed they did, but as they long as they were occupied that way, it would be hard for Winn to strike back with magic at my fighters, who were advancing steadily in her direction. At least, that was what was supposed to happen. I ought to have known there would be at least one more hitch that night.

Yeah, I could see clouds forming with unnatural speed above us, but I thought it was just another effort to rain on White Hilt's parade, and I was ready for that. What I didn't see coming was a barrage of lightning. Thank God it started slowly, but I knew it might speed up as Carrie Winn got rolling.

After one uncannily close lightning strike, Vanora directed all her attention to countering the storm, but it was more intense farther away from us, where our four champions had been beating the shifters until they had had to start dodging lightning bolts. I was so proud of how much they had learned to work as a team when I realized that they moved into tight formation around Shar. Zom would prevent a lightning hit close enough to affect him, and he could swing the blade to cover someone else if the need arose. Supporting his tactic, I cast a major burst of speed into him, giving him a better chance of deflecting the blasts. He probably still wasn't literally fast enough to deflect oncoming lightning, but his rapid footwork effectively prevented any lightning strikes nearby.

Then the rain poured down in gallons, soaking all of us in seconds, pounding us harder than any natural rain would have. However, this tactic produced mixed results, since the shifters were as much affected as we were. To be sure, it was harder to keep White Hilt going, but I had it blazing with such intensity that so far even such a heavy rain was creating massive amounts of steam—and also creating weather I could exploit to create another hurricane. Winn must have remembered that, because pretty soon the rain stopped abruptly, though the lightning continued, more or less a waste of energy on Winn's part, since Vanora was keeping it off us, and Shar was still keeping it off the fighters.

By now the shifters had realized that simply increasing size and muscle mass wasn't enough to win this battle, especially as their numbers were becoming depleted at what to them must have seemed an alarming rate. One of them farthest away from our advancing fighters was even trying to become a dragon, an effort that was clearly beyond him, and the result so far was more like a slowly churning blob. Others more realistically seemed to be trying to grow dragon scales as a way of protecting themselves from sword blows—not a bad idea, except that we had Zom, and no magic countermeasure could prevail against that. A few tried becoming gigantic, but that too was a transformation requiring time they did not have, and if some seemed close to succeeding, I redirected my fireballs.

I was tiring, however, and I could feel the energy reserves ebbing away. After all, I had been burning through magic like crazy for the better part of an hour, and I had already been nearly spent before this battle started. It was a miracle that the extra help I was getting had lasted this long. I looked at the students standing behind me, and the strain showed clearly on their faces, not only in their expression but also in their pallor.

I looked back at the battle. The shifters were nearly done. Seeing through Stan's eyes for a moment, I could see that Winn looked nearly as exhausted as I was, and Morgan was spent. We had clearly given Winn more than she had bargained for. Yes, we could not keep up the magic much longer, but neither could she, and at this point the physical side of the battle was ours. It would not take longer than five minutes for my brave friends to reach her, and her wind defense could not hold back Shar. Check and mate.

And then Winn spoke to me through the thunder, no doubt an attempt to be intimidating. "Taliesin, surrender yourself, or your friends will suffer!"

"Your attacks have failed," I shot back through the wind. "My friends have nothing to fear from you. It is you who need to fear them!"

"I don't need to hurt them physically to make them suffer. I can just awaken all their past lives and watch their minds shatter. I did it with you, after all. You had a strong personality like the original Taliesin in there to help you hold everything together. They may not. Do you want to take the chance?"

"You can't hurt them mentally or physically," spoke Nurse Florence in the wind. "If anything happens to them at your party, you could ruin the life you've built."

Only one row of shifters stood between my men and Carrie Winn. I was surprised she was continuing this conversation rather than making good her escape. But perhaps she had been too arrogant to have an escape plan.

"Really? For such clever people, you are incredibly dense sometimes. I have enough shifters downstairs to double for all of them. That was the plan to begin with, you know—they all end up dead, and the shifters fill in long enough to divert any kind of suspicion from me."

Yeah, I know—we hadn't taken that strategy into consideration. All our calculations about the safety of my friends went up in smoke in seconds.

"I see we need a demonstration," thundered Winn. I switched to "Stan cam" and realized to my horror that she was aiming right at him. Fortunately, so did Shar, and Zom swept between Stan and Winn, dissipating the reddish blast of her spell before it could strike him.

One of the shifters had managed to become a nine-foot giant and had a sword—Mordred's sword, Clarent, to be exact. It rang against Dan's blade and pushed him back. Unfortunately, the shifter should have thought more about speed than strength. Yes, he could deliver a mightier blow than even Shar or magically muscled Stan, and he could have beaten any one of them, but he was facing all four by this point, and he couldn't move fast enough to parry all of their thrusts. He focused on Shar to ensure that Zom couldn't touch him and shift him back to human form. His skin was toughly scaled enough to deflect Dan's and Stan's blades, but he had no defense against Carlos's blade's drowning effect—one nick, and he started running out of oxygen. Winn managed to heal that wound and stop the effect, but Carlos struck again and again and again, faster than Winn could heal him. The few surviving shifters were imitating his example, though, which meant more work to get to Winn than I thought. I had to consider moving up closer and bringing White Hilt to bear on the remaining shifters while I still had the energy.

Winn must have realized that she couldn't heal her minion fast enough and that she couldn't hit anyone near Shar with her awakening spell. She shot a wild blast in our direction, catching us by surprise. Apparently, this spell was not as influenced as most by distance. I had time to realize it was pulsing toward Carla and moved to step in front of her.

What might have happened if someone already awakened had been hit by that blast I didn't get to find out then because Vanora tripped me. I was out of position, and Carla took the full blast. Her scream tore my heart in half, and she clutched wildly at her temples. The other band members stopped singing and looked at her in horror.

"Carla, Carla! I'm here!" I tried to yell over her screaming, but my attempted yell came out like a hoarse croak.

Then I got a psychic blast of the chaos in Carla's mind. If her earlier broadcasts had been uncontrolled, these were a thousand times worse. Used as I was to this kind of thing from my own experience, the collision between my mind and the fragmented pieces of what used to be hers almost made me lose my grip. They did shatter the energy-sharing ties Vanora and Nurse Florence had built up so laboriously, and my fatigue crashed into me so hard I almost dropped Carla.

"I'll take care of her!" said Vanora, trying to pull her away from me. "Focus on the battle!"

"You, you did this! I could have…"

"Died," said Vanora firmly. "I don't think you could have survived a second shot of a spell that powerful."

I wanted to question how she could possibly know that, but I was too furious to really have a coherent conversation, and Vanora was right about one thing—I needed to focus on the battle. That would be hard to do even if I cared nothing about Carla, given the amount of psychic static she was putting out, but other lives might be at risk if I didn't find a way to shield myself from her. Vanora was trying to put her to sleep, which at least took the edge off the chaos.

Moving more sluggishly than I wanted, I looked out through Stan's eyes. He and the others were on the verge of finishing off the shifters, and the lightning storm was fizzling out, so Shar had used his enhanced speed to outflank the shifters completely and was throwing himself straight at Carrie Winn, whose shield of fast moving air would not stop him. In seconds Winn would be dead.

As focused on Winn as Shar was, I missed until it was too late the fact that Morgan had been making herself inconspicuous nearby. Shar never saw the blade coming, but it dug deep into his side, and he crumbled to the ground. I switched to his perspective long enough to realize that his hand was still clenched tight on Zom's hilt, so at least no one could hit him with a spell while he was down. I could feel warm blood leaking from his side at a frightening rate, though, and he was very near to losing consciousness. I had to get closer!

This time it was Jackson and George who helped me reel in the direction of the battle. Everyone else was moving, except for Vanora, who was still tending the now sleeping Carla, but they moved in slow motion. Gordy was up and carrying his sword, with Nurse Florence cautioning him that he was not fully healed yet. The others, drained of energy as a result of their contribution to the battle, were half staggering, half walking, like zombies in a cheesy horror flick, but they were all moving, as I was, toward what was left of the battle.

When I got close enough, I used what fire I could muster to help finish off the shifters. Carrie Winn, her own strength fading, her own reflexes slowing, was not fast enough to stop me.

She was, however, fast enough to zap Stan with what I recognized, with a sickening jolt, was the awakening spell.

He too screamed and fell to his knees, dropping the sword of David and becoming just plain old Stan again. Well, physically at least. Psychologically he was dissolving into recollections of hundreds of past lives.

I grabbed him and forced his head in my direction. "Stan, I will help you get through this," I said, my voice trembling, but with just a little undercurrent of magic to back me up. I think he heard, but I wasn't sure.

Surprisingly, Nurse Florence and Gordy were almost upon us. Carlos and Dan were both poised to take on Winn, but she was holding them at bay with the threat of the awakening spell, though it was clear they would charge her anyway. Morgan lay nearby, seemingly unconscious. I realized that, even having seen her stab Shar, Dan and Carlos had both still hung on to the fact that she was human and tried to avoid killing her.

"You can't take down both of us before we can get to you," said Dan, softly but menacingly.

"Fighting your way through this high wind? I can take down both of you without giving it a second thought."

"Stop this!" I said, cautioning Jackson and George with a glare not to follow me. "All right, Ms. Winn, I'm ready to bargain."

This time Stan was in no position to argue, but Dan said, "The hell you are," and it was clear he and Carlos might try to block me if I moved forward. I could feel Nurse Florence's scrutiny, but her real focus was on Shar, whose side she reached while I was still contemplating my options. That also put her in between Carrie Winn and me. Well, she would probably have to focus all her energy on Shar to save him, particularly in her current state. That just left Dan and Carlos, both tired and relatively sluggish. Gordy had finally made it to the scene, but he was even more sluggish and completely focused on Stan. He held Stan in big brotherly arms and whispered reassurance to him. Stan seemed to be twitching more or less mindlessly. I forced my attention back to Carrie Winn.

She had dropped any pretense of friendliness or even civility. "Why should I bargain for something I can now so easily take? The awakening spell is a surprisingly low drain on me. I can just cast it on the rest of your friends, and then you will be alone, and you will be mine."

"Surely it would be easier without all that spell casting. Same deal as before?"

"Oh, you mean before you and your allies killed almost all of my shifters? I think not. The best I could do now would be an oath to use the awakening spell on no one else here."

Carla and Stan would be stuck coping with what Winn had done, probably without my support, because whatever Winn wanted, I doubted I would ever be free to just walk away—if I were even still alive. But at least no one else would suffer the same fate. I had to put my faith in Nurse Florence and Vanora to be able to nurse Carla and Stan back to health. I had made it back on nothing but emotional support from Stan and my parents. With more help, surely they would eventually be all right.

"Everyone here also goes free, and you never make a move to harm them again?"

"This grows tiresome," said Winn irritably. "Call off your little foot soldiers, and come to me."

"He doesn't give me orders," snapped Dan. "And I'm under a *tynged* to protect him."

"Pity," said Winn, raising her hand to strike him too with the awakening spell.

"NO!" I yelled, trying to move forward, but doing so with frightening slowness. "This is between you and me, and I'm surrendering. Just let them go."

Winn seemed hell-bent to hex Dan, but at that moment Carlos threw his sword straight at her. His strength plus the inertia of the sword traveling forward kept the blade from being completely deflected, though it struck Winn in the shoulder instead of the heart as he had probably intended. Having prepared no protection against the sword's drowning effects, she immediately began struggling for breath. She was also bleeding fairly profusely from the wounded shoulder. Her air currents began to subside as she labored to heal herself.

Dan saw his opportunity and moved in, but just as he reached her, she demonstrated she had been faking to some extent. With uncanny speed, she scratched Dan in the arm with Carlos' sword, and Dan immediately fell backwards, gasping for breath, though at least his own sword kept him from bleeding. Winn was not even short of breath, so clearly she had already healed the wound inflicted by Carlos's sword. Carlos moved forward, but now Winn's magically animated air began to stir again, and she waved his own sword at him, forcing him to back off. Nurse Florence, still working on Shar, whose bleeding she had at least stopped, lunged for Dan to heal him before he drowned.

I was close enough to see how old and tired Winn looked. Perhaps my bargaining position was better than I thought. I'd bet my tired fire could kick her tired wind's butt. Morgan was still unconscious, and I had at least the currently unarmed Carlos, who, even exhausted from the fight, was still easily able to overpower Winn. Together we stood at least a chance of getting the sword away from her.

"Maybe," I said to myself, "I don't even need to surrender. Maybe we can still win."

I noticed Winn was backing up a little. Carlos followed, which worried me, but he was being cautious, ready to dodge a spell if the need arose, and Winn's attention no longer seemed directed at him, or even at me.

It was then I noticed what was behind Winn, what she was trying to inch toward inconspicuously.

Or rather, which two things—I wasn't sure which one was her immediate objective.

Right behind her appeared to be an ancient altar carved from dark gray stone. I could see it vaguely; most of it was in shadow. But there was something disquieting even about its outline. No, not disquieting, downright sinister. Something more than merely optical, something instinctive. I wanted to get away from that altar. It was taking me every ounce of will I had not to run screaming in the opposite direction. Instinctively I knew that this altar had been the source of Carrie Winn's new, very un-Celtic forms of magical attack.

Almost next to the altar was an enormous cauldron, faintly glowing, at least to my magically attuned eyes. It was not so much frightening as oddly familiar, tugging at a very distant memory.

Carlos tried to charge the seemingly preoccupied Winn, but the storm around her held him back. I moved forward, running various plans over in my mind.

From somewhere Winn had picked up a darkly gleaming *athame*, and before we really knew what was happening, she slashed her own left palm, then slammed her bleeding hand down on the altar surface.

The whole altar began throbbing redly, radiating a light that seemed more like darkness, a hot color with a bitingly cold feel. The air filled with screams, and I knew with absolute certainty that this was some kind of sacrificial altar. Well, not some kind. The human kind.

Bathed in that reddish glow, Winn no longer looked old and tired. Too late I realized that she was drawing power from the blood sacrifice. I raised White Hilt, and its flames pierced the darkness, but I had already waited too long. The wild winds around Carrie Winn intensified and expanded, knocking Carlos aside effortlessly, blowing White Hilt's fire almost sideways. I doubted her renewed energy would last long, but it didn't seem as if it would have to.

Then I remembered Zom. It should still be near where Shar lay. Perhaps he was even still holding it. If I could find it fast enough, I could counter whatever Winn had planned. I cursed myself for not remembering it sooner.

I turned away from the altar. My eyes had started blurring, and I tried to remember where Shar had fallen in relation to where I was now. It should be a relatively straight line if I could manage one in this wind. I took a few uncertain steps forward—and then a darkness blacker than the night blocked my path.

No, it was not another effort by Winn to animate the darkness. It was my old friend, the *Gwrach y Rhibyn*, ugly, long-clawed, and dark as always—and it looked mad enough to chew swords.

Well, it had, after all, predicted my death weeks ago, and I was still very much alive. From what I recalled, *Gwrach y Rhibyn* sometimes fulfilled its own prophecies if they weren't coming true fast enough. I held White Hilt between us, but the creature made no hostile move. Instead, it looked at me with its piercing eyes and wailed, as if it were me, "My friends! All my friends!"—a clear prophecy of the death of everyone who had joined me on this quest.

White Hilt flashed, and with one good swing I lopped off its head, which thudded onto the roof and rolled a bit. Its body shuddered, then dropped emptily, its neck still burning a little from White Hilt's fire.

"Oh, shut up!" I muttered as I pushed myself forward.

"Come back here!" yelled Carrie Winn, once again through thunder. "If you don't, I'll awaken the rest of your party before you can reach me with that damned sword."

She had guessed my strategy and my psychology. I was no more able now than I had been a few minutes ago to let more of my friends suffer. I turned back toward her and walked slowly in her direction, giving myself time to make sure there was nothing I was overlooking.

Winn seemed to have used some of her renewed energy to charm my nearby friends to sleep. Nurse Florence and Dan, for instance, were both out cold, though thankfully Dan was breathing normally, so Nurse Florence had gotten his wound healed. The band members and the people who had donated their energy to the earlier battle had all fallen more or less where they stood, too tired to have much hope of resisting a sleep spell. I think Carlos had been knocked out earlier when he got blown off his feet. Shar, even if awake, was only partially healed when Nurse Florence had had to switch to Dan, so I doubted very much that he would be able to intervene. I thought I could hear Gordy talking to Stan, so Gordy might have been out of range when Winn cast the spell, but he wasn't exactly working at one hundred percent of his normal fighting capacity either. Anyway his presence was maybe the only thing holding Stan together, so it was just as well if he stayed with him. I assumed Vanora was doing the same for Carla, and better she also kept doing what she was doing.

In the end, I guess I always knew it would come down to Winn and me.

And I guess I knew I probably wasn't going to make it.

No, I didn't have a martyr complex, and I certainly wasn't suicidal. But, except for my parents, practically everyone I really cared about was right there, on that roof. What would you have done? Let them all die? Probably not.

The closer I got to the altar, the more I could hear the screaming, presumably echoes of the victims sacrificed on it for God knows how

BILL HIATT

many millenniums. The cacophony was almost more than I could bear, but I knew I had to keep thinking clearly.

"Your oath?" I said as she kept motioning me forward.

"I swear not to awaken anyone else here. Now, come here! I grow impatient."

"Swear not to harm any of them and to let them go, or there is no deal."

She looked at me disdainfully. "Okay, have it your way—there's no deal!" Before I could react, she hit me with a sleep charm on steroids. I resisted falling asleep, but the unexpected attack stunned me. Already shaky, I dropped to my knees, and White Hilt clattered to the ground, its flames winking out. Belatedly, I realized I should have handled things differently, but it was too late now.

I would die—and everyone else would die, too. I would die for nothing.

I reached for White Hilt, but a shoe painfully crushed my hand against the surface of the roof. Looking up, I saw that Winn had evidently summoned a couple of the shifters she had been holding in reserve to take our places after she had killed us. The battle over, she must have decided she could risk bringing a couple of them out.

They dragged me to my feet and then toward the altar. I struggled, but my attempts were far too feeble to be more than a minor annoyance to them. I started to sing, and predictably one of them smashed me in the mouth. I should have been getting used to that by now.

Before I knew it, they were tying me spread eagle on the altar and ripping open my shirt.

Though the altar was stone, I could feel it pulsing hungrily beneath me, waiting to drink my blood. By now the screaming was deafening.

I suddenly became aware of Carrie Winn looking down at me.

"Pity you didn't let me bed you," she said, brushing her hand across my chest with surprising gentleness and sounding almost wistful. "Well, no time now, I'm afraid. It is almost midnight. Gwion Bach, it is at last time for you to pay back what you owe me."

Gwion Bach?

Finally, I realized who Carrie Winn was.

BACK TO THE BEGINNING

Gwion Bach was one of the few lives I could not remember clearly. I had read the stories. Hell, I had read every word about my earlier lives I could find. But in the case of Gwion Bach, the stories seemed just that: stories, too mythical to be true, even in a universe in which magic existed.

Yet here was the artifact I now recognized as the cauldron of inspiration, where the witch Ceridwen had brewed the great potion, the first three drops of which would grant wisdom and poetic inspiration. Ceridwen had planned to give those three drops to Morfran, her incredibly ugly son, as a way of compensating for his ugliness. Unfortunately, she had a boy named Gwion Bach continuously stirring the potion, and he inadvertently splashed it on himself. Reflexively, he licked his burned thumb, in the process drinking the three precious drops. According to the story, Ceridwen pursued Gwion, presumably to find some way of undoing what he had done. However, he had already figured out from his new knowledge how to shape-shift, and so Ceridwen pursued him from form to form, until at last, he tried to hide as a single grain of corn, and she became a hen and swallowed him. (You can see why I had trouble swallowing this story—pun intended.) As often happens in Celtic tales, after swallowing something strange,

Ceridwen found herself pregnant. She knew the unborn child must be Gwion Bach, and she resolved to kill him, but when he was born, she did not have the heart to. She did have the heart to sew him in a bag and throw him in the ocean, though. Go figure! Anyway, as often happens in myth, he did not die but was found on the coast of Wales by a prince, Elffin ap Gwyddno, who named the child Taliesin and raised him as his own.

Yup, Gwion Bach was me, though I still couldn't remember that life. Clearly, though, Carrie Winn could remember, and at least the potion of wisdom part of the story must be true; the presence of the cauldron confirmed that much.

Except for those of you who can't figure out a book without *Spark-Notes* by your side, I'm sure you have realized by now that Carrie Winn was Ceridwen (the witch in the story, not the Wiccan goddess of the same name.)

I tried hard not to dwell on the fact that Ceridwen, who was in at least one sense my mother, had been trying to have sex with me just a few weeks ago. Yuck! Way too Oedipal for my tastes.

"So, what's the plan, Mom?" I asked, my voice dripping with sarcasm, trying to sound disdainful in a desperate and probably not completely successful effort to cover up the fear clawing at my heart. Okay, so this might not have been the best time for sarcasm, but I was already tied to a bloody altar vibrating with the screams of its previous victims, my chest bared for the knife. I doubted I would have ended up playing Canasta with her no matter what tone I used.

"You always were a saucy one, Gwion—at least in any of your lives in which I have encountered you. Well, the plan is simple. Apparently, the cauldron of inspiration cannot produce another potion as long as its previous recipient still lives."

"The original Taliesin died 1500 years ago or so."

"Yes, you did, but you kept reincarnating, and the cauldron somehow knew you were out there, even when you yourself had forgotten the incredible knowledge that you possess." Behind her, the two shifters had lit a fire under the cauldron and started stirring.

"I have been waiting all these centuries for a way to separate you from the knowledge you stole. I had a spell that should have done the

trick, but I tried it and failed more than once. I finally realized that you
need to not only have that knowledge but remember it. The spell for
awakening your past lives took years to perfect, and several people I
tested it on died. Eventually, I found a way to cast the spell without
killing the target. Even so, I couldn't get the spell to work on young
children, so I had to wait until you started puberty."

"You've been watching me for four years?" I asked. The thought
made my skin crawl. I thought she had only been aware of me since
Stan broke my *tynged*. For the first time, I began to question that whole
idea. Where had I gotten the notion of a *tynged* requiring secrecy in the
first place? Could Ceridwen have planted it in my mind herself as a way
of keeping me isolated? Perhaps.

"Silly boy. I have been watching you since you were born. One of
the advantages of the wealth I amassed over the centuries is the
resources it affords me to keep track of you each time you reincarnate.
Those resources also built a town I knew was just perfect to attract your
parents, so I could keep you in one place and close to me without
arousing suspicion." I must have looked incredulous at that point.
"Don't underestimate your importance, or rather, your wisdom's importance. Yes, Santa Brígida was built as a trap for your family, built from
hints I drew from their own minds in various ways."

Santa Brígida was based on what my parents wanted? Damn, and I
thought my mom at least had better taste!

"We'll be ready in a few more minutes, Ms. Winn," said the shifter
stirring the cauldron.

"So, what does this spell involve?" I asked, doing a pretty good job
of keeping my voice steady.

"I won't bore you with all the details. The key part of the ritual
involves cutting your heart from your chest and throwing it, still beating, into the cauldron, then casting a powerful spell amplified by your
blood running onto this very ancient altar."

"Just killing me in some more mundane way wouldn't do it?"
Damn, my voice cracked a little on that one.

"I'm afraid not, Gwion. There is that pesky reincarnation to think
about. You see, the best part about this spell is that it traps your soul in
the cauldron. No reincarnation. No cozy Episcopalian heaven. No

sipping apple juice with the old gang in Avalon. Whatever you might have expected after death won't happen. Just one endless stretch in the cauldron, knowing you are trapped but having no way to escape."

I had steeled myself for death, but now the adrenalin numbness was wearing off, and I had not expected to be condemned to some kind of claustrophobic hell inside Ceridwen's cauldron.

I had never been so scared in any of my lives. I started to pull against the ropes, but they were thick and well tied, and I was exhausted anyway. Ceridwen laughed at my pathetic efforts.

"Ah, not as brave as you thought? I knew it all along. You were a coward as Gwion Bach, you were a coward as Taliesin, hiding behind Arthur's warriors and singing your songs, you were a coward more than once when I caught up with you in other lives. Crying, begging, pleading. I thought maybe this time would be different, but I guess not."

Abruptly someone nearby started cursing Ceridwen in fluent Italian. The tone was very different from what I was used to, but the voice had to be Carla's. She was coming up rapidly, and I had been right about the magic. I could feel her power even through the frenzied outbursts of the altar.

I wasn't sure whether to be pleased or horrified. Carla seemed to have bounced back faster than I could have hoped. Except it wasn't Carla. A possible danger in pulling oneself together after an awakening is that a past life personality is stronger than your present life one might be in charge. There were a few days when I literally was Taliesin 1. He relinquished control in the end, but a more determined, less ethical past self might theoretically stay in control for a whole lifetime. The personality controlling Carla's body at the moment was very strong from what little I could tell. On the other hand, it did seem to be listening to present-day Carla. I knew Italian well enough to know whoever Carla was at the moment was trying to defend me.

If Carla was up and around, surely Vanora was about to pop up. From my admittedly limited view, it looked as if Ceridwen and two shifters were the only enemies around, though I knew there were a few more in the house. If I could get free, though, there might still be hope.

Under normal circumstances, someone operating at Carla's power level would have given Ceridwen pause, but unlike Ceridwen, the person controlling Carla hadn't been steadily researching magic for hundreds of years. Whoever it was was not necessarily less powerful than Ceridwen, but definitely less skillful.

Really, the battle was over before it began. Ceridwen raised her hand and cast what I realized with horror was the awakening spell.

What had Vanora said? "I don't think you could have survived a second shot of a spell that powerful." Well, if I couldn't, how was Carla going to do it?

I screamed and thrashed, another pathetic display, but Carla hit the ground with a sickening thud, perhaps dead, perhaps just broken beyond repair. I almost passed out at that point. (Yeah, screaming and fainting, just the sort of things heroic deeds are made from.) However, I was dimly aware of Vanora starting to attack Ceridwen, and then realizing Carla's plight and becoming distracting by it. Silence fell too quickly. At best Vanora was unconscious. At worst, she too was dead.

"Is it time?" said Ceridwen in obvious impatience.

"Two more minutes," replied one of the shifters.

"Well, I guess it wouldn't work to rush. My, Gwion, you do have a surprising number of allies for someone trying to hide who he really is."

I thought that I could say the same about her, but I was too weak and overwhelmed now even to talk. What would be the point? What energy I had I focused on a little prayer for Carla. I wondered if I could still pray when my soul became trapped in the cauldron. If I could still think, perhaps. Ceridwen had implied I could. As much hell as that would be—certainly, oblivion would be better—maybe it would somehow be worth it if I could still pray for Carla. My mind felt as if it were unraveling, but I didn't care.

Two minutes passed with uncomfortable rapidity, and Ceridwen raised the *athame*, ready to plunge it into my chest.

"I'll never get to say goodbye to my parents. They won't even know I'm gone at first. They'll think some shifter is me," I thought to myself in what I was sure would be the last few moments of my life.

However, I had made a number of miscalculations that night, and that was one of them.

Much later, Gordy told me what had happened. Stan had come to, well sort of—as with Carla, the controlling personality in the body wasn't really Stan at that moment, but current Stan seemed to have some input, again as with Carla. In any case, "Stan" convinced Gordy he was all right and that they both needed to defeat Ceridwen, which Gordy was more than happy to do. Both of them were relatively far away on the roof and effectively off Ceridwen's radar. Stan had them sneak cautiously toward where Zom and White Hilt had fallen. Carla and Vanora inadvertently created the perfect distraction. There was not much cover on the roof, but it was dark, and Ceridwen's attention had been pulled away at the very time she would have been most likely to see them. Then, at the point when Ceridwen was awaiting the precise moment to tear my heart out, they reached the swords. Stan grabbed White Hilt, and Gordy took Zom.

All my focus had been on the blade ready to descend on me, but a battle cry in ancient Hebrew captured my attention, and Ceridwen's. (You might think, wow, typical unrealistic villain move—why didn't she finish you? Actually, though, just killing me wouldn't serve her purpose. She needed to make sure whoever was attacking did not disrupt the ritual, or she would have to go through the whole process again in my next life.)

Ceridwen darted away from me to intercept a new set of attackers, dropping the *athame* and picking up Carlos's sword. I twisted my head as much as I could. I didn't have the best view, but I could see Stan carrying a flaming White Hilt. Whoever he had been in the past included at least one person the sword chose to respect. I wasn't sure, but I thought I sensed something else, a new power vibrating within the sword as well. Stan couldn't do all the tricks I could with it, but at the end of the day, a flaming sword through a shifter's heart does get the job done. Gordy took the other one down, and then both of them turned on Ceridwen.

Stan was fighting without all the extra muscles, but there was something different, some new agility to his movements. He had been practicing with a sword, and he had been working out, but there was still something uncanny about the way he moved.

Gordy, on the other hand, was not fully healed, just as Nurse Florence had said, and the combat with the shifter had not left him in good shape. He coughed, and a little blood came out. I didn't think he could hold up too long if his lung wound had opened up again.

Ceridwen seemed to have made a bad strategic choice by charging Stan and Gordy with a sword. Even with Gordy rapidly losing strength, she was no match for them with a blade, but with both of them on her, she could not retreat very easily. Then I realized what she was doing. With both shifters down, she needed to position herself to attract their attention and keep them from knocking over the cauldron or doing something else that would wreck the spell before it could even begin. The winds raged around her again, keeping Stan's blows from connecting. Gordy hung back, confused and obviously forgetting he was holding a sword that could cut right through her defenses. I didn't think I could yell loud enough to make myself understood.

I searched quickly for Shar and Carlos. Both of them seemed conscious...barely. They wouldn't yet be able to do much, and it probably wasn't safe for Shar, only partially healed as he was, to try.

I tried sending a message to Stan, but the odd state of his mind at the moment cut me off. I tried sending one to Gordy and realized that the blood loss was pulling him toward unconsciousness. He may have heard me, but he just swayed a little. Clearly, standing up was an effort.

Pulling at my bonds was clearly not doing anything, so I tried singing to them. I didn't have much music left in me, or much magic either, but I did feel the ropes begin to loosen. If only Stan and Gordy could keep the witch busy long enough, I might just be able to do it.

But then the altar itself started resisting me. It wasn't exactly sentient, but it wasn't your typical inanimate object either. The dark magic for which it had been a tool over the millenniums had built up a mindless but formidable hunger within the stone, a hunger that would not be denied. It wanted my blood, it needed my blood, and it was going to get it one way or another. I could feel it fighting me, holding the ropes in place, needling me in the back with tiny stone slivers.

Ceridwen had risen into the air, an astute move just in case Gordy came around enough to use Zom properly. She seemed to be inviting them to throw their swords at her, but neither fell for that ploy, and Zom, which would have made it through her defenses, Gordy probably wouldn't be able to throw with enough force to do the job. At least Stan was feeding whichever past life persona was in charge of his body enough information that he stayed close to Gordy, in case Ceridwen tried to hit him with a spell. Once she was airborne, she did try more than once, but Stan reached over and touched Zom's hilt, which seemed to be enough to ward him effectively.

The altar continued to claw at me, so much that it tore through the back of my shirt in several places. The tears were tiny, but they were enough to let those stone splinters gouge me. I started bleeding from several tiny cuts, and I could feel the altar getting stronger, more aggressive, with each drop of blood that hit its stone surface.

Knowing I could not use a direct mental connection with Stan, I sent my voice to him on the wind. "Stan, Gordy's about to drop. Take Zom, and use it to destroy the cauldron."

The unfortunate part about using the wind like that is that someone else who is nearby and magically sensitive can also hear what you are saying. Ceridwen raised both cauldron and fire into the air in a single, elegant gesture. They soared until they were out of reach of any possible attack by Zom.

"Stan, the altar!" I yelled through the wind. I doubted Ceridwen could lift such a massive stone slab as easily as a metal pot.

She did, however, try. I felt the altar shudder, and I could swear it got a couple of inches off the ground. I looked up and could see Ceridwen's face twisted with pain. She needed more power, but the only obvious source was the altar. It had plenty, but she seemed to have to touch it to tap that power, and that would mean descending to within reach of Zom.

Stan tried to get Zom away from Gordy, but Gordy, confused and not much better than semi-conscious, did not let go. The real Stan could have gotten through to him more easily, but whoever was in charge at this point evidently didn't know how to talk to him. Seeing the confusion, Ceridwen shot down toward the altar, clearly intending to power up and then levitate the thing out of reach.

I might have stopped her if I had just been free, but what power I could muster was not nearly enough to beat the altar, and it kept getting stronger, using my own blood against me. By now I must have had a hundred cuts on my back, and the altar kept jabbing away, making more by the minute.

"Ceridwen," I croaked when she got close enough, "this damn altar is killing me." She was certainly an odd person to appeal to, but she desperately needed me alive until she could cut out my heart herself. As horrified and exhausted as I was, I could still appreciate the irony.

She could see I was right, but her solution was to drain the altar, taking all of its power into herself. As she pressed her palm against it, and become surrounded by its red non-light, I did indeed feel the jabbing and cutting beneath me begin to slow.

Abruptly Stan loomed up with Zom in his hand. Ceridwen had strategically placed herself on the other side of the altar, so she could fly up out of the way if needed before he could get to her, but even if she had the strength, she couldn't possibly raise the altar fast enough.

Zom came crashing down on it with a dull thud and its signature green flash. On some level, I had hoped that one blow would turn the whole altar instantly to dead stone, but it was too powerful for that. Just as Zom initially killed only the flames in one spot when it hit White Hilt, so on the altar, the red glow faded out only in the immediate area where Zom had hit. Stan struck again and again and again, each time dulling a new piece of the altar. I felt it convulsing beneath me, but it did not give up. Indeed, my bonds grew tighter, until I feared the ropes would cut off circulation altogether.

Ceridwen could see that if she kept draining the altar, she would only hasten Stan's effort to kill it completely. Instead, she rose slowly into the air, taking the altar with her. At least that was the plan, but every blow of Stan's shattered her levitation spell and let the altar crash down into the roof, which would eventually collapse in that spot if the battle continued for very much longer.

When it first crashed down, Stan deftly slit the bonds on my left hand and tossed me White Hilt. Using it left-handed was awkward, but that had been the only side Stan could reach, and in three quick, flaming strokes I had freed myself.

Desperate from the steady sapping of its energy, both from Ceridwen and from Stan, the altar had tried to strengthen the ropes, but they were after all just ropes, and no match for a flaming sword, even backed by whatever force the altar was putting out. As I was about to jump off, however, the altar made one last, desperate attempt to stop me. Where it had been using mere splinters of rock, it thrust a dagger-sized chunk up into my back, piercing me between the ribs and causing blood to gush out. I managed to roll off the altar, but I knew the wound was serious—as if I hadn't been in bad enough shape already.

I expected to hit the ground awkwardly. Instead, I found myself rising upward, drawn into the air by Ceridwen. I was so taken by surprise that I let go of White Hilt, making my situation even more dire. Below me, Stan was doing his damnedest to finish off the altar, newly refueled by yet another dose of my blood, but it was now all too clear that he was moving too slowly, too worn down himself to really get the job done. He was unable to deliver the kind of forceful blows he had been accustomed to using without the increased muscle mass derived from his own sword. Worse, as he got sluggish, the altar began to regenerate its power faster than he could take it away. Eventually, it would run out of energy if it drank no more blood, but before then Stan looked as if he might drop. We seemed to be losing on all fronts.

Ceridwen flew close to me, just far enough away to be out of range of my sword.

"Well, Gwion, your friends are a more potent force than I gave them credit for. But it won't matter. I don't really need the altar for this spell —it was just insurance. Besides, it is stronger than even I understood. I think it will exhaust Stan despite his sword. Then perhaps it will drain his blood if he falls too near it and happens to lose his grip on that sword.

"As for you, well, here is the *athame*, and there is the cauldron, very near to us. It would have been easier to do this on the ground, but I can just as easily cut your heart out from here—and this time none of your friends can intervene."

I saw that Ceridwen intended to cut out my heart by using her levitation skill on the *athame*. I could probably have beaten back that attack if I had still had White Hilt, though my mind was getting progressively fuzzier. Before long I would be less use than Gordy. If I intended to make a move, it had to be now.

The weakness in Ceridwen's position lay in the different objects she had to control separately. Focusing on one levitation would be okay, but levitating multiple objects—herself, the athame, the cauldron, me—and doing something different with each would drain her far more quickly than she realized. I was willing to bet she had seldom if ever actually done something like this, but I knew from the experience of sculpting White Hilt's flame in multiple directions simultaneously just how taxing such concentration could be. It would be easy to err, easy to lose control. That's why I pretended to be unable to dodge when the *athame* flew toward me, that's why I let it cut into my chest, dangerous as that was. Doing that kind of maneuver would require even more intense concentration from Ceridwen and make it even more difficult for her to control everything else. I could already tell that she had allowed the whirlwind shield to dissipate, believing herself safe from any conceivable attack.

As soon as Ceridwen committed to trying to cut out my heart through telekinesis, I reached out with what little magic I had left, grabbed hold of the air current she was using to raise me, and propelled myself right at her, colliding with her as forcefully as I could. She tried to grab the handle of the *athame* and finish cutting out my heart— result-driven to the very end—but I knocked her hand away and pulled out the *athame*, then turned it on her. I was probably too weak to drive the knife into her chest, and I knew it, so I struck at her arm instead, making a sizable gash and forcing her to divert part of her concentration to stopping the bleeding. She did manage to grab my right arm and keep me from attacking again with the dagger, but I managed to punch her in the face before she grabbed the other arm. She was amazingly strong, certainly stronger than I was in my current condition, but the blood loss would weaken her soon enough, and I kept struggling, so she had to keep part of her focus on me, which in turn slowed down her effort to stop her own bleeding.

As we struggled, she lost control of the cauldron, which went crashing to the roof below, probably not breaking, but certainly spilling its precious potion. At this point she realized that she was not going to be able to complete her plan tonight; there would simply be no way to complete the cauldron preparations again, and I could tell from the look in her eyes she could not complete the process of binding my soul in the cauldron without whatever the fluid was.

I was dimly aware of Stan below us hacking away at the altar. It was still regenerating, but much more slowly without a blood source, and he was using the hardness of his blade to actually knock chunks of it loose. Whoever was in charge of Stan's body was every bit as determined as he could be. He might just beat the altar after all.

I felt a subtle shift in Ceridwen's energies and realized that she was about to open a portal into Annwn, presumably to escape there. I knew if I let her get away, she would raise another army of shifters and come at us again and again, and if she couldn't trap my soul in her cauldron, she could at least take from me everyone I cared about. But if I clung to her and went through the portal with her, I wouldn't probably be strong enough to deal with her on the other side, let alone whatever awaited me there.

I could feel the portal opening, and my struggling against her was not breaking her concentration on it. However, to concentrate on it, she had let her control of the air currents grow very slack. I knew the altar was directly below us. Again I grabbed the currents, this time dissipating them and putting us into free fall with her on the bottom. She had not expected this move, and she tried to fight back, but we fell too quickly for her to entirely counter the move. She slowed her descent, just as I had hoped she would—I really wasn't trying to die. Still, we hit the altar with a bruising thud. I managed to roll off quickly, but Ceridwen did not fully realize her danger until it was too late.

You see, by now the altar had been thrown into blind panic. Even the most loyal dog may bite its master at such a time, and Ceridwen was only the latest of many masters. Stunned by her fall, she lay still for a moment, and the altar, having tasted a few drops of blood from her arm wound, reacted to the blood source as a necessary way to renew its power and fight back against Stan. Like me, her back was pierced with a hundred splinters, but this time they were larger and more insistent.

Whoever was controlling Stan tried to reach for her, but I managed to warn him back.

"It is God's will," I said in the same ancient Hebrew he was using. "Let God's will be done, for is it not written, 'He who lives by the sword will die by the sword?'" Too late I remembered I was quoting the gospel of Matthew, which someone speaking ancient Hebrew would neither know nor acknowledge, so I hastily changed direction. "She has brought this abomination among us. Surely it is only just to let her suffer from that which she would have inflicted upon us." I think Stan's current persona was skeptical, but there must have been enough of my Stan still present that he was willing to trust me on this. He went back to hacking away at the altar, making it all the more frantic to drain Ceridwen of every last drop of blood, which is what it did, or so I'm told. When I passed out, her raucous screams were still filling the air.

THE END?

WE WON THAT NIGHT, and Ceridwen would trouble us no more, except in the nightmares most of us had for some time after. Well, unless she caught up with some of us the next time she reincarnated, but I decided it was better not to dwell on that idea too much.

The altar had in its own way been even harder to beat. Whatever Ceridwen had thought she was going to do with it, it had proved more powerful—and more evil—than even she had ever imagined. Stan knew that, as did whichever past self of his was controlling his body. While I was out cold, he was hacking away at that altar, chipping it away one splinter at a time. The others revived one by one and helped as much as they could. Having drunk Ceridwen's potent blood, its power flared again, and it was nearly dawn when Stan, praying fervently in ancient Hebrew, finally dealt the blow that killed the last of the magic within it. By that time, I was conscious again, as was almost everyone else. Vanora and Nurse Florence had done as much as could be done to heal the worst of the injuries and get all of us back on our feet. Soon we would go home to make what excuses we could. This time there would be no shopping trip to buy replacement clothes, but the fact that we had been at Carrie Winn's dealing with an emergency, as verified by Nurse

Florence and by Carrie Winn herself, would probably get us all off the hook.

And how, you might ask, would we explain Carrie Winn's bloodless corpse? The short answer is, we wouldn't have to. Ceridwen wasn't the only one who could shapeshift. Vanora had apparently always foreseen the possibility that she would need to stay here in Carrie Winn's form in the event Winn died in some kind of showdown with us. The few shifters still left in Awen would be sent packing back to Annwn, believing that Ceridwen was sending them back. Her human staff, who had all been given the night off, would come in from their quarters at the back of the estate, or from their homes in places like Carpinteria or Santa Ynez, to find a kinder, gentler Carrie Winn. They would not find evidence of battle, which would be tucked away beneath illusions until Awen could be properly repaired. The extra artifacts, like Mordred's sword and Morgan's dagger, as well as the fragments of the dark altar, would be sent back to Wales, to be dealt with appropriately by the ladies of the lake. Morgan herself had disappeared sometime during the climactic battle, but I couldn't summon up the energy to worry about that yet. Aside from that, pretty neat and tidy, huh? Well, not quite!

My mom is always telling me to count my blessings, so here they are.

First, and miraculously, everyone lived, and with no permanent physical damage.

Second, I got Stan pulled back together, though it took quite a lot of effort. My mental state had been chaos most of the time when I was first awakened. The problem with Stan was, his condition looked an awful lot like really severe multiple personality disorder, with the part I thought of as the real Stan very seldom in outward control. The Israelite warrior who had been so helpful on Samhain seemed to be the default personality in the early days, and though he drew enough on Stan to accommodate modern life, his characteristics and desires were almost nothing like Stan's. I couldn't get him to even touch a computer at first, and you can imagine how Stan's parents reacted when he announced he was dropping out of school to join the Israeli army. Oddly enough, they didn't institutionalize him right away. His mom turned to me, of all people, to help, and I did. I talked with him, sang to him, magicked him, and eventually the Stan I knew reemerged, with quite a lot of school work to catch up on, but otherwise unscathed. Oh, like me he was not exactly the same person he had been before the awakening, but he was back into being the math-science genius, back into working his recently developed popularity with cheerleaders, back on track for Stanford, though he still talked occasionally about joining the Israeli army after he finished his under-grad work. "We'll see," was the most he got from his mom on that one. Most important, at least from my point of view, we were back to being best friends—the Israelite warrior knew who I was to Stan but never warmed to me himself; I think the suspiciously unbiblical nature of my abilities was off-putting to him. Anyway, Stan treated me like a brother, and a brother from whom he had been separated for years and finally managed to rejoin. Like me, he could access memories and skills from his past selves but remain in control himself, so there was little danger that any of them would come between us again. There was one change in our relationship, but it was a good one. Back when school started, he was in some ways more my sidekick than my equal—he had been right about that, though I never consciously tried to put him down. Now we could be not only friends, but equals as well. For some reason, he wouldn't tell me who the warrior inside him was, but White Hilt thought enough of him to flame for him, so clearly the sword viewed us both as worthy. Also, perhaps because he was working out so hard, perhaps because of all the magic that poured through his initially frail adolescent frame, he was finally catching up with me physically. With Gordy's encouragement, he even made the wrestling team. I know, who would have thought!

Third, I didn't have to hide who I was anymore, at least not as much. Aside from my bound allies, the band knew, and the rest of the students who had been in Annwn on Founders' Day had had their initial, seemingly crazy vision of me confirmed. Nurse Florence had wanted to call them in one at a time and erase those memories, but I talked her out of it. They all agreed to keep my secret, and frankly, it was nice to have at least one person in each class who knew what was really going on. It made me feel less like an intruder from some other plane of existence.

Fourth, besides Stan, I now had other strong friendships that I could rely on. Dan and I were as close as we had ever been, even in the inno-cent childhood days playing soccer together. Shar, Gordy, Carlos—we all hung out with each other and with Dan and Stan, of course, when-ever we could, and we all knew that any of us had all of the others' backs. Even Jackson from the band became closer to me than ever before. Musicians in the same band aren't automatically friends, but we were now.

Fifth, my relationship with my parents, while not perfect, was better than it had been for four years. They both made every one of my soccer games—yeah, I did end up going out for soccer, just like Dan wanted— and I knew Dad had to do some pretty elaborate schedule juggling at work to make that happen, but he always pulled it off. If my dad still wondered about my sexual preference, he gave no outward sign. They were both as proud as could be of all my accomplishments, and, damn, when I thought about it, I could really pat myself on the back for quite a few things now.

Okay, so you've noticed I haven't mentioned Carla. If you really want to know, it's hard for me to even think about her situation, let alone talk about it. The second blast of the awakening spell was not fatal, as Vanora had feared, but it did leave her comatose.

I visit her every day after practice, and if I'm late for dinner, my parents never bust my chops about it. She has a doctor who believes strongly that any kind of familiar company helps, so the nursing staff doesn't bug me too much, even if I stay a little after visiting hours. I bring her flowers. I talk to her. I sing quietly to her. I hold her hand. I kiss her every so often when none of the nurses are around. I know, it's probably childish to play Prince Charming and try to awaken her with a kiss, but I've seen more desperate ploys than that work, and you know it. Not this time though. Her lips are warm but unresponsive. I look into her eyes, but no one looks back. I try to read her, but I hit a blank wall. And that powerful magic I felt from her before? Gone without leaving a trace.

At least I know Carla is getting the best care possible. "Carrie Winn" has been donating massive sums to the facility Carla is in, which now has state-of-the-art equipment and a considerably larger staff than it used to. I suppose I should go thank Vanora some time, but I haven't spoken to her since Samhain. I know she thought she was doing the right thing when she tripped me and kept me from taking the spell meant for Carla, but I can't make myself forgive her. Yeah, I could be in that bed instead of Carla—but most of the time I wish that is the way things had turned out. I know I sound ungrateful. I know God probably thinks that, but I hope he understands.

I didn't used to be much of a churchgoer, but now I go every Sunday, without fail, and I pray like it is going out of style, I sometimes pray at night until I fall asleep. I know my friends pray, too, even the atheists, though I'm pretty sure they're just humoring me.

The funny part is that everyone assumes I'm Carla's boyfriend. Unless you count our brief encounter in the band van on Samhain, we've never really had a conversation about much besides music, and we've never really had a date, much less had sex, though for some reason the guys all seem to assume that somehow we've been intimate. When that was supposed to have happened in those last, hectic days before Samhain, I don't know, but even Stan at one point seemed to have bought that theory, and I know my dad does—but if you think about it, he would be the most eager of all to embrace it. For the other guys, it might have been the only way they could explain the intensity of my feelings toward Carla. Hell, even I couldn't explain them to myself. I was beginning to have feelings for her, sure, but now it felt as if we had been in love for years.

Even stranger, her family operates on the same premise—well, except for the sex part. I often have dinner at the Rinaldis', and aside from consuming more pasta than I have before in six lives, I feel surrounded by their love, just as if I were a member of their family. Yeah, really weird, because I'm not even sure they knew my name before. At most, they knew that I was in the same band with Carla, and I know they didn't much approve of her singing because they never showed up to any performance. Now, damned if Mr. and Mrs. Rinaldi and Carla's little brother, Gianni, don't show up for most of my soccer games, and sit with my parents just as if they are all in-laws. Gianni plays soccer himself, insists on calling it "football" as Europeans do, and wants to be on the team in high school. Sometimes we kick the ball around a bit in the park closest to his home, though I usually have to stop those sessions faster than he wants and go somewhere else quickly. I don't want him to see me cry. I know, more macho silliness, but that's the way it is. He does remind me so much of her, and of what happened on Samhain, that there are times when being with him is like trying to crawl through barbed wire. That isn't his fault, of course. It's ironic that whenever I read him, he has the same feeling of gut-wrenching help-lessness, of wanting to save his big sister and not knowing how to. He feels guilty for absolutely no reason, his guilt a childish reflection of my own, much deeper, much more realistic guilt. Somehow, I should have protected her better, maybe found a way to keep her away from Awen completely. Well, I can't change her past. Maybe I can change his future. I know he is lonely without his big sister, and I know he always wanted a big brother. Maybe I'm a poor substitute for the real thing, but I'm going to do my damnedest to be whatever he needs me to be. I guess I need to spend more time with him, and if that means he'll see me cry from time to time, so be it. Besides, Stan kind of graduated from that "little brother" spot in my heart to "brother." That leaves a hole that is just the right size for Gianni. When I was counting my blessings, I should have included the Rinaldis, perhaps a bittersweet blessing now, but I'm betting it is the sweet part I will remember years from now.

As I leave Carla's room, I sometimes lean over and whisper in her ear, "Don't forget, you still owe me a shower!"

There are times after that whisper when I can see the ghost of a smile on her lips. At least that's what I tell myself, anyway. Everybody else calls it a trick of the light, or something like that.

And sometimes, when someone tells me that, I go home, lock myself in my room, and don't come down for dinner. My parents have never bothered me during those times, even if perhaps they've heard a sob or two. I could tell they wanted to, but they left me alone, gave me some space, which was really what I wanted.

Most of the time, though, I successfully paste on a fake smile for my friends and family. Yeah, there is a lot to smile about for real, and I do have many blessings to count, but it's hard for me to feel anything but miserable. I have tried, I really have, but the best I can manage these days is numb. People tell me that time heals all wounds. I don't know whether that's true or not, but right now I kind of doubt it.

But you know what? I don't care what anyone says. I don't care if every flicker of consciousness I see is just wishful thinking. I won't give up on Carla, I just won't. If I have to keep coming back to her bedside until I'm ninety, and nothing changes, and I finally die there, well, so be it. I'll tell you one thing, though—if I die that way, I will be smiling... for real.

Because if I die that way, at least I know I will have done everything I could.

And somewhere, somehow, she will know it, too.

ACKNOWLEDGMENTS

As John Donne wrote, "No man is an island, entire of itself." My students over the years have provided much of the inspiration for this novel, and my colleagues have made its creation possible, because without them, I would be a very different person now, and probably not one with the desire to write—or teach. They have kept me sane during good times and bad.

A NOTE ON THE GEOGRAPHY

The story is set in Santa Brígida, an imaginary coastal town between Summerland and Coast Village, just a little east of Santa Barbara. There wouldn't really be enough room for such a place to fit, so you have to imagine a somewhat longer coastline that what exists in reality, with inland territory to match.

A NOTE ON WELSH FOLKLORE AND OTHER MATTERS

I began this novel with the intent of being true to the Welsh folk tradition. In other words, though this is fantasy, not a factual work on Welsh mythology or folklore, I wanted to draw the details for material such as the nature of monsters and the way magic works as much as possible from early Welsh sources. I suppose my teaching background pulled me in that direction; in the classroom one of my goals has always been to get students to learn as much as they can about other cultures. Unfortunately, modern readers have different expectations than those of early medieval audiences and are certainly curious about different things, with the result that relying on unaltered medieval material as the basis for a modern novel leaves gaps a modern reader would find unsatisfying, particularly since I was not creating a retelling of Welsh myths but a story set in modern times. In addition, with regard to the Arthurian materials, modern readers are used to later versions that draw on the early Welsh tradition but include many other elements as well. Finally, I had to come to terms with the fact that I was writing fiction, not a factual study of the early Welsh tradition. In the interest of the story I wanted to develop, I ended up keeping as much Welsh material as I could but also used some non-Welsh sources and a considerable dose of imagination. I hope if any lovers of the early Welsh literary tradition honor me by reading my work, that they will not be too offended by my deviations from that tradition. I take comfort from the fact that early Welsh writers handled the sources before them in much the same eclectic way.

Since the novel presupposes that figures like Arthur are historical, I had to wrestle a little with differing theories of chronology and location, as I have had to do with issues regarding the original Taliesin. Inevitably, I had to make choices. These choices do not necessarily reflect my judgment of the best reconstruction of whatever history may lie behind the original stories, but rather my attempt to create the best framework for the story I was telling.

Finally, I had to wrestle with how to render Welsh names from some of the early sources. I am not a speaker of Welsh myself and pretend no expertise in the pronunciation of the language, but I know some of the names will be puzzling to readers unfamiliar with Welsh. If it helps, comparison of various forms of the same word suggests that *w* (in words like *pwca*) seems to be pronounced somewhat like *u*. (Yes, I could have just Anglicized it as *pooka*, but that choice would inevitably have conjured up for some readers an image of giant invisible rabbits derived from the movie, *Harvey*, and the original *pwca* was not that warm and fuzzy.)

ABOUT THE AUTHOR

As far back as he can remember, Bill Hiatt had a love for reading so intense that he eventually ended up owning over eight thousand books-- not counting e-books! He has also loved to write for almost that long. As an English teacher, he had little time to write, though he always felt there were stories within him that longed to get out, and he did manage to publish a few books near the end of his teaching career. Now that he is retired from teaching, the stories are even more anxious to get out into the world, and they will not be denied

For more information, visit
https://www.billhiatt.com

facebook.com/writerbillhiatt
twitter.com/Billhiatt2

OTHER BOOKS AND BOOKLETS BY BILL HIATT

Spell Weaver Series

(Shorts set in the Spell Weaver universe are inserted where they belong in the storyline but are not numbered.)

"Echoes of My Past Lives" (0)

Living with Your Past Selves (1)

Divided against Yourselves (2)

Hidden among Yourselves (3)

"Destiny or Madness"

"Angel Feather"

Evil within Yourselves (4)

We Walk in Darkness (5)

Separated from Yourselves (6)

Different Dragons

Different Lee (1)

Soul Switch (2)

Soul Salvager Series

Haunted by the Devil (1, also includes *The Devil Hath the Power*, originally published separately)

Mythology Book (hybrid mythology text/young adult urban fantasy)

*A Dream Come True: An Entertaining Way
for Students to Learn Greek Mythology*

Anthologies

[The name(s) of the piece(s) by Bill Hiatt are in parentheses following the anthology name.]

Anthologies of the Heart, Book 1: Where Dreams and Visions Live

("The Sea of Dreams")

Flash Flood 2: Monster Maelstrom, A Flash Fiction Halloween Anthology

("In the Eye of the Beholder")

Flash Flood 3: Christmas in Love, A Flash Fiction Anthology

("Naughty or Nice?" and "Entertaining Unawares")

Hidden Worlds, Volume 1: Unknown, a Sci-Fi and Fantasy Anthology

("The Worm Turns" and "Abandoned")

Great Tomes Series, Book 6: The Great Tome of Magicians, Necromancers, and Mystics

("Green Wounds")

Education-related Titles

"A Parent's Guide to Parent-Teacher Communications"

"A Teacher's Survival Guide for Writing College Recommendations"

"Poisoned by Politics: What's Wrong with
Education Reform and How To Fix It"

Made in United States
Troutdale, OR
08/09/2024